From the Author of the Beloved National Bestseller

THE JANE AUSTEN SOCIETY

NATALIE JENNER, the #1 Canadian and *USA Today* bestselling author of *The Jane Austen Society*, returns with a compelling and heartwarming story of postwar London, a century-old bookstore, and three women determined to find their way in a fast-changing world.

"Through superior research and brilliant creativity, Jenner deftly crafted intriguing, well-rounded, relatable characters.... *Bloomsbury Girls* is a delightful, heartening story that I recommend to all historical fiction lovers!"
—GENEVIEVE GRAHAM, #1 national and *USA Today* bestselling author

"The charm and warmth of Natalie Jenner's *Bloomsbury Girls* transports readers to postwar England, and to a most remarkable bookshop where three women must learn a valuable lesson: not how to make it in a man's world, but how to remake that world in their indelible image. This story of sisterhood and self-determination had me cheering for Vivien, Grace, and Evie throughout. A must-read!"
—BRYN TURNBULL, #1 national bestselling author

"A powerful and moving novel that explores the tragedies and triumphs of life, both large and small, and the universal humanity in us all.... Destined to resonate with readers for years to come."
—CBC BOOKS on *The Jane Austen Society*

"[*The Jane Austen Society*] delivers a world reader escapism."
—PEOPLE

"A charming and memorable debut, which reminds us of the universal language of literature and the power of books to unite and heal."
—PAM JENOFF, *New York Times* bestselling author of *The Lost Girls of Paris*

"Anyone seeking an antidote to contemporary chaos will find a welcome respite among the members of a group whose outer lives may appear simple, but whose inner lives need the kind of balm Austen knew well."
—*THE WASHINGTON POST* on *The Jane Austen Society*

BLOOMSBURY GIRLS

Also by Natalie Jenner

The Jane Austen Society

BLOOMSBURY GIRLS

NATALIE JENNER

ST. MARTIN'S PRESS
NEW YORK

First published in the United States by St. Martin's Press, an imprint of St. Martin's Publishing Group

BLOOMSBURY GIRLS. Copyright © 2022 by Natalie Jenner. All rights reserved. Printed in the United States of America. For information, address St. Martin's Publishing Group, 120 Broadway, New York, NY 10271.

www.stmartins.com

Designed by Gabriel Guma

Map © Andrea Nairn

Library of Congress Cataloging-in-Publication Data

Names: Jenner, Natalie, author.
Title: Bloomsbury girls / Natalie Jenner.
Description: First Edition. | New York : St. Martin's Press, 2022. |
Identifiers: LCCN 2022000925 | ISBN 9781250276698 (hardcover) |
   ISBN 9781250283221 (Canada & international, sold outside the U.S.,
   subject to rights availability) | ISBN 9781250276704 (ebook)
Subjects: LCGFT: Novellas.
Classification: LCC PR9199.4.J448 B56 2022 | DDC 813/.6—dc23
LC record available at https://lccn.loc.gov/2022000925

Our books may be purchased in bulk for promotional, educational, or business use. Please contact your local bookseller or the Macmillan Corporate and Premium Sales Department at 1-800-221-7945, extension 5442, or by email at MacmillanSpecialMarkets@macmillan.com.

First Edition: 2022

10 9 8 7 6 5 4 3 2 1

For my daughter,
the original Evie

—and—

in memory of
Malkit Leighl,
the very best of men

All life worth living is difficult. . . . It is a by-product of brave living, and it never comes in the form we expect, or at the season we hoped for, or as the result of our planning for it.

—Katherine Anne Porter

This sense, of everyone working for, or with, or around, the same people, was exquisitely London.

—Adam Gopnik

The worst of a bookshop is it has to be all or nothing.

—Nancy Mitford

BLOOMSBURY GIRLS

Inside the Shop

Evelyn Stone . . . Former servant girl & Cambridge graduate
Grace Perkins . . . Secretary to the general manager
Herbert Dutton . . . General manager
Vivien Lowry . . . Disaffected staff member
Alec McDonough . . . Head of fiction
Ashwin Ramaswamy . . . Head of science & naturalism
Frank Allen . . . Head of rare books
Master Mariner Simon Scott . . . Head of history

Outside the Shop

Fredrik Christenson . . . Vice-master of Jesus College, Cambridge
Lord Baskin . . . Owner of Bloomsbury Books
Ellen Doubleday . . . Widow of American publisher Nelson
Doubleday, Sr.
Lady Browning . . . English aristocrat & author
Sonia Brownell Blair . . . Widow of George Orwell
Mimi Harrison . . . Movie star
Samuel Beckett . . . Irish playwright
Peggy Guggenheim . . . American heiress & collector
Stuart Wesley . . . Research assistant to Vice-Master Christenson
Yardley Sinclair . . . Director of museum services at Sotheby's
Elsie Maud Wakefield . . . Deputy keeper of the Kew Herbarium
Dr. Septimus Feasby . . . Principal keeper of printed books,
British Museum
Robert Kinross . . . Junior fellow of Jesus College, Cambridge

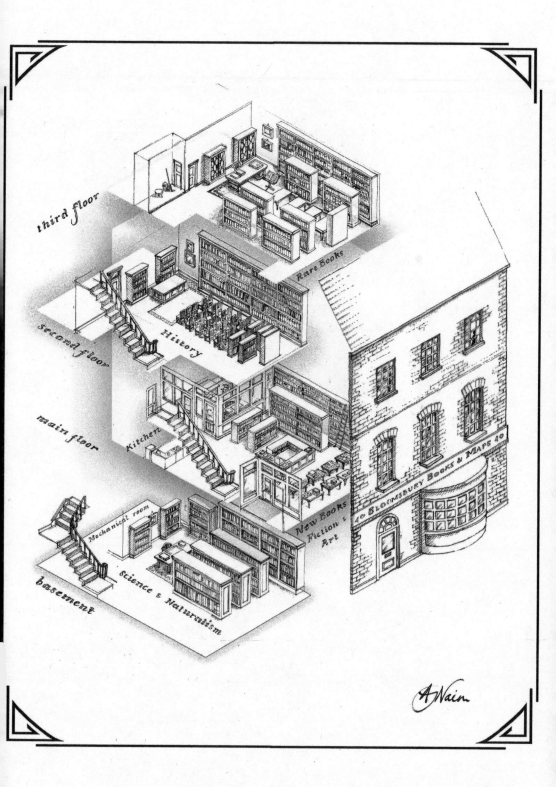

third floor

Rare Books

second floor

History

main floor

Kitchen

New Books
Fiction
Art

Mechanical room

Science & Naturalism

basement

40 BLOOMSBURY BOOKS & MAPS 40

A Nain

PROLOGUE

Cambridge, England
December 19, 1949

E vie Stone sat alone in her tiny bedsitter at the north end of
Castle Street, as far from the colleges as a student could live
and still be *keeping term* at Cambridge. But Evie was no longer a student—she remained at the university on borrowed time.
The next forty minutes would decide how much she had left.

The room's solitary window was cracked open to the cool December air, which was about to vibrate with the sound of Great St
Mary's striking two o'clock from precisely three miles away. The
interview with Senior Fellow Christenson was for twenty minutes
past that—exactly as long as it would take her to arrive at Jesus
College. Evie always had her walks perfectly timed.

Christenson scheduled his appointments for twenty minutes
past the hour, one of many famous eccentricities for which he was
known. The students jokingly referred to this arrangement as
CMT or Christenson Mean Time. Resounding bells of St Mary's or
not, Evie could have guessed the exact minute almost down to the
second. She had honed this skill as a servant girl at the Chawton Great House, where for two years she had secretly catalogued
the family library. Without the benefit of a clock, she had passed
hours every night going through all 2,375 books, page by page. At

a clear two-foot distance, Evie could now eyeball anything from a Gutenberg-era tome to a carbon-copy document and not only predict how long it would take her to summarize the contents but to quickly skim each page as well. These were skills that she kept to herself. She had long known the value in being underestimated.

The male faculty around her only knew Evelyn Stone as a quiet, unassuming, but startlingly forthright member of the first entry class of women to be permitted to earn a degree from Cambridge. After three years of punishing studies at the all-female Girton College, Evie had been awarded first-class honours for her efforts, which included a lengthy paper on the Austen contemporary Madame de Staël, and become one of the first female graduates in the eight-hundred-year history of the university.

Christenson was the next hurdle.

He needed a research assistant for the upcoming Lent term, and Evie had applied before anyone else. She also needed the job more than anyone else. Since graduating with a First in English, she had been assisting Junior Fellow Kinross with his years-long annotation of William Makepeace Thackeray's 1848 novel, *Vanity Fair*. With this project finally at an end, Evie's current stipend was scheduled to dry up on the very last day of 1949. As Christenson's newest research assistant, Evie could continue to spend countless days on her own, without supervision, methodically working her way through the over one hundred libraries at the university—a prospect that remained more exciting to her than anything else at this stage of her academic career.

The minute the bells started to ring out, Evie—already clad in her thick woollen coat for winter—stood up, grabbed her leather bag, and headed for the door. Twenty quick steps down to the street, five and a half minutes until she passed the Castle Inn, and then a clear ten before she saw the bend of the River Cam. There the Bridge of Sighs loomed above the river, Gothic and imperious, the stonework tracery in its open windows designed to keep students from clambering in. This was the type of campus foolery that Evie would never seek to join—or be invited to.

Jesus College, Evie's immediate destination, was rich in history, having been founded in 1496 on the site of a former nunnery. The grass beneath Evie's feet had been kept long for centuries, reflecting its historical use as fodder. During the Second World War concrete shelters had been situated under the gardens to offer protection from German air raids. In this way, the medieval university had begun to bear the scars of modern existence, as well as its fruits: only a few years later, the women of Cambridge were finally permitted to graduate.

Evie didn't think about any of this as she crossed the grounds. Instead, her brain kept time to the rhythmic crunch of frost-covered lawn beneath her lightly booted feet. With every crisp, measured step, her weathered leather bag swung steadily against her hip, weighed down by the writing sample inside: nearly one hundred pages dissecting individuality and resistance in the works of de Staël for which Evie could not have done better, having received the highest mark possible. The bag also contained a letter of reference from Junior Fellow Kinross. This time Evie could have done better, but didn't know she needed to.

Mimi Harrison had written to Evie earlier that fall in anticipation of her upcoming need for employment. Mimi had urged the young girl to accept a letter of referral from her husband, who had recently finished a three-year professorship at Jesus College and returned to Harvard along with his new wife.

"But I only ever met him once," Evie had answered Mimi over the phone in the downstairs common room.

"Nonsense," Mimi had replied with an indulgent lilt to her voice. "When I arrived in Hollywood twenty years ago, it was with a letter from my father's former law partner, and I'd only met him one time more than that. Besides, Geoffrey desperately wants to help you."

"But why? He don't—I mean, he does . . . not . . . know me." Evie often slipped back into Chawton vernacular when conversing with Mimi, whose friendship remained so rooted in their time together in the small farming village.

Mimi had laughed, always trying to keep things light with the serious young woman. "But he knows *me,* and he knows that I know a good egg when I see one."

Still, Evie had refused. And still, Mimi had had the letter sent through, just as she often did with theatre tickets, and rail fare, and the many other things that she had tried to give the girl over the years. The generosity of Mimi Harrison, a famous film and stage actress, knew no bounds.

But neither did Evie's pride. So today she carried the letter of referral from Professor Kinross instead. Kinross gave out many such letters each term, but poor Evie did not know that. She had been perfectly content when he had offered her one. She had done solid research work for him on his annotation of *Vanity Fair,* and he had called her capable and efficient. Surely that would be enough for Senior Fellow Christenson.

It was now 2:22 p.m. and Evie sat feeling smaller than ever in the large swivel chair that faced her entire future. Christenson put Kinross's letter down, tapped the top of the one hundred pages on de Staël, and sighed.

"The research here . . . all these obscure women authors. Even de Staël is no George Eliot."

Evie found this comment interesting, given Christenson's noted expertise on the latter.

"After all, the cream always rises to the top, hmm?" He leaned back in his chair. "And the joint paper . . . on Mr. Thackeray . . ."

Evie sat up. She was particularly proud of the research work for Professor Kinross, which she had completed alongside Stuart Wesley, another recent graduate. Kinross had commended her on the note-taking and impressive indices she had assembled to support his annotation. He had encouraged her to spend as much time with the original sources as possible, often stressing how critical accurate research was to the entire project.

"Your colleague Mr. Wesley contributed a large part, I understand."

Evie sat up even straighter. "We both did."

Christenson paused, his eyes narrowing against both her lack of demurral and the all-too-familiar letter of reference before him. Kinross did none of his students any favours with these rote little missives.

"Yes, well, I understand that you carried out the research and such, but the writing . . ." Christenson smiled, so genially and unlike him, that Evie finally grew concerned. "As you know, what I need is a certain facility with text, with, ah, *language*." He gave the last word an extra syllable in the middle, and Evie became even more conscious of her rural accent, which was apt to shorten everything instead.

"What you may not know is that I am assuming Vice-Master Bolt's role in the New Year. Less time for my own writing, more's the pity." Christenson picked up the papers before him, tapped their bottom edges decisively against the blotter on his overflowing desk, then passed the entirety of a term's work back to her.

"Thank you, Miss Stone, for your time." He gave a cursory nod at his closed office door, which everyone knew to be his cue for dismissal, and Evie gave a quick nod back before hastily leaving.

On the walk home, it started to snow. The windows of the shops and pubs glowed from within, their golden electric lustre in soft contrast to the early-winter darkness making its descent. For Evie, however, the day was fully, and terrifyingly, at an end.

She did not feel the tiny flakes of snow falling about her hatless head and shoulders—did not notice the figures scurrying home, the baskets full of rationed goods, the brown-paper packages hinting at the Christmas week just ahead. Instead, she pulled her coat tighter about her, wondering what had just happened, mulling it over again and again. She now knew she had missed something, not just in her time with Christenson, but with Wesley, and Kinross, all along. She felt a sense of distrust starting to form from her confusion, which bothered her by its sudden—and delayed—appearance.

Evie knew that she had worked harder than any other student these past three years. Her marks reflected that. Christenson would never find a better research assistant. And yet.

She stopped in front of the window of the Castle Inn. Inside she could see students laughing and drinking, piled about different tables, celebrating the last day of term and the Christmas festivities already in full swing. She stood there for a while and watched through the frosted glass, confident that no one would notice her small, indistinct form against the snow-speckled night.

When Evie returned to her bedsitter at the very north end of Castle Street, her mother's weekly letter lay on the worn carpet a few feet from the threshold of the door. Evie put the leather satchel on its anointed hook on the coatstand, which contained nothing else but her sturdy black umbrella, then stood aimlessly in the middle of the sitting room, looking about. She would need to start packing up soon. She had no idea for where.

Her brothers were all scattered far from home except for the youngest, Jimmy, who was only ten. Their father was dead these past two years from an infection in his gimp right leg, which he had shown the local doctor one week too late. After that, the family farm had finally been sold, and her mother and Jimmy had moved to a small two-up, two-down terrace house on the main village road. But Evie had not worked this hard to go backwards.

She walked over to the upright dresser, the top drawers of which she had fashioned into a makeshift filing cabinet, having few clothes to keep inside. She pulled open the first drawer and started at *A.* She proceeded apace, going through each carbon copy, each sheet of notepaper, each trade card and pamphlet that she had retained over the years. She never threw anything out.

When she got to *AL,* she found the small trade card for a Mr. Frank Allen, Rare Books Acquirer, Bloomsbury Books & Maps, 40 Lamb's Conduit, Bloomsbury, London. Mr. Allen had been introduced to Evie by their mutual contact, Yardley Sinclair, during the landmark dispersal of the Chawton Great House library by Sotheby's in the fall of 1946. Along with Mimi Harrison, Yardley Sinclair and Evie had been founding members of the Jane Austen Society, which had acquired the library as part of its efforts to save the Chawton cottage where Austen once lived. During the auction, Allen had bid on and acquired a handful of nineteenth-century books for the London store that employed him. As assistant director of estate sales at Sotheby's at the time, Yardley had proudly been showing Evie off to all the various dealers and agents in attendance at the sale. She recalled how Allen had briefly complimented her meticulously handwritten catalogue, which Yardley also often showed around.

Evie stared at the embossed silver lettering on the cool white card, running her stubby, ink-stained fingers over the raised name. She could hear the bells of Great St Mary's strike half past three. Standing there in her woollen coat, she felt the cold draught entering the room from the window she had left open. The satchel dangled from its lonely perch; the letter from her mother remained unopened on the floor. She heard the word *lan-gu-age* still reverberating in her head, then took a deep breath with all the assurance and certainty she could muster.

She would not be going backwards; she would not be looking back.

CHAPTER ONE

RULE NO. 17

Tea shall be served promptly four times a day.

T
he Tyrant beckons."

Grace looked up from her small desk at the rear of the shop. Here she marshalled all manner of what the bookshop staff called *couches:* the piles of letters, requests, adverts, journals, newspapers, trade cards, catalogues, magazines, announcements, invitations, and all the rest of the paper ephemera that kept Bloomsbury Books in commerce with the outside world.

Her colleague Vivien stood in the doorway, swinging the kettle in her right hand. It was Monday morning, and Vivien was always on elevenses duty on the first day of the week.

"And now the fuse to the cooker's gone again." She made a face. "You know they can't function without their tea. The Tyrant's in a particular *mood* today."

The Tyrant had a name, but Vivien refused to use it in private, and Grace often found herself failing to do so as well—just one example of how Vivien's attitude at work sometimes seeped into her own. Grace stood up and stacked a pile of papers neatly before her. "If he were ever to catch you calling him that . . ."

"He can't. He can't hear anything but the sound of his own voice."

Grace shook her head at the younger woman and stifled a grin. They had been working at the bookshop together since the end of the war, and Vivien's friendship was a big reason why Grace stayed. Well, that and the wages, of course. And the fact that her unemployed husband could not begrudge her the opportunity to earn those. And the time away from her demanding boys. And the fear of drastic change. In the end, Grace supposed there were quite a lot of reasons why she stayed. She wasn't quite sure why Vivien did.

"Is Dutton not in yet?" Vivien asked, glancing past Grace to the empty office behind her.

Herbert Dutton, the longtime general manager of the shop, had never been given a nickname by Vivien, let alone a term of endearment. He wasn't the kind of man one would ever bother to put in a box, being so fully contained on his own.

"He's at the GP."

"Again?"

Vivien arched both eyebrows, but Grace only shrugged in response. As the two female employees of Bloomsbury Books, Grace and Vivien had mastered the art of silent expression, often communicating solely through a raised eyebrow, earlobe tug, or barely hidden hand gesture.

Vivien placed the kettle on top of a nearby filing cabinet, and the two women headed wordlessly for the basement. Whenever they strolled the shop corridors together, their matching height and tailored clothes gave them an indomitable appearance from which the male staff instinctively shrank. Both women were unusually tall, although very different in physique. Grace had broad shoulders which did not need the extra padding so fashionable at the time, an open, un-made-up face, and a peaches-and-cream complexion—her one inheritance from a family that had farmed the upland hills of Yorkshire for generations. She dressed in a simple manner that flattered her height: the strong lines of military-style jackets and pencil skirts, with low-heeled pumps for walking. Her most delicate features were her calm, grey eyes and fine brown hair with just the slightest hint of auburn, which she always kept neatly pinned back at the crown.

In contrast, Vivien was as angular and slender as a gazelle, and just as quick to bolt when impatient or displeased. She preferred to dress in formfitting monochrome black—most often in tight wool skirts and sweaters embellished by a striking Victorian amethyst brooch, her one inheritance from a beloved grandmother. Vivien's face was always dramatically made-up, intimidatingly so, which was part of the point: by looking so in control of herself, she succeeded in keeping everyone else at bay.

On their way to the basement, the two women passed by the rear, glass-windowed office belonging to Mr. Dutton, who was both the store's general manager and its longest-serving employee. To reach the back staircase, which Vivien had nicknamed Via Inferno, they had to brush up against the towering boxes of books that were delivered daily from different publishers, auctions, bankrupt stocks, and estate sales across central England and beyond. The shop turned over five hundred books a week on average, so a healthy and frequent replenishing of stock was required from all these sources.

The misbehaving fuse box was in the mechanical room, which was adjacent to the infrequently visited Science & Naturalism Department. The entire basement floor was unseasonably warm and humid due to the inept workings of the prewar boiler. Through the open doorway of the mechanical room, Grace and Vivien could spot the small wire-rimmed spectacles and placid brow of Mr. Ashwin Ramaswamy, the head of the Science Department and its lone staff, peeking above the table where he always sat behind piles of books of his own.

"Has he said a peep yet today?" Vivien almost whispered, and Grace shook her head. Mr. Ramaswamy was notorious for keeping to himself within the shop, which was easy enough to do given how rarely his department was visited. The basement collection of biology, chemistry, and other science books had been there since at least the time of Darwin, but remained the most forgotten and least profitable floor of the shop.

A trained naturalist and entomologist, Ash Ramaswamy did not seem to mind being left alone. Instead, he spent most of his day organising the books in a manner that put the other department heads to shame, and peering through a microscope at the slides of insects stored in a flat wooden box on his desk. These were the creatures of his homeland, the state of Madras in southeast India. Ash's late father, a Tamil Brahmin, had been a highly placed civil servant in the British colonial government who had always encouraged his son to consider the opportunities offered by a life in Great Britain. Ash had emigrated after the war in the hopes of securing a post at the Natural History Museum in London. As a member of the most privileged caste in his home state, he had not been prepared for the overt prejudice of the British people towards him. Unable to obtain even an interview at any of the city's museums, he had ended up employed at the shop instead.

"You said a mood," Grace started to say, as she fiddled around with her head inside the fuse box.

"Hmm?"

"A mood. The Tyrant. What is it now?"

"*It* is Margaret Runnymede."

Grace poked her head out from the fuse box. "The new book is out?"

"The way she bustles in here every release day, just so he can give her that ridiculous posy of purple violets to go with her latest purple prose and tell her everything she already thinks about herself. It's nauseating. He wants everything in the shop *just so* for her today."

Grace raised an eyebrow at the younger woman. "Is that all he wants?"

Vivien made a disgusted noise from the back of her throat. "He's so full of himself. As if she'd ever."

"Enough women do. Have an interest in him, I mean." Grace shut the door to the fuse box and wiped her hands together. "All done."

"As he's plenty aware."

"Well, one can't necessarily fault him for that." As much as Grace herself did not care for the head of fiction, Vivien expressed a degree of dislike that Grace thought best to temper, for all their sakes.

They headed back up the stairs together, pausing in Grace's office for Vivien to retrieve the kettle before going her separate way. Through the glass divider to the farthest rear room, they could see the moonfaced Mr. Dutton sitting idly behind his desk as if waiting for someone to tell him what to do. Above his head hung, slightly askew, the framed fifty-one rules for the shop that Mr. Dutton had immediately devised upon his ascension to general manager nearly twenty years ago.

"One biscuit or two?" Vivien asked loudly and officiously, suddenly all work as Grace settled down into her chair, delicately pulling the folds of her A-line skirt out from under her.

Grace hesitated. She was nearly forty years old, and lately she had noticed just the slightest increased weight about her hips. Her husband, Gordon, had noticed it, too. He was never one to let something like that slip by.

She held up one finger with a sigh. Vivien scoffed as she ambled back to the kitchen, swinging the kettle widely to and fro by her side, as if hoping to hit something along the way.

Grace looked about her, at all the familiar papers, the boxes of books, and the bills of lading she had yet to type up. It would be pointless to start anything this close to the hour. So, she waited.

After a few minutes, she heard Mr. Dutton call her from the back room at exactly 11:00 a.m. Right on schedule.

"Miss Perkins," he announced in his usual formal manner. He always combined the spinster prefix with her married name to reflect Grace's unusual status as a working mother. It would make Grace feel like a film star—*Miss Crawford, Miss Hepburn*—if she didn't know better.

Grabbing her notepad and pencil, she stood back up and walked into his office through the open doorway that connected with hers.

"Good morning, Mr. Dutton. Everything went well, I hope." She said it kindly but declaratively, knowing he would not directly answer her.

"Lovely morning," he said with a smile so small that one could hardly detect it within the wide expanse of his face. "I trust you had a pleasant New Year's."

"And you?"

He nodded. "Might I now have a second of your time?"

Grace nodded in return and held up the notepad and pencil in midair. They had done this routine a thousand times. He went through the schedule for the day—his schedule alone, as everyone else in the shop worked in service to the customers—and when they came to the 2:30 p.m. slot, he halted.

"A Miss Evelyn Stone?" he inquired.

"Yes, remember? That strange call right before the holiday. Mr. Allen vouched for meeting her through Yardley Sinclair, and you agreed to interview."

Mr. Dutton just stared at Grace. She knew that his memory was lately not what it had been, and she prompted him again.

"A formality, you called it—out of respect for Mr. Sinclair. As a most valued customer of the shop."

Mr. Dutton tapped the name in his appointment book, then nodded. This was her cue to seat herself and take dictation while he drafted his correspondence.

They were on their seventh letter when he concluded with "'And while we appreciate the job the Broadstreet Signs Company has done in promoting this latest sales success, we are sorry to say we must decline your kind offer of competitively priced signage at this time. Most sincerely yours . . .'"

He paused and brushed his fingers over the right side of his balding head. Grace must have had one of her *looks* on her face, as Gordon liked to call them.

"Yes, Miss Perkins?"

"It's just that—well, I do think the front window has been looking somewhat shabby of late, and Viv and I strolled over to Foyles last week to check out theirs, and I must say, they have done rather a clever job."

Mr. Dutton sat there watching her with one of his own looks, a strange tightrope walk between terror and indulgence that ran across his round features whenever she proposed something new. Even more than losing out to Foyles, the shop's most envied competitor, Grace suspected that Mr. Dutton's greatest fear was of any tumble being somehow cushioned by *her*. Grace's ideas for improving the shop seemed to do nothing so much as put him on edge.

"And . . . well . . . I thought, with some proper signage such as that provided by the Broadstreet Company, suspended from the ceiling so as not to block the view from the street, and with different shelving—more open-backed, to let in the light—we could promote the upcoming New Year sale quite effectively."

Mr. Dutton just stared. Grace had worked at Bloomsbury

Books for nearly five years and, to her knowledge, a sales sign had never once been placed in the front window or, for that matter, anywhere else in the shop. Instead, the staff were trained to mention sales only most discreetly, in demure, elegant asides to the customers, as if even the mere idea of money had no place around books.

"There's also the matter of our upcoming centenary this summer," continued Grace in the face of his silence. "It's never too early to start celebrating. Vivien and I were thinking of another display: *One Hundred Years of Books*. A selection of top titles from every decade."

Mr. Dutton was a creature of habit and rules who, due to the daunting uncertainty of the future, resisted spending time or money too far in advance. This was one of many differences between him and his trusted secretary when it came to matters of business.

"Thank you, Miss Perkins," he finally replied, looking almost pained by her suggestions. "That will be all for now."

It was indeed all for now. It would be all for tomorrow, too, and for the day after that. She would go back to typing up his unnecessarily long letters, organising his voluminous paperwork into alphabetical files, and fetching his tea. Then she would go home and do a version of the same for her family.

Grace looked down the corridor at Vivien, who was leaning on the edge of the front cash counter, her hips swaying as she alternated between jotting something down in a green coil-bound notebook and chewing on the end of her pencil. Vivien was essentially caged behind that counter, only occasionally allowed out front to assist with the customers. She, like Grace, had joined the shop just as the world was emerging from the ashes of war. Life back then had seemed full of possibility and freedom, especially for the women who had taken charge while the men were off fighting.

This was the social contract that had been forged to sustain each of them during a time of great pain and sacrifice: of whom much had been asked, much would later be given.

But the past had a way of slipping back through even the thinnest of cracks in a fractured world. Women such as Vivien and Grace had hoped for a fresh beginning for everyone; but five years on, new opportunities for women were still being rationed along with the food. Those in power would always hold on to any excess supply, even to the bitter end.

CHAPTER TWO

RULE No. 12

First-aid procedures shall be strictly adhered to
in the event of an emergency.

The Tyrant was Alec McDonough, a bachelor in his early thirties who ran the New Books, Fiction and Art Departments on the ground floor of Bloomsbury Books. He had read literature and fine art at the University of Bristol and had been planning on a career in something big—Vivien accused him of wanting to run a small colony—when the war had intervened. Following his honourable discharge in 1945, Alec had joined the shop on the exact same day as Vivien. "By an hour ahead. Like a dominant twin," she would quip whenever Alec was rewarded with anything first.

From the start Alec and Vivien were rivals, and not just for increasing control of the fiction floor. Every editor that wandered in, every literary guest speaker, was a chance for them to have access to the powers that be in the publishing industry. As two secretly aspiring writers, they had each come to London and taken the position at Bloomsbury Books for this reason. But they were also both savvy enough to know that the men in charge—from the rigid Mr. Dutton and then-head-of-fiction Graham Kingsley, to the restless Frank Allen and crusty Master Mariner Scott—were whom they first needed to please. Alec had a clear and distinct advantage when it came to that. Between the tales of wartime service, shared grammar schools, and past cricket-match victories, Vivien grew quickly dismayed at her own possibility for promotion.

Sure enough, within weeks Alec had entrenched himself with both the long-standing general manager, Herbert Dutton, and his right-hand man, Frank Allen. By 1948, upon the retirement of Graham Kingsley, Alec had ascended to the post of head of fiction, and within the year had added New Books and Art to his oversight—an achievement that Vivien still referred to as the Annexation.

She had been first to call him the Tyrant; he called her nothing at all. Vivien's issues with Alec ranged from the titles they stocked on the shelves, to his preference for booking events exclusively with male authors who had served in the war. With her own degree in literature from Durham (Cambridge, her dream university, still refusing in 1941 to graduate women), Vivien had rigorously informed views on the types of books the Fiction Department should carry. Not surprisingly, Alec disputed these views.

"But he doesn't even read women," Vivien would bemoan to Grace, who would nod back in sympathy while trying to remember her grocery list before the bus journey home. "I mean, what—one Jane Austen on the shelves? No Katherine Mansfield. No Porter. I read that Salinger story in *The New Yorker* he keeps going on about: shell-shocked soldiers and children all over the place, and I don't see what's so masculine about *that*."

Unlike Vivien, Grace did not have much time for personal reading, an irony her husband often pointed out. But Grace did not work at the shop for the books. She worked there because the bus journey into Bloomsbury took only twenty minutes, she could drop the children off at school on the way, and she could take the shop newspapers home at the end of the day. Grace had been the one to suggest that they also carry import magazines, in particular

The New Yorker. Being so close to the British Museum and the theatre district, Bloomsbury Books received its share of wealthy American tourists. Grace was convinced that such touches from home would increase their time spent browsing, along with jazz music on the wireless by the front cash, one of many ideas that Mr. Dutton was still managing to resist.

Vivien and Alec had manned the ground floor of the shop together for over four years, circling each other within the front cash counter like wary lions inside a small coliseum. The square, enclosed counter had been placed in the centre of the Fiction Department in an effort to contain an old electrical outlet box protruding from the floor. Mr. Dutton could not look at this eyesore without seeing a customer lawsuit for damages caused by accidental tripping. Upon his promotion to general manager in the 1930s, Dutton had immediately ordained that the front cash area be relocated and built around the box.

This configuration had turned out to be of great benefit to the staff. One could always spot a customer coming from any direction, prepare the appropriate response to expressions ranging from confused to hostile, and even catch the surreptitious slip of an unpurchased book into a handbag. Other bookshops had taken note of Bloomsbury Books' ground-floor design and started refurbishing their own. The entire neighbourhood was, in this way, full of spies. Grace and Vivien were not the only two bookstore employees out and about, checking on other stores' window displays. London was starting to boom again, after five long years of postwar rationing and recovery, and new bookshops were popping up all over. Bloomsbury was home to the British Museum, the University of London, and many famous authors past and present, including the prewar circle of Virginia Woolf, E. M. Forster, and Lytton Strachey. This made the district a particularly ideal location for readers, authors, and customers alike.

And so it was here, on a lightly snowing day on the second of January, 1950, that a young Evie Stone arrived, Mr. Allen's trading card in one pocket, and a one-way train ticket to London in the other.

Vivien saw her first.

The bell at the front door gave its customary curt *ting* sound as the worn pair of girl's boots tripped the line across the inner vestibule door. Just as curtly, Alec McDonough looked up, then down, from his perch on a ladder nearby.

The hatless small figure failed to notice him. Instead, she took her time as she walked slowly past the fiction tables in the front half of the store. She did three things with every book she touched: first she would run the palm of her hand across its face almost in rapture, next tap on the title thoughtfully, and then with both hands gingerly lift the volume to minutely examine its contents and back cover.

Vivien had stopped writing in her notepad and was now absentmindedly chewing on the end of her pencil, observing the young woman with interest. She had a poorly cropped simple bob haircut and penetrating dark eyes that fixated intently within a narrow field of vision. She didn't look like someone from the city, but she didn't look completely out of place, either.

She moved methodically in the direction of the front counter, while Vivien slouched against it in the way that most irritated Mr. Dutton. When the girl finally reached the counter, Vivien put her pencil down.

"Hello."

Vivien raised her right eyebrow. "Hello," she replied slowly, and waited.

The girl put her gloved right hand on the edge of the counter and, as if in silent conspiracy, slipped forward a small white card.

Vivien cocked her head to the right before picking up the card. Surprisingly, it belonged to Frank Allen, from the Rare Books Department.

"I am Evie Stone," the girl offered by way of explanation.

Vivien watched her, entranced by the contrast between the girl's plain demeanour and that deep, intense gaze.

"I'm afraid Mr. Allen's away today and tomorrow at an estate sale. I hope you've not come far."

The girl shook her head insistently. "I am *Evelyn* Stone. To see Mr. Dutton."

"Ahh," Vivien exclaimed pleasantly, causing Alec to look down from his ladder at the sound of her voice brightening for once. "I see. You have an appointment then?"

Now Evie cocked her own head to the right, as if concerned that no one had been told to expect her.

"If you would wait right here, I shall see about getting him."

Vivien's slender figure departed through a small swinging door at the back of the counter and down a long corridor, before eventually disappearing into a rear glassed-in office. Next Grace popped her head out of the same office to peer down the corridor, and then she, too, disappeared from view. A few seconds later Vivien reappeared, walking back towards Evie as if she had all the time in the world.

"We're so sorry, he was indeed expecting you. I'll lead the way." Vivien motioned for the girl to follow her. "Here, let me take your coat, shall I?"

The girl declined the offer, pulling her woollen coat tighter about her in a slightly nervous manner that Vivien found endearing.

After passing the young girl off to Grace, Vivien returned to her post at the cash counter to find Alec now standing there. He was leaning against the counter in the same casual manner for which she was so often reprimanded. Mr. Dutton did not seem to mind it so much in a man. The girls in the shop were expected to have an elegant comportment, the men to be easy and approachable.

"Yes?" she asked sharply.

"Who was *that* queer little thing?"

Vivien sighed and picked up her pencil. She always had to look up at Alec, which she resented. No one should be that tall.

"A Miss Evie Stone to see Mr. Dutton, if you must know."

"Whatever for?"

Vivien put the pencil back down and made an exasperated noise. "A job, apparently. Grace said there was a referral by Yardley Sinclair. The director of museum services, over at Sotheby's? Is that enough name-dropping for you?"

Alec gave a smirk back to match her own. "Surely not for anything front of store, I should think. She doesn't look much older than sixteen, if that."

"Don't worry, Alec. I'm sure she has no interest whatsoever in your *dominion*."

Alec was about to say something in retort when the strangest shout rang out. Every single head in the bookshop shot up from a book as Alec reached forward for Vivien's arm in alarm.

"My God!" Alec exclaimed. "Was that Grace?"

He rushed around the counter to pull open the swinging door for Vivien before they raced down the corridor together. There they found Grace standing outside the general manager's office, frozen in place, her hand over her mouth.

Inside the doorway lay Mr. Dutton on the floor, his face and body stiff as a board. Evie Stone knelt there beside him.

"What on earth . . ." Alec made a move towards the manager, but Evie put out her left hand to stop him.

Just then, Mr. Dutton began to convulse, his arms and legs violently twitching.

"Call an ambulance," Evie said calmly to Grace while loosening his tie. "And stay back."

Grace just stood there in the doorway along with Alec and Vivien, all three of them stunned by the figure now writhing on the frayed carpet at their feet.

"Now!" Evie cried.

Grace finally jumped with a panicked start and rushed over to the phone on the desk, while Alec, looming behind Vivien in the doorway, called out, "Put something—put something in his mouth—a book, or—"

The young girl was shaking her head. "No," she replied firmly. "Just keep back." She looked up and nodded towards the large antique table on which Mr. Dutton reviewed his constant correspondence. "And move the desk away. Now! Before 'e hits himself!"

Alec came forward and shoved the desk corner hard, just as Grace hung up the phone.

"The poor man . . . they're on their way. How—how did you—"

The young girl put up her left hand again to silence Grace. The three shop employees could only stand there, watching helplessly, as Evie placed her right hand on his chest. "His heartbeat's quite slow."

"Grace," Alec asked, "did he say anything earlier? Anything at all? Did you know about this?"

Grace shook her head, her hand again suspended, quivering, over her mouth. "He'd just been to the GP, that's all I know. Wait—" She pulled open the top drawer of his desk and rummaged around, then ran to the coatstand and fished her hands into his trench coat pockets. "Oh, wait, yes, here's something. . . ."

She held out a small prescription box for them all to see. "'Phenytoin,'" she read aloud.

"Get Ash," Vivien cried out. "His medical dictionary!"

Alec gave her a look, then quickly ran to the back staircase.

"He's stopped convulsing," Evie suddenly announced.

All three women watched as first Mr. Dutton's round eyes began to flicker, and then the rest of his facial features started to relax in turn.

Alec now returned with Ash Ramaswamy, who held a thick medical dictionary in his hands.

"It's phenytoin—for epilepsy—yes, miss?" he asked Evie. "Low heartbeat?"

Evie was staring so openly at Ash that everyone else in the room grew suddenly uncomfortable. Vivien wondered if Evie had never seen anyone from India before, then felt a strange sort of shame for even having such a thought.

"Yes, quite low," Evie eventually replied, but Ash did not seem to notice her hesitance or her reddened cheeks. Instead, he seemed to be equally astonished by her being there, too.

"Put something under his head then, miss, to align his spine and jaw."

They all watched as Evie hurriedly took off her blue knit cardigan and gingerly placed it under Mr. Dutton's head as he slowly returned to consciousness.

"You're all right, sir, it was just a little fit." Evie reached out and patted his hand as if trying to console a small animal or child, which seemed to only increase Dutton's mortification at his present state.

Everyone watched with relief as Evie now helped ease Mr. Dutton up onto his right elbow.

"Your heart rate's low, sir. Please, stay still," Evie urged him.

At the unfamiliar voice, a dazed Mr. Dutton turned about to see his interviewee kneeling behind him. "I'm terribly sorry. How awful for you. How awful for you all."

Evie gave the first smile any of them had seen on her face yet. "Don't worry 'bout me, sir."

"Yes," Vivien spoke from the doorway, keeping an eye on the front of the store as the bell rang out to announce the arrival of the ambulance attendants. "Miss Stone certainly coped better than any of us lot."

Vivien moved to the side as the two attendants rushed down the corridor with a stretcher and began ministering to Mr. Dutton, who was still resting on the floor. Alec returned to the front of the shop to attend to the few customers, Ash left for the basement, and Vivien, Grace, and Evie remained clustered together in the hall.

Remembering how difficult the entire situation must be for their visitor, Grace was about to ask if she could get Evie a cup of tea when a booming voice thundered down the upstairs staircase, the one that Vivien mockingly called Via Dolorosa.

"What the devil is all the racket?"

CHAPTER THREE

The General Manager shall have sole authority and discretion
regarding the hiring, elevation, and firing of staff.

At the bottom of the staircase stood a man well into his sixties, wearing a jacket decorated with a series of naval pins along both lapels.

"Mr. Dutton's had some kind of attack," Grace explained with a nod towards his office. Through the open doorway, the two ambulance attendants could be seen kneeling on the floor next to the general manager and helping him to sit upright against one of the legs of the desk.

"An *attack*?" the old man almost spit out. "What kind of attack?"

"Epilepsy, most likely," Evie answered.

Peering over the rim of his reading spectacles, the man finally took note of her small form sandwiched between Grace and Vivien, who were both rather tall for women.

"And who are *you*?" he thundered again.

Grace took a small step forward. "This is Miss Evelyn Stone. Referred to Mr. Dutton by Mr. Sinclair for a position. Mr. Yardley Sinclair, of Sotheby's? The director of museum services?"

The man made a dismissive noise. "Not for my department, she's not. Second floor's no place for a girl."

Vivien gave an audible sigh. She was used to such stonewalling by the men in the shop. Alec wouldn't have the young girl on the store's main floor, Master Mariner Scott wouldn't allow her on the second.

"Perhaps she's not interested in a bunch of dusty old maps, hmm?" Vivien asked him with a taunting tone. "Has anyone even thought to ask her?"

Vivien was the only employee of the shop who remained unafraid of Master Mariner Scott, despite his frequent outbursts. She was fairly certain that beneath his crusty exterior was a man who loved women, particularly pretty women, and had built up a wall of defense against them to protect his ego. Vivien was writing a character just like him in her novel—the novel that no one else knew she was writing in that green coil-bound notebook of hers.

Master Mariner Scott looked ready to respond in kind to Vivien's words, but something about her aggressive manner seemed to change his mind.

"Still, she looks too slight to be up to much of anything." He turned to Grace. "Attack or not, it's time for tea," he added gruffly.

"One biscuit or two?" Grace asked in her overly deferential manner, the genuineness of which the men in the shop had begun to seriously question of late.

"Two," he barked back, then headed up the stairs.

"You're probably wondering who that was," Grace said to Evie in an apologetic tone.

Vivien laughed at her side. "Oh, I think that get-up was explanation enough."

Grace peered into the office where the two attendants were now packing up their gear. She was relieved to see Mr. Dutton already back at his desk, pen in one hand, trying to act as if none of the last few minutes had happened.

"That was Master Mariner Simon Scott," Grace continued. "Fought in the Battle of Dover Strait in the Great War and, to his great chagrin, sat out the Second. He rules the second floor: history, travel, topography, genealogy. But mainly naval and military history."

"I don't care much for cartography," Evie replied.

Vivien patted her on the back. "Lucky for you. What are you interested in? Book-wise, I mean."

Evie looked up the staircase. "Rare ones."

Emerging from the back room, the attendants brushed past the three women standing in a line as they carried the empty stretcher through the corridor. The sound of a slight cough came from inside the office, and Grace knew this was Mr. Dutton's cue for her and Evie to come back in.

"His heart rate has stabilized," the first attendant, a tall, jovial-looking young man, stopped to inform Grace. "Probably in reaction to the new medicine."

"It wasn't epilepsy, then?" Vivien asked.

The man turned to look her up and down approvingly. "No, miss, it was—the one beget the other. Did you not know he's an epileptic?"

Both older women shook their heads at him, while Evie remained entirely missed standing there between them.

"Well, whoever took care of him did everything right and proper."

Grace stepped back with a motion to Evie, and the man leaned down to get a good look at her. "I understand you were interviewing for a position when it happened."

Evie nodded.

"Well"—he straightened up and gave Vivien and Grace both a wink—"after all *that* fuss, they should at least hand you the job."

———————

vie was back in the visitor's chair across from Mr. Dutton's desk. He was writing something down for Grace, who remained standing in the doorway.

Evie looked about the room as Mr. Dutton labouriously composed his message. She noted the glass-covered case of old books that stood next to an extensive set of filing cabinets, the type of organising system that she could only dream of. On the walls were several certificates for bookselling success of some commercial nature, a cricket trophy from grammar school days decades past, a photo of the shop staff picnicking on a beach, and one of an austere-looking older woman with the same roundish features as Mr. Dutton. Most prominent of all was a large framed set of shop rules that hung high on the wall behind his desk.

Evie felt as if Mr. Dutton had his whole life contained within the walls of Bloomsbury Books. Before collapsing onto the floor, he had been telling her that he had first been employed by the shop as a delivery boy. He had worked there on weekends throughout university and then, upon failing his civil service exams, had ended up permanently joining the shop. This was right after the Great War, in which Mr. Dutton had been too young to fight. He had worked his way up to general manager of Bloomsbury Books & Maps by the 1930s, which is when he had first hired Frank Allen, now the head of rare books, as an assistant buyer. They remained the two longest-standing members of the staff.

Mr. Dutton had then given her the rest of the history of the shop. Evie had not been quite sure why. What she most wanted to hear about was the antiquarian collection on the third floor, which she now knew to be one floor safely removed from the purview of Master Mariner Scott.

Folding up the paper he had been writing on, Mr. Dutton held it out for Grace to take.

"You must post this to Mr. Allen. He is at Toppings today and tomorrow morning, but he needs to be made aware, should I . . ." His voice trailed off as Grace carefully took the note from him.

"Mr. Dutton, please, don't exert yourself. I'll see to everything. And I am sure Miss Stone here might also like the chance to catch her breath."

Evie shook her head pleasantly. "No, ma'am."

"I'm terribly sorry," Mr. Dutton broke in. "I've not even thanked you. They told me what you did. How did you know?"

Evie shrugged, thinking back on the many seizures that her father had suffered following his first stroke. Mr. Stone's health had never recovered from the trauma of the tractor accident on their family farm. One by one, different parts of his body had simply started to fail him and fall apart. It had been a difficult lesson for his family, that bad luck could be followed by even more.

"You learn what you have to."

"And you had to learn rare books?" Mr. Dutton asked simply.

"In a way, yeah—*yes*."

"And you want to sell them, now, after all your studies?"

"No, not at all."

She watched as Mr. Dutton and Grace looked at each other in confusion.

"I want to catalogue them."

Mr. Dutton leaned back in his chair, and in the fading afternoon light both women could make out the small beads of sweat still left on his brow from the stress of the recent attack.

"Grace, the letter." He stared at her until, recollecting herself, Grace nodded and quickly left.

"How do you know they need cataloguing?" he turned to Evie to ask.

"Well, they always do, in a way. As things change. Provenance, rarity, value. Something always comes along and changes the future for an old book."

Now Mr. Dutton was staring at her, too. Evie knew that she talked about books as if they were alive. As alive, as changeable, as people themselves.

"Your academics are impeccable. I wonder that you would settle for a role in a shop." Mr. Dutton gave a weak smile. "But I suppose I am just as guilty of that myself."

The former servant girl and the portly general manager shared a strange congruence, in addition to their compulsive natures and strong sense of duty. Mr. Dutton's entire life was on display within the four small walls of his office; Evie was known for saving her affections in life for dead authors and relationships that were socially constrained. She had adored her schoolteacher Adeline Gray and former employer Frances Knight. Even Kinross she had trusted, it turned out, to a fault.

As Evie sat there, she could feel herself already warming up to the sickly older man sitting pale and worn at his desk, trying so valiantly to continue with his work in exactly the way that she would have done.

"Sir, perhaps I should return another time—"

"I'm afraid there won't be another time." He put up his hand in a most supplicating manner at the alarmed look on her face. "Terribly sorry, Miss Stone. I only meant I'm told I need to rest for a bit. A few weeks at least, it seems. I will be informing the staff in the morning. It will entail some shifting about, and I'm afraid not all the changes will be to everyone's liking."

Somehow Evie already knew that he was talking about Vivien and Grace.

"Our head of rare books, Mr. Allen, has been my right-hand man for nearly two decades, and we always act in partnership. But as you know, he is away, quite far north, and I shan't be expecting to get ahold of him before tomorrow. The, ah, changes will be significant for Mr. Allen perhaps most of all. He will need"—here Mr.

Dutton paused for so long that Evie started to fear another attack was coming on—"he will need reinforcement in his department. All the staff will."

Evie sat there quietly, recalling her recent meeting with Senior Fellow Christenson, and how she had not caught on in time. Not asserted herself over his preference for Stuart Wesley. Not done what was necessary to secure the job.

"I can help in any way," she offered. "Not just rare books, as I said. Just . . . whatever you need."

These were the words that Mr. Dutton always most wanted to hear. He sought complete dedication and compliance from his staff. He had written the fifty-one rules so prominently displayed on his office wall to ensure that his voice—parental, authoritative, godlike if need be—was constantly in the ears of his employees. Nothing could go wrong, he believed, if everyone simply followed the rules.

CHAPTER FOUR

RULE No. 14

Departure time for staff is subject to the needs
and progress of the day.

Grace Perkins and Vivien Lowry departed together that chaotic day at precisely 5:30 p.m., just as they had done every workday for the past four years. No matter the goings-on at the shop, managerial collapse or otherwise, the staff always kept to their exact routines.

The gentlemen in the shop could set their watches by the moment when Grace arrived at the front cash counter, plain black handbag over her left arm and hands elegantly clasped, and Vivien immediately stopped whatever she was doing to grab her own black bag. They then marched out together and headed straight for the Russell Square bus stop. They would spend the first leg of their journey home commiserating over the events of the day and fortifying themselves against the one ahead, grateful to be out of earshot of the men who managed them. At Camden Town, Vivien always disembarked and transferred to the Hackney rail line. She could have headed straight home by bus from Bloomsbury, but the time saved was less appealing to her than the time spent airing her grievances to Grace.

Tonight, however, the two women were oddly silent as they sat together in their row of two seats. Grace stared out the window at the evening sky, its darkness punctuated by a blur of streetlamps and lit windows. Nights in the city hid so much of the grime and shadow cast by the pollution that constantly hovered above London, a permanent cloud that seemed to reflect the national mood.

The Camden Town bus inched slowly northwards, passing first Russell and then Tavistock Square. The borders of these perfectly geometric parks were towered over by buildings housing all matter of public services: hospitals, universities, the British Museum, even the former site of George Orwell's infamous Ministry of Information, where Grace's husband had worked during the war.

She felt Vivien tap her left arm and looked back at her.

"They say Orwell's dying, right down there, at University Hospital. I overheard one of the Secker and Warburg editors in the shop."

Grace sighed in remembrance of their own invalid. "Poor Mr. Dutton. He must be so mortified by everyone seeing him like that. I wonder what the doctor will say."

"Whatever it is, Dutton's sure to ignore it."

"Maybe he'll surprise us."

Vivien let out a dismissive laugh.

"Well, he should rest up, all the same. January is never a busy month."

"He could hire that girl, Evie. I do like being proven wrong about a person."

Now Grace laughed just as dismissively. "You do *not*."

"No, I don't suppose I do."

"Still, it'd be nice to have another girl in the shop."

"You are quite surrounded by men." Vivien hesitated. "Everything all right over the holidays?"

Grace gave a quick smile. "The boys were spoiled by my mother."

"And Gordon? Although I suppose he's spoiled enough already by you."

Grace could feel Vivien watching her closely. "As for the men at the shop," she replied instead, "they'd be wise to install Evie on the third floor and let Frank run everything until Mr. Dutton returns."

"You have it all figured out. As always." Vivien winked, then stood up for her stop. "They certainly won't be elevating the pair of us."

As Vivien got off the bus, Grace discreetly put her handbag on the seat next to her, hoping for some quiet time alone before returning home.

Did Grace even want to go home? The mere fact of this question had been troubling her for years.

Her husband, Gordon, was a difficult man, needing the whole of daily life joylessly cut into pieces to fit his unpredictable moods. Things had only become worse following his service in the war, when, as part of a propaganda department with hundreds of highly educated employees, he had found even more people to complain about. Grace and Gordon had met back in 1937, when she was employed as a secretary at the reinsurance firm where he worked as a mid-level manager. At age twenty-seven and keen to have children, Grace had been starting to fear spinsterhood (a fear she now questioned in view of younger, more modern women such as Vivien, who practically embraced her unmarried state) and had agreed to marry Gordon after only a few months of dating. Gordon, inching up on forty himself, had seemed intent on moving fast, which Grace only later realised had been due to the constant pressure to start a family from Mother Perkins and not at all to being swept away by *her*. Their first son had followed one year later, the second son even faster than that. And then the war had happened, and everything in family life had ground to a halt.

As Gordon spent long hours doing wartime tasks he could not talk about, Grace was left to raise both boys mostly alone. They grew up increasingly annoyed by how much she worried all the time: about the bombs that fell randomly over their neighbourhood, the trench being dug in nearby Kent to ward off the threat of invasion, the men heading off to Europe who never made it back. She was grateful her two boys would, God willing, never have to fight in a war like this, while they in their childish naivety openly resented this same fact.

After the war ended, Gordon's sense of victimhood continued. His moods only darkened as the skies above England finally opened back up, and Grace spent most of her energy trying to keep him from exploding at her or the boys. Or the leaky rain barrel. Or the milkman for treading too close to Gordon's front rose bed. Or the thousand other things that Gordon believed were in conspiracy against him. If only everyone and everything would *behave,* then he, too, could be happy. Was that asking too much?

Of course it was, but Grace never said those thoughts aloud because that would have been impertinent and unsympathetic, the two qualities in her which Gordon railed against the most. Grace didn't see the world remotely as her husband did. If she could give Vivien any romantic advice at all, it would be to find someone who shared the same horror at the world as you, and the same sense of curiosity and fun.

Any impertinence with Gordon she had learned to suppress over time, but Grace had never seen herself as unsympathetic. She simply didn't think the world owed anyone anything. Life was difficult for everybody in their own way—she herself could be envied for having a family by the hearth and a roof over her head, yet no one would ever suspect that sometimes she just wanted to stay on that bus and keep going.

Her ambivalence towards her life confused her because she

loved her sons, now ages ten and eleven, more than anything else.
She loved their sun-browned, strappy bodies in the summer and
the little eggbeater legs that were constantly jumping off of a vari-
ety of gravity-bound objects: overturned chesterfields, the tin roof
of Gordon's garden shed out back, the old knotted walnut tree on
the lawn out front. She loved how their faces lit up when she made
them warm Ovaltine before bed in the winter, and the warm cen-
tres of their foreheads as she kissed them each goodnight. But
she felt as if she represented only the beginning and the close to
their days. Worse still, to Gordon, she was the hole in the middle,
the source of his disappointment and despair, the person who—if
only she had been kind enough, loving enough—could have made
it all better for him, but instead resisted doing that. He couldn't
for the life of him figure out why: *why* she wanted to make him so
unhappy all the time.

By taking the job at the bookshop, for one thing. Gordon had
been prescribed his own period of convalescence near the end of
the war. *Nervous exhaustion* had been the official reason, but he
asserted that they had simply been working him far too hard.
He was to receive a weekly stipend that barely covered their gro-
ceries, and by 1946 his wife had started to despair, especially as
prices after the war began to soar.

One day Grace had headed early into Camden Town for her
weekly shopping day. Just as her bus approached the line of green-
grocer, fishmonger, and butcher shops up ahead, she impulsively
decided to stay on. The double-decker bus travelled next towards
the King's Cross and St Pancras stations, winding and winding its way farther south into the city's West End, farther than
Grace ever had reason to go. She sat at the very front of the top
deck, staring through the clear gridless window as all of London
whirled about below. She thought of the book she was currently
reading to the boys at bedtime, Jules Verne's *Twenty Thousand
Leagues Under the Sea,* and in a rare moment of whimsy that fit

her suddenly impulsive mood, Grace could imagine being at the front of a futuristic submarine roaming the sea in exile, far from the reach of everyone for whom she had been made responsible.

When the bus reached Bloomsbury, Grace recognised the name Great Ormond Street as the location of the children's hospital to which author J. M. Barrie had famously donated the copyright to *Peter Pan,* another favourite book of her sons'. As the bus continued to sputter its way along the increasingly narrow streets, Grace decided to get off and walk around. In this way she found herself for the first time in a quiet, cobblestone lane called Lamb's Conduit, stretching between the much more bustling Guilford Street at the north end and Theobalds Road to the south. Since Georgian times, this street and its seventy-eight establishments had housed all manner of high street shopping delights, from confectionery, cheese, and wine, to jewellery, books, and no less than two rival toy shops.

Grace treated herself to a morning bun and mug of steaming black coffee from a nearby street vendor and strolled about aimlessly, letting the coffee burn the end of her tongue, sipping it all the same. Finally, sitting on a wrought-iron bench, she found herself face-to-face with a notice pasted at eye level in the front window of a bookshop.

HELP WANTED

Mature, responsible & diligent lady secretary
for administrative duties in assistance of the general manager.
Pitman shorthand & typing speeds of 100 WPM a <u>must</u>.
For further information, please enquire inside.

The bookshop itself was exactly what tourists came to London to find. The exterior woodwork was painted a glossy dark indigo blue, there was a street-level bow window and two floors of symmetrical Georgian windows above, and the Victorian fanlight above the front door had been stained in the pattern of a rising sun. The only other signage besides the notice for help were the words Bloomsbury Books & Maps painted in gold and stretching the entire width of the shop, from above the door on the left to the other side of the front bow window.

The books in the window that caught the eyes of most pass-ersby were not of any particular interest to Grace. She enjoyed reading, but what she most enjoyed was money—or, rather, how to make more of it from less. A resourceful and sensible woman, Grace was well suited for her role as the default keeper of her family. She had always appreciated the economics of household management and the striving to reuse what one could: the saving of food scraps for tomorrow's supper, the jar of buttons, the ball of different string. Grace believed strongly in making the most of one's given lot. The only thing that defied her enterprising spirit was the family's grocery list: with rationing still in place, the Per-kins family's meals rarely varied from a rotation of meat, vegeta-bles, and one monthly egg each.

Just then a quite pleasant-looking man of about Grace's age stepped right in front of her, fishing around in his briefcase for something while muttering under his breath. Realising that he was blocking her view of the bookshop window, he took a step back.

"Oh, I'm terribly sorry, am I in your way?"

Grace looked up at him to smile politely and shake her head, causing coffee from her mug to spill onto the lap of her tweed pencil skirt.

"Oh, dear," the man said with concern. Reaching for a perfectly pressed handkerchief from his front jacket pocket, he dropped the key he had finally found and watched helplessly as it skipped un-der the bench where Grace sat.

She held out her mug with one hand and instinctively bent

down to retrieve the key with the other, and now they both smiled as their heads almost bumped together.

"We're rather a clumsy pair," the man said in a most elegant manner. Grace warmed to him immediately and the way he seemed most intent on keeping her at ease. The more frustrated he became with himself, the more solicitous he became with her. The complete opposite of Gordon, whom she had once thought elegant, too, in the manner of Charles Boyer or Basil Rathbone, until it had turned out that he was merely fastidious.

Just then a well-dressed tall blond young man with the face of an angel appeared in the front vestibule to the shop, holding the street door wide open.

"Excuse me, your *highness,* are we in need of assistance?" he called out with a laugh as the other man triumphantly held up the key now back in his grasp.

Grace watched the two men joking about in their jocular, familiar manner before disappearing together inside the shop. She remained sitting on the bench and read the posted advertisement again. She could do all those things—she had been a competent secretary in her day. Her Pitman speed was excellent and she would certainly qualify as *mature,* which she took to mean either too married, or too old, to pose a threat to delicate staff relations.

Grace took another sip from the mug, returned it to the coffee stall, and reluctantly started on her way. She got as far as the bus stop when something made her turn back. To this day she had no idea what. She had enjoyed the foreignness of the morning bun, the taste of coffee not prepared by her own hand for once, the Captain Nemo–like sensation of the bus ride. The elegance of the clumsy man, the affability of the other.

This is how they tricked you, Vivien would later decry.

CHAPTER FIVE

RULE No. 6

The shop's historic reputation as a purveyor of the
finest books must be upheld at all times.

The owner of Bloomsbury Books was Jeremy Baskin, the 11th
Earl Baskin, whose great-grandfather had won the shop
during a protracted card game in a West End private club exactly one hundred years ago. For the earldom of Baskin, Bloomsbury Books had ended up just one more asset on a centuries-old
ledger, along with several generations of racehorses, an original
Hogarth, and a row of worker cottages in the nearest village to
the family's ancestral Yorkshire seat.

Having been acquired in a fit of whimsy, the shop had been
held on to in much the same spirit ever since. Until the present
Earl Baskin, the family had not paid much attention to Bloomsbury Books and the property on Lamb's Conduit that housed it,
nor spent much time in the city at all. But Jeremy Baskin loved
London, loved walking the crowded, twisting streets and stumbling upon something he hadn't noticed before. The city was full
of endless surprises; one had to keep one's head up at all times, for
fear of what might get bumped into or missed.

Lord Baskin held a paternal affection for the bookshop and its
staff, who often struck him as a collection of lively but squabbling

children. He himself was childless, divorced, and alone. He had returned from service in North Africa with an injured left arm and a wife who, in his absence, had run off with a young American soldier. It had been a scandal worthy of his friend Evelyn's book *A Handful of Dust*. But instead of plunging into the depths of the Amazon rain forest to escape from all the gossip, the earl had taken shelter inside Bloomsbury Books while high society had fled London and the Blitz for their country estates. As different young men on staff were called up to serve and women often hired in their place, Lord Baskin had ended up working in the shop for the remainder of the war.

Unlike the other men in his family, Jeremy Baskin loved meeting people from all walks of life. He was the essence of geniality: he could find something interesting in just about anyone. Whereas his late older brother, father, and grandfather had all kept to one extremely narrow class of society—the idle aristocracy—Jeremy went out of his way to hear other people's stories, big or small. He believed that there was no better place to learn these than in a bookshop.

Behind the cash counter where Vivien was now begrudgingly stationed, Jeremy Baskin had been made privy to a few of the possible reasons for her discontent. The role of customer seemed to bring out the worst in certain people. There was something wonderfully—yet woefully—democratic about it all. One minute a harried housewife with a lollipop stuck on her sleeve would be demanding her money back for an obviously used book; another minute, a professor from one of the nearby universities would be criticizing the disarray on the rare books floor. Lord Baskin could never anticipate when the awkward or aggressive moment would arise, but this was when his years of preparation for inheriting the family estate served him best. He saw the bookshop—and the world—as a series of interconnected parts. His job was to keep it all running smoothly together, and his natural amiability helped him accommodate the momentary needs of others, while managing not to give up any real ground. The present Earl Baskin could not afford to lose much more of *that*.

For one thing, the Finance Act of 1949 had placed an 80 per cent death tax on amounts in the family estate in excess of one million pounds; when Baskin's grandfather had died, the taxes facing his son and heir had been only a fraction of that. The result for the earldom was a new imperative to sell nonessential family assets to help defray the costs of less dispensable ones. The bookshop should have been the first to go, having annually yielded only a few thousand pounds of profit since the Great Slump of 1930. Things remained so tight that both Mr. Dutton and Mr. Allen, as the most senior members of staff, received a small part of their annual salaries in shares in an effort to keep the bookshop liquid. Soon the two men would be in a position to acquire majority ownership of the shop by pooling their equity, and the Baskin family's involvement with Bloomsbury Books would come to an end.

Recently Mr. Dutton had mentioned doing this very thing in conjunction with Mr. Allen. Lord Baskin, however, wasn't sure that they were the best choice for shepherding the shop into the second half of the twentieth century. Much as he genuinely liked and respected both men, Baskin couldn't help but wonder if it was time for a change. Frank spent more and more time on the road, while Herbert swatted away the ideas of his younger staff like so many pesky flies: *no* to special sales, *no* to ticketed events, and *absolutely not* to personalized subscription and home library services. Lord Baskin's mother, a famous and generous hostess, had taught him the importance of putting others at ease and providing an experience. Dutton and Allen were selling only the memory of the past, and the past was no longer worth as much. Lord Baskin understood the financial side of the book business better than most, and his family's historic shop was hardly worth more than the land it rested on.

Fortunately for Lord Baskin, he still owned *that*. The majority of the land in England remained largely in the hands of a few thousand hereditary peers like himself. But Lord Baskin suspected a reckoning was ahead for the "landed gentry," as his father had preferred to call himself. *Gentry* as in gentleman; *landed* as in lucky. Having inherited his father's sangfroid and his American mother's free spirit, Jeremy Baskin was not troubled by the idea of change; he knew he would always have enough. But for many of his peers, the prospects of the new decade, only two days in, were highly unsettling. The aristocracy were starting to sell family homes when they could, and demolishing them when they couldn't. Invitations were being scooped up and sought out: a country weekend away or London townhouse party at the host's expense could solve many a temporary cash-flow problem.

That was where the earl found himself tonight, standing near the bar in the main drawing room of his hostess's townhouse in Belgrave Square. The guests were celebrating Vivien Leigh's return to the stage that night in *A Streetcar Named Desire* following a short convalescence. Baskin planned on making a relatively early evening of it. The message left for him at the front desk of the Hotel Russell in Bloomsbury had been quite disconcerting: Herbert Dutton had telephoned to explain a temporary shuffling of staff to accommodate what he was sure would be a short but regrettable leave on his part. Knowing both Mr. Dutton's dedication to his job and his tendency to minimize anything else, Lord Baskin was worried enough to have less patience than usual for the social niceties swirling about him.

He was relieved to spot Yardley Sinclair coming towards him through the crowd of shimmering jewel-toned cocktail dresses and black dinner jackets with nary a tailcoat in sight. This was just one of many postwar changes in dress that Lord Baskin was having to adapt to in his early forties. Despite the new informality, Yardley looked as elegant, and as impish, as ever. As the highly respected but notably avaricious head of museum services at Sotheby's, Yardley split his time between London and the small Hampshire village of Chawton, where he had recently acquired several acres of farmland. Rumour had it that he shared his home there with another man, a local farmer and fellow member of the Jane Austen Society. Lord Baskin had known and liked Yardley for years, ever since their time together at Cambridge.

"Sinclair, you're back from the farm, then?"

Yardley nodded while merrily taking a flute of champagne from the tray being discreetly held out by a waiter who, unlike the company, was still in tails.

"Yes," Yardley purred in his Scottish drawl, an accent that Lord Baskin could swear was only thickening with time. "There's nothing like celebrating New Year with an assortment of villagers drunk on cider."

"Was the society all together again?"

"All except the wee one. She's still up at Cambridge, far exceeding our own paltry efforts there. But I brought Mimi back with me. She's around here somewhere. And you? Were you in town for it all?"

Baskin finished his glass of champagne but declined a second one. "Need my wits about me," he explained at Yardley's inquiring look.

"Lady trouble?"

Baskin laughed as if the idea were absurd. "Hardly. Who would want an aging divorcé with a crumbling estate?"

"An estate's still an estate, old chap. And divorce is clearly on the rise." Yardley raised his eyebrow playfully while glancing about the room at several women straining to overhear Lord Baskin, who was so tall and attractive that he stood out in any crowd.

Following his gaze, Lord Baskin spied Lady Browning listening intently, with a mischievous expression, to the two men's
conversation. She purposefully caught his eye before whispering something in the ear of her close friend Ellen Doubleday,
the recent widow of the American publishing magnate. Baskin
wondered what gossip the two women might be saving up from
tonight. Fortunately, he knew that his love life, which of late had
started to perplex even him, was safe from prying eyes.

"The trouble's the shop, actually," he now answered Yardley.
"My GM's taken off sick, and Frank Allen will need to be called
back."

"Allen won't like that. He's been on a right tear of late over at
Sotheby's with new acquisitions."

Baskin nodded. "Dutton will have to rearrange all the roles,
what with staff being so lean. The girls in the shop are sure to be
overlooked yet again for any advancement—Dutton's far too old-
fashioned that way."

"Perhaps he'll finally loosen up."

"Not likely." Lord Baskin smiled ruefully. He had known Herbert Dutton for decades, with his fifty-one rules and shaky but
iron fist; the man was incapable of impulse or initiative.

"Your family's had the shop for, what, a hundred years? Perhaps it's time to let go."

Baskin shook his head slowly. "What will happen to the
women? The country's still in such a slump. And then there's Mr.
Ramaswamy, joining us all the way from India, hoping for a job in
the sciences and having to settle for us. No, I must somehow keep
it in the right hands."

"How very paternal of you."

Baskin laughed. "I'm sure I do sound presumptuous. But each
of them needs this job to put food on the table, they're stretched so
thin. We're lucky, you and I. I mean, look around you. Everyone is
here. One can always drum up opportunity."

It was true. On any given night in London, hotel bars, theatre lobbies, and drawing rooms all teemed with the same assortment of people: politicians and press barons, aristocrats and American socialites such as Ellen Doubleday, writers, artists, and actresses such as Lady Olivier and Mimi Harrison. In America, Hollywood controlled the film industry, Washington was the centre of politics, and New York of the arts—but London was the centre of everything. A city built on the ghost versions of earlier ones, you could plumb its soil and find centuries of relics from Roman, Anglo-Saxon, Viking, Norman, Elizabethan, and Victorian times.

Lord Baskin surveyed this particular drawing room and wondered if the lords and ladies gathered about were soon to become relics of another kind. The London outside of these gilded rooms—the one that belonged to his employees—had been worn down and bombed out. But change was afoot, even he could see that. Lord Baskin didn't know what to expect from the decade ahead, but he had an inkling it would end up looking nothing like the last one. High-density housing, employment, immigration, and exports were all rapidly on the rise, along with national health care for all. That meant more money for holidays by the sea, trips to the cinema, and books. More money for the new nylon hosiery that Vivien and Grace could now afford, despite the scuffed toes of their patent leather pumps.

His two female staff were highly competent women who made the most of what they had, which wasn't much. Lord Baskin admired them both greatly and feared that Mr. Dutton did a disservice to the shop in putting only men in charge. But Baskin was nothing if not a hands-off owner: his heart was in the game, but he knew his place in the world and respected the autonomy of others. His conception of noblesse oblige was complete, unchallenged, and about to come in for a reckoning of its own.

CHAPTER SIX

Arrival time for all staff must be strictly adhered to.

amb's Conduit Street had been named in tribute not to the quaint image stirred up in tourists of a crossing for sheep, but to a cloth merchant and an Elizabethan dam. Four hundred years ago, the wealthy William Lambe had financed the building of an actual conduit, now long since demolished, to supply water to the city from springs and meadow rivers. A noted philanthropist, Lambe had also provided over one hundred pails to poor women for the collecting and selling of the water, a dreary employment that Vivien often sarcastically compared to her and Grace's own.

Near the base of the street, at No. 40, was Bloomsbury Books. When Vivien arrived late for work the morning after Mr. Dutton's attack, she was surprised to find both the outside and the inner vestibule doors to the shop still locked. The customers weren't due to arrive until on the half hour, when the shop officially opened. Mr. Dutton always asked the staff to start their day at precisely 9:00 a.m. instead, although Vivien often encroached well past that time. From what she could tell as she entered and looked about, no one else was at work yet to ask for tea, spy from ladders, or fiddle with decrepit fuses. The entire main floor of the shop was eerily quiet.

Vivien went to place her black patent leather handbag under the squarely situated cash counter. She let the register swing fully open instead of stopping it with her hip. There was still no response from anyone else, not even the cough of acknowledgement that Mr. Dutton always gave the first sound of the register each morning without ever leaving his office.

Vivien peered under the counter as she hung up the front door keys on their little metal hook. Alec's briefcase (real calfskin leather and monogrammed in gold, a gift from his adoring parents) was not hidden in the corner where he always kept it.

Vivien's keen eye shot up at this discovery, her mind racing.

Alec was never tardy, not unless he had been entertaining guest authors the night before with the permission and encouragement of the much less social Mr. Dutton. In fact, Alec was the first to arrive at the shop most mornings and often the last to leave at the end of the day, and on Monday nights he worked extra late. Vivien was sure it was to gain some kind of an advantage over everyone else for the rest of the week.

She thought back on all the commotion of the previous day. How the small, strange Evelyn Stone had left Mr. Dutton's office with hardly a word goodbye, and Vivien and Grace had followed soon after. Most days, Ashwin Ramaswamy would leave shortly after the women; no one had taken the time to learn for where. Master Mariner Scott usually headed out next, to one of the two pubs that had been a feature of life on Lamb's Conduit for centuries: the Sun at No. 63 near the corner of Great Ormond Street, and the Lamb at No. 94, said to have often been frequented by Charles Dickens and therefore a particular favourite with the men of Bloomsbury Books.

The last employees to leave each night were always some combination of Herbert Dutton, Frank Allen, and Alec McDonough. When Frank was not off on his travels to various estate sales, he would wait behind for Herbert so that the two men could end their day by talking over the affairs of the shop. Alec stayed behind even longer than that, ostensibly to occupy himself before an evening event, but also gaining valuable time alone with both Dutton and Allen, much to Vivien's irritation and dismay.

But yesterday had not been most days. Vivien had been taken aback by her level of panic and concern for Mr. Dutton as he lay writhing on the floor, the rest of them at a loss over what to do next. All of them except for Evie Stone.

Just then Vivien heard a noise from the back of the shop. Mr. Dutton must be at his desk after all, bright and early as usual. She headed straight to his office, surprised at this sudden and new desire to check in on him. When she reached the open doorway, she stopped in her tracks.

There, seated at Herbert Dutton's large desk covered in towering piles of paperwork and bills, sat Alec McDonough.

"God, Alec, the body's not even cold. Get up from there," she spat out, then noticed the lengthy sheaf of papers in his hands. "What do you have there?" she asked suspiciously.

"Notes of instruction. From Mr. Dutton." Alec put the pages down and spread them out fanlike on the blotting paper before him. "Fourteen pages."

"What on earth for?"

"It appears . . . it appears that he is having to take an extended leave. Doctor's orders."

"He is not! It was just a seizure—presumably not the first."

Alec shook his head. "I think things with Mr. Dutton are far more serious than he'd ever let on."

Vivien stared at him. "All the same, Mr. Allen will do just as well in the role."

Alec patted the papers with both hands, as if in finality. "It appears Mr. Dutton would like an acting general manager who is always available for the floor."

Vivien stood there, silently glowering down at Alec and enjoying the advantage of height for once over his six-foot-plus frame, until it dawned on her.

"You're not—"

Alec gave a small but confident shrug.

"Well, I'm not—"

"That's your prerogative."

They stared at each other.

"Fine. I'll just have to resign."

"Are you quite sure?" Alec finally spoke.

Vivien watched him carefully. He wasn't telling her everything. Fourteen pages was a lot, even for Mr. Dutton, and not a very resounding endorsement of the capabilities of his staff.

"What else is in those notes? Here, give them to me."

Alec shifted about in the large banker's chair but did nothing further in response. "It's addressed to me. As acting general manager."

Vivien sighed in defeat, then sat down across from him.

"As a matter of first instance, Evelyn Stone is hired."

"I should hope so."

"And there's to be a new head of fiction." Alec paused. "You, apparently."

He was watching her carefully in turn. She saw something deliberate cut loose from his usually cool demeanour and quicken in his gaze.

"I retract my resignation," Vivien countered quickly.

"Can you do that?"

"Yes. Yes, I think I can." She stood up and left the office before he could say another word. She practically bumped into Grace rushing in late from the street, her hat and coat still on. Vivien raised her eyes at Grace as they passed in the corridor, knowing Alec could hear through the open door, then walked straight to the front of the shop to face the tables and shelves before her with pent-up anticipation.

Almost immediately, she walked over to the bookcase marked *A* and picked out the two-volume *Little Women* and a thick anthology on Jane Austen that sat surprisingly neglected on the bottom shelf. First things first, she would pull together that table of classic women authors she'd always wanted to create. Anne Brontë would gain her rightful place next to her sisters, Katherine Mansfield would join her longtime pen pal Virginia Woolf, and Elizabeth Gaskell would emerge from the Victorian shadow of Dickens, Thackeray, and Trollope.

A knock at the front door brought Vivien out of her reverie. She glanced at her Cartier Tank watch, a gift from her late fiancé: one of the first ever made by the luxury French designer. Grace had once asked if the 18k-gold-and-diamond watch wasn't too painful a reminder, especially given its design based on the tanks of the earlier war's battlefields. But Vivien liked the sharp pang of emotion that she felt whenever she saw the watch and was forced to remember. It made her feel strangely alive, when little else did.

The watch showed exactly 9:30 a.m.: time to open. With the Austen anthology still in her hands, Vivien went over to unlock the front door from the small anteroom that preceded the entrance into the shop. She gave a quick greeting to the first man in line, then headed back to the cash counter, where Grace now stood waiting.

"You didn't quit?" she asked in a hushed tone.

Vivien shook her head and peered down the corridor. "The Tyrant told you everything?"

Grace nodded. "Poor Mr. Dutton must have been here for hours last night, writing all that down."

"I'm sure he had a draft in his filing cabinet ready to go. In case of emergency."

"So, you're in charge." Grace looked down at the Austen book that Vivien was playfully cradling. "Don't get dizzy with power."

They smiled at each other, and Grace gave Vivien a quick, affectionate pat on her shoulder before returning to her desk.

An hour went by, an hour in which—for once—Alec McDonough was nowhere to be seen. Vivien could almost cry from the freedom. She stood there coming up with mental lists for all the authors she would now bring in: Gertrude Stein and her fellow postmodernists; American realists including Sarah Orne Jewett; out-of-fashion Victorian sensation novelists such as Mary Elizabeth Braddon and Ellen Wood.

"Miss?"

Vivien looked up at the American accent to see a young woman standing before her, wearing thick-rimmed glasses and a beret cap on her head.

"How can I help you?"

"I'm sure you don't, but any chance you carry *The Age of Innocence,* by Edith Wharton?"

"No, I'm afraid not."

"It won the American Pulitzer Prize."

"Yes, I know. I'm frightfully sorry."

The younger woman gave an understanding smile and returned to the farthest aisle in the fiction section. Vivien watched her poking around the shelves marked *W,* knowing the best she would be able to find would be Virginia Woolf, the only woman whom the male staff did not seem to mind taking up valuable shelf space.

Vivien had lost count of the number of times young female students and staff from the surrounding universities and museums had come into the shop asking for certain women authors, only to be met with an unexpected lack of success. Only Agatha Christie, Nancy Mitford, and Daphne du Maurier could reliably be found on the shelves, mostly because they continued to produce and sell and were therefore harder to ignore.

Hard to ignore felt like the best that anyone could expect from the shop when it came to women authors. Vivien had always wanted to change all that. Suddenly, she could. If one could rely on anything at Bloomsbury Books, it was hierarchy. Mr. Dutton had committed it all to the page, and in so doing, he had freed Vivien's ambition to secure his own. Furthermore, as acting general manager, Alec could only push back so hard on any of Vivien's choices: she had his own record as head of fiction to lord over him.

Vivien not only suddenly felt free—she felt emboldened. She could take the structure and the strictures in place, the framed fifty-one rules of the shop, the many pages of notes that Alec was already eagerly administering, and turn them in her favour. She wondered if the men fully understood what they had done, in their fervour to elevate Alec.

It was to be a significant miscalculation on their part.

CHAPTER SEVEN

RULE No. 9

Any interruption of a customer's thoughts
risks interruption of a sale.

t was mid-afternoon when Frank Emsbury Allen returned to
London from North Yorkshire, where he had been attending the
two-day estate sale at Toppings alongside dozens of other rare
book buyers from across England. Emerging from St Pancras Station into the early dusk, Frank treated himself to a cab. Normally
he would have sprinted the fifteen minutes down Judd Street
towards the shop, but it had been a long day and he was eager to
get home.

While at Toppings, Frank had quickly but meticulously gone
through the entire family library of one thousand books. There
had been no catalogue to prepare from—no auction house such as
Sotheby's involved. It was what they in the book business called a
fire sale. The last of the family had passed away with no immediate male heir, and the executor was quickly selling everything off
to make up the punitive death taxes now owing. Frank suspected
that within the decade, the stunning but dilapidated Georgian
Palladian home would itself be torn down to make way for even
more of the prefab bungalows already circling the estate.

Frank entered the shop at 40 Lamb's Conduit and found everything much the same as always. Two American ladies in rose and yellow Dior day dresses with matching hats and bags stood looking over the front table of art books with the dull air of obligation. These were the kind of women who tended to pop briefly into the shop after a day spent lunching, shopping, and touring the National Gallery with a private guide. For once, Alec McDonough, with his floppy blond hair and tall trim form always in jacket and trousers, was not to be found high up on one of the rolling ladders ("like God," Vivien liked to complain). Vivien herself stood at her regular station inside the front cash counter, scribbling furiously away in her green coil-bound notebook.

Frank passed her with a quick and mutual nod, everyone on staff always aware of the need to stay as silent as possible for the browsers. *Any interruption of a customer's thoughts risks interruption of a sale* was the ninth rule of the shop, and one of many mantras that management had instilled over the years.

Frank knew from the morning post at Toppings, passed to him by the head butler just shortly after breakfast, that Herbert Dutton would not be in that day. Frank did not know anything more than that. He had slid the note off the silver tray being held out to him just as Lady Bradbury, at least fifteen years his senior, had given him another of her looks. He had not taken her up on them, as easy as it would have been to indulge in a night away from home. A pleasant-looking man with sharp, aquiline features and a smoothly seductive manner, Frank had found himself declining the attentions of many estate widows over the years as he rummaged about their late husband's libraries.

Frank bounded up the stairs to the upper two floors of the shop. Full of high, unflappable energy, he was quite the counterpart to the subdued Herbert Dutton, with whom Frank had unofficially co-managed Bloomsbury Books for the past eighteen years. As he turned the corner of the second-floor landing, he didn't bother to peek his head in at Master Mariner Scott, who would greet him at most with a grunt. When Frank finally reached the third-floor landing, which led into a large open loft, he went to hang his bag and suitcase on a nearby coatstand, whirled around in relief to be back, and stopped so suddenly that one foot hung suspended mid-stride before him.

There, in the middle of the floor, sitting on a three-legged wooden stool, was a small nondescript girl who looked to be still in her teens. She had left the Regency-panelled glass doors to the bookcase wide open as she poked her head about inside.

Frank's mouth opened, then shut, and he whirled around again to run back down to the second floor.

"There's a girl in my department."

Master Mariner Scott did not look up right away at Frank's outburst. Instead, Scott held up his left forefinger and made a shushing sound as he continued his reading.

"A girl. A right tiny thing. This big." Frank held out his own left hand flush to the floor and three feet up.

Scott finally put down his magnifying glass to stare at his colleague. "Come on, man, she's a mite bigger than that."

"What on earth's happened around here while I've been gone?"

Scott briefly recounted for Frank the details of Mr. Dutton's seizure and collapse, while Frank sank slowly down into a nearby reading chair.

"I had no idea—his note simply said he wouldn't be in today."

"There was no need for alarm." Scott coughed. "It's all worked out well enough."

Speaking with the former navy officer often felt like chipping away at an iceberg floating in the arctic seas, but at that moment Frank thought he caught a slight thawing in the older man's demeanour.

"So, he handed her a job, just like that, without consulting me?"

"Without consulting anyone. She showed up this morning. Went straight to work and hasn't been heard from since. A Miss Evelyn Stone."

"Evelyn Stone," Frank repeated almost absentmindedly. "Oh, of course, I remember now—the telephone call right before Christmas. I'm afraid she's not at all what I expected."

"But you did meet her once?"

"Scarcely. It was during the dispersal of the Chawton Great House library. Autumn of . . . '46, I think? Yardley Sinclair of Sotheby's introduced her to me. I can hardly fathom why." Frank let out a heavy sigh from his chair. He liked to travel in part because he did not like feeling watched over in any way. Being on the road allowed Frank to do whatever he wanted, when he wanted. And he did not want a girl going through all of his valuable books, degree from Cambridge or not.

"I suppose the women put Herbert up to this," he added, placing his right thumb and forefinger between his eyebrows and pushing out the vertical frown line that tended to appear in times of stress.

Master Mariner Scott shrugged. "Herbert was in a fairly demented state."

Frank sighed again.

Things for Miss Evelyn Stone were not off to an auspicious start.

At 10:29 a.m. on January 3, 1950, Evie Stone had arrived at the front door of Bloomsbury Books exactly one minute before Mr. Dutton had instructed her to. The night before, she had exited the shop as its newest employee and carefully timed the journey back to her friend Charlotte Dewar's tiny Richmond flat. When Evie had telephoned over Christmas and explained her need for work, Charlotte had immediately offered her a foldable camp bed in her flat until Evie could afford a room of her own.

Evie and Charlotte had grown close as servant girls on the Knight family estate in Chawton. After the estate had been sold off to a developer, Charlotte had swiftly secured new employment in London as a hotel chambermaid. The move to London had been prompted by a romance that had ended just as swiftly. There had been a few other dalliances since then, but Charlotte seemed in no hurry to marry and start a family, which confused Evie. She couldn't otherwise see the point of men.

Walking home along Lamb's Conduit Street as the shopkeepers put down their blinds for the night, Evie kept her pace steady as she passed the row of shops without glancing around. She had been to Bloomsbury on enough research trips to no longer notice any of the buildings or landmarks about her. Even when somewhere new, Evie tended to look straight ahead as she walked, focused on her ultimate destination and determined never to be late. She had never been late for anything in her life. She planned everything out so that she always arrived one minute beforehand. The idea of making anyone wait, even for a few seconds, was as foreign to her as being late to work was for Mr. Dutton, or being on time was for the petulant Vivien.

It was Vivien, however, who was there to greet Evie when she arrived the next morning for her first day of work at Bloomsbury Books.

"Why, hullo, Mr. Dutton wrote you'd be by."

Vivien seemed much warmer than when they had first met. She had a large pile of books in her hands and a cleared table before her, and was happily laying everything out according to her own design.

Not knowing what else to say, Evie asked after the man who had been part of yesterday's emergency, the one always on the ladder.

"Oh. You mean the new general manager with poor Mr. Dutton in absentia." Vivien twisted a pencil about in her hands. "Quite the opportunist. You know the type."

Evie pictured Stuart Wesley back in Cambridge, his arm around Senior Fellow Christenson's daughter, the two of them ambling drunkenly along the crumbling cobblestone streets in black tie and silk dress, exaggeratedly stepping over the champagne corks and confetti strewn about their well-heeled feet.

"Ah," Vivien observed with a conspiratorial smile. "I see you do know the type. Never mind. You needn't worry about *him*."

Evie stared at Vivien, at her quick vacillations between hostility and humour, at the hair cropped even shorter than hers but in a much more beguiling way. Whereas Evie used sewing shears to maintain her plain bob, Vivien's hairstyle had a shape to it that flattered her oval face and wide-set eyes, with bangs that crested just above the brows to bring out the matching darkness of her mascaraed lashes. As the two women spoke, Evie found herself often staring at Vivien's eyes, which were more made-up than Evie was used to, even on her actress friend Mimi Harrison. The mascara had been thickly layered on, and a dark pencil had added both an arch to the brows and long winged tips to the outer corners of the eyes, until Vivien's gaze seemed to dominate the entire landscape of her face. Evie felt as if Vivien could see everything about her, like one of the many beagles they used to have on the family farm. Evie wondered if that was the point.

"Mr. Dutton left lengthy instructions—thank God McDonough can't fabricate it *all*. I am the new head of fiction, and we understand you're to help Mr. Allen."

"Yes, miss."

Vivien looked as if she was waiting for Evie to say something further, before amiably persisting, "We understand you *know* Mr. Allen."

"Yes, miss. I met 'im at an auction. At Sotheby's."

"You worked at Sotheby's then?" Vivien's voice had a note of surprise that Evie missed.

"No, miss, I was attending the auction. With Mr. Yardley Sinclair."

"Oh, yes, Grace told me. How delightful. And . . . how do you know him?"

Evie was not sure she had ever met anyone as curious as Vivien. "We are members of a society together."

Vivien stared at her. "What kind of society?"

"The Jane Austen Society."

Vivien gasped. "You are not!"

"I am."

"You are one of the famous eight, that saved the cottage? You and Yardley Sinclair, and actress Mimi Harrison?"

Evie nodded.

"Well, I never. I'm a dues-paying member of the Brontë Society myself. I seem to better relate to their rage." Vivien checked her watch. Mr. Dutton did not permit a clock on the walls of the shop, lest customers suddenly recall their other commitments. "It'll be time soon for elevenses. Care to join me in the kitchen? New head of fiction or not, we women will always be entrusted to make the tea. Although that's no small operation around here, let me assure you."

As they walked down the corridor to the kitchenette, located across the hallway from the two back offices, Evie noticed the tall blond man from the ladder the day before now sitting comfortably in Mr. Dutton's chair.

Vivien was noticing him, too. "Like I said, don't mind him," she repeated with a sigh.

Leading the way into the small storage room that had been converted into a kitchen, Vivien took down a canister of black tea leaves and plugged in the Swan kettle while Evie watched intently.

"We always leave the kettle filled with water to get stale. Just one of many small acts of rebellion around here."

Vivien started pulling down a sugar bowl and various mismatched cups and saucers from the open cabinet above their heads.

"And now we wait right here, as the kettle's apt to boil dry. I once set the counter on fire that way."

She gave a strange laugh, her gleeful hostility leaving Evie unable to think of anything to say in response.

"With rationing still at two ounces a week, or twenty-five cups, Mr. Dutton has all seven—now eight!—of us on a very strict accounting. But if you remember four trips a day, you shan't go wrong."

As Evie stood there, the most unfamiliar scents seemed to flavour the air.

Vivien, with her unceasing observance, noticed the girl's nose twitch.

"Spices," Vivien said simply, giving a nod to a stack of small cube-shaped wooden boxes on the highest shelf above. "Mr. Ramaswamy's. The Indian fellow. You met him yesterday. Well, only slightly, given our sudden lapse in hospitality."

Evie drew in a deep breath and picked up on the smell of cinnamon and cloves. The powerful scent reminded Evie of her mother's famous Christmas cake, and she felt an unusual pang of missing home.

"It's to make his tea," explained Vivien. "His *masala,* he calls it. Lovely word. Lovely man, actually."

Evie watched as Vivien scooped out the tea leaves from the canister with a measuring spoon and added them to a large Brown Betty teapot. When the water had boiled, she unplugged the kettle before filling the teapot to the very top.

"We have a slight problem with the fuse," she was saying to Evie. "If we lose that kettle, all hell will break loose around here, so Grace and I keep it unplugged just to be safe."

Vivien took a creamer jug from the white under-the-counter fridge and teaspoons from a nearby drawer, laying everything next to the cups and saucers. "And now we leave it out for the men to make up themselves. They're all very *particular,* this lot."

Evie returned to the Rare Books Department with her own cup of tea and two biscuits, then stood there for a minute in the middle of the large open floor, ruminating quietly. Although she was always one for routine, Bloomsbury Books seemed to have a lot of unnecessary rules—and violations—in place. After the relative freedoms of Cambridge, for all its faults, Evie was starting to wonder what she had gotten herself into.

Behind the large desk at the east end of the room, Evie noticed a small dustbin closet. Inside she found a little wooden stool, just perfect for her work. Settling into her new routine and regular seat, she was thankful to be free at least to resume the secret task she had set herself.

She had actually set it months earlier, long before Christenson, Kinross, and Wesley had interrupted her preferred academic path. It had been no moment of coincidence that Evie had opened the top drawer in her makeshift filing cabinet, started at *A,* and retrieved Mr. Allen's card shortly after.

She had kept it for a reason all along.

CHAPTER EIGHT

New staff shall dedicate themselves entirely to learning
their roles and responsibilities.

Evie Stone spent her first day at Bloomsbury Books going
through the shelves of the Rare Books Department. Just before he had left for his extended convalescence, Mr. Dutton
had informed Evie that there were nearly ten thousand volumes
on the uppermost floor of the shop which, it pained him to admit,
were in need of organising.

"Frank—Mr. Allen—is an excellent acquirer. We rely upon
him greatly. He does, however, lack some, ah, diligence where cataloguing is concerned."

As Evie now began to sort through the disarray of the third
floor, she recalled the last time she had been left alone with so
many rare and neglected books. As a servant girl at Chawton
Great House on the Knight family estate, she had been desperate for education of any kind, having left school early due to her
father's accident and resulting misfortune. A precocious reader of
Jane Austen and other classic authors, Evie had been the first in
the village to consider the possible significance and value of the
Knight family library, which Austen herself had regularly used
and which over a century later sat neglected as part of the dwin-
dling estate.

For two years, as everyone else in the Great House slept, Evie had gone through every one of the 2,375 books in the library page by page, looking for marginalia and markings of any kind—perhaps even traces of Austen herself. The resulting handwritten catalogue would become the basis of the eventual evaluation by Yardley Sinclair on behalf of the newly founded Jane Austen Society. The society had purchased the entire Knight family library following the appraisals by Evie and Yardley, who were the least surprised out of everyone when two thousand of the books sold through Sotheby's in the fall of 1946 for a record-setting four hundred thousand pounds. With these profits, the society was able to turn the neighbouring Chawton cottage where Austen had once lived into the Jane Austen's House Museum.

Frank Allen had attended the Great House dispersal on behalf of Bloomsbury Books. By the end he had acquired, with little competitive bidding, five volumes from the Knight family library. Evie had kept track in her notebook of the two thousand winning bids that had been made during the course of the lengthy auction. She had been relieved when the Third Folio edition of the collected works of Shakespeare had been won by Dr. Septimus Feasby on behalf of the British Museum, following an extremely heated battle with a phone buyer from the University of Bonn; dismayed when Blake's *The First Book of Urizen* headed off to a wealthy private buyer on the California coast; and crestfallen when a handful of female-authored books barely met their reserve pricing.

During this exciting time, Evie had also been preparing for her university equivalency exams under the keen and exacting eye of schoolteacher and fellow society member Adeline Gray as her private tutor. Yardley Sinclair had attended Cambridge decades earlier, and Mimi Harrison's fiancé was currently on sabbatical there from Harvard. All three society members—unbeknownst to Evie—had made sure her application received a complete and proper review. The admitting professors could not dismiss the achievement by Evie, at only age sixteen, of the historically significant Chawton Great House library catalogue. The society had sent her off to Cambridge, hopeful that her prodigious work ethic, single-minded ambition, and high moral standards would result in a long and rewarding academic career.

Instead, Evie Stone was back to cataloguing books. But she did not look dismayed as she sat there, only hours into her first day of work, already forgotten on the top floor of Bloomsbury Books. For all her aspirations, Evie was most comfortable alone, surrounded by these simple physical objects that held far more exploration, and explanation, of the world outside than she had ever acquired from people.

She turned to the next cabinet to go through. She knew exactly what she was looking for—she could only hope that she would find it.

Ironically, she had Professor Kinross to thank for both her current job *and* her secret mission. While doing unrelated research work at Cambridge, Evie had discovered that one of the books from the Great House library had been worth far more, historically and financially, than either she or Yardley would have had reason to suspect. By so diligently recording all two thousand winning bids in her notebook during the monthlong auction by Sotheby's, Evie had been able to independently confirm that the undervalued book had been purchased at the Great House dispersal by Mr. Frank Allen of Bloomsbury Books.

Evie was grateful not to have to ask Yardley—and, by extension, Sotheby's—about the acquisition of the book. Although Evie trusted Yardley as both a friend and fellow member of the Jane Austen Society, she also knew that he had an ethical obligation as an employee of Sotheby's to disclose anything he might learn about one of its sales, past or present. As a result, Evie was hesitant to involve him or anyone else in her current search.

This time, whatever she discovered would be solely for herself.

The top floor of Bloomsbury Books was poorly lit to protect the rare books, and Evie spent much of that first day sitting comfortably in shadow. Eventually the sky grew gloomy with the onset of both snow and dusk, and she went to turn on the copper banker's lamp on Mr. Allen's desk. When nothing happened, Evie followed the lamp cord that snaked along the floorboards, between the piles of books, and into an electrical box protruding dangerously from the middle of the room. After fiddling with the plug and socket, she headed downstairs to reluctantly inquire of Grace.

"Oh, no worries—it's that blasted fuse again." Grace stood up from her small desk and headed towards the back staircase, nodding amiably for Evie to follow her.

"Miss Lowry named these stairs Via Inferno for all the fires we've nearly started over the years. Dante's nine circles of hell."

"She told me about the kitchen-counter one," Evie piped up from behind as they proceeded carefully down the rickety wooden stairs until reaching the mechanical room at the bottom.

"Viv's nicknamed most things—and people—that irritate her. Which are quite numerous, I'm afraid."

Grace's head disappeared into the fuse box, and Evie looked around while waiting patiently. Through the open doorway she could see the back of Mr. Ramaswamy, who was standing at his desk.

"Has there been any word from Mr. Dutton?" Evie wondered aloud, thinking back on how she and Ash Ramaswamy had first met.

"Not a one. There. All fixed. Evie?"

Evie turned at the sound of her name to see Grace watching her in amusement.

"Shall we?"

"Actually, I might have a look around while I'm down here, if that's all right?"

"Of course. Now, officially, rule number twenty-two says you mustn't leave your station unattended unless you are on a break." Grace winked. "But you didn't hear that one from me."

As Grace's footsteps could be heard treading carefully back upstairs, Evie entered the Science and Naturalism Department just as quietly. Ash Ramaswamy appeared deep in thought and concentration, which Evie thoroughly respected. She detested nothing more than being interrupted in the middle of a task.

At the sound of her approach, Ash straightened up and turned around to face her.

"I hope I'm not bothering you."

When he didn't immediately say anything in response, Evie looked about herself and then down at his desk. She was surprised to discover that he had been peering through a microscope and not at a book.

"So, you came back," he finally spoke, putting his little wire-rimmed spectacles back on. "You must not frighten easily."

She continued to stand there awkwardly before him.

"Yes, Miss Stone? Do you need anything?"

His desk was covered in glass slides and a large wooden box containing several slim labelled drawers, on top of which rested magnifying glasses, tweezers, and several less familiar metal instruments.

"What are you looking at?"

He moved aside and motioned to the microscope between them. "Would you like to see?"

Evie had never spent a minute of her life thinking about the things she could not see. Her vision was always gravity-bound and concrete. Life on the farm had taught her to pay attention to what was right before one's eyes: the rain clouds looming on the horizon, the burr in the side of an animal's coat, the exact right time for reaping wheat before the head shattered. Her subsequent years immersed in books had taught her to fixate on words and their placement as objects and makers of meaning. This was one reason why more esoteric studies such as philosophy and religion left her cold. She had to be able to run her hands over something to believe it was true.

Evie had also never looked through a microscope, having left school before any significant study in the sciences. Ash helped her adjust the lens and the height of the instrument, and suddenly the object on the slide came into focus. Evie caught her breath at the aqua iridescence and detailed symmetry of the pair of wings before her.

"Oh. That's quite lovely, actually. A dragonfly?"

"No, miss, it's a damselfly. Not quite the same thing." He removed the slide to show her. "Smaller, see? Less than an inch, this one."

"Is that what's in all these trays, then? Insects?"

He nodded. "There are a million different species in the world. It keeps me busy."

She looked over at him curiously. He sounded as if he was making fun of himself.

"I would never have thought a fly could be that beautiful up close."

"Perhaps that's the point." Ash put the slide away in its little drawer.

"Were you a scientist then, back home? In India?"

"I know where home is." He followed these curt words with an equally sudden, conciliatory smile. "And, yes, I was. At the University of Madras."

"Really? How long have you been in London?"

He adjusted his little wire-rimmed spectacles. "Exactly one

year ago this month. Thanks to your government, I can—for the first time—live and work, or at least sell books here, with no restrictions."

"Oh," she said haltingly, not sure how to respond.

"And you, as a woman, can finally keep your British citizenship no matter whom you might marry."

"I didn't know I could lose it," Evie replied with surprise.

He gave her the funniest look. "How lucky."

"Why?"

He started to answer, then stopped himself. "Perhaps I'm just envious."

"All the same, I have no plans to ever marry. Or to leave London."

"You are indeed very lucky then."

Evie moved away from the desk and acted as if she were examining the Science Department's many shelves of books, but her mind was too confused to take anything in. Ash made her feel as if she lived in a whole other world, and an easier one at that. He couldn't know how her family had suffered, and how hard she had worked for the little she had. Part of Evie resented his presuming so much about her, when he seemed to resent anyone making presumptions about *him*. But part of her wanted to understand him better, and to make him see her more clearly, too.

With each of them having failed to secure employment in academia, Evie wondered if she and Ash might be trying to come at the same thing but from completely opposite directions. Evie didn't think this was necessarily the best foundation for a friendship. Her years with the Jane Austen Society had shown her that a shared pursuit or mindset was a wonderful way to bond with someone, but she had absolutely no interest in bugs, however beautiful they might microscopically be. Doubtful that she and Mr. Ramaswamy would ever find much to talk about, Evie felt relieved but also strangely vexed as she returned alone to the top floor of the shop.

CHAPTER NINE

RULE NO. 2

The customer is, without exception, always right.

Vivien had been watching the middle-aged woman for a while. Vivien could tell she was American from the small *London A–Z* map peeking out of her luxury handbag, the lack of a trench coat over her tailored black suit, and the extremely long umbrella tucked perilously under one arm.

The woman was making her way along the stacks, having first examined all the new fiction laid out on tables at the front of the shop. Her elegant hands with their red-polished nails had picked up or otherwise touched every single volume within grasp without hesitation and, seemingly, any intention to buy. Her movement through the stacks appeared equally unambitious. When the new section devoted to Classic Women Authors was only cursorily examined, Vivien grew hurt.

Finally, she approached the woman.

"May I help you?"

The woman was holding a copy of *The Heat of the Day* by Elizabeth Bowen. "This was just released in the States last year—any good?"

Once again, Vivien suspected the interest was less in purchasing than in some form of surveillance. "It's one of my favourites."

"But is it any good?" This time the woman spoke with the hint of a teasing smile.

Vivien gave her own practiced smile of indulgence for moments such as this. "Well, I suppose that depends on what you're looking for."

"*That,* my dear, I can't find in a book."

Vivien's eye was now caught by the stack of rings—engagement, wedding band, a stunning anniversary diamond—on the woman's left hand, all of which were in dazzling contrast to the sombre black outfit and drawn features that undermined the ease of her address.

"It will be a year next Wednesday," the woman offered, "since my husband died."

Vivien was caught off guard by the woman's casual offering of such intimate and personal information, which struck Vivien as unusually forthright and unquestionably American.

"I'm so sorry."

"That's why I'm here, actually. To tidy up some things. He was in the book business, too, like you."

"Oh, not like me, I'm sure. I just work in a shop."

"Didn't I hear you call yourself a manager on the phone just now?"

Vivien wondered if the woman had been eavesdropping all along. "It's just temporary."

The woman gave a sad smile. "Isn't everything?"

"Not around here. Things haven't changed around here in a hundred years."

"Ah, then it's a true British bookshop. My husband loved them so. He would drag me all over London, snooping over the latest stock."

"A corporate spy? This street is full of those."

The woman laughed. "Not from the retail side. But the family does have a . . . let's say *professional* interest."

"He was a writer, then."

"No—but you are, aren't you?"

Vivien was surprised. "What makes you say that?"

"You keep scribbling away in that little notebook of yours. Shop life can't be *that* interesting."

"Actually, there's been quite a lot of frenzy of late. I'm only manager because of it."

"Don't sell yourself short, my dear."

"Oh, I'm not. It has nothing to do with me. It's *them*." Vivien caught the bitterness in her own voice. "The men in charge, I mean."

The woman now smiled fully at Vivien, a smile so sympathetic and wide that it left deep creases about her lips where the sallowness would surely soon return. "I suspect they're no match for you, my dear."

A cough came from behind them, and Vivien saw two other American tourists waiting impatiently at the cash counter. Vivien immediately recognised these women from the day before, when they had perused the art books section in matching Dior. This time they were attired in houndstooth and brocade Chanel, with perfectly paired handbags and pumps made of dark brown crocodile leather.

The taller of the two women leaned across the counter as Vivien entered the cash area, letting the little half door swing violently behind her.

"My sister," the woman said loudly, nodding at the smaller woman at her side, "lost her watch here yesterday."

"I'm terribly sorry," Vivien replied calmly. "We haven't had anything turn up, I'm afraid. But if you'll leave me your details where you—"

"Agnes!" the woman now exclaimed, motioning again to her sister. *"Look."*

The two women were staring down at Vivien's slender wrist, balanced against the inside edge of the counter.

"My God, you thief."

Vivien braced herself and bit the inside of her lip to keep from exploding. "I'm afraid I have no idea—"

"Where's the manager?" The taller woman's voice was now raised loudly enough to attract the attention of the other early-morning customers, who lifted their heads up from tables, newspapers, and shelves to see what the commotion was about. Out of the corner of her eye, Vivien noticed the woman in mourning moving along the stacks in her direction, clearly eavesdropping once again.

"I *am* the manager."

"Nonsense."

"Excuse me?"

"Where is the man in charge?"

"Excuse me, madam, but I am the one in charge."

"This is ridiculous—excuse me—hello!" the woman called out towards the back of the shop, while her sister stood next to her looking increasingly embarrassed.

Vivien could feel all the eyes of the shop on her. She rarely cared about what others thought. But once in a while even she couldn't help it. Vivien was being forced to care about these insolent women and what was going to happen next, merely because of the power they held by virtue of their position. A sickening, unavoidable sensation took root in her stomach.

At the angry clamour of the woman's voice, Grace was first to emerge from the back offices with a stack of paper in her hands. She always tried her best to convey the impression of efficiency. She had long ago learned that looking busy was the best stronghold against the men in the shop.

"Vivien, is everything all right?" Grace asked, giving the hard stare that was code for offering reinforcement.

"I'm afraid this woman's sister here has misplaced her watch."

"She's done no such thing!" the American customer cried loudly at them both. "It's on your wrist and you know it. A shop-girl, wearing a Cartier, of all things!"

Vivien stood there coolly, refusing to break the woman's gaze but saying nothing.

"It was a present—" Grace started to respond, and Vivien looked down at her feet while shaking her head.

"No, Vivien, this is ridiculous," Grace persisted, then turned back to the irate customer. "It *was* a present. From her late fiancé. Lord St. Vincent. Heir to the Earldom of St. Vincent. Son of the 7th Earl St. Vincent, his father? Of Skillerton Hall?"

Grace caught Vivien smiling at the many aristocratic titles that Grace was lobbing at the two determined sisters. All the other customers in the shop, including the grieving American, were now listening openly and unabashedly.

"We want to talk to the man in charge," the woman repeated angrily to Grace.

"I'm afraid Mr. McDonough is on a telephone call at present."

The woman motioned to her sister and started heading for the back office. Through its large window, Alec could be seen sitting comfortably in Mr. Dutton's swivel chair, his ankles crisscrossed and perched on the outer corner of the desk. Grace followed the two customers quickly, Vivien trailing behind at a resentful pace.

"This woman has stolen my sister's watch," the American woman said again as she burst into the general manager's office.

Alec put his right hand over the mouth of the receiver. "I'm sorry?"

For once the female staff were grateful for Alec's complete obliviousness to a woman's dangerous mood.

"My sister's watch—her Cartier—the exact same one she lost here yesterday. Sitting on this girl's wrist. I mean, it's obvious what's going on here, and if you won't do something about it, we'll have no choice but to call the police to press charges."

Alec looked over at Vivien, who stood in the hallway a few feet behind Grace.

"Vivien."

"No."

"Vivien, please. It will do us all good."

Now Grace was watching Vivien and Alec in confusion as Vivien stared wordlessly back at him, her arms folded. For once, Grace felt left out of Vivien's silent signalling.

"Vivien." Something in Alec's tone caught Grace's attention. Something she had never figured out, until now.

Giving a frustrated sigh, Vivien came forward, took off the watch, and held it before her with one taut, outstretched arm.

"See, Agnes," the woman exclaimed in triumph. As she went to snatch the watch out of Vivien's hand, Alec stopped her.

"Let me," he said surprisingly softly, taking the watch from Vivien. He looked at it for a second in the palm of his left hand, then turned it over to display the back of the face to both women.

The smaller one called Agnes stared at the inscription, then stepped back with a reddened face and pulled on her sister's arm to leave.

"Now that's an end to it, ladies," Alec said firmly, barely hiding his irritation.

As the two sisters stormed out together, Grace remained standing in the threshold to the office, staring wordlessly as Alec returned the watch to Vivien. She snapped it back on in a fury, then turned on her heel and left, too.

"That will be all," Alec said to Grace in an unusually curt manner.

Grace walked away as well, returning to her smaller windowed room with its view of the shop and the other customers reluctantly resuming their browsing. It wasn't all, she thought to herself, fully bewildered. And it certainly wasn't the end of it.

But what on earth could have been the beginning?

CHAPTER TEN

RULE No. 28

Relations between staff members must remain
strictly professional at all times.

The beginning had been a mistake.

A few months into Vivien's tenure at the shop, Graham Kingsley, the head of fiction at the time, had arranged an event on the second floor to celebrate the release of a new book by Evelyn Waugh titled *Brideshead Revisited*. This was quite a coup for Bloomsbury Books, due entirely to the influence and connections of its owner, Lord Baskin.

Evelyn Waugh had returned to London in the fall of 1945 from war service in Yugoslavia, and Vivien was, to put it mildly, starstruck by his appearance at the shop. In an effort to relax, she took a glass of champagne despite being at work, but instead of ennobling her as she had hoped, the alcohol only increased her nervousness. She never did approach Mr. Waugh to ask him the many questions she had about his latest book, which she had read that summer in a single day on a beach near her grandmother's flat in Hastings and then taken apart chapter by chapter like a well-constructed set of Meccano. Questions about the symmetry of the plot, the perfect internal title—*Et in Arcadia Ego*—and whether siblings Sebastian and Julia functioned only in relation to each other. Instead, as Waugh and the other shop staff mingled together after the event, Vivien had sat down on the steps to the History Department, looking so crestfallen that Alec had come over and crouched down to face her.

"I say, are you all right?"

It was the first time Alec had really spoken to her, even though they had both joined Bloomsbury Books earlier that summer on the exact same day. Sitting together in Mr. Dutton's fishbowl of an office, Alec had immediately struck Vivien back then as just another social-climbing privileged schoolboy pretending at being a man. By now, everyone at the shop had figured out that he was also a writer. That wasn't unusual in a bookstore employee— Nancy Mitford had recently written her next novel while on leave from the Heywood Hill bookshop in Mayfair.

Alec, however, treated his literary aspirations as just one more rung on the ladder to success, using his job to connect with the well-placed editors, publishers, and authors who attended events such as tonight's. With Graham Kingsley hinting at retirement, Alec was considered to be first in line for the head-of-fiction role, despite his tenure being equal to Vivien's. The shop rules clearly stated that the head of each department shall have final say on guests and special events, which would enable Alec to further his connections, while Vivien would be relegated behind the cash counter to stand prettily and watch.

Tonight, Alec's leaving such a celebrated gathering to inquire after Vivien was having an unexpected effect on her. Maybe it was the champagne, or the brush with literary celebrity, or her own writerly hopes, but in that moment, with Alec's blue eyes steeled by desire, Vivien saw him differently. Positively. Even, to her later regret, unreservedly. She wondered if he had yearned for her all along, and as a beautiful woman who had once been well and truly loved, Vivien had a weakness for being yearned for—a weakness only strengthened by her disappointment in herself tonight.

Alec had offered to call her a taxi. As he stood there at the kerb gently helping her in, their eyes met again. Alec turned away in hesitation, gazed up at the second-floor windows of the shop, then gazed back down at her. Suddenly and wordlessly he had climbed into the back seat of the cab and taken her hand, so sweetly that she had foolishly let her guard down against any new kind of entanglement.

Vivien had lost her fiancé, the late heir to the Earldom of St. Vincent, in 1942. He had been attacked in ground battle at Gazala with the 50th (Northumbrian) Infantry Division and his body had never been found. This had given the loss a unique emotional dimension that had rattled Vivien far more than she understood. She had been only twenty-two at the time, and she and David had wasted their entire engagement dealing with his titled family's distress over it. Since his untimely death, Vivien had committed herself to feeling as little sentiment and as much anger as possible. Her hatred of Hitler and the war would eventually reach such a critical boiling point that those around her feared she might never recover.

All Vivien had to remember David by were a locked-away diamond solitaire, the Cartier watch, and the memory of a single night on leave in a rather dodgy seaside hotel. That one night in January 1942 had in some ways been unremarkable, being the first time for them both. It had, however, given Vivien a taste of intimacy, and of the way being physically vulnerable could bind you to someone in a most delicious, and secretive, way. She had never understood or condoned adultery, but that one night of sex had shown the budding writer that love might be the least of it. That the hidden nature of the experience, the heightened sense of doing something forbidden—and enjoying it—could be the real draw for a certain kind of person.

Within hours of the Waugh literary event, Vivien and Alec would realise that they were both a certain kind of person. Instead

of bringing them closer, this awareness of how similar they were
had divided them. If Vivien recalled any of their lovemaking, it
would cause her to blush. So, she didn't. Instead, she recalled how
Alec had, immediately upon waking, acted as if she had done
something wrong, or made him do so. Their working relationship
had never recovered. Vivien had renamed him the Tyrant and
chopped off her hair, and Grace—the one married member of the
shop—had found herself the mediator between them, when what
was really called for was a tribunal, once and for all.

It was as if that one night had never happened. No one at the
shop had any idea; it was quite the opposite. Vivien and Alec were
both tacitly—and fiercely—determined to keep it that way.

A lec had awakened first and lain there next to Vivien, watching the way her long hair tumbled in natural waves about
her shoulders. Hair that he had let brush and fall against
his chest during their lovemaking and grabbed at hard with
his hands and lips as if grasping for breath, having no idea that
within the hour, she would hack it all off in what he could only
surmise was also the complete repudiation of his desire for her.

Following their collapse in each other's arms, Alec had endured surprisingly fitful and disturbing sleep. He was glad that
Vivien remained dozing at his side because it gave him time to
think. He spent it, however, mostly thinking of her. He marvelled
at her beauty and repose, at how content she appeared in sleep
when, awake, her features barely treaded above disdain for her
surroundings.

Alec let his eyes travel from Vivien's hair to her naked right
shoulder and exposed back, which had the loveliest creamy hue in
the soft morning light. Finding himself now staring at her skin,
he forced himself to blink and roll over to face her bedroom wall

instead, which was covered in peeling paper in faded blue-and-white damask. A substantial dresser with a large makeup mirror tilting on its surface covered the entire expanse of the wall, and scattered about the looking glass was an array of perfume bottles, brushes of varying sizes, and several little pots. From this assortment of tools, Vivien made up her dark, almond-shaped eyes—eyes so brutally assessing, and startling, that until last night Alec had done his best to avoid directly gazing into them. Lying there that morning in her bed, he now fully understood the wisdom of his earlier ways.

Scrunching the right side of his face hard into the pillow from confusion and distress, Alec let his one open eye rove over the tower of books on Vivien's bedside table. The stack included several titles that Alec recognised from their ordering disputes at the shop: a foreign edition of Radclyffe Hall's *The Well of Loneliness,* which had long been banned in England, *The Death of the Heart* by Elizabeth Bowen, and *A Traveller in Time* by Alison Uttley—a book for girls, and therefore both surprising and strangely endearing in its presence. He did not recognise Anna Kavan's *Asylum Piece,* but knew her short story "I Am Lazarus" from a recent issue of his favourite literary journal, *Horizon.* Much of Kavan's writing drew from her experiences working with invalided soldiers in mental wards and displayed an absurdity and disinterest in pleasing the reader that struck Alec as distinctly masculine. Intrigued, he tried to gingerly slide the book out from under the Cartier watch that rested on top.

The watch slid too fast and Alec had to reach out to grab it mid-flight. He had always been surprised that a girl like Vivien would own a watch like this. He didn't know much about her lower-middle-class background, only that her father had been in trade of some kind. Alec's father had been a radiologist and might easily have given Alec a Cartier watch for his twenty-first birthday to go

along with the boarding school education and the year abroad before the war, if Patek Philippe had not been the family mainstay.

Vivien's watch was studded in diamonds around its rectangular face, which was made of 18k gold. It was a fairly recent
design by the French luxury house and therefore unlikely to have
been inherited. Alec recognised the model because he always paid
attention to matters of style. He knew that appearances made
a difference in life—how one dressed, how one looked, how one
displayed success. So he wore his perfectly tailored crisp white
shirts and jacket from Gieves & Hawkes at No. 1 Savile Row and
his perfectly polished and shined brogues from Barker Shoes in
Jermyn Street, shops long frequented by his father, grandfather,
and great-grandfather before him.

Sitting up now, still naked in the bed, Alec turned the watch
over in his hand. On the back was a single date: January 22,
1942. He wondered what to make of it.

"What are you doing?"

Alec flinched as he put the watch and book back down in their
place. He turned around slowly to face Vivien, who had rolled over
and propped herself up onto her right elbow to question him.

"Good morning."

"I asked what you were doing."

"It's a lovely piece. And I didn't recognise the book. Any good?"

Vivien gave him one of her usual suspicious looks. Alec felt as
if the preceding ten hours were in danger of slipping away just as
the watch had done.

"I doubt you were interested in the book."

She raised herself up fully, dressed only in a thin mint-green
underslip.

"As I said, it's a lovely watch. A present?" He knew enough about
Vivien to not run scared—that would only antagonize her more.

"Yes." She pulled the covers back and slid off the edge of the bed away from him before heading to the sink in the corner. He watched as she tied her long hair up into a hasty bun and splashed cold water on her face, then patted it dry with a blue-and-white-striped towel hanging nearby. She threw on an orange knitted housecoat and walked with eerie calmness into the small front sitting room and kitchenette.

Alec watched silently through the open door as Vivien lit the gas stove and started up the kettle. He continued to watch as she made them both a pot of tea, just like in the shop, and just as sullenly. On the one hand he loved the domesticity of it all, the feeding and caring of him, as if he were something more to her than a mere colleague or brief encounter. But part of him feared the deceptive normality of the gesture as well, being fully attuned by now to Vivien's quick shifts in mood.

She returned to the bed and placed the tray of tea on the crumpled sheets between them. She didn't say anything, just poured out the tea and started to sip hers while he sat there quietly, and increasingly, panicked.

"A present from a relative?" he finally asked, fully exasperated by this new, unreadable mood of hers.

"Of sorts."

"A man?"

"Mm-hmm. My fiancé actually."

Alec practically jumped up out of the bed. "Your *what*?"

"Relax. He's dead."

But her abrupt words made him do nothing of the sort.

"Why am I only learning this now?"

"It's really no one's business, is it? The things that don't happen in life?"

Now his own mood caught up with him, and Alec said something he already knew he shouldn't—the one thing that would push her away for good. Years later, he still had no idea why.

"Well, I suppose it explains some things."

She stared at him. "You're not really—"

"You're just—you know—quite forthcoming, in bed."

Vivien stood up without a word, as if pulled by an invisible long string, and left the small bedsitter for the bathroom in the hallway. Alec listened warily as first her bedroom door, then the front door, and then the bathroom door each slammed loudly shut behind her.

Alec smacked his forehead hard with the heel of his hand.

When Vivien returned, she had cut off most of her hair, unintentionally making herself even more attractive to him.

The inscription remained unexplained, although Alec would torture himself about its meaning for years.

And now, four years later, his intimate knowledge of the watch had become known to the entire shop and at least three American citizens, in an effort to keep Vivien out of jail.

CHAPTER ELEVEN

Ever since moving to London, Evie Stone had taken to spending Sundays at the British Museum.

Her flatmate, Charlotte, worked all weekend as a chambermaid, leaving Evie alone on her one day off from the shop. She quickly established the following routine: a simple bowl of porridge and milk and then a long bus ride to the museum, where she would conduct hours of research in its library.

This Sunday, however, Evie was heading to the Natural History Museum instead. Having recently hit a dead end in the British Museum, she wondered if information helpful to her search could have ended up in the archives of the famous botanist and horticulturist John Claudius Loudon. All part of the puzzle that Evie Stone had been trying to solve, on and off, for the past year.

The Botany Department had its own independent library collection of specialist literature and records, located adjacent to the scientists' working areas. Evie went straight to the front desk of the library, signed the visitors' book, and asked to see the files belonging to John Loudon for the years 1825 to 1830. This required the librarian to write down Evie's name in the account of removal

records, a moment that always made Evie hesitate. She wanted
to avoid leaving behind any clues or written record as to what she
was looking for. Her natural suspicion and doggedness were now
working in combination with the knowledge that Stuart Wesley
had landed a position rightfully hers and had access to all of her
prior hard work. She was determined never to make that mistake
again.

Evie was handed two long wooden boxes, which she spent
the next several hours poring over. It would take her days to go
through all of the Loudon archives, given the amount of material
housed there, which included drawings of leaves, twigs, and fruits
by the famous botanist, correspondence relating to the gardening
and natural history magazines that he had founded, and stacks
of miscellaneous paper.

Evie, however, was not interested in the writings of John
Loudon. She was trying to find any information she could on his
wife, a writer in her own right, of whom there was little paper
record left. Evie often found herself frustrated by the discrepancy
between the archival preservation of male writing and that of
their female counterparts—how every sketch of a twig that John
Loudon had ever even whimsically composed was being carefully
safeguarded by several British museums, while an entire novel
by his wife had become only a minor footnote in the record of her
husband's work.

Evie had learned from cataloguing the Chawton Great House
library that what got salvaged over time, and what fell prey to
it, was subject to the whims of the age. During her research at
Cambridge, she had combed through listings of all the novels
published in specific eras and noted how the proportion of female
novelists had suffered a slow and steady decline over the past hundred years. The heyday for female novelists appeared to stretch
back even further than that, to the turn of the previous century,

when famous women such as Jane Austen and Maria Edgeworth had dominated the early evolution of the novel.

As Evie went even deeper in her research, she discovered forgotten female authors from that period such as Charlotte Lennox, Eliza Haywood, Rachel Hunter, and Elizabeth Inchbald, several of whom Jane Austen herself had read and admired. These names meant little to the reader of the day. But value often accrued over time; Evie herself, a former servant girl and recent Cambridge graduate, was proof of that. The book she was secretly searching for was not a classic in the traditional sense, having no recognised or established literary value. Evie's ambition, however, exceeded that. Her aim was to confer new value on it, through its very rescue.

Evie had spent several hours quietly working through Loudon's voluminous correspondence, hoping to find anything that could shed light on his wife, when she opened a handwritten journal to find this:

January 1830

I am reading a strange, wild novel in which the author, a man of most rigorous intellect and imagination, lays the scene in the distant future and attempts to predict the state of improvement to which this country might possibly arrive. I plan a review shortly for the magazine. Meanwhile I have written to the publisher, Henry Colburn, of my interest in meeting the unknown author. I am particularly intrigued by the mention he makes of various labour-saving devices such as a digging machine run by steam.

February 1830

As I write this, I am still recovering from shock—the author of the book has turned out to be a lady, a Miss Jane Wells Webb! How typical of Mr. Colburn to keep that information to himself and do nothing to disabuse me of my presumption. Everything always, with him, is in the interest of increasing curiosity and hence sales.

After my initial reaction, I had a most pleasant and educational discourse with Miss Webb. She was recently orphaned and wrote the book aged only seventeen, to raise both her income and her spirits. I must say, it is difficult to conceive of so much imagination and sagacity coming from one so young. She is, however, quite charming, and kindly agreed to another meeting as I have much more I want to learn and discover.

October 14, 1830

My beloved and I have been married one month today, and I have never been happier. Like myself, Jane is an enthusiast in all things, which greatly suits my own imagination and temperament. I often forget how young she is, her mind moves so rapidly from one project or thought to another!

To my great relief and excitement, Jane has offered to help me with the completion of my arboretum. My goal is for the encyclopedia to present a comprehensive account of each and every shrub and tree growing in our kingdom and their history, all drawn from life, which shall entail a great deal of travel and effort for us both. This will require my beloved to put aside her own writing to act as amanuensis, given my pathetic crippled state. According to Mr. Colburn, sales of Jane's recent stories of a bride are not strong and her first book has long been forgotten, despite the promise of its start. . . .

Evie was so immersed in her discovery that she barely heard a man's soft but deliberate voice speak her name from a few feet away.

She turned to see Ashwin Ramaswamy standing there. In her surprise, she could feel that same strange warmth rising to her cheeks as when they had met standing over Mr. Dutton's convulsing body on the office floor. Evie had not seen Ash since her one visit to the Science Department on her first day of work. He spent all his time in the basement of Bloomsbury Books, and she kept to herself on the uppermost floor.

"Hello, Miss Stone," he repeated a little more loudly when Evie said nothing back.

She looked about herself quickly, closing the journal pages as she did so, then gravely brought her right index finger up to her lips. The rules about speaking in the reading room were strict, even though there were few other people to worry about disturbing so late in the afternoon.

Ash seemed aware of this, as an uncomfortable look now crossed his features. Reddening slightly himself, he gave an immediate nod of acquiescence and started to back away.

"Wait," she cried out loudly, and this time one or two heads among the group did pop up from the pages before them.

Evie inwardly berated herself for this habit of hers: sticking so close to the rules that she occasionally and unintentionally ended up breaking them. She had been watching Vivien at the shop, how she subverted or ignored the rules altogether, and with such outward brio that the men were stunned into silence. Evie wished she had that knack.

Ash continued walking towards the main marbled corridor. Evie felt miserable, a combination of her constant fear of being caught and of having somehow disappointed this man she hardly knew. Normally she would have cared only about the two little wooden boxes and the discovery that lay inside. Ash had intruded into all of that, yet for once she didn't feel resentful at the interruption. Something about the man made her want to please him. It was most confusing.

Returning the files to the front desk, Evie forgot to try to discreetly cross her name out in the removal ledger; tiny as she was, she often took to sidling about the librarian's desk looking for a moment of distraction in which to do so. Instead, she ran out with her notebook and leather satchel to follow Ash. When she entered the cavernous open hallway, he was standing by a glass case containing a display of several brightly coloured coral specimens. His back was turned and she noticed that he was not much taller than her own five feet, a half dozen inches at most. His boots were quite scuffed, like hers, and he had on several layers of sweater. A thin trench coat rested over one arm.

"I'm sorry," she called out, and he turned around, slowly, to stare appraisingly at her. She sensed approval in his gaze as well, and her cheeks warmed again, this time with a new emotion that felt so intense, it could only be anger—whether at herself or at him she could not tell.

"Why?" he asked simply.

"You were just being friendly."

"Perhaps not. Perhaps I was just surprised."

"I was surprised, too. To see you, of all people."

His lips twitched in amusement. "I'm not sure you're helping matters."

"Why are you here?"

He now looked fully amused by her persistence. "I might ask you the same thing." He nodded at the leather satchel hanging from her right shoulder.

"Research."

He raised one eyebrow at her. "Are you still studying, then?"

"No, not officially. I—I have my interests, is all."

"Ah, yes, well, I know something about that."

Evie still knew little about Ash, just that he had formerly been a naturalist and entomologist with the University of Madras. This was the only substantive information that he or anyone else at the shop had so far offered up regarding his past.

Ash motioned for her to resume walking ahead of him, and they proceeded along the corridor. When they reached the main Hintze Hall, with its soaring, cathedral-like ceiling and display of elephants, he checked his watch and looked about awkwardly.

"Well, I best be going—"

"Would you like to join me for tea?" Evie heard herself say, impulsively and quite unlike her. When he didn't immediately reply, she quickly added, "Of course, you must have plans—"

"No," he stated simply. "No plans."

"Oh."

He hesitated and looked about himself again.

"Are you not hungry?"

"No, *that's* never a problem." He brushed the bottom of his chin with the edge of his forefinger thoughtfully. "There's a tearoom across the street where I sometimes grab a sandwich when I'm here. Shall we?"

He motioned again with his right hand, indicating that she should continue to go first, and they left the museum together. With each turn in their walk, Evie felt as if Ash hung ever so slightly back from her.

There was no one to greet them at the front door of the tearoom just off Exhibition Road and, given the late hour, they had the place to themselves. Evie headed straight for a table along the window where they could both sit with a view of the street.

"Excuse me."

Evie looked over her left shoulder in the direction of the strong Scottish accent to find an elderly female waitress standing a few feet back from their table.

"Yes, hello, a pot of tea for two and—"

Evie looked inquiringly at Ash, who interjected, "And some sandwiches."

"Yes, and some sandwiches, please. And lettuce? With salad cream?" This she directed towards Ash, who nodded amiably back.

It was as if they had ordered together like this many times before, which put them both more at ease. The waitress, on the other hand, seemed increasingly annoyed.

"You've been in 'ere before," she finally spoke to Ash, not sounding at all pleased by the realisation.

Evie watched silently as he sat up ever so slightly in his chair. "Yes."

"But not with ' er."

Evie noticed that everything the woman was saying to Ash sounded like an accusation of some kind. Evie was confused but one thing was clear—the two of them were not having a conversation.

"No, not with the young lady."

The woman made a noise under her breath and walked off.

"Is she always so rude?" asked Evie.

"She's consistent." Ash shrugged. "So. You said research. What kind of research? I thought you were a scholar of obscure eighteenth-century women writers."

Evie stared at him. "They're not obscure. They're neglected."

"Sorry." He smiled. "*Obscure* sounds deficient. I am corrected."

"You're right, though—I've no interest in rocks and bugs and such. I'm trying to track down some archival material that moved here from the British Museum. Why are you here?"

"I suppose for the rocks and bugs."

"Oh, I didn't mean to sound dismissive."

The waitress returned and plopped the teapot down between them without a word. Evie started to pour out both their cups, then watched as Ash added quite a bit of milk to his.

"The spices in the kitchen smell so lovely. For your masala."

He stopped midpour as if to gauge her meaning. "*My* masala?"

"I just meant—"

He finished pouring the milk and made a motion with his

hand that was both dismissive and forgiving. Evie felt confused as to which it really was. Perhaps that was the point. Perhaps someone like Ashwin Ramaswamy found it best to shield himself against people like their waitress—and even, Evie feared, herself—by keeping his thoughts impenetrable.

"My family ships them here for me. Impossible to find otherwise, what with the rationing and all."

"Your family?"

"My mother and grandmother, and my sisters. My father is dead."

"Oh. My father is dead, too."

They both became quiet as the waitress returned to noisily place the plates of sandwiches and greens about the table, then retreated wordlessly again.

"Do you come to the museum often?" Evie asked.

"Quite often on my Sunday. Or I walk."

"You walk? Where?"

"All over."

"All over . . . ?"

"Yes, all over. Wherever I feel like. Wherever the day takes me."

"Don't you get lost?" Evie now thought of her own, specific routes.

"I always have time. To redirect course."

"I'm still getting to know my way around." Evie picked up one of the sandwiches and gave it a small investigative nibble before assuring herself that she liked it. "London feels endless. Like you could walk for days and days and only the sea would stop you."

Ash smiled. "There's actually been some talk of doing that. Of making a path the entire length of the Thames, from where it starts to where it ends."

"I will wait for that day."

"You prefer that, then—knowing your way around?"

She nodded. "I grew up in a village of just a few hundred

people and one main road barely two miles long. *Very* different from here."

"Here *is* very different." He shrugged again. "But isn't that why we come? To find things we can't find anywhere else?"

"You mean rocks and bugs?"

He laughed. "No, not just that."

She waited for Ash to say something more. She felt quite comfortable sitting there with him, almost as if they were alone but together. As they talked, he didn't barge into her thoughts. Instead, he would listen intently, then take her little sentences and finish them off for her. Usually, she felt spoken *at*.

"Whatever it is," he finally added, "let's just hope we'll know it when we see it."

CHAPTER TWELVE

RULE No. 35

The head of each department shall choose which books to carry.

E arly the next morning, Grace arrived at the shop to find Alec already in his office and deep in conversation with Lord Baskin. Grace was not surprised at the earl's sudden appearance. Every January he made the trek down from Yorkshire to inspect the shop's accounting records for the prior calendar year.

"Grace, how *are* you?" Jeremy Baskin asked, seated comfortably on the edge of Mr. Dutton's desk while Alec leaned back casually in his chair. Grace was starting to miss the way Mr. Dutton had always sat upright at the table, poker straight and at attention, wearing spectacles only because he sat so far above the papers at hand and could not tolerate slouching in himself or anyone else.

"I'm fine, Lord Baskin—and how are you and Lady Baskin?"

"My mother is as sprightly as ever." He smiled, then straightened himself and looked down at Alec. "Do you mind if I go over the newest bank statements with Mrs. Perkins before we talk further? Grace, care for a spot of coffee first from Jonny's cart outside? I need to warm myself up."

Still in her coat and hat, Grace followed the tall, stately figure

of Lord Baskin as he strode purposefully towards the front entrance and held open the street door for her.

"Alec seems at home in his new role," he said with a knowing
smile as she caught up to him. One always had to catch up to the
earl—he walked fast even though there was ostensibly nowhere
he needed to go. It was one of the things Grace liked about him—
unlike the wealthier visitors to the shop, he did not put on that air
of unconcerned indolence, as if nothing were to be worried over,
and weren't the rest of them so foolish for having their cares. Instead, Lord Baskin gave the impression of perfectly understanding why the staff were always hurrying about. Grace supposed
this was because of his own days working at the shop during
the war. Since then, he still popped in occasionally, especially at
Christmastime, when his favourite thing to do was get back behind the cash counter next to Vivien. He often declared amid the
commotion and bustle that there was no better time to work in a
bookshop than the holidays.

As they waited for a few early-morning shoppers to clear
the pavement, Lord Baskin examined the crate of books at reduced prices that Grace and Vivien had recently set out to entice
passersby.

Picking out two books by Henry Miller, along with Hemingway's *For Whom the Bell Tolls,* Lord Baskin shook his head in
amusement.

"Vivien's been clearing house, I see."

"She calls them the Misogynists—says the bin is exactly where
they belong."

"Do you think that?" He had a gleam in his eye.

Grace shrugged. "I don't really know much about the books. I
hardly have time to read, except to my boys before bed. Awful of
me, I know."

"Not at all. Herbert's the same, as far as I can tell. I actually think that's the mark of a great bookseller—the ability to *appear* as if one has read all the books."

Lord Baskin left for the vendor cart while Grace waited on the pavement, looking about the quiet narrow street. It was nine in the morning in Lamb's Conduit, the preamble to its busiest time of the day. Only a few of the shops had opened their doors, and most of the people rushing by were on their way to work at various Bloomsbury institutions: Great Ormond Street Hospital, the British Museum, and the many colleges of the University of London scattered about. A few blocks north, a gaggle of toddlers and their nannies were descending on Coram's Fields, the large children's playground situated on the former grounds of the Foundling Hospital. This was the charitable institution established in 1739 by philanthropic sea captain Thomas Coram to house and educate the children of unwed mothers. Thinking of her own two boys as the prams and pull toys passed by, the scent of baby powder and pablum in the air, Grace was grateful to have spent her sons' most tender years at home. Gordon would certainly not have been up to the task.

Lord Baskin was now walking back towards her, still managing to look elegant as he struggled not to spill the two mugs brimful of steaming coffee in his hands. They took a seat on the bench in front of the shop, just as they always did whenever he visited. Lord Baskin would tell her that he needed to warm himself up before dealing with the accounts, which were always in the same worrying state, and they would sit together and watch the world of Lamb's Conduit pass by.

"So, any word on poor Herbert yet?" he asked.

"I'm afraid not. I do worry that he shouldn't be alone. I think Alec was planning a visit, but for some reason Mr. Dutton keeps putting him off."

Grace leaned back to allow a large pram to pass by, causing

her coffee to spill slightly. She then watched as Lord Baskin did the most startling thing: he casually reached forward with his left forefinger and ran the beads of coffee back up towards the rim of her mug, then licked off the small bit of coffee left on his finger.

Grace stared at him in surprise.

"Oh, I'm sorry, how rude—that's what this thing is for, after all." Removing a monogrammed handkerchief from his front jacket pocket, he proceeded to dab at the rim of her mug again and then at his own hand. It occurred to Grace that both Herbert Dutton and Frank Allen, and even Alec McDonough, were much more formal than the earl.

"So, Alec and Vivien. What's the latest there?"

Grace gave a sigh and for once broke rank with her girlfriend. "It's unceasing. I've always understood Vivien's grievance—you were a top seller here, you know how that should be rewarded. But I'm not even sure that's what any of this is about." Recalling the recent incident with the watch, Grace stopped herself. She worried that she was saying too much, while also wondering how much the perceptive Lord Baskin might already suspect.

"I understand she's turned the department around in one week flat."

"One can do a lot of change in little time—if there's a will."

Jeremy Baskin now gave an unusual sigh of his own. Beneath his unlined brow, he had lovely, deep-set hazel eyes that changed colour with his every mood; when he was happy or carefree, his quick smile would light the room. His liberal and unguarded manner reminded Grace of the many Americans who visited the shop. She recalled that his mother, Lady Baskin, had been a famous New York socialite before marrying into British aristocracy. In one romantic swoop, she had saved the 10th Earl Baskin and his failing estate with a substantial dowry from her industrialist father: the *Buccaneers,* Vivien called these women, after the title of an unfinished Edith Wharton novel. Grace wondered if Lord Baskin's engaging demeanour was another part of his significant inheritance from the American side of the family.

"And we've brought on new staff, I understand. I hope we can afford it. I'm fearful for this year's profits, what with all this rationing *wear and tear* still in place."

"Yes. Evelyn Stone. A Cambridge graduate, like yourself. Although I understand *she* got a First."

Lord Baskin threw his head back in mock hurt. Grace knew he appreciated her directness and willingness to tease him, being so playful and affable himself.

"Evie's quite dedicated," continued Grace. "Mr. Dutton wants her cataloguing the entire third floor and then rearranging the thousands of volumes into categories of some kind. Things have become a little disorganised up there of late."

"I understand Frank's away more than ever, which can't help matters." He hesitated. "Is everything all right there?"

Grace took a sip of her coffee in silence, unwilling to say anything about her superior's protracted absences of late.

"You know," Lord Baskin said in a teasing tone, "when you first joined us, I thought for the longest time that Frank had a little crush on you."

She laughed. "I am a married woman, Lord Baskin."

"How is Gordon," he asked, sounding more serious, "and your two boys?"

"Fine, thank you. Everyone's back at school or work, now that the holidays are over." She hadn't told anyone, not even Vivien, about Gordon's breakdown and subsequent unemployment. He would explode if she ever did.

Just the idea of Gordon tired Grace, and what an awful thing to feel as a wife. Worse still, after years of irrational behaviour from her husband, Grace had been forced to accept that there would be no hoped-for change. Whatever mysterious demons he was battling, Gordon was by now comfortably mired in his own complaints. They had become his most reliable companions; trying to talk him out of his worries would only leave him bereft and un-moored. Mother Perkins was the exact same way, and this was just one part of her husband's own family inheritance.

"And you—how are you doing with all the big changes of late? New employees and all that."

Grace sipped her coffee. "I'm better with small changes."

"Me, too. Although I prefer to think of it as nicely stable." Lord Baskin smiled. "Vivien and Alec, on the other hand, appear trans-formed by all the chaos. I hardly recognise the front tables. Or Alec's lack of good cheer. Those two are both so ambitious, for all that they accuse and deny in the other."

"I do envy them that long view. They rarely get bogged down by the mundane or the everyday."

"Ambition is all well and good, but there are some parts of everyday life that one should never miss. You must see that, with your children. How fast they grow."

On this plaintive note, Lord Baskin returned their mugs to the vendor cart and escorted Grace back to her office.

As they reviewed the shop's dismal accounts together, they fell back into another familiar routine. They would suddenly and si-multaneously stop what they were doing, take a sip of the tea that Grace had since made them, and observe the rest of the staff through the large glass window to her office. At one point they both watched in amusement as Alec sidled up to Vivien at the cash counter and inquired about something, only to have her re-spond by throwing down her pencil and storming off.

"Those two need to find neutral ground of some sort." Lord Baskin laughingly shook his head. "Not all relationships, I would hope, need to end in war."

Grace again questioned how much Lord Baskin might know

about Vivien and Alec's mysterious past, given how close the two men were. Lord Baskin's words also made her wonder about his present love life, given that the scandal of divorce was long behind him. As a middle-aged member of the aristocracy, he might not be quite the "deb's delight" he had once been for the young ladies presented at court each year to the king and queen, but Lord Baskin clearly appreciated the fairer sex. Over the years, she and Vivien had occasionally caught sight of a silk-gloved, swanlike arm fluttering through the cab window as Lord Baskin disembarked before the shop.

Grace wondered at his never having remarried. Perhaps divorce made the whole enterprise of marriage so fraught and unforgiving that one never dared enter the institution again. She thought often of how costly marital estrangement could be, both financially as well as socially, whether aristocrat or housewife. Staying with Gordon might keep Grace at the end of her wits, but it also kept a man in the house for her two sons and at least the impression of respectability. She still firmly believed this was for the better.

CHAPTER THIRTEEN

RULE No. 27

Fraternizing with customers outside of the shop
is strictly prohibited.

V ivien was returning to the cash counter from yet another
summons to the back office when the shop bell rang out to
announce the entrance of the wealthy American woman
from the previous week. Not the one dressed in Chanel who had
accused Vivien of being a thief, but the one in mourning who had
openly been surveying the contents of the shop.

The woman gave Vivien a smile of familiarity upon entering,
and Vivien responded with a quick smile and nod back. The staff
were under strict orders to never verbally initiate conversation
with customers upon arrival. Instead, they were to wait an appropriate length of time, hope for some sign of hesitation or confusion
in the customer's manner, and only then approach with the most
passive of inquiries.

Vivien resumed writing in her little notebook at the cash
counter, and a few minutes later a stack of art books was placed
before her.

"Hello again," the American woman greeted her. "You can arrange shipping overseas, I presume?"

Vivien stood up straight. "Of course, madam."

"Please, call me Ellen."

Admiring the woman's taste in books, Vivien started to tally up the trio of gorgeous volumes on Picasso, Matisse, and Cézanne that had been released in England the previous year.

"I'm most sorry for what happened here last week," the older woman said.

Vivien kept at her task with a tight smile. "It was a simple mistake."

"It was nothing of the sort. Although you handled yourself very well. You must have been David's girl, then?"

Vivien put down her pen and stared in astonishment at the woman's sleuthing abilities.

"I know Lady St. Vincent. An awful, tragic loss."

"It all was," Vivien merely replied, hoping to move past the woman's concern.

"I just ran into Angelica yesterday, actually."

These ladies were all the same, thought Vivien. Lunching, gossiping, and interfering with the lives of others. For some reason, she had hoped this one was different.

Ellen seemed to pick up on Vivien's dismay because she took off her hat and gloves as if planning on staying for a while and laid them on the space of bare counter between them.

"Two years of engagement during a world war is both long and unwise, given the circumstances. Bertie and Angelica should have known better."

Vivien was again caught off guard by the woman's disarming manner and willingness to raise such intimate subjects. "I should have, too."

"Touché, my dear. Listen, I am holding a small reception at the Dorchester tonight. Not too many lords or ladies as such, but there will be a few people an aspiring young writer should meet. I am told I need to re-enter society after my year of mourning, the

first anniversary of which—wouldn't you know—was yesterday."
Ellen paused and surveyed Vivien's downcast and frustrated features. "I suspect you need to do the same."

"That's very kind of you, but—"

"Won't you at least consider it? Please?" There was that very
American openness and eagerness again. "Oh, and you may ship
those to my home address. I believe my late husband had an account here."

Intrigued, Vivien took out the accounts book and held the
cover open between them. "Your late husband's name?"

"Mr. Nelson Doubleday, Senior." The woman gave her a warm
and intimating smile before adding, as she turned to leave, "Of the
Doubleday Publishing House. So, you see, you really must recon-
sider tonight."

V ivien exited the elevator doors on the eighth floor of the
Dorchester Hotel. She was both surprisingly nervous and resentful of it; she had not attended a party in such elegant
surroundings in many years. As she dropped the heavy weight of
the door knocker to Ellen Doubleday's suite, Vivien involuntarily
took a breath. After several seconds of no response, she knocked
again, and again was met with silence. In frustration, she tried
the heavily polished handles to the doors to the suite herself.

"You'll have no luck there," Vivien heard a voice say.

Looking down the corridor, she saw a slim, striking woman in
her forties with a wavy short bob, sitting in an alcove below a gilt-
framed mirror that matched the golden colour of her hair.

"Am I early?"

The stranger laughed. "No, but Ellie's always late. Better to
learn that now."

The woman stood up to her full height, which was impressive, and tucked a black-beaded clutch purse under her left arm as she came forward to shake Vivien's hand with her right. Even from a distance, Vivien was entranced by the woman's most remarkable sky-blue eyes.

"And I am always early. How do you do? Lady Browning."

Vivien took the gloved hand in her own, but before she could respond in kind, the elevator doors slid open and Ellen Doubleday emerged in full evening attire, followed by three men carrying large silver trays of food high above their heads.

"However did you all fit in there?" Lady Browning called out in amusement as Ellen blew right past her in a most intimate and familiar manner to unlock her private suite.

"We're running a little behind schedule," Ellen replied merrily, then swung open both painted-and-gilded doors as if unveiling the scene to a stage. "But you know me—I'll make up the loss. Vivien my dear, so glad you could come."

Vivien found herself trailing inside behind Ellen, the other woman, and the three young—and quite handsome—male servers from the hotel. Even in her days around the St. Vincent family, Vivien had rarely seen a hotel suite as luxurious as this one. Rooms opened onto other rooms in a gallery-like manner, all of them fronted by a row of doors leading outside to an impressive balcony with a view of Hyde Park. The furnishings were a mix of various antique styles, and Vivien recalled something David's mother had once condescendingly pointed out to her in front of a roomful of guests at Skillerton Hall: "The key, my dear, just so you know, is to decorate English, eat Italian, and dress French."

While Ellen Doubleday instructed the servers on where to unload their trays and set up the bar, the woman from the hallway removed her fur coat and reached out for Vivien's plain woollen one. "Here, allow me."

Vivien felt herself watched over as she slipped out of her coat
and let it pass into Lady Browning's elegantly outstretched arms.

"Let's have a seat, Miss—"

"Lowry. Vivien Lowry."

"Ah. Lovely name. Lovely girl. I can see why Ellie grabbed on
to you."

Vivien always preferred to be in real, if not nominal, control of
her surroundings, but something about both of these women and
their proprietary manner was making her feel incredibly off keel.

Lady Browning now patted the stretch of embroidered love
seat next to her, and Vivien duly took her place. She could hardly
meet the woman's eyes—she had never seen a gaze so beautiful
or piercing.

"Your hairstyle flatters you, my girl. I keep threatening to go
violently short, but my husband—a man of few demands, and even
less presence—always seems to have an opinion on at least that."
Lady Browning spoke so frankly, and entertainingly, that Vivien
wished she could take her notebook out to copy all of it down.

There was a loud knock at the door and Ellen quickly reappeared from another room to answer it, her merry mood increasing with each new arrival. The door opened to a handful of invited
guests, who moved into the room while tearing off silk scarves
and gloves, evening cocktail hats and fedoras. Rachmaninoff was
now playing from a record cabinet near the bar, the chandeliers
had been lowered, and suddenly a party was in full swing.

"Ahh," Lady Browning said, patting Vivien's left knee lightly
beside her. "Everyone is here. We all do love Ellen so. This party is
mostly for us, of course. I doubt she would have done it otherwise."

"She seems very solicitous, and kind—and quite glamorous."

"I couldn't agree more."

"Lady Browning!" a voice called out brightly.

Vivien watched as her companion kneeled up onto one leg on

the seat cushions and grabbed both hands of the newly arrived guest from over the back of the love seat.

"How long are you in town?" the new woman was asking, looking about. "Is Tommy here, too?"

Vivien soon learned that Lady Browning's husband had recently been appointed head of the personal staff of Princess Elizabeth, Duchess of Edinburgh and heir to the British throne. This must have been the source of Lady Browning's own regal composure and air of authority, and the corresponding deference being shown her by all of the other guests.

As Vivien sat there silently, watchfully, having little to contribute to the rapid-fire conversations swirling about her, the suppressed memories of a long-ago life came flooding back. The disastrous first meeting with David's parents, the incredibly tense engagement party, the sixtieth birthday celebration for Lord Albert St. Vincent at which his wife, Angelica, had had both too much to drink and nothing to say to her future daughter-in-law, only days before David had shipped out for what was to be his final mission. Vivien had never heard from the family again.

"Beverley, you little misfit," Lady Browning was now calling out to someone else, "come meet my new friend. Miss Vivien Lowry of—"

"Bloomsbury Books" was the best Vivien could muster in sudden response.

"Oh, how wonderful! Yes, of Bloomsbury Books!"

The other women chatted amiably while Vivien continued to quietly observe the rest of the guests. A few dozen were now gathered, having arrived largely en masse from an earlier cocktail reception at another hotel across the park. Vivien knew no one there, although she found herself genuinely starstruck when someone called out to Somerset Maugham and shortly thereafter Noël Coward sat down to play the piano to familiar applause.

Lady Browning introduced Vivien to Coward's good friend, Clarissa Spencer-Churchill, niece of the former prime minister, and again Vivien found herself unusually overcome. She had always adored Winston Churchill's bullish energy and had been both devastated and angered by his election loss after the war.

A handsome young woman close to Vivien in age, Clarissa bore a striking resemblance to Greta Garbo and had yet to settle down in marriage. She was currently rumoured to be embroiled in an affair with the much-older Anthony Eden, the deputy leader of Churchill's Conservative Party in opposition. Clarissa reminisced happily to Lady Browning and Vivien about living on this same top floor of the Dorchester during the war at a reduced room rate due to the threat of air raids and pined over that month's closure of the literary journal *Horizon,* where she had once worked as an editorial assistant.

Vivien said little in return, and nothing about having submitted writing last fall to this same journal, only to be politely but summarily rejected by the editor Cyril Connolly. But as she looked about the room and saw how everyone else was connected by multiple overlapping social and political strands—*my father while up at Oxford; my older sister's season just before the war; the undersecretary's reception in honour of my school chum*—Vivien understood yet again how much of an orphan in the storm she would always be.

Lady Browning did her best to keep Vivien engaged in conversation the few times it was possible, given all the talk of wintering in Cap d'Antibes, the announcement that day of new elections by Clemmie (as they all referred to the current prime minister), and the passing the previous week of American publisher George Putnam, husband to the presumed-dead Amelia Earhart.

Late in the evening Clarissa Spencer-Churchill sat down at the piano next to Noël Coward to sing, enthusiastically but rather poorly, his latest composition, "I Like America."

"In tribute to our hostess!" Clarissa announced vivaciously to the room, and Vivien could only be impressed by how all these women lacked any social compunction whatsoever. They said what they wanted, dripping in irony or sarcasm but with a strange earnestness all the same, gamely grabbed at the trays of drinks and food, and took up space in the room as much as any man.

"Poor Coward can only play in three keys," Lady Browning was whispering quite intimately in Vivien's ear, "and poor Clarissa can't sing in any of them. Although she doesn't suffer for admirers all the same."

"Is the affair with Mr. Eden true?" Vivien lowered her own voice to ask.

Lady Browning nodded. "They say it's a romantic infatuation—on his part—going back many years. But that seems rather an unkind distinction to me."

"'What the world stigmatises as romantic is often more nearly the truth,'" quoted Vivien.

"*The Tenant of Wildfell Hall,*" Lady Browning replied, surprising Vivien. "Anne Brontë—the neglected one of the pack."

"Emily is my favourite."

"Mine, too. But then, I always root for the tempestuous one." Lady Browning smiled, patting Vivien's left knee again in knowing sympathy. Vivien wondered exactly what Ellen Doubleday may have shared with her titled girlfriend about the St. Vincent family, or last week's incident with the watch.

"I am quite obsessed with the entire Brontë family. My daughter Flavia and I are planning a trip north to see the parsonage—you should join us."

This was something else that Vivien remembered well from her time around the St. Vincents: how quick the wealthy were to throw out invitations such as this, whether they truly meant them or not.

The balcony doors had been left open to the brisk night air, while the drawing room filled with cigar and cigarette smoke from the continual stream of wealthy and convivial guests. Vivien had once been so close to this life—but in the end only close enough to know what she was now missing. It was a chapter from her past that she had resolutely tried to put behind her, this type of mannered and social interdependency, the way in which one's value was determined by one's connections to others. Her treatment over the years by the upper crust—the limited admittance based on her looks, the hasty dropping of her whenever it suited—had made Vivien the antithesis of someone such as Alec when it came to cultivating favour with the rich. It was one reason why the encounter in the shop with the two American sisters had unnerved her—she despised the presumptuousness, the recklessness, the incessant sizing up of others.

Vivien angrily pictured Alec sitting in her bed, eating her toast, and calling her *forthcoming,* all based on his narrow sense of how a woman like her should behave. She wondered if he would ever dare to similarly judge any of the wealthy women currently lounging about Mrs. Doubleday's suite, flirting openly, indiscriminately, and often. Vivien also wondered, not for the first time, at the total obliviousness of Alec's self-sabotaging attitude. She had paid him back in spades ever since for the brutal hypocrisy of his words in light of his own actions in bed, which made her blush yet again in recall.

"My dear, you're looking a little flushed." Lady Browning's gaze was fixed on Vivien quite intently. "I'm feeling rather worn-out, too. Shall we share a cab back home?"

They said their farewells to whomever they passed on their way out. One of the servers informed them that Mrs. Doubleday had gone to the bedroom to take an overseas call from her daughter, and Lady Browning requested that their gratitude and goodbyes be passed along. After retrieving their coats, Vivien followed Lady Browning into the corridor and towards the elevators. She got the sense that Lady Browning quite liked being followed around. She did not strike Vivien as being particularly maternal, but instead almost godlike in control. In her magnetic presence, everything and everyone seemed to subtly shift towards her will and her wants.

It was starting to rain. As the head doorman to the Dorchester held an oversized umbrella above both their heads and escorted them to the kerb, Lady Browning asked where she could drop Vivien off. She quickly gave the most central location to her bus line home, something she regularly did with various gentlemen on her nights out.

"And then the Savoy," Lady Browning called out to the cab-driver, before settling back in the seat next to Vivien. "How I detest London. I grew up here, in Hampstead, but only stay because of Tommy's work. I much prefer the house in Cornwall."

It was already well past midnight as the cab raced through the emptied London streets, the city lights shimmering starlike through the mist and drizzle all about them.

"When I was little, my night nursery faced Katherine Mansfield's bedroom across the way—I could see her lights on at night, while she wrote. . . ."

Despite her obvious wealth and stature, Lady Browning was beginning to strike Vivien as a little lonely, even wistful. As if on cue she turned to Vivien and confessed, "I really am not one for parties, especially in the world of publishing. Much as I adore Ellie."

Vivien grinned in agreement. "I certainly am not."

"But you should be. After all, you are of Bloomsbury Books."

Vivien glanced quickly at the other woman to see if she was teasing her, but there was something oddly sincere about Lady Browning. It was as if she had taken full measure of the world about her, found most of it wanting, and was at no pains to give undeserved praise.

"I understand literary events are all the rage in London," Lady Browning continued. "They're still talking about last April's dustup between Roy Cameron and Spender."

"Such events do tend to showcase the men."

"I say no to enough of them myself," Lady Browning remarked simply, while Vivien stared back at her, uncomprehending. "I understand from Ellie that you are an aspiring authoress. As am I," Lady Browning added with a conspiratorial nod.

Vivien found it hard to picture the woman aspiring to anything, so completely at ease did she appear to be with her place in the world.

Lady Browning often seemed able to read Vivien's mind, because she quickly clarified herself by adding, "Authoress, I mean. Fortunately, no longer aspiring. Ah, I see I've surprised you. And I suspect you don't surprise easily. So, you haven't guessed? *C'est bon.* It is genuine then, our little rapport tonight."

Vivien tilted her cropped head to the right and noted again the golden hair styled so curiously, and attractively, to compliment the high cheekbones and perfect lines of the pert nose and well-defined lips.

"I would always much rather talk like this, one to one, wouldn't you?" Lady Browning continued.

Various magazine and newspaper articles were now reassembling themselves inside Vivien's head, which was still slightly buzzing from the glass of champagne she had enjoyed on an empty stomach. She saw the actor Laurence Olivier, of all people, in her mind's eye, and a mansion aflame, and a news article about a recent plagiarism trial in New York.

"Oh my God," Vivien heard herself say.

"No, my dear, not quite."

It was Daphne du Maurier.

CHAPTER FOURTEEN

All shop events must be held after hours.

L iterary luncheons."

Alec looked up from the purchase orders on his desk, bewildered week to week by all the new author names. And not just women's names, either. Fantasy and science fiction authors; writers of twisted psychological fiction; questionable imports from the smaller American publishers.

"I'm sorry?" he answered Vivien, not sounding apologetic in the least.

"I want us to hold literary luncheons here. Like Foyles do. They do such a smart job."

The women in the shop mentioned Foyles as much as possible when making their requests of management. The six-floor, two-million-volume behemoth on Charing Cross Road never failed to raise the competitive spirits of the men of Bloomsbury Books.

"Foyles actually holds them at the Dorchester," Alec insisted. "A much more elegant venue, as you know."

"I know," Vivien said with irritation before smugly adding, "I was just there."

Alec gave her a suspicious look, while Grace suddenly appeared behind Vivien in the doorway.

"It will bring loads more people into the shop, Mr. McDonough," Grace chimed in. "Plus, special events make the customer feel like they're getting something for free."

"So, they spend," added Vivien.

Alec stared at the two women. Mr. Dutton had been off for two weeks now, and the lengthy list of ideas and demands from the Fiction Department was becoming hard to keep up with.

"We have events," Alec persisted. "In the evening. So as not to cut into customer hours."

"Events full of men," Grace pointed out.

"Remember when Stephen Spender got punched in the nose at that poetry reading last year?" Vivien asked Grace with a playful nudge at her side.

Spender was Alec's favourite poet, and he had been in the audience that infamous night. He grimaced in recollection while the two women stood before him, laughing uproariously over the incident.

"Mothers always have more time during the day," Grace said once she and Vivien had composed themselves.

"Bookshops during the day are not a place for people to *speak*," Alec insisted. "They're a place for people to read, and to buy."

"And I know exactly whom to invite to the first one," Vivien said.

"I said *to read*."

"Du Maurier."

"Daphne du Maurier? The romance writer?" Alec asked with a dismissive noise.

"She is no such thing!" Vivien scoffed back at him. "What does that even *mean*? Oh, I just hate that—"

Grace stepped forward to rest her left hand on Vivien's forearm. She reluctantly stopped talking to take a breath before continuing more calmly.

"She's only one of our few international stars, is all—highly prolific, and everybody reads her." Vivien paused to glare at him. "Whether they'll admit to it or not."

Alec sat back in his chair. "And how do you propose securing Miss du Maurier for an event at our little shop?"

"Leave that with me," Vivien replied in that assuring manner she put on with customers. "Leave it all with me."

Alec was hesitant to do that, even though he knew this was the point of their current assignment of roles. He couldn't help but be impressed by Vivien's unique and escalating goals as acting head of fiction, but the gains often came at his expense. The department had become undeniably busier since Vivien had emerged from behind the cash counter to walk the floor as he had once done, offering assistance and assurance in hushed, solicitous tones.

Her themed tables were a particular hit. With Grace's help, Vivien had been depleting their stale back stock by arranging books on the flat front tables according to a themed concept and accompanied by relevant objets d'art: vases or paintings on loan from the antiques shop across Lamb's Conduit, hothouse flowers from the Inverness Street Market a few blocks away, even domestic items such as co-ordinated teacups or decorative tins.

The displays were sometimes more of a hit than the books themselves. Grace had recently approached him with a department-wide purchase order for specialty cushions to be placed strategically throughout the shop. Customers had been caught fawning over the ones that Grace had brought in from home, needlepointed at night during the war to keep her fears at bay.

Alec, on the other hand, was now stuck in the back office with only the subtly disgruntled Grace at his service. It was not the promotion he had dreamed of. There was no time to persuade, to sell, or to observe: all the things he had enjoyed doing at the front of the shop. Sure, he had more time to write (he kept his own coil-bound notebook now in one of Mr. Dutton's many filing cabinets), but nothing to write about. He hardly saw Vivien anymore, which did not help his imagination.

Then there was the matter of their newest employee, Evie Stone, hiding away on the top floor where no one could see her. Frank Allen was away more than ever, although purchasing far less, and Alec knew he would have to raise this with Dutton, too. Ash continued to intimidate any visitors to the basement with his wall of silence, while Master Mariner Scott did so with his thunderous tones.

Things felt askew at Bloomsbury Books, and Alec wondered not for the first time how Herbert Dutton had kept everything from imploding with his fifty-one rules. Before Alec agreed to let a lady romance writer take over the shop during its busiest time of the day, he would run the idea by Mr. Dutton, along with several other growing concerns. In the meantime, he would politely ask Grace to visit the top floor, fetch him Frank Allen's appointments book, and check in on Evie Stone.

Frank Allen had hardly been seen in the shop since Evie Stone's first day of work. Following the Toppings sale, he had left for a three-day scouting trip to Ireland. The entire staff had been surprised by his lengthy absences of late, given the recent shake-up. Three weeks into her new job, Evie continued to work happily alone on the top floor, quite at home on her little stool cataloguing the books, just as Grace found her now.

"Mr. McDonough asked me to fetch Mr. Allen's appointments book," Grace explained as she took a quick peek at the series of hasty scribblings inside. "How strange . . ."

Evie watched as Grace flipped ahead several pages, then back again, before looking over at Evie with unusual consternation.

Grace was normally so calm and relaxed, which suited Evie well. She was extremely averse to drama or conflict of any kind. She had not enjoyed the barely hidden competitive energy of academia, let alone the outright feuding going on at the shop.

"The entry for this week . . . the Roundtree warehouse sale. I'm sure that was already held last autumn. Same with next week."

Evie shrugged and returned to the book in her hands. She didn't mind Mr. Allen's being away so much. She was starting to feel as if the top floor of Bloomsbury Books was her own private research library.

"No matter, I must have it wrong." Grace picked up the appointments book and turned to Evie. "Tea?"

At that exact moment Ash appeared on the landing, to the surprise of both women.

"I thought I'd introduce Miss Stone to a cup of chai," he announced formally, nodding down at the steaming mug on a small melamine tray next to two Bourbon biscuits, Evie's favourite.

Evie stood up hurriedly as she felt Grace's eyes upon her.

"How very kind," Grace observed. "Isn't that kind, Evie?"

Evie felt as if Mr. Dutton's secretary was prodding her to say something. When she didn't, Grace turned back to Ash with an encouraging smile.

"I shall get out of your way then," she said as she squeezed past Ash's slight figure to head back downstairs.

He remained standing on the landing, looking about the disarray of the third floor. "I haven't been up here in ages."

Patting down the creases in her navy knit dress, Evie came over to take the tray from him and place it carefully on the floor next to her stool. *Never near the books* was the one shop rule they all unanimously abided when it came to their many cups of tea.

"Mr. Allen's still travelling." Evie watched as Ash treaded

carefully between the piles of books on the floor. "The boxes just keep coming."

Ash made his way towards the row of glass-fronted cabinets positioned along the back wall. "Everything well protected. Like my rocks and bugs." He turned and gave her a knowing smile.

For the first time in her life, Evie felt her heart leap over something other than a book. "Well, books are precious in their own way."

"May I?" He waited for her to nod before opening the cabinet behind Mr. Allen's desk. Carefully removing an old atlas, he placed it on top of an oak lectern from the Victorian era that had probably been in the room since that time.

Evie watched as Ash lifted each page carefully, almost reverently, then motioned for her to join him.

"This map here. This is from before the Raj. How interesting. And this is where I was born, along the Coromandel Coast. Madras, see? *George Town* as written here." He returned to the frontispiece of the book. "Yes, this is from long before the Raj. Sixteen hundreds, I should think."

Evie's knowledge of literature was tremendous, and her recollection of American cinema almost as impressive, but having to leave grammar school at age fourteen had left a few notable gaps in her education. Hard as her tutor Adeline Gray had tried, Evie still had a lot to learn when it came to geography, astronomy, and anatomy in particular.

"Is it really that old?" she asked in astonishment.

"Master Mariner Scott should be able to tell you. The price marked down is certainly generous." Ash closed the dusty volume and looked about them. "Mr. Allen may have slightly undervalued a few things in his busyness."

Evie knew the top floor was a disastrous mess, but she already took pride in all its possessions and appreciated Ash's careful choice of words.

"How old were you when you learned English?" she asked him out of the blue.

Ash put the atlas back inside the glass cabinet and closed the door. "English is one of our languages."

"Oh, I didn't know."

"Not at all. Why would anyone here know something like that?"

Evie did not know how to reply to the curtness in his tone, so they just stood there, staring at each other, until something in Ash's gaze softened at her discomfort.

"I'm sorry. That was unnecessary of me."

"No, I'm sorry. I am sure there is much I should know. Geography, for one thing."

"It's not you." He waved a hand about them. "It's everyone. And it's me, as a result." He sighed. "Besides, I doubt a girl who graduated from Cambridge has many gaps in her education."

"I had to leave grammar school early."

"How early?"

"Fourteen. I had to catch up fast to sit the exams for Cambridge. I know plenty about women writers of the eighteenth and nineteenth centuries, but other stuff got missed."

Ash leaned back against Mr. Allen's desk with his arms crossed and observed her thoughtfully. "Fourteen. Catching up must not have been easy. And all for this?" He nodded about at the mess of books surrounding them.

Evie's face darkened at the memory of Professors Christenson and Kinross, and the hiring of Stuart Wesley over her.

"No, this was . . . not planned."

He smiled knowingly at her. "But you do have one, don't you? A plan?"

"What makes you say that?" Evie began to inwardly panic that her activities in the shop were not going completely unnoticed.

"Researching nineteenth-century botanists on one's day off."

Evie smiled from relief. "Oh, that. That's just . . . finishing something I started at Cambridge. My real interests lie in rediscovering writers, women writers, who've been overlooked."

"Overlooked?"

"Forgotten. Ignored. Dismissed."

"That's quite the mission. How do you propose to do that?"

"Oh, I forgot the chai!"

Ash watched with amusement as Evie plopped back down onto the stool and took a few sips of the now-warm drink before replying,

"I plan to publish."

Ash stared at her. "That is *not* what I thought you were going to say."

"Doing literary research, you stumble across so many lost and forgotten books. No one even remembers their titles anymore. I read fast, always have done, 'n' if I can find a copy, just one copy anywhere, I can assess it 'n' reprint the important ones."

"Reprint?"

"Mm-hmm. Typeset and print it, just like Virginia Woolf 'n' her husband did."

"Virginia Woolf published?"

"Mm-hmm," Evie repeated with increasing excitement. "With a handpress, in her *drawing room*! So, it must be possible. I've researched it all."

Ash shook his head at her admiringly. "I am sure you did. We are biding our time here together, then."

"It's not such a bad place to be."

"No"—he smiled directly at her—"it certainly isn't. Well, I better leave you to your work—Allen's left quite a mountain to go through."

As Ash headed back downstairs, Evie wished she could have told him more. She had a feeling Ash Ramaswamy would understand her compulsions—not everyone did. Most people spent their few hours of leisure time seeking entertainment and distraction, but Evie had set such a large goal for herself that she dared not waste a second in its pursuit. Few people would be willing to comb through materials as she did—she just had to stay ahead of everyone else, and beneath their notice, until what she wanted was safe and secure.

Looking at the piles of books on the floor and in boxes stacked against the walls, Evie thought about the atlas and wondered how many other centuries-old treasures she might find buried beneath the years of Mr. Allen's neglect. Unfortunately, she was beginning to fear that the one book for which she was secretly searching on the third floor—the real impetus for her applying to Bloomsbury Books—had been lost, and not for the first time.

CHAPTER FIFTEEN

RULE No. 21

Staff shall not peruse other departments without permission.

The first time had been only a few years after the book's anonymous publication in 1827, following which *The Mummy! A Tale of the Twenty-Second Century* by Jane Wells Webb had disappeared from the world.

From her research work, Evie knew that this was often the case with anonymous or woman-authored texts. Mary Wollstonecraft's *Vindication of the Rights of Woman,* now acknowledged as the single greatest work of early feminism in human history, had similarly fallen out of print and from cultural memory until its reprinting many decades later.

This lack of a public record was one reason why Evie had missed the significance of *The Mummy!* during her late-night cataloguing at the Chawton Great House library, where the book had been hidden in plain sight for over one hundred years. There had been no reference to it in the listings of publications that Evie had consulted in various libraries during her two years of cataloguing. For all Evie knew at the time, *The Mummy!* was merely an obscure, second-rate attempt to capitalize on the Gothic novel as with many other works of its era. While preparing for the dispersal of the Great House library by Sotheby's, Yardley Sinclair and his colleagues had similarly assessed and dismissed the book as one of many lesser novels written in response to the revolutionary *Frankenstein*.

Along with the rest of humanity, Evie had forgotten all about the book until three years later, when she was immersed in her research work for Professor Kinross and his voluminous annotation of Thackeray's greatest masterpiece, *Vanity Fair*. Evie had stumbled across a letter by Thackeray in the archives of Trinity College Library in Cambridge, where the famous poet and writer had also been a student, describing a dinner at the home of his good friends botanist John Claudius Loudon and his wife, the former Jane Wells Webb. In the letter, Thackeray mentioned how Mrs. Loudon's current work alongside her husband, as well as her recent manuals *Gardening for Ladies* and *Botany for Ladies,* had caused her to turn her back on her own fiction writing. Thackeray had then praised one of her early novels, written when she was just seventeen, as a most riveting account of life in a future century, centerd around the revivification of a mummy, of all things.

Thackeray had also laid out several of the technological advances that Jane Loudon's first book had foretold, advances that Evie—reading this letter one hundred years later—now knew to be eerily prophetic, including railway lines with mobile houses, a form of communication that loosely resembled television, and steam and electricity as primary sources of power. According to Thackeray, the book took place in 2126, when "England enjoyed peace and tranquility under the absolute dominion of a female sovereign" who establishes a reign based solely on female ascension. The political and philosophical themes described by Thackeray struck Evie as having more in common with modern works of science fiction such as Orwell's *Nineteen Eighty-Four* than with early eighteenth-century Gothic texts. With three years of higher education behind her, Evie could now fully appreciate the potential historical, literary, and monetary value of such a work.

Rushing home from Trinity College Library to her bedsitter on the north end of Castle Street, Evie had made straight for her makeshift filing cabinet in the old upright dresser drawers. There she retrieved the notebook in which she had diligently recorded every one of the two thousand books sold during the Sotheby's Great House dispersal. Flipping furiously through the pages of her notebook, Evie quickly confirmed to herself that an anonymously authored book called *The Mummy! A Tale of the Twenty-Second Century* had indeed been acquired, along with four other nineteenth-century texts, by a Mr. Frank Allen on behalf of Bloomsbury Books.

Throughout last fall, Evie had investigated backwards, attempting to discover any recent critical evaluations of Webb's book. First, she found a short summary in a text by Andrew Block, released amidst the chaos of the Second World War, called *The English Novel, 1740–1850*. Evie still could not forgive herself for missing this reference text during her initial cataloguing of the Great House library. Next, she tripped across a recent and extensive review of the one known abridged edition in the spring 1949 issue of a Wisconsin literary gazette called *The Arkham Sampler*. From these two evaluations, which provided the sole modern record of the existence of Jane Webb's first novel, Evie was mortified to discover that she had thoroughly devalued one of the most important science fiction novels ever written—and by someone her own age, no less!

As the newest employee of Bloomsbury Books, Evie had used her first days of work to search through every sinking shelf and ramshackle crate on the third floor, eager to find the book Mr. Allen had bought. Mr. Dutton had not been exaggerating during her interview when he had described the head of the shop's Rare Books Department as lacking some diligence where cataloguing was concerned. But Evie was becoming worried that Mr. Allen had done worse than fail to catalogue the book—she feared he had lost it.

Within a week of starting work, Evie had exhausted her third-floor search for the book so colourfully called *The Mummy! A Tale of the Twenty-Second Century*. It was not on any of the shelves, or in the boxes or piles of books that Frank Allen left lying around. There was also no record of its purchase in the annual ledgers that Mr. Allen and the other department heads were required to keep. The only other possibility was that the book was somewhere else in the shop. If ultimately decreed by Mr. Allen to be of little value, old or rare books were sometimes moved to the other floors, most often according to subject matter.

Evie had lost no time in turning next to the New Books, Fiction and Art Departments. For all their squabbles and opposing temperaments, both Alec McDonough and Vivien Lowry were notoriously scrupulous when it came to organising their respective areas. Vivien had taken advantage of her new role as acting manager to create a slate of impressively narrow genre categories (contemporary feminist literature, modern expressionist drama, and late nineteenth-century French realism, among many others), which helped further narrow Evie's search. A few quick visits during her lunch break over the past few weeks had so far yielded nothing.

Next was the basement and the Science and Naturalism Department, which was also kept in pristine order by Ashwin Ramaswamy. Evie had learned how to make a decent cup of chai in order to spend more time down there and discreetly examine the relevant collections. Even better organised than that of fiction, Ash's department was arranged on taxonomic principles along Linnaean lines. With the entire basement floor divided into various "kingdoms" and each shelf categorized according to Darwin's notion of common descent, Evie was able to methodically work through the few sections that looked relevant to her cause and quickly glance over the rest.

Only the second floor of Bloomsbury Books remained completely unexamined—and, unfortunately, out of bounds as far as Master Mariner Scott was concerned. Evie knew she must never be caught perusing the history floor without a purpose sanctioned by its departmental head, pursuant to shop rule twenty-one.

Evie was just going to have to continue biding her time, waiting for the perfect moment when she could venture onto the second floor without fear of reprisal and finish her self-appointed task once and for all.

CHAPTER SIXTEEN

RULE NO. 16

Clerical staff shall have Saturdays off to spend time
with their families.

Grace stood in the front hallway of her small semidetached home in Camden Town, pulling on her gloves and smiling down at her sons, who were fidgeting with excitement.

"Gordon!" she called up the stairs. "Gordon, we must hurry!"

No corresponding noise came from the master bedroom, and Grace motioned to the two boys to wait for her. As she trudged upstairs, the dusty-rose carpeting dulled the sound of the low-heeled shoes she wore for shopping, making the prospect of another of Gordon's moods feel even more ominous than usual.

Gordon was sitting on the corner of their bed as if he had been waiting for her.

"Gordon, please." She sighed.

"I told you not today."

"It's not up to you. It's Teddy's birthday tomorrow and this is what he wants."

"You'll go without me."

At his accusatory tone, Grace felt her back stiffen with resolve. "Yes, we will."

"You're always doing what you want now . . ." he hissed, and she saw the winding up in his eyes that came faster and faster all the time. It hardly took anything now to set him off.

"Gordon, I'm sorry, we don't have time for this. And I won't let Teddy down, not for you, not for anyone."

Gordon's willingness to use their sons as pawns was a recent development. Grace had learned to ignore the impact of his mood swings on herself, but feared the effect of his cruel deprivations on Nicholas and sensitive Teddy, especially as they grew older and more aware of the strain at home.

Gordon made a dismissive gesture, as if she were the one hiding behind their sons and not the other way around.

Grace turned on her heel and headed back downstairs without a word. She rushed the boys out the front door, hoping the lengthy bus ride to Soho would restore both her sense of calm and Teddy's special day. It was her youngest son's eleventh birthday, and he asked for the same thing every year, being as habitual a creature as his father: an excursion to pick out more toy soldiers for his Second World War battle set. They were off to Regent Street and Hamleys, the oldest and largest toy store in London.

As the three of them walked down the lane to the bus stop, Grace knew they must be an object of interest and speculation to the neighbourhood. No one ever came straight out and asked her where Gordon was, or how he was doing; they were far too polite to do that. Still, Grace preferred to never stand out in any way. She had to wonder how much her natural reserve had factored into the decision to marry Gordon as the spinster years drew closer. How ironic that the decision to tread the expected marital path had come to such an aberrant end.

This was one reason why she admired Vivien, who rarely paid much heed to what others thought. The younger woman particularly refused to allow the snobbery of the shop's more fashionable clientele to push her aside; if anything, it made her dig her heels in. No one could ever accuse Vivien of lacking in confidence or needing the approval of others. Following the incident with the watch, however, Grace now wondered whether Vivien's enmity towards Alec belied a degree of caring about what he, at least, thought of her.

In contrast to Vivien, Grace had let her husband erode her confidence over the years. He had been most effective in flattening her spirits because he should have been her most reliable ally. His undermining of her gave the lie to the maxim to keep one's enemies closer. Only when she was away from him did she feel happy or free. Yet even away from him, she was unable to regain her old sense of self. She had hoped the job at Bloomsbury Books would help, but the limited expectations and responsibilities entrusted in her by Mr. Dutton failed to motivate. Instead, her position made her the one woman on her street who went to work each day along with the other husbands—and the one woman whose husband did not.

All of this made the idea of leaving Gordon too big for Grace to contemplate, even as his behaviour towards both her and the boys continued to escalate. It would mean not only being the sole working woman among their acquaintance, but the only divorced one as well. The shame of divorce could be difficult even for men, although the wealthiest of them seemed to cope well enough. Look at Lord Baskin and his love life: plenty of society ladies of a certain age still seemed to set their cap at him, and Alec in particular was full of rumours from various outings and events that the men at the shop indulged in together.

As if the universe could read her usually unreadable mind, there stood Lord Baskin himself on the London pavement before her, escorting a woman into an idling cab in front of the Hotel Café Royal.

"Grace—Mrs. Perkins!" he called out happily upon seeing her, then looked down from his estimable height at her two boys. "And who might have we here?"

Grace self-consciously started to wipe down the unwieldy cow-
lick that always rose up from Teddy's brow.

"Lord Baskin, what a surprise." She continued to fiddle with
her youngest son's hair while letting her eyes dart slightly ahead
to the waiting cab. The woman inside looked to be around Vivien's
age and as smoothly made-up and co-ordinated, but in ravish-
ing shades of red instead of Vivien's morose black. "These are my
boys, Nicholas and Teddy." Grace put a hand proudly on each of
their outside shoulders as they stood before her.

For a second she caught Lord Baskin's eyes similarly wander
about as if he, too, was searching for someone else in their small,
lopsided party. "How nice to meet you both. Out shopping?"

"It's Teddy's birthday tomorrow, his eleventh, so we're on our
way to Hamleys. Toy soldiers, isn't that right, Edward?"

Teddy looked back up at his mother at hearing his given name.
"You don't call me that," he said simply.

Grace smiled over the tops of her sons' heads at Lord Baskin
and shrugged, while his hazel eyes lit up in playful commiseration with her son.

"I prefer Teddy, too," he said to the younger boy, kneeling down
to address him.

"I didn't say I did," the boy stated, again so simply that Grace
and Lord Baskin could only gesture at each other helplessly in
amusement. "I said nothing of the sort."

"Teddy, hush, please."

"If you'll allow me"—Lord Baskin motioned the three of them
over to his side of the pavement and away from the press of the
crowd—"I just need to see someone off. Wait right here?"

Grace watched as Lord Baskin leaned down into the cab to address first its occupant and then the driver before stepping back
onto the kerb. She noticed that he waited for the cab to disappear
in the heavy traffic before turning back to them.

"Right, may I join you? It's been too long since I ventured inside Hamleys. My grandfather often treated me there himself."

They proceeded up Regent Street together, a surprising foursome on a family afternoon, and Grace couldn't help but notice that the crowd about them was similarly mixed. Stretching from the circus at Piccadilly to Oxford Street in the north, Regent Street had been designed by John Nash as another type of conduit, one that connected all of the major shopping, theatre, and cultural areas of central London. The pavement was full of parents and children exiting from Saturday-afternoon matinees in the West End, well-dressed society matrons tired by shopping and seeking respite over afternoon tea, and young people enjoying the cinema and arcades with their allowance, something many families had only recently found themselves able to afford.

Several of London's finest restaurants and hotels were located in this hub of leisure activity, and the Hotel Café Royal, from which Lord Baskin had just emerged, was the grandest of the lot. Over the years its patrons had included royalty, movie stars, artists, and writers such as Shaw, Kipling, and Yeats; the most notorious of them all was Oscar Wilde, who had first encountered his future lover Lord Alfred Douglas in the Grill Room restaurant itself. Leaving the hotel, one could stroll north to Regent's Park or south to Buckingham Palace along a route of established boutiques nestled amongst newer retailers. As one approached Piccadilly Circus to the south, the illuminated signage—BOVRIL, COCA-COLA, WRIGLEY'S CHEWING GUM—managed to look both flashy and common. With large portions of the street having been rebuilt following catastrophic fires and German bombings during the Blitz ("Hamleys was hit at least five times!" Teddy often boasted), nowhere in London was its hope for the future, and quest for global dominance, more visually apparent.

"I hope we haven't kept you from anything," Grace offered after a few seconds of silence, feeling the oddness of walking out with Lord Baskin so far from the shop.

"I wouldn't let you put yourself in any such position. Fortunately for myself, I'd just finished dining."

"At the Grill Room?"

"Yes. Do you know it?"

Grace laughed and noticed Teddy glance back at her with new suspicion. Although only a year older, Nicholas stayed focused on looking ahead, being much more interested in the young girls passing by in bell skirts and stockings.

"No, not really. We aren't here very often."

"Neither am I. Like you, I try to avoid Regent Street when I can," Lord Baskin replied with that strange mixture of gallantry and humility that so amused Vivien and Grace both. "However, I had an early luncheon I could not extricate myself from."

Grace wondered who the woman in the cab might have been and grew silent at his side. Soon they reached the toy store, with its series of large glass panes surrounding a central emblem of the King's Royal Warrant. Lord Baskin looked up at all seven storeys of the shop with a charmingly nostalgic air, then stood back to let Grace and her sons enter first. Before he could follow, a small mob of children pushed in ahead of him, and Grace and Baskin smiled at each other over their heads as she waited for him to catch up.

"That's what you get for being a gentleman," she teased, although it did not come out quite as she had intended, and she quickly fell silent again.

The toy soldiers were at one end of the miniatures floor, the train sets were in the middle, and at the other end were dollhouses from different eras: baroque Queen Anne, stately Georgian, and ornate Victorian. While Grace and Lord Baskin lingered in the central corridor, Nicholas and Teddy quickly ran over to the Second World War section and disappeared behind the displays.

"They can't seem to forgive me for birthing them too late to fight," she mused aloud.

"I'm afraid I was once the same way." He was watching her sons keenly. "The idea of war is always exciting to young men. All my own toy soldiers were from the Crimean, where my grandfather fought. Which of course makes me feel quite old."

Teddy was now gesturing pleadingly to his mother with his right hand while holding up a long box of eight painted lead soldiers with the other. She shook her head and held up four fingers instead. This led to some foot-stomping by the birthday boy, followed by Nicholas whispering conspiratorially in his ear.

Lord Baskin was watching all of this with great amusement. "Now I see where you and Vivien get it from. All that silent gesturing."

"I'm sure we're quite childish sometimes."

"Not at all. It keeps the shop young." He leaned back against a nearby counter. "I would have liked to have had children."

Once again, Grace found herself wondering who the woman in the cab could have been.

"We—Anna and I—were to have a son, but we lost him. I suppose that's what set a lot of it off."

"I'm so sorry."

"Thank you. It was a long time ago. Still . . ."

His voice trailed off and a sad silence fell between them. Grace watched her two boys playing happily with the toys on display, a wave of gratitude washing over her for their presence in her life. She would not have been blessed with these children if she hadn't married Gordon. The unanswerable question now was whether—if not for the children—Gordon would still have her.

Grace let her gaze drift off to the elaborate dollhouses that she had yearned for as a child. How strange to think that she and Lord Baskin might once have stood together on this same floor decades ago, despite coming from such different family backgrounds. The dollhouse her parents had eventually bought her had been a simple and affordable square shell, with four dolls inside representing the perfect Edwardian family, everyone in his or her place.

She looked back at Lord Baskin, who was watching pensively as her sons and the other children ran about the department.

"We've been coming here for Teddy's birthday for years now, even in the war," she finally spoke. "During the Blitz, the staff wore tin hats and cashed you out in front of the store, running back and forth to get the toys."

"How very Churchillian." Lord Baskin smiled, then nodded to her as Teddy held up his final choice from across the aisle.

Grace headed over with her handbag to help with the purchase. While the clerk wrapped the box of four soldiers, Grace looked about at the different battle scenes—some of them from the Crusades, others from the Napoleonic or Boer Wars—set out on display. So many centuries of bloodshed as sport, and so very different from what she had played with as a girl.

There was not a single injured toy soldier in sight. In grown-up life, of course, no one escaped war unscathed. Grace thought back on Lord Baskin's dropping of the keys, the way he always struggled when fetching their coffees, and how he still clearly favoured his left arm and hand. Alec refused to talk about the war, Vivien had lost her fiancé to it, civilian Gordon had possibly lost his mind.

For the first time, Grace wondered what Gordon might be up to in his family's absence. She was grateful that Lord Baskin hadn't asked where her husband was—he was far too gallant to do that. Even so, he could have no idea that the life she was holding on to was as primly furnished as a dollhouse and just as unreal. Grace wished she could talk to someone about her marital problems—if not the earl, then at least Vivien. But talking about it would also make it painfully real.

In all their years of working together, Grace had only ex-changed harsh words with Vivien once. At the argument's zenith, Vivien had accused Grace of using calm detachment as a shield. *"No one can be this unflappable!"* Vivien had finally cried out in a huff before storming off. The two women would never discuss it again, but Grace knew that *not* reacting to others could be just as effective, and deceptive, a shield as saying something. She had learned to suppress her emotions the hard way, at home. Just like the men in the shop, she was fully capable of not feeling—and thereby of deceiving—herself. At this moment in the toy store, happily watching her boys without their father and not missing him at all, Grace allowed herself a small but dangerous inkling of what she truly wanted. And it wasn't at all what she had.

The sun was setting by the time the four of them finally de-parted Hamleys. As she and Lord Baskin hesitated on the front pavement together, Teddy finally remembered his hunger in all the excitement and leaned against his mother's side with a dra-matic groan.

"Why don't I treat the birthday boy to tea?" Lord Baskin of-fered. "We could cut down Sackville Street and be at Fortnum and Mason in just a few minutes."

Her sons' faces lit up, but something about the situation struck Grace as not quite right. She was surprised that Lord Baskin would want to accompany a married woman and her children to a place where his own social circle—and the four of them—would be out on full display. Besides, she was expected home herself. And in that moment, she finally had the answer to something that she had wondered about for years, during all those bus rides from work.

She did not want to go home. If she was honest with herself, she wanted to take her boys and run.

As if worried Lord Baskin could intuit such betrayal in her

thoughts, Grace pushed them aside and gave a pleasant smile and polite shake of her head. "How terribly kind of you. But I'm afraid we must catch our bus home. Come along, boys."

This was followed by more groans, at which Lord Baskin turned and held his right forefinger up to an approaching cab. "Allow me to at least treat you to the journey home."

The cab came to a hard stop. He pulled open the rear door, and the boys clambered in excitedly ahead of her. As she settled into the seat, Grace watched Lord Baskin chat amiably with the cabdriver while discreetly passing him several pound notes. He did this with his usual smooth elegance—again, that gallantry—which always left Grace feeling as if nothing mattered more to him, at that moment, than the comfort of others. It wasn't just about money, although of course the money helped. It was his constant thoughtfulness and concern that made Lord Baskin unique.

Her sons had never been in a London cab before—their London was one of double-decker buses and musty underground tube stations. As the two boys roughhoused on the seat next to her, Grace looked up at Lord Baskin standing on the kerb, the cab door latched but the window still open between them.

"Thank you."

"For what?" she asked with surprise.

"For letting me spend time with you and your family."

As the cab sped off through the busy London streets, Grace wondered at his words. Lord Baskin seemed to yearn for what she had—if only he knew. He suddenly struck her, for all his wealth and glamorous life, as deeply lonely. She had never sensed this about him before, during the many stop-ins at Bloomsbury Books. There Lord Baskin seemed to be quite at home, enlivened by all the activity and employees about him. Around her he seemed particularly content. She pushed the thought away and turned back to her boys just as her nerves started to roil about inside. She desperately hoped the cabdriver got them home to Camden Town in time to make Gordon his tea at precisely 4:00 p.m., just as he demanded it.

CHAPTER SEVENTEEN

RULE No. 29

The personal lives of staff are to remain private and confidential.

Alec McDonough had never been to this part of London before. It had taken subway, train, and bus to find the handsome Victorian terrace house on a winding road in the leafy enclave of Dulwich Village, across the Thames from central London.

The front garden was immaculate, its perimeter of hawthorn and hydrangea bushes trimmed against the winter frost. In the centre of the small square yard was a cracked stone urn on a pedestal base, giving the space an exotic look enhanced by ornamental honeysuckle vines that draped over the front stone wall. Alec opened the entrance gate, freshly painted in a rich mulberry colour, and latched it behind him as gently as possible. Everything about Herbert Dutton's well-appointed home struck Alec as demanding both diligence and care.

He let the front brass door knocker, shaped like an eagle, fall against the matching mulberry-painted front door. After waiting several seconds, he heard a loud noise inside, followed by Mr. Dutton's voice calling out for whoever was there to let themselves in.

Alec entered the front foyer to find a china umbrella stand just inside the threshold, full of an assortment of antique walking sticks, and a basket of several pairs of men's leather gloves, which rested on the long shelf built over an old cast-iron radiator. Feeling his feet kick at something on the floor, he looked down to see a few pieces of forgotten mail from the front-door slot. Alec picked up the envelopes and stacked them next to a small porcelain bowl full of different sets of keys, then looked along the corridor walls covered in multiple framed lithographs of Roman and Greek ruins—famous sites that Alec knew Mr. Dutton had always hoped to visit one day, but had never allowed himself enough vacation time to do so.

Alec wondered how such a conscientious and hardworking man as Herbert Dutton was faring, stuck at home for weeks on end. Turning in to the passageway to the front drawing room, he discovered the patient sitting upright on a lovely antique chaise lounge, warmed by the nearby fireplace. On the coffee table before him rested a tray amply stocked with tea, a bowl of fresh dates, bananas, and oranges, and a large plate of slices of pound cake and various other breads.

Mr. Dutton must have caught Alec's look of surprise at all the food because his first words, after his own expression of astonishment, were that he had recently received a crate of fruit from an aunt residing in Spain.

"How kind of her," Alec replied, not recalling any tales of such an aunt before.

"I was not expecting you today." Mr. Dutton looked away, busying himself with the cushions about him.

"As you know, I've been wanting to visit for some time now. To make sure you are being well taken care of—which, I gladly see, you are."

"Yes, as I said on the telephone, my neighbours are most solicitous. So, there is no need to worry." Mr. Dutton glanced quickly at the clock on the fireplace mantel. "I'm afraid I will need to rest soon, however, and cut our visit short."

Alec had been watching Herbert Dutton carefully as he spoke, while he in turn was resisting looking straight back at Alec. Dutton looked worn and tired, as if he had aged overnight, which might explain his sudden diffidence around Alec. But Alec also had the strange sensation that, for the first time in their professional and personal relationship, his presence was not entirely welcome.

"Here," Alec said as he walked over to the front window, "let me open the curtains a bit to let in some sun."

"Really, there's no need . . ." Mr. Dutton began, but Alec ignored him and continued to casually explore the room while looking for clues. Scattered across the seat of an armchair were sections of that morning's *The Sunday Times* and an import copy of *National Geographic* magazine. Through a Victorian archway, the dining room table could be seen in all its stately mahogany, intimately set for two.

Alec came back to stand above Mr. Dutton, who was now looking even more pale and nervous than usual. He was wearing striped silk satin pyjamas and a plaid dressing gown beneath a luxurious lambswool blanket pulled up high around his waist. What Alec did not notice were any books nearby, which also struck him as strange, given the amount of time the older man was having to spend on his own.

"You're very missed."

Mr. Dutton gave one of those small smiles that hardly left a dent in the moonlike features of his face. "The doctor says a return in February might be possible, with some stipulations. Can you and Vivien survive until then? How is she faring in the new role?" Mr. Dutton's eyes darted again at the clock.

Alec shrugged. "Miss du Maurier is charging ahead, of course. Pulling out all the stops for the du Maurier luncheon this week. I fear we'll be hard put to relegate her back to cash."

"I was afraid of that." Dutton gave a small cough. "Mr. Allen's of the opinion that she should get a promote to assistant manager."

Alec thought about what such an advancement would mean to Vivien, and how little it really was, in the context of both her ambition and her abilities.

"What do you say to that?" Mr. Dutton asked, always eager for Alec's opinion.

Alec found himself torn between the years of feuding with Vivien as rival colleagues and his undeniable admiration, as acting general manager, for her hard work and initiative. The latter feeling caught him off guard.

As he hesitated, Mr. Dutton answered for him. "I have to say not. I suppose I am just old-fashioned. And Evie Stone?" The decision on Vivien was clearly no longer up for debate. "I've received the occasional note from Miss Stone, memoranda of a sort, updating Frank and myself on her cataloguing progress, but with little mention of the other staff."

"She keeps quite to herself on the third floor, easy enough with Mr. Allen away so often. Which reminds me—"

"And Grace?" Mr. Dutton gave an odd cough at the sound of the front door opening, followed by the clanging of keys against the small porcelain bowl.

"Grace is fine, as always. . . ." Alec's voice trailed off as he looked up to see Frank Allen standing in the doorway to the drawing room. "Oh, what a coincidence." Alec took a step forward to greet his colleague, then stopped himself.

Frank was holding a brown bag from the local chemist in the crook of his left arm and in his right hand the small stack of mail that Alec had gathered up.

"Oh, hullo." Frank also took a step forward but then, seeming to make eye contact with Mr. Dutton from behind Alec, froze back in place. "I was just doing some errands for the invalid here."

"I see that," Alec offered in as casual a tone as he could muster.

"Let me put this down and then join you both for a catch-up."

Frank stepped back into the front hall and disappeared. Alec waited a few seconds in confusion, then turned to see Mr. Dutton looking quite flushed.

"Let me tamp down the fire a bit." Alec went to poke at the coal, keeping his gaze on the dying embers as he thought through what was happening. Mr. Allen had looked quite at home, mail and medicine in hand, strolling through the house on a Sunday morning as if he had been there many times before. As if he lived there.

Something in Alec's nature—a tendency to judge, mired in a lack of self-awareness—now entwined itself with this sudden knot of new and unnerving knowledge. It all combined to strangle the easy charm he usually wielded. He hastily took his leave of Mr. Dutton, who looked visibly relieved at Alec's vague explanation of having another stop to make. Without looking back, he exited each of the mulberry-painted doors to the exquisite terrace house and front garden, then hurried down the road in the direction of the village centre.

As Alec walked, taking in deep breaths of the cold January air, he felt disappointment in Mr. Dutton and Mr. Allen, and even deeper disapproval. The three men had spent many hours together after work, discussing the precarious finances of the shop, as well as politics, travel, and books. They had become close, Alec thought, although not as close as Vivien and Grace, who in their intimacy possessed the silent, subversive language of siblings. Alec suddenly saw the shop as two different and increasingly warring factions of the same family. He had had no idea, however, that Herbert and Frank had also been living as one.

Alec's ego was strangely hurt. He didn't like being lied to; even less did he like learning this particular truth. He wondered at the two men putting so much at risk just to share a bed. Any resulting scandal could mark the ruin of both and, by extension, the business of Bloomsbury Books.

The irony of Alec's allowing his own time at the shop to be fraught with physical memories of Vivien entirely escaped him. Instead, he continued to let his judgmental mind complicate unfairly what he had just realised, standing in the drawing room by the fire that Frank Allen had lit for Herbert Dutton before leaving him to the lovingly compiled breakfast. Unfortunately for Allen and Dutton, Alec's notions of sex and propriety were as fixed in him as anything. These notions did not include two men secretly living together as a couple. Fortunately for Alec himself, his ideas on sex lined up nicely with majority rule.

That the rules of the majority could, by definition, never fit the intrinsic beliefs and needs of everyone, was meaningless to Alec. What was illicit in others was, for him, often the just deserts of being a man. He would always warmly recall losing his virginity to a schoolmate's older sister under a garden pergola after an equally memorable cricket match. During the war, he had been grateful to seek refuge in the arms of a very young Norwegian woman following a protracted land battle near the village of Kvam, where dozens of the 15th Infantry Brigade now lay buried. Finally, Alec would never forget the intimate exploration of Vivien's coltish, cream-coloured body in her own bed, with all the things that made up her mystery scattered about the bedroom, to also be explored by him when the sun came up.

Alec continued to treat the loss soon after of Vivien herself as just another casualty in his life, rather than a cause of deep, self-inflicted pain requiring inner reflection. By not seeking to understand his role in his suffering, he was doomed to keep hurting others as well as himself. He had let Vivien's sexual history ruin a moment of genuine closeness between them, and he would do the same with Herbert and Frank. Alec never questioned whether those less advantaged in life should conform to his uniquely advantaged one. Like the bookshop he worked in, Alec was a perfect fit for the world as it still stood, teetering on the cusp of the second half of the century.

CHAPTER EIGHTEEN

RULE No. 30

Staff shall be addressed by formal title at all times.

G race had not expected to see Lord Baskin striding happily towards the back offices so early on the morning of the literary luncheon. His most recent visit had completed the annual review of the accounts, and the London season was not yet in full swing. Grace knew he preferred being up in Yorkshire in January with his elderly but lively mother and had heard many tales over the years of hunting and ice-pond parties gone awry with the sudden hard flashes of English winter weather.

Passing by the glass window to her office, Lord Baskin must have noticed the look of surprise on her face. Motioning to Alec in the back office to hold on for a second, Baskin leaned forward in the open doorway and smiled. "All ready for the notorious Lady Browning?"

Grace shuffled about the many papers on her desk. She and Vivien had been working hard to ensure the imminent event went off without a hitch. This greatly amused the men about them, who thought only a few extra chairs were needed to accommodate any high-profile guests.

"Do you know her?"

"A little. Our parents were quite friendly. If I recall correctly, she and I are the exact same age."

Of course he knew her, Grace thought to herself. How foolish of her to ask.

"Which is forty-two," he added in a playful tone. "Not that you inquired."

Something in his voice here—a new personal note—surprised her. The recent spontaneous outing to Hamleys seemed to have broken down an invisible barrier of some sort between them. Grace was also surprised to learn that Lord Baskin was only a few years older than herself, when he seemed to have lived—and lost—so much, with an entire married life fully tucked away in his past.

"How's Miss Lowry faring?" he asked in that teasing way he had of inquiring after Vivien.

"Chomping at the bit."

"But not you, hmm? You never get fussed. Dutton's very lucky to have you."

"And to have Mr. McDonough. Or the Little Usurper, as Vivien now calls him."

Lord Baskin looked back at Alec, sitting glumly behind a mound of paper on his desk, and laughed. "Yes, him, too."

"Shall I get you some tea? I'm on elevenses today, but we could move it up. Alec—unlike Mr. Dutton—doesn't seem to mind a lack of schedule."

"Then why don't I treat you instead? Jonny's cart, à deux? I need to warm myself up."

His affable tone suddenly sounded slightly more artificial than Grace was used to. She wondered if he had come down from York-shire to impart bad news of some kind to the acting general man-ager. Earlier that week, Alec had shared an update on Dutton's continuing recovery with a similar oddness to his voice. Vivien had remarked on, and worried over, that—too much so, Grace had thought at the time. She now wondered if more change was indeed afoot amongst the management of the shop.

Grace nodded and got up from her desk, not bothering to grab her coat given the thick tweed suit she was wearing for the day's big event. Usually saved for christenings and Christmas Eve service, this outfit was her favourite: a red-plaid-and-gold-threaded two-piece that always brought out the subtle ginger highlights in her hair and the blush to her cheeks. Given Vivien's tales of Ellen Doubleday's party at the Dorchester, as well as today's impressive guest list, Grace had added matching red lipstick and her one string of pearls to the ensemble. She knew she looked her best, leading to a caustic comment from Gordon that morning as she had headed out the door, and an openly admiring glance from Lord Baskin as she now met him in the corridor.

A few minutes later they were sitting down together on the bench that faced the shop, two steaming mugs of coffee from Jonny's cart warming their hands. Looking up, Grace thought she saw young Evie Stone for a second in the upper-floor window, then turned to see Lord Baskin noticing the same.

"I think we have a spy in the house," he stated ominously.

Grace looked back up at the now-empty window. "Really? However do you mean?"

He shook his head with a smile. "Nothing in particular. I understand from Alec and Frank that Miss Stone is wonderfully diligent. Very focused. Perhaps . . . a little too focused?"

"I wouldn't have thought that a negative around here, with fifty-one rules and ten thousand books to master."

Lord Baskin laughed. "You put me in my place. As always."

A strange silence fell between them at his words, which again struck her as surprisingly intimate. Grace was not used to this and could not understand where it was coming from. Uncertain as to what to say next, she looked up Lamb's Conduit to her left, where Vivien could be seen haggling with the antiques dealer on the corner of Emerald Street.

"I wonder what she's fired up about now," remarked an amused Lord Baskin.

"Ellen Doubleday told her that Lady Browning loves Limoges, so Viv's determined to wrestle a tea set on loan for today."

"Ah, yes, I heard about the new acquaintance with Mrs. Doubleday as well. How'd that all come about?"

Grace was starting to wonder if the men in the shop gossiped even more than she and Vivien did.

"She was in the shop for that whole horrid incident with the watch."

Lord Baskin took a thoughtful sip of his coffee. "Such a shame, although sadly not surprising—I've seen the way the wealthier women tourists size her up."

"They're just jealous, absurdly so. Vivien would never want anything of theirs."

"But you're not. Jealous, I mean."

"How could one be jealous of such a devoted friend?"

"The two of you are indeed very close." He paused. "Tell each other everything."

He gave her an indecipherable look, and something started to dawn on Grace, something that she had successfully—and unknowingly—kept at bay until now. In a last-ditch effort to keep it there, Grace forced herself to picture Gordon at home instead, still in bed, still upset with her for leaving the roll-up blinds askew instead of straight. The boys were fully back in school and her husband had no plans for the day, except to putter about in his garden and write the municipal authority regarding the loud roadworks down the lane.

As if Lord Baskin were picking up on the thread of her silent and suppressed thoughts, Grace heard him say, "Do you remember . . . no, I don't suppose you do . . . but you were sitting right here when we first met."

"When I came in to apply for the position. I do remember."

"I had locked myself out. Again."

"And I had spilled my coffee. As usual."

"You seemed quite forlorn, then, if you don't mind my saying."

"And you were ever so affable and accommodating. Vivien says that's how you tricked me."

"Tricked you?"

"Into applying. For the position. I'm still not sure what came over me."

"I've always wondered that, too," he replied softly.

The indecipherable look now turned so heartfelt, so intimate, that his emotions from that moment four years ago on this exact same spot suddenly became crystal clear to Grace, just as the rest of Lamb's Conduit fell away: the coffee cart and its row of creamware, the Queen Anne dining chairs being placed in front of the antiques shop, the hothouse market flowers gathering condensation on their ruby-red petals in the chill January air.

"Well, we best get you back inside to start the *preparations*," Lord Baskin announced, sounding like his regular lighthearted self again.

Standing up, he reached out his hand, and Grace stared at it awkwardly until realising he simply meant to take her mug. He headed quickly for the coffee cart, as if knowing she was in need of rescue from the moment. Grace rose slowly from the bench, confused by what had just happened. Could she really be attractive to a man like Lord Baskin? She let the idea first flatter her, before it terrified her.

The notion was in many ways preposterous. If anything, Grace had sometimes wondered whether the earl—like so many men who frequented the shop—had an interest in the much more captivating Vivien. Certainly, his past taste in women was typical for his class. In her elegance, Lord Baskin's ex-wife stood out in the staff picnic photo from before the war that Mr. Dutton kept up in his office, the way one would a family photo. Her fine, symmetrical features and high cheekbones dominated the frame, brightened by makeup and professionally set hair. In Grace's family photos at the beach, her strong, square features—attractive enough— looked sunburned and windswept in comparison.

But it wasn't just a matter of looking right for the part. She had nothing in common with Jeremy Baskin, a titled peer and divorced man who worked at the shop purely because he wanted to and from no pressing need. He lived in a state of constant anticipation—of the next weekend shoot, the next charity ball, the next commemorative ceremony. For years now, Grace had been doing a good job of never thinking about the promise of the future or the disappointment of the past. Instead, she stayed focused solely on the day ahead: the breakfast dishes, the bus route exchanges, the laundry neglected on the line and hanging wet from the rain. Not even in her darkest moments had Grace contemplated the possibility of something—or someone—else.

But that that person might be Lord Jeremy Baskin, the 11th Earl Baskin, would never have occurred to her, not once, not even in a thousand years.

Through the glass window to the back offices, Alec was keeping an eye on the fiction section until Vivien returned from her break, Limoges china in hand.

"You're going to a lot of effort," he remarked as she carefully placed the expensive cup and saucer in the cabinet behind Mr. Dutton's desk.

"It's the little things, Alec. You should know all about *those*."

"Which reminds me, I almost forgot. . ." Reaching into his trouser pocket, Alec fished out a small object wrapped in tissue and placed it in the palm of her hand. "I had it engraved."

Vivien jerked her head up at him.

"I'm sorry." Alec hesitated upon realising the unintentional reference to her Cartier watch. "Poorly worded."

"To be expected," she replied curtly. She unwrapped the small brass nameplate with a metal pin affixed to the back, then looked at him curiously and—did he imagine it?—almost softly.

"'Miss Vivien Lowry, Manager,'" she read aloud.

"I had Colworth across the street make it up for you."

He did not mention his recent visit to Dulwich or Mr. Dutton's resistance to any future promotion for her. This resistance had led to Alec's ordering the nameplate earlier that week, as well as finding it increasingly difficult to watch all of Vivien's enterprising efforts at work. At the same time, Alec was starting to develop his own vision for the shop, one that he hoped would soon make ineffectual Mr. Dutton's decisions with regard to Vivien or anything else.

"This is a very interesting move on your part, Alec."

"It's not a game of chess, Viv."

"It's not?" She gave a rare but short-lived smile before adding flatly, "But I'll have to take it off when Dutton returns."

"Just enjoy it, for now. Who knows what will happen."

Paying close attention to his vague words, she reverted to her usual suspicious self. "What do you know?"

"Just that I saw Mr. Dutton on Sunday," Alec replied, choosing his words now more carefully. "The poor man looks awful. Things could continue without him for quite some time. I thought a more formal acknowledgement of your new role was called for under the circumstances."

Vivien's eyes were still narrowed against him, but he could see a small, pleased look starting to curl about her lips. He averted his eyes as she caught his gaze.

"How *did* you come up with du Maurier?" he asked quickly instead.

"A customer introduced us. Ellen Doubleday. A great friend of Lady Browning's." Vivien paused, clearly enjoying the look of surprise on his face.

"Better brace yourself, Alec."

CHAPTER NINETEEN

Shop events shall be conducted with the greatest decorum
by staff, attendees, and speakers alike.

really don't see how that has any bearing on the matter."

Daphne du Maurier sat in a low-slung armchair on the second floor of Bloomsbury Books, addressing the male journalist standing before her with notepad and pen in hand. On a small round table next to the famous author rested the Limoges teacup and saucer. The entire History Department had been given over to the event, Master Mariner Scott having grudgingly taken himself off to the local pub for the rest of the afternoon.

The newspaperman let the tittering about him die down before speaking again. "Critics would argue that operating within the confines of genre—the mysterious house, the threatening landscape, the attractive but unreliable man—reduces the value of the text in terms of innovation and, shall we say, psychological penetration."

"But what does it do in terms of *story* . . . ?" Du Maurier elongated the final word in her barely hidden frustration.

It was 1:30 p.m. on a Thursday and the famously private authoress of *Rebecca* and *Frenchman's Creek* was facing a crowd of mostly women sitting in wooden fold-up chairs, with several male journalists standing in formation behind them. Vivien had been thrilled when Evie had mentioned a vague contact in the London theatre community who could arrange the provision of extra seating for the event at no expense. At the time, Vivien had not probed any further into this surprising connection. The staff of Bloomsbury Books were quickly learning that Miss Stone would not offer up information on herself unless absolutely pressed.

"The novel as a form is not just about plot," the journalist persisted. "Some might argue that by overly stressing setting and landscape, and using fantastical notions such as dreams or visions to create suspense . . ."

Du Maurier leaned forward ever so slightly and clasped her hands together in her lap. "I believe the word you are struggling for is *Gothic*."

The male critic from the *Daily Mail*, whom Alec had insisted be invited to the event, gave a slight clearing of the back of his throat. "Do you not mean *romantic*?"

Grace, standing off to the side of Miss du Maurier, bit her lip.

"I think I know my own intent. *That*"—the guest of honour smiled disarmingly towards the women in the audience—"is an author's, and a woman's, prerogative."

Vivien thought this the perfect moment to move on from what was becoming a fairly charged conversation. She took a step forward from where she stood next to Grace and announced, "We have time for one more question from the audience."

An attractive woman, who was dressed fully in black like Vivien and close to her in age, stood up. She had warm, brown doe-like eyes, full lips painted a deep morocco red, and rich brunette hair so luxurious that Vivien for once regretted her own closely cropped head.

"'The Doll.'"

Miss du Maurier leaned back in her chair while the fingers

of her right hand appeared to move involuntarily to her lips in sudden remembrance.

"I see. How interesting. And you are . . . ?"

"Sonia Brownell Blair."

Everyone in the audience turned their heads to gaze at the prepossessed woman in their midst.

"And might I ask how you came upon my little story?"

"At *Horizon*. I was an assistant to Mr. Connolly."

"Cyril's magazine? You only just disestablished, yes? You have my condolences." Du Maurier, however, did not sound at all upset by the news.

"Yes." The woman hesitated.

"You were telling me how you came upon it."

"Yes." The woman hesitated again. "Mr. Connolly brought it over with the files from *The Criterion*, after Mr. Eliot ceased its publication as well."

Vivien mouthed the letters *T* and *S* to Grace, who stood with her mouth open as they watched the two women discussing what was most assuredly a private matter of submission.

"So, you are one of two people in the world to have read it," Miss du Maurier remarked with unusual humility. "Although I will admit, I circulated it far more widely than that. To no avail, I might add."

"It's a powerful short story."

"I always say, 'Women want love to be a novel, men a short story.'" Du Maurier smiled brightly at the room as the women in the audience gamely laughed. Vivien looked over at Alec, who was watching from the other side of the makeshift stage. He did not look so amused.

"You were, I believe, only twenty-one when you wrote it."

"Actually"—Miss du Maurier corrected her with a proud smile—"I was only twenty."

"With all your remarkable success since then, will you not try again for its publication?"

Miss du Maurier looked about the room of middle-aged matrons and housewives who had been thrilled to learn of an event that they could conveniently fail to mention to their husbands, taking place as it did in the middle of their shopping day. Vivien and Grace had been most correct on that supposition, as well as on the entire initiative. Having someone of Daphne du Maurier's repute read from her latest work in progress, a new manuscript called *My Cousin Rachel,* as well as take random questions from the audience, was turning out to be a categorical triumph for the shop.

"I think 'The Doll' both too much a creature of the past, and too far ahead of its time, for those in charge of the publishing world."

"You mean men."

Du Maurier laughed. "Yes, I most certainly do."

"My late husband would have agreed with you. He said one day a man will write this same story, fifty, sixty years from now, and then everyone will sit up and take notice."

Vivien saw Ellen Doubleday, sitting anonymously in the audience, lean forward at these words from her seat in the back row.

"Your late husband?" Du Maurier asked.

The woman nodded. "Eric Blair. He was a huge fan of these shorter stories of yours. He says they are indeed decades ahead of their time."

Vivien took in a deep breath, then mouthed to Grace the words *George Orwell.*

"Ah, then you must be Julia." Du Maurier and the other woman now smiled at each other as if in secret commiseration.

"I thought she said her name was Sonia?" a confused Grace whispered to Vivien.

"Oh my God. I think they mean Julia in *Nineteen Eighty-Four*," Vivien whispered back, her voice catching at the magnitude of the encounter unfolding before them. She hoped the local press in attendance were connecting the dots as quickly as she was. Bloomsbury Books' first literary luncheon might possibly go down in history even without the sight of two male poets coming to blows.

"Well, my dear, now you genuinely have my condolences. It must be very difficult, attending here so soon."

The younger woman gave a small smile of gratitude that quickly faded. Only then could one detect how much her otherwise beautiful features had recently been cast down by grief.

"Shall I describe a bit of 'The Doll' before we end?" Miss du Maurier turned to the room as the audience quickly murmured their assent. Vivien found this attempt at distraction especially endearing. When she had invited the famous author to inaugurate Bloomsbury Books' literary luncheon series, du Maurier had at first demurred, citing her lifelong need for privacy. Ellen Doubleday had eventually intervened, explaining how such an event would surely entrench Vivien in her new managerial role. As today's luncheon proceeded, Vivien was greatly relieved by the audience's respectful questions about du Maurier's writing process, which the author was undeniably enjoying discussing. Vivien had met Daphne du Maurier a couple of times by now and knew that she was nothing if not attuned to a crowd. Every single answer she was giving today only intrigued her delighted onlookers even more.

"'The Doll' is about just that: a mechanized automaton of sorts that is able to fulfill a woman's bodily desires."

There was an audible, collective gasp from the audience. Vivien's face lit up—Alec visibly started to panic.

He took a quick step forward from where he was standing, and Vivien immediately motioned for him to stop. According to Mr.

Dutton's intractable shop rules, the manager of each department had final say on all aspects of any event that they might choose to promote and carry out.

"But of course," du Maurier happily continued, "it is not really about *that*. It is about how women are made to feel shame, largely by men, for wanting the very same things as them. For providing men with the very things that they tell us *they* want. The doll is, possibly, a solution."

Alec was now outright glaring at Vivien and pointing at the face of his Patek Philippe watch. Vivien looked at him blankly before turning her attention back to their featured guest.

"A solution?" one of the male journalists in the audience called out.

Miss du Maurier sighed. "Yes, for the female character in the story, who lives in Bloomsbury and is named Rebecca. Take from *those* coincidences what you will." She winked at her audience in partial reference to her most famous book.

"You're not seriously proposing that real-life wives and mothers—"

Miss du Maurier put up her hand to silence the man. "I'm so bored of this nonsense. Please allow me the same consideration you give the writing of my male colleagues in not assuming there is any connection to real life. Or to my own."

The sound of murmuring agreement started to ripple through the audience, followed by the beginning of what soon became thunderous applause for this final statement by the author on the subject.

Still ignoring Alec's glares, Vivien decided that this was the absolute best note on which to end the event and stepped forward to address the room.

"Allow me to thank Miss du Maurier for sharing her work and her valuable time with all of us here today. I know I speak for everyone when I say it's been the greatest of privileges. On behalf of Bloomsbury Books, I'd like to extend our best wishes and most heartfelt thanks."

The room erupted again into applause. Several women in the audience rushed forward in the hope of having a word or two with the famous authoress. One of the newspapermen called Vivien over and asked if he could have a photo of her and Miss du Maurier together. Vivien requested that he also include Evie and Grace, who had each helped her with setting up the event. The resulting photograph ended up in the foremost society section of the morning issue of *The Times*. This led to an immediate increase in customers by 20 per cent over the previous week and a cascading chain of events from which Bloomsbury Books was never to recover.

CHAPTER TWENTY

RULE No. 18

The imbibing of alcohol or spirits on shop premises
is strictly prohibited.

That evening, Vivien and Grace did not leave together at precisely 5:30 p.m. for their bus journey home. Instead, the staff of Bloomsbury Books, minus the long-departed Master Mariner Scott, held an impromptu gathering after hours to celebrate the success of their first literary luncheon. Grace telephoned home to tell the boys that she was working late and to wish them goodnight without her, something she had never done before in all her years at the shop. Meanwhile Vivien brought out the tray of crystal sherry goblets and matching decanter that were kept in a cupboard in Mr. Dutton's office. Over the years he had yielded to their usage on only two occasions: a Christmas Eve drink to ring in the start of the holidays, and a toast each twelfth of May to celebrate the 1937 coronation of King George VI.

Evie joined the other women from the third floor and Alec from the rear office, partly to keep his eye on the victorious Vivien. Lord Baskin reappeared from a late-afternoon appointment elsewhere in the city, and Ashwin Ramaswamy surprised everyone by emerging from the basement to participate as well. Mr. Allen was reportedly in Devon for the latter half of the week; Mr. Dutton continued to convalesce at home.

At 7:00 p.m. the staff were all gathered together about the front cash in a rare show of collegiality, using the counter as a bar of sorts on which to rest their drinks, when there was a loud banging on the shop's outside door.

Grace took in a loud breath. "Gordon," she muttered, giving Vivien a look of desperation mixed with warning.

Without another word, Grace walked up to the front vestibule and closed the inner door behind her before unlocking the one to the street. At first no one could tell what she and her husband were saying. They could only see Gordon gesturing pointedly behind him in the direction of home and Grace trying unsuccessfully to placate him with both hands on his chest. Despite Grace's attempts to calm her husband down, however, their voices eventually rose together in unison.

"Perhaps I should intervene . . ." Lord Baskin said.

Vivien shook her head. "Please don't. I think that's the last thing Grace needs." Vivien didn't say why or how she knew this. She hadn't thought of her mother's similar behaviour for quite some time. But from the little Grace had said about Gordon, Vivien had recognised the signs: the incessant whining, the blaming of others, the constant testing of a family's bonds and affections. Vivien's rebellious nature had been grown in the hothouse of her mother's turbulent and oppressive moods. Vivien had moved to Durham for school, and then London for work, partly to escape all that. She had always wondered how Grace managed to live with it, and Vivien now understood that Grace didn't. She suffered with it instead.

The rest of the staff continued to watch uncomfortably as Grace finally threw up her arms in frustration and opened the inner vestibule door. She was about to lock it behind her when Gordon pushed his way inside, causing Grace to stumble.

"That's it." Lord Baskin stormed over and took Gordon by the elbow. "Hello, mate, why don't you and I step out into the street and have a little talk, hmm?"

Lord Baskin did not wait for an answer. Instead, being a full four inches taller than Gordon Perkins, he used his advantage of size to hustle the man onto the pavement outside. Grace stayed behind, head bowed, unable to look Vivien or anyone else in the face.

After a minute of awkward silence, Vivien came over and put her right arm gently about Grace's shoulders. "Perhaps you should be getting home," Vivien said under her breath. "Evie and I can do the washing up."

Grace shook her head firmly. "No, I'm fine. I'll help."

"Grace . . . it's best you settle him down, for now, don't you think?"

At the more insistent tone in Vivien's voice, Grace silently went to retrieve her coat and bag from the back office, then said not a word in parting as she left the shop.

The party clearly over, Alec downed the rest of his sherry. "I need to get some air." He turned to Ash. "Heading home?"

The two men left together, leaving Evie and Vivien alone in the shop.

"I'll wash up and let myself out," Evie said to Vivien. "You've worked plenty 'ard enough already today."

Vivien saw in the girl's eyes the confusion and disappointment they were all feeling over Grace's marital situation.

"Don't worry about the glassware, Evie, thank you though." Vivien gave her a grateful smile. "Maybe just resituate everything in the History Department so Scott doesn't have a fit tomorrow when he comes in."

As Evie headed upstairs, Vivien remained behind the cash counter, waiting for Lord Baskin's return. She was not surprised when he re-entered the shop a few minutes later visibly peeved.

"I put them in a taxi," he stated with unusual bluntness.

"That was wise."

"Vivien."

"Yes, Lord Baskin."

He shook his head, then retrieved his monogrammed handkerchief from his jacket pocket to wipe his hands thoroughly, as if in disgust.

"It hasn't happened before," Vivien added, "if that's what you're wondering."

He gave her a most curious look. "I should hope not. I should hope someone would have told me if it had."

Vivien had always found the earl's continued presence at the shop intriguing. As first she had wondered if he might fancy her. She was not above wondering such things—it happened often enough. But it had long been obvious to her that Lord Baskin's attentions must lie elsewhere. Having caught him glancing at Grace several times during the luncheon when he thought no one was looking, Vivien's suspicions had recently and most happily been confirmed.

"I should think that would be the last thing to happen, if you don't mind my saying."

"Because I'm an earl?"

Vivien laughed. She liked Lord Baskin, but he did have his moments. "No, because you're the owner."

"I do still sometimes work here."

"Which is even more curious. Why keep holding on? Unless there's something else of interest to you here." Vivien raised one lovely, arched eyebrow. "Besides the books."

Lord Baskin shook his head in amusement. Vivien knew that she could talk to him like this and there would be no hard feelings in the end. He clearly enjoyed the banter, and in turn she enjoyed his palpable appreciation for women, which was always inherently respectful. Vivien suddenly thought about Alec for no particular reason, which brought a sudden flash of anger to her face.

"Sentimental reasons, then," he offered.

"Rubbish—if you don't mind my saying so."

Lord Baskin was eyeing her carefully. Vivien could tell he had no idea whether to trust her. The fact was, he shouldn't. For one thing, her allegiance lay wholly with Grace and her happiness. For another, Vivien had no interest in making things easier for any of the men of Bloomsbury Books, not even Lord Baskin and the surprising matter of his heart. If the earl were ever to confide in her, Vivien would only respond in her girlfriend's best interests. For the longest time, Vivien had grudgingly accepted that those interests extended to Grace's staying in her marriage.

Tonight, however, had changed that; tonight, Vivien had something new to be angry about.

She had always resented how an adherence to rules and hierarchy served mostly to protect and promote the men of the shop. She had done her best as acting manager to use Dutton's absolute strictures to her own advantage. In the meantime, Evie Stone seemed intent on operating under the radar, out of the way and forgotten, and Grace remained ever conciliatory, believing things were best done through consensus. Vivien desperately disagreed with her good friend on that approach. What pained Vivien now was the realisation that this same approach at home had led to tonight and, as she herself knew from experience, far too many other nights as well. But if Grace needed to leave her marriage, where or what could she turn to, with two little boys in tow?

"That's why today was so important, for Grace and me both," Vivien said aloud, wondering how much she could get Baskin to see things from their perspective. "A chance to do something of our own for once."

"You two certainly pulled off a real coup. Alec was green with envy. I'll miss that when Herbert returns."

Vivien was packing up her coil-bound notebook into her handbag, looking forward to later working out her anger through her writing, when she stopped to stare at him. "When Herbert returns?"

"Yes, I've just been to see him. He is intent on returning as general manager next month, despite doctor's orders."

"Presumably Alec will have to step back down to his former role. As will I," Vivien added with a huff.

"Presumably," Lord Baskin replied gently.

"You and I both know that Mr. Dutton will never elevate me to assistant manager, no matter how much I've proved my mettle this month, what with customer visits and sales both up and all the success and publicity from today."

Lord Baskin could only nod reluctantly in the face of Vivien's persuasiveness. "You've done an exemplary job, no one can argue with that."

"What is the argument, then?"

He cleared his throat. "Mr. Dutton as general manager would never put a woman permanently in that role."

"You agree with that?"

"Not at all. But it's not my decision."

Vivien looked at the binder of shop rules and procedures tucked away in a corner of the counter. "Rule forty-four."

Lord Baskin now had to laugh.

"I'm glad you find it so funny."

He put his right hand on her forearm in such a friendly manner that it caught her off guard. All of a sudden, Lord Baskin did not feel like the enemy.

"You're the owner—can't you change any of it?"

"Sadly, no. I voted to reapprove the current rules and procedures at the last annual shareholder meeting. Yes, believe it or not, Herbert makes us hold those, too."

"You're kidding."

"Vivien, you know how he is. Everything's approved until the next fiscal year commencing the first of January, 1951."

"Who are the shareholders, then?" Vivien couldn't believe she had never wondered about the ownership structure before. She doubted that Grace knew anything about it either, having access only to the accounts. As far as Vivien knew, the corporate records and minute books were kept in one of Mr. Dutton's many filing cabinets under lock and key.

"Just myself, Herbert, and Frank. I presently retain majority ownership at fifty-one per cent, Herbert has thirty-two per cent for each of his years of service, and Frank has seventeen for each of his."

"Only fifty-one per cent? That's cutting it close."

Lord Baskin leaned his elbows forward onto the counter before giving Vivien an almost impish grin.

"What's going on?" she asked suspiciously.

"I never intended to hold on to the shop this long. I mean, Mother certainly doesn't care."

"Why have you then?"

He laughed again. "No, Vivien, much as I like you, you are not going to get all of my secrets tonight." He hesitated. "Frank and Herb have been planning to buy the shop from me ever since the war ended. Well, the assets and goodwill, at least. The family is loath to let any more property go."

"Mr. Allen and Dutton together?"

"Mm-hmm. I suspect they want to merge the managerial and ownership roles. As you know, we haven't made much profit in years—at least not until this month, thanks to your and Grace's enterprising ways. Only enough to keep paying off everyone and everything."

"So next year . . . ?"

"Next year was to be the handover. Herbert and Frank would

go to fifty-one per cent together and then could buy me out as part-ners, in business at least." Lord Baskin seemed to catch himself at these last words because he stopped talking, leading Vivien to put her notebook and handbag down to cross her arms.

"Why are you telling me all this?"

Lord Baskin stood up straight and tapped the fingers of both hands almost whimsically on the countertop.

"I like Herbert and Frank, always have. They've served the shop well."

"But . . . ?"

"But so have others, and under quite trying circumstances, as we saw tonight." He paused. "Are you familiar with the notion of share capital?"

It pained Vivien to shake her head. She had never paid much heed to the financial side of her employer; she realised now how much she should have done.

"I have fifty-one shares, right? Currently valued on the books at fifty pounds a share."

"So they can buy you out for roughly twenty-five hundred pounds?"

"Exactly. The shop's always treading just above water, and giv-ing away a couple of shares a year kept us in the black."

"But how would Mr. Dutton and Mr. Allen, as sole owners, keep that up?"

"They'd take less salary, I suppose, and continue to tread along."

"But why would they do that?"

Lord Baskin shrugged. "I think they're banking on things fi-nally starting to improve the further we get from the war. But I agree: there has to be aggressive growth, some kind of significant change and improvement, for anyone to keep the shop going much longer."

He went over to the stand near the front door and grabbed his hat and coat, then turned to her with a smile. "Not everyone can pull that off."

Vivien was left alone at the counter, still flush from the success of that day's event, locked out from the corporate records, and no longer mindful that Evie Stone was still one floor above.

CHAPTER TWENTY-ONE

RULE No. 24

Staff must not use knowledge gained at work for personal benefit.

Evie Stone was finally alone in Bloomsbury Books.

She had long ago given up on finding such an opportunity during the actual workday. Alec or Ash always arrived first each morning. Any career motivation of Alec's aside, the two men lived closest to the shop: Ash in a hostel for Indian men in the nearby East End, and Alec a short subway ride away in Knightsbridge, where he had inherited an apartment from a doting, spinster aunt. Evie's commute from Charlotte's rooms in Richmond took her far longer, even though she remained an early riser from her family-farm and servant-girl days.

Alec was also the last one to leave each night, especially now as he struggled to keep up with the responsibilities he had inherited as acting general manager. Mr. Dutton's correspondence alone was so vast that Alec spent most of the workday reading through all the *couches* and dictating his responses to Grace, leaving any solitary tasks for after hours.

In searching for *The Mummy!*, Evie had tried to lie low as the newest employee and not draw attention to herself. Having already searched through the thousands of volumes stored on the third floor, she had used her scheduled breaks to explore the other departments as casually, yet thoroughly, as possible. Ash seemed merely happy to have the company, and Vivien was too busy officiously reorganising the entire Fiction Department to pay much notice to anything else. Until tonight, only Master Mariner Scott's department had remained off-limits, with Evie's occasional appearances in his doorway always being met with a grunt and a gruff reminder of rule twenty-one.

While folding up the extra chairs for the luncheon on the heels of the cut-short celebration, Evie listened for the sound of the shop bell marking the departures of Lord Baskin and Vivien for the night. Evie had actually been listening for more than that as she did the tidying up: she often wondered if the dapper but older Lord Baskin had a romantic interest in Vivien, which would not be surprising, given how charismatic and attractive the acting fiction manager was.

Instead, theirs had been a most tedious conversation, all about share capital, annual meetings, and fiscal years. Evie could only hear bits of it clearly, just enough to know that they were talking about business, a discipline in which she had never had much interest. Evie refused to believe that value could be drummed up or artificially grown: something was either special, or necessary, or it wasn't. This was one reason why Grace's constant efforts to better market the shop went straight over Evie's head. The books, she believed, spoke for themselves. You just had to find them—and the fun was in the finding.

Evie's heart now quickened at the possibility that here on the second floor was where *The Mummy!* had been hiding all along. The main reason Evie had applied for the position at Bloomsbury Books might soon be within her grasp—she had no idea what she would do if it wasn't.

Ironically, Evie wasn't even sure what she would do if it was.

She did not have enough money to meet its purchase price, which presumably was no less than the twenty pounds that Mr. Allen had bid and paid for it nearly four years ago. Evie didn't dare confide in anyone else the book's potential value or solicit help to purchase it. To her mind, this would be an implicit violation of rule twenty-four: *not using knowledge acquired in the course of employment for personal gain or benefit.* Although she could try hiding it elsewhere in the shop, in the hope of staving off a random customer sale, Evie considered this akin to stealing and no way to treat a book.

She decided that she would worry about her next steps should she be lucky enough to find the long-forgotten text. Hearing the shop bell ring out first for Lord Baskin and then a minute or two later for Vivien, Evie immediately started combing the second-floor shelves for any books on Egyptology, knowing how much fascination British readers still held for that subject. She strongly suspected that Master Mariner Scott did not read any of the books under his care. Instead, he could most often be found examining old maps of his former navy voyages, magnifying glass in hand. Evie wondered if Scott might have taken one look at the title of the book and its anonymous authorship and unthinkingly shelved it away. Perhaps next to a book on the Napoleonic campaigns, or Champollion's deciphering of hieroglyphics.

As Evie moved among the different bookcases, she ran her fingers methodically along the spines of the books, one right after the other. According to her handwritten catalogue, she was searching for three volumes, each of them bound in leather with marbled boards and lettering embossed in gold. It should not take her long—most of the books on the shelves in the History Department were from between the wars, often with more modern dust jackets enveloping their bindings.

After rummaging through the bookcases at the back of the

room closest to Scott's desk, Evie diligently inched along, book by book, until she reached the west wall, which overlooked the street. Lamb's Conduit lay still and empty below, the row of gas streetlamps giving an eerie glow to the lightly falling snow. After a mild start to January, the weather in London had dipped well below forty degrees Fahrenheit in recent days.

The heat in the shop had been turned off for the night, and Evie pulled her blue cardigan tighter as a chill ran through her. She was experienced enough to know, however, that the tingling she felt wasn't just the cold—it was the sensation of *fingerspitz-engefühl,* something she had felt only a few times before in her young life, despite the thousands of books she had handled. This sensation was the holy grail for a rare book lover like herself: the awareness that one was in the presence of something special or ominous.

Sure enough, she turned to the next set of shelves, and there it was, tucked away between a book on the Giza monuments and an old atlas of the Nile. Evie's hand froze midair before the three matching volumes, and her heart started to pound so loudly that at first she didn't notice the strange sounds coming from one floor below. She gently slid out the first volume and turned it about in her hands, letting the gold lettering on the spine catch the moonlight before opening the book to the title page. It was indeed the first edition from the shelves of the Chawton Great House library, but before Evie could read any further, a sharp banging noise reverberated through the floorboards beneath her feet.

It was now well past 8:00 p.m., and the entirety of Lamb's Conduit would be deserted except for the pubs farther up the street. Yet someone was inside the shop.

Evie slipped the first volume back in its place on the shelf and started to tiptoe down the stairs. Reaching the small landing that marked the turn in the staircase nearest the front door, she scanned the main floor for signs of a robbery. Both vestibule doors looked shut and secure, the front bow window unbroken, the cash register on the counter firmly shut.

The noise was clearly coming from the rear offices. Evie shuffled haltingly along the wall, keeping her head below the shaft of moonlight that trailed along the corridor ahead of her. She had not been back there since the day of her interview, when she had tended to Mr. Dutton on the frayed carpet of his office floor and soon after been hired, as if it had all been somehow preordained. All part of her destiny, from the finding of the letter from Thackeray in the archives of Trinity College Library, to the walk home in the snow following the disastrous interview with Christenson, to the eventual discovery here in the shop tonight.

Glancing through the windowed wall that Grace shared with Mr. Dutton, Evie still couldn't see anything. She had hoped not to have to get too close—she couldn't imagine all the explaining she would have to do if another member of the staff had returned only to find her crouching there, tiptoeing about in the dark.

Evie reached the doorway to the general manager's office, took one look down at the same frayed carpet, then quickly ran out of the shop. She didn't stop to catch her breath until she was as far from sight as her little legs could carry her.

CHAPTER TWENTY-TWO

Staff shall behave in a manner befitting their station,
both on and off shop premises.

It was two in the morning and neither Vivien nor Alec could sleep. She was wandering about the front of the shop with only a small desk lamp on the cash counter to light her way, naked under Alec's tan trench. He himself was wearing only trousers and braces as he stood in the kitchenette making a pot of tea.

"One biscuit or two?" Alec playfully called down the corridor towards her. Peeking from the kitchen doorway, he caught her smiling at the familiar shoptalk phrase, which calmed him down greatly. Given the sudden and passionate détente between them, he was determined not to make any missteps this time.

He had returned to the shop just as Lord Baskin was leaving. Alec had waited until his lordship was safely out of sight before approaching the front door, suppressing wild feelings of jealousy over what Baskin and Vivien might have been doing alone together so late at night.

Now nearing her with a tray of tea awkwardly balanced between his bare arms, Alec set it on top of the cash counter in violation of shop protocol.

Entering the swinging door at the rear of the cash counter,

Vivien announced with surprising cheerfulness, "We're breaking all the rules tonight." She took a seat on a nearby stool rarely used during shop hours, Mr. Dutton preferring the staff to stand at their stations at all times.

"Number nineteen," added Alec, before they both repeated in unison, "'Never allow food or beverage near the books.'"

Alec looked down almost shyly at his naked chest beneath the braces. "I should think that would be the least of Dutton's concerns at this moment."

Vivien instinctively pulled Alec's trench coat tighter about her, and he marvelled at the unusual sight of her cheeks beginning to blush.

"Lady Browning was quite something today," he said, pouring Vivien's tea first. "She had those women eating out of the palm of her hand."

"Don't lie. You were terrified."

"Where's your nameplate, by the way . . . ?"

Vivien wrinkled her nose while looking about the counter. "It must have come off in all the, um, commotion."

Alec laughed and headed for the back office. There he glanced down and caught the glint of brass on the carpeted floor, next to several papers from his desk also strewn about.

He returned to the front counter, tossing the nameplate about in his hand. "Here, let me put this back on you before we forget. . . ."

He fiddled with the backing until the nameplate was securely pinned on his coat just above her left breast, then allowed himself to trace one finger along the curve of her chest, bringing her to a sigh of remembrance that made him exhale sharply in turn.

Overwhelmed by his emotions, Alec looked around at the many empty spaces on the darkened fiction shelves. "You'll be on a right ordering spree after today."

"The till was so busy after the luncheon—we cleared out half of the Gothic section, most of Contemporary Feminist, and all of Romance."

"While I suspect the *Daily Mail* lost subscribers."

Vivien laughed, so brightly that Alec felt as if his heart would burst. Determined to stay composed, he put down his cup of tea and wandered over to the bookcase devoted to classic women authors.

"Did you know Evie specialized in eighteenth-century women writers while at Girton?" Vivien asked, taking a sip of tea from the Limoges china cup and saucer he had retrieved for her from the back cabinet.

"No," he replied absentmindedly. "I must say I'm not surprised."

"She's been helping me shore up those shelves with some of the lesser-valued books from the third floor. We've added Burney—Fanny—she lived just a few blocks from here, you know—and Madame de Staël, and Mrs. Radcliffe, too."

"Should we really be mixing new fiction and old books like that?"

"Ever the shopboy," Vivien murmured.

He could feel her watching his naked back from her side of the counter. While he wandered about, she stayed sitting on the high stool, unusually placid and content, her bare legs fetchingly crossed at the knees. Alec felt more genuine happiness in that moment than he had felt in years, which both aroused and terrified him in equal measure.

Looking for a quick distraction, he pulled down one of the new arrivals and flipped it over.

"Elizabeth Lake?"

"Literary realism. Very unsentimental."

"Like you," he said simply, placing the volume back on the shelf. Vivien stayed silent, and he found himself resorting to a more familiar pattern of behaviour as he added, "George Orwell's widow was quite attractive."

"Shame about the *Horizon* disestablishing." Vivien slipped down from the stool and left the cash counter for the periodicals section, across from where Alec now stood. "I wonder if the last issue is still here."

Alec knew it wasn't. He'd bought up all four copies the day they arrived. "Doubt it," he replied, trying to sound as disinterested as possible. "Grace keeps a tight rein on the monthly returns, as you know."

Vivien was shaking her head. "She told me she brought in a few more copies once news of its closing made the rounds."

Alec bit his lip, inwardly cursing himself for even mentioning Sonia Blair in a juvenile effort to toy with Vivien. He could only watch with increasing panic as she happily ran her painted nails along the tops of the various magazines, literary journals, and newspapers.

"Ah, here it is. November 1949." She pulled out the last copy of *Horizon*'s final issue to examine the table of contents while Alec turned away from the shelves.

"Alec . . ."

He kept his back turned, still silently swearing at himself.

"Alec, you got published?"

He shrugged his shoulders in a gesture hinting at defeat. It wouldn't take long.

"'The Girl in the Shop,'" he heard Vivien mutter to herself as she started furiously turning the pages until finding the story.

He finally looked back to watch silently, sullenly, as her beautiful lips, lipstick smudged and so recently inviting, mouthed each word as she read. He could do nothing to stop her or this moment. It was the watch slipping off the bedside tower of books, and his failing to grab hold of it, all over again.

And then, as if in a bad movie, the literary journal was thrown to the floor and stomped underfoot, followed next by the sound of the nameplate being pitched into the empty wastepaper basket under the counter, rattling in a little death spin to the bottom.

The détente was over.

CHAPTER TWENTY-THREE

RULE No. 32

Staff shall not permit friendship to interfere with work.

Between the discovery of *The Mummy!* and the clandestine goings-on in Mr. Dutton's back office, Evie Stone was keeping even more to herself than usual on the third floor of Bloomsbury Books. Only Ash seemed to pick up on her change in mood whenever he brought her the occasional cup of chai. One day, in an effort to cheer her, he made the surprising suggestion that—as two people with a day off and no family in London—they meet for Sunday lunch at his favourite restaurant in the East End.

Having never been to that area of London before, Evie was relieved to find Ash waiting for her on the pavement when she exited the Aldgate station at exactly noon. Wearing a suit instead of his usual wool jumper over an oxford shirt and tie, Ash looked distinguished with his wire-rim spectacles and wavy black hair. Something inside Evie lightened at just seeing him. He didn't move to greet her physically in any way, but instead gave a nod and a smile. Just then, Evie felt her heart make a small but perceptible leap for the second time in her life.

It was a rare crossing of the emotional and social chasm that Evie had created about her, after being forced to leave school at fourteen and fend for herself. She had learned the hard way that ambition must come from within, so that no one could take it away from you. The many years of study and absorption in old books had given Evie purpose and comfort; keeping to herself had given her the fuel to succeed.

But was a shopgirl's existence worth the sacrifice, when the most she could hope for was the caring and dusting of books? Having mapped out her entire life upon matriculation, Evie was getting her first bitter taste of irony. She also wondered if she had built the chasm for another, less deliberate reason: because one always had to leave some of the past behind to make way for something new.

To reach the restaurant, Evie and Ash walked south from Whitechapel High Street, then turned right onto a quiet lane of Georgian residential buildings. At the intersection of Alie and Saint Mark Streets was the Halal Restaurant, in a house at the end of an eighteenth-century terrace. Ash explained that the restaurant, one of only six Indian ones in all of London, had been conceived out of necessity.

"Originally it was the mess in a hostel for merchant seamen lodging in the rooms upstairs. They would cook different types of curry, and their mates would come round, and eventually it turned into the first Indian restaurant for the area."

Evie had not been to many restaurants, her small childhood village having only one public house and her stipend at Cambridge providing little money for indulgence. A more pleasant irony of Evie's young life was that her few times dining out had been by invitation of Mimi Harrison and at some of London's finest establishments. Mimi's personal favourite was the Thames Foyer at the Savoy Hotel, where she always stayed when in town. Here she would take afternoon tea in a discreet corner of the dining room, hiding her famous features behind a set of potted palms.

The Halal Restaurant was very different from that. The tables were so close together as to be practically communal. Evie could smell the different spices of her neighbours' meals and hear the many voices and dialects that filled the room. The restaurant specialized in three curries, which were nonetheless written out on a board: meat, meatball, and mince curry. Ash was the one to order this time, and he had specific instructions for the kitchen, which made the waiter laugh with familiarity.

Watching how Ash directed her when they walked, interacted with the waiters, and arranged his glass of water and napkin not from nervousness but a sense of order, Evie had no doubt that he was a born scientist. He was so precise and grounded in facts. Over lunch, she tried to discuss their work colleagues, particularly Alec and Vivien—Evie still couldn't figure out what on earth was going on there. But Ash wasn't interested in judging or assessing the behaviour of others—what her mother would have called *idle talk*. Evie wondered if Ash had always been this way, or whether his reserve came from being constantly judged now himself.

It certainly didn't come from lack of observation. At first, Evie had assumed that Ash was just like her: so focused on the details of the tasks before him that larger, less tangible matters passed him by. But the more time that they spent together, the more Evie realised that Ash actually did notice everything. He was always on high alert, poised to be defensive. She didn't blame him: the looks they received when out together failed to escape even her.

Perhaps this was why, like her, Ash largely kept to himself at work, staring at the many slides of insects, pursuing secret tasks very different from her own. Evie's mind lived so often in the past—the musty scent of books, the torn or disintegrating pages, the records of objects no longer to be found—that the discovery of a new type of insect species, or what it could teach us about our world and its history, was lost on her. Similarly, Ash seemed bemused by Evie's preoccupation with what he called "stories," as if the contents of the books were merely tales to pass the time, rather than the most direct and lasting evidence of what the human species had felt and thought across the ages. This was what she and Ash often discussed when alone at work together, and they were doing it again now: a playful comparison of their fields of discipline, to which they each devoted all of their personal time and energy.

When the food arrived, Ash showed Evie how to eat with one hand while keeping the other hand dry to take water. The curry was a mix of flavours both familiar and new to her. She recognised the ginger, coriander, cardamom, and fennel from the chai that Ash made at work. He now explained to her the additional seasoning of curry, turmeric, and cumin, as well as the potent chili powder that gave it all such intense heat. Evie's mother's cooking at the farm, with only onions or salt and pepper to season the meals, suffered greatly by comparison.

As they ate, Evie finally noticed the lack of women dining about them and mentioned this to Ash.

"It is not so unusual. Although *this* is." He motioned at the space of table between them.

She stared at him uncomprehendingly. "Our being here is unusual?"

"To dine together without a chaperone, yes." He paused. "To do anything alone together."

She tilted her head to the right in her confusion, but he only gave her a small, cryptic smile, and they both fell quiet. Evie did not like the silence for once—it made her feel even more nervous.

"Does it make you miss home?" she asked as their cleaned plates were taken away.

He gave his usual shrug. "I was hoping London would feel more like home by now."

"At least you have this."

"I don't need more of the same. It's certainly not about something as trivial as spices. I do, however, enjoy being understood."

Evie thought about the Jane Austen Society back home, founded by people also from such different walks of life. A doctor, an auctioneer, a movie star, a servant girl, a farmer, a teacher, a lawyer, an heiress: somehow, they had connected and bonded over their shared love of Austen and her books. Evie had never felt more understood. She had failed to find that feeling while at Cambridge and had lately started yearning for it at Bloomsbury Books. This gave her pause. What if her move to London hadn't been just about finding a book?

Evie and Ash were heading back to Aldgate station after lunch when he stopped and put his finger to his lips in thought.

"Can you manage getting home from Whitechapel station instead? There's something you should see" were his ominous words before motioning her east along the high street.

It was one of the last surviving trees in all of London, a four-hundred-year-old mulberry that had been planted in the garden of the bishop who had helped Henry VIII to separate his crown from the Roman Church. The black mulberry tree had survived the Great Fire of London in 1666, only to be left a charred stump by the German Blitz centuries later. In the near-decade since, the tree had regrown significantly but gained a strange new shape, as the gnarled and damaged main trunk leaned forward with a crest of green shooting lifelike out of its head.

"We call it *munja pavattay* in Tamil. Indian mulberry. Or"— here Ash gave a rare smile—"*ach.*"

Evie watched silently as he reached forward to rest his hand on the tree just as she did with books. They each had a tactile appreciation for the reliable elements that make up the world: the things we can excavate and explore. The hidden traces of our history that so many others choose to ignore or, worse, devalue.

"I once saw some nurses from the hospital here, holding hands and dancing in a ring all around it," Ash said, taking a step back from the tree and nodding at the newer building behind them. "It was last Easter when I first arrived. I thought you were all *barmy,* as you Brits like to say."

"The child's nursery rhyme." Evie laughed. "Ring-a-ring-a-roses."

"I know it well. My father loved all things English and had a picture book of rhymes when we were young—Mother Goose. I, too, fell in love with England from that book."

She let him talk. She loved listening to him.

"It's how I first learned English. My father would read the same rhymes over and over again, and I remember having the sounds memorized, and then one day putting the sounds to the letters, and the letters to his words—and then the words to the pictures. I felt like I was unlocking a secret code. The code to the British." Ash gave a laugh of bitter amusement at himself. "I was wrong."

Evie had been wrong, too. She now knew that learning the language—mastering the books—was only one key to the people around her. She also needed to understand them to get what she wanted. Mr. Dutton was so rigid as to hopefully be predictable, but Alec in his stead was a different matter. Evie suspected Alec of not having the best interests of the bookshop at heart, so intent was he on his own quest for success. On the other hand, both Mr. Allen and Lord Baskin appeared only minimally concerned with the goings-on at the shop, given their predilection for socialising and travel. And no one understood Master Mariner Scott's desire to still work at all. His miscalculation in retiring from the navy—only to miss out on the entirety of the Second World War—might have something to do with it, but he seemed most interested in frequenting the local pub.

Evie wondered what Ash thought about the other men at work.

For all the time that the two of them spent discussing the business of the shop, he showed little interest in the habits and relations of the other employees, let alone the different romances brewing on the various floors. She wondered what that said about the two of them, and his intention in asking her to lunch today. Perhaps they were simply two lonely people, far from home and family, who shared a common bond in their preoccupation with the past. Evie only knew that she didn't want to say goodbye to Ash when they reached the Whitechapel station, went over their lunch together in her head the entire way home, and couldn't wait to return to work the next day.

CHAPTER TWENTY-FOUR

The head of each department shall have sole authority
and discretion regarding the organising of events.

Against his GP's advice, Herbert Dutton returned to his general manager duties on the first day of February. He had been hearing from both Frank and Alec that overall morale in the shop was on a dangerous seesaw. At times the women in the shop seemed energized, even ennobled, by the various victories piling up before them. Other times, they appeared increasingly resentful and distrustful of the men in charge. Vivien was making noise about a deserved ascension to assistant manager, which Mr. Dutton believed would require his full presence on the ground to tamp down. Grace was reported to be quieter on this and other points, but a sharp uptake in signalling between the two women was leaving the male department heads on edge, as if everything of import in the shop were happening behind their backs.

From the inaugural literary luncheon and the resulting newspaper coverage to the subsequent boost in customer visits and sales, Vivien's and Grace's efforts were yielding the kind of financial results that had escaped Bloomsbury Books until now. One day Lord Baskin had hinted as much in a casual comment to Frank, who was temporarily back at his desk between travels. From that point on, Frank and Herbert had started to worry about the future of their respective roles as well as the yearly increase in their shareholdings.

Herbert Dutton decided that the sooner he came back to work, the sooner things would return to the way that they had always been.

Unlike Vivien, Alec did not mind resuming his former role as head of the Fiction Department. Being acting general manager had fallen far short of his expectations. Alec had thought he wanted to manage things, only to discover that he derived little satisfaction from bringing out the best in others or attending to their complaints. What he really wanted was to feel in control, like the shop's owner, Lord Baskin, with all the other benefits that ownership conveyed: the status and prestige, the autonomy, the ability to hedge his bets.

Alec had originally planned on a career as a great writer for these very reasons. He had been encouraged throughout his youth by teachers and the positive response to his writing amongst select personal connections. A few years ago, one of his stories had even been accepted by *Gangrel,* a small literary journal, following submission by Evelyn Waugh on Alec's behalf. Alec had done his best to solicit the famous author as a mentor after his event at Bloomsbury Books in the fall of 1945. Unfortunately, *Gangrel* had shuttered in 1946 before publishing Alec's story.

The story had been called "The Girl in the Shop," written in the wake of his first morning-after debacle with Vivien. Over the past three years, Alec had continued to refine the piece, as if, in trying to figure out Vivien on paper, he could regain some of what he had lost in real life. When the leading literary journal *Horizon* had stunned him last fall by offering to publish the piece, Alec had at first hesitated over how personal a portrait of Vivien it was. But by then he had no hope for a future with her and was increasingly doubtful about one as an author as well. Any further intimate encounter between them seemed just as unlikely. The timing could not have been worse for Vivien to find that last remaining issue of *Horizon* buried deep inside the shop's magazine stand.

It had been only a short piece, however, and its brevity spoke volumes of the even larger failure at hand: the failure to write a novel. Now in his early thirties, with only this one short story to his name, Alec wondered if the time had come to try his hand at something else. Although he planned on keeping secret what he had learned about Mr. Dutton and Mr. Allen, Alec thought there might be a career opportunity for him in all of this. Dutton had confided in him the share structure over the years, and Alec knew the time for transfer must be getting close. He had money himself—what better way to use it? His secret plan for taking over the shop had since started taking shape, born out of frustration and—if Alec could only see it—aimlessness and fear.

For now, as the newly reinstalled head of fiction, he would focus on the selection of a speaker for the midwinter evening lecture held every February at Bloomsbury Books. Alec had learned that Samuel Beckett was in town to shop around a new play he had written for the Paris stage, the enigmatically titled *En attendant Godot*. Early supporters were claiming that Beckett's latest work would revolutionize the stage for decades to come. Now the top London agents and theatre impresarios were keen to meet with Beckett and acquire British stage rights on the strength of that early excitement.

Samuel Beckett led just the sort of life that Alec had always wanted: Continental, peripatetic, and free. Time with the infamous author, scholar, and former research assistant to James Joyce could only benefit Alec in his own hunger for these things. It was the perfect invitation, and the perfect counterpoint to the fur-coat-and-pearls-filled du Maurier event, from which the men in the room had still not fully recovered.

Vivien surprised everyone by not balking at Alec's choice of Samuel Beckett for the upcoming evening lecture at Bloomsbury Books.

"I like Beckett" was all she said from behind the cash counter at Alec's announcement as the newly reinstalled head of fiction. Her tone was so amiable that it immediately raised his suspicions.

By now, everyone in the shop knew that Vivien was no fan of the legendary male Irish writers who had held their own in drinking bouts across Europe between the wars. She especially did not get the fuss over James Joyce, Beckett's avowed literary idol as well as one of Alec's. But according to Lady Browning, who knew Beckett's agent and lover, Suzanne Déchevaux-Dumesnil, the Irish writer had recently overhauled his craft. His latest writing was reputed to be a daring new approach to the theatre, aggressively dispensing with norms and convention to the point of absurdity.

Alec, spurned by Vivien all over again, was clearly throwing down another gauntlet by inviting a known Irish gadabout and hero of la Résistance to be their next lecturer, at an evening hour beyond the reach of the average housewife. As if marshalling reinforcements, Vivien had requested that special VIP invitations be sent out to Mrs. Doubleday, who was in London until the middle of March, as well as to Daphne du Maurier and Sonia Blair, the recent widow of George Orwell. Both Daphne du Maurier and Ellen Doubleday immediately accepted, especially when it was rumoured that Peggy Guggenheim, the former paramour of Beckett, would also be attending the event.

Having both come of age in Manhattan at the tail end of the First World War, Ellen Doubleday and Peggy Guggenheim were notorious rivals. Accepting the Beckett lecture invitation by phone, Ellen had mentioned Guggenheim's time in a Manhattan bookstore following her famous inheritance ("She claimed it was either do *that,* or get a nose job!"). Lady Browning, stopping by the shop to personally accept her invitation, gleefully informed Vivien that the primary goal of most debutantes in 1920s New York had been to land a husband before he'd become embroiled with the notorious heiress and collector ("of art and *other* things, my dear!").

"Ellie calls that time period BP, for 'Before Peggy,'" Lady Browning further explained to Vivien. "She was apparently merciless in taking lovers. She came out the year before Ellen did, in 1919—the year she inherited half a million dollars. After that, the world was Peggy's oyster and she did not stop at one. I must admit, even I am a little envious."

Vivien was convinced that the idea of so many women on the second floor of Bloomsbury Books would again set Alec's teeth on edge. But just as Vivien's reaction to the selection of Beckett had surprised Alec, his game reaction to the prospect of all these female guests surprised her. In truth, Alec felt an undeniable anticipatory thrill for the fireworks that would inevitably ensue amongst such a collection of former rivals, widows, ex-lovers, and friends. No punched-in noses perhaps, but surely a female equivalent of some sort.

Alec was half-right about all of this, but as was so often his luck, it wasn't the half he was counting on.

CHAPTER TWENTY-FIVE

RULE No. 23

Staff must dedicate their time to the business
and profits of the shop.

Evie Stone was sitting alone in the Thames Foyer of the Savoy Hotel. She was surrounded by an assortment of British high society and wealthy American visitors, who were all enjoying afternoon tea under the striking glass-domed atrium high above their heads. Evie was not paying attention to anyone else around her, though. She rarely did. Otherwise, she might have noticed how out of place she looked.

Tugging on the bottom buttons of her cardigan, Evie sat as upright as possible at the corner table hidden behind a large potted palm. The seating had been at the request of her hostess, Mimi Harrison. Whenever she was in London, Mimi delighted in treating Evie to the kind of indulgence that was beyond most people, let alone struggling shopgirls and students.

As Evie watched the bubbles in the pink champagne that the waiter had brought her without asking, she thought about the college balls that she had never once attended. For days afterwards, champagne corks and confetti would lie strewn about the streets of Cambridge. On her way to the library Evie would grudgingly have to step around the discarded bottles and other debris from the celebrations. Like an annoying itch she couldn't help but scratch, Evie recalled bumping into Stuart Wesley escorting Senior Fellow Christenson's daughter home from the May Ball last spring at the end of their final academic year.

It had been early in the morning on the day before Evie's and Stuart's research papers for Professor Kinross were due. Stuart had gleefully recounted for Evie how he and his date had capped off the evening with a midnight walk to the Orchard, the tea garden in Grantchester, falling asleep in green-canvas deck chairs under the blossoming fruit trees and then traipsing back through the meadows along the River Cam. How free and easy and likable Stuart had seemed at that moment, whereas Evie had not slept in two days. He hadn't either, but was clearly running on a different kind of adrenaline. Evie had not been surprised when he had handed in his own paper late.

The Thames Foyer now started to buzz with excitement. From her seat facing the entrance, Evie knew immediately why. Even with her hair dyed blonde, Mimi Harrison was unmistakable to her many fans. The Americans in the room could be counted on to be most voluble in their reaction as the famous star crossed the room in an extremely high set of heels.

Mimi was back from New York with her newly blonde hair. As a personal favour to Sir Laurence Olivier, she had agreed to be on standby should Vivien Leigh fall ill again while starring in *A Streetcar Named Desire* at the Aldwych. Mimi was also using her time in London to pursue a possible comeback to film after a five-year absence. Still refusing to ever return to Hollywood, she was taking meetings regarding various upcoming British productions including *Pandora and the Flying Dutchman* and *My Cousin Rachel,* which was currently under development. Daphne du Maurier had hand-selected Mimi Harrison for the role of the older mysterious woman who marries the hero's cousin, but the studios were once again disappointing the authoress by focusing on Olivia de Havilland instead, who was on the right side of forty compared to Mimi.

But to Evie, Mimi always looked eternally young, the wartime cinema star whom Evie had grown up watching on-screen long before their becoming friends.

"Evie!" Mimi exclaimed, rushing over to pull the young girl up for a hug and a quick peck on the cheek, then patting her wig as she sat down.

"Larry has me trying this on for size, in case I need to step into the toppling heels of Blanche DuBois." Giving Evie's features a quick, motherly sizing up, Mimi sighed with concern. "Evie, you're working too hard again. What's going on?"

Evie bit her lip. She trusted Mimi implicitly, but was still hesitant to tell anyone what she was doing at the shop.

"Adeline wrote me you'd left Cambridge. Geoffrey was so certain you would land another research position there."

Evie nodded. "Things didn't work out. I'm employed in London now."

"So Adeline also wrote. Selling books."

"No, actually, cataloguing them. The rare ones. At Bloomsbury Books."

Mimi took a sip of the pink champagne that had also been presented to her by the headwaiter upon arrival.

"But that's not why you went to Cambridge, though, is it?"

Evie made a funny face.

"Evie . . ."

"I think I found something."

"More Austen?" Mimi's face lit up.

"No, something entirely different. But a very valuable book, in its own way. And extremely rare. One of a kind, actually." As the waiter put down a large three-tiered silver tray of tea sandwiches, pastries, and scones between them, Evie lowered her voice. "It was in the Great House library to start. Sotheby's sold it for just a few quid, to Bloomsbury Books."

Mimi sat back in her gilt-edged chair. "Ahh. I see. You've been chasing after it."

Evie nodded.

"And you and Yardley both missed it, back in Chawton? You're slipping, the two of you."

"It's mortifying." Evie sighed and Mimi laughed delightedly, causing several of the American tourists in the room to gaze even more obviously in their direction.

"How much money are we talking about here?"

"That's the thing. I've no clue. I'm not even sure it can be valued. It might be the only first edition left in the entire world."

"Well, thank you for trusting me with all that. I do worry that you keep too much to yourself." Mimi poured out the steeping teapot between them. "Do you remember taking tea together like this, with Frances Knight at the Great House, the first time we met? You've come a long way since then. You seem more confident now, more . . . purposeful, if that's even possible. Perhaps, even, a little sad." Mimi paused with that sense of dramatic timing that Evie knew so well. "Is there something more?"

It was hard to deny Mimi Harrison anything. She was a most complex combination of vivacity, otherworldly beauty, and compassion. Evie finally relented and told her all about Christenson, Wesley, and Kinross, the three nemeses so often in her mind.

"That Kinross," Mimi replied with irritation. "Geoffrey tells me he's such a dope. Harmless, though, I should have hoped. Christenson, on the other hand, is notoriously mean."

"Christenson Mean Time. CMT." Evie had to smile at the recollection. "That's what the students called his office hours."

Mimi laughed again so charmingly that even a few of the British patrons, trying to ignore the famous actress in their midst, finally glanced over at the mismatched pair.

"Giving Fredrik the vice-master role was a huge mistake. Like feeding the beast. They do it at the studios all the time." Mimi started to fiddle absentmindedly with the little silver cross on her necklace, as if recalling something to herself. "So, do you at least have the book, after all that?"

Evie shook her head and explained to Mimi the crux of the problem: how to acquire the book without raising suspicion or violating several of the shop's well-worn rules.

"Well, we learned a lot in our early society days. First and foremost, not to go it alone. Isn't there anyone whom you can trust?"

Evie grew silent.

"What is it, little one?"

She now told Mimi everything else that had been bothering her about Bloomsbury Books: the warring staff, the ponderous rules, the late-night assignation she had stumbled upon. Mimi listened carefully while Evie spoke, clearly not wanting to confuse the girl any further.

"Well, from what you're saying, the men in charge don't sound mean so much as misguided. You at least have that working in your favour. Much easier to manage."

Evie nodded reluctantly.

"And this ridiculous rule against employee purchases. Why don't I just send someone over to buy the book for you, as a gift?"

Evie vehemently shook her head. "I'd still be benefitting from using knowledge I gained in the course of my employment. There's a rule for that, too."

"As we Americans like to say, rules are made to be broken. After all, what if the book got sold out from under you? Better to act fast and confide in the other women, even this Vivien, than to risk that."

Mimi hesitated, then placed her right hand over Evie's. "You're still so young. Try not to judge too much, hmm? I know you always keep to the straight and narrow, and that's one of the things I love about you. But not everyone is the same, and goodness knows, it takes all kinds." Mimi gave Evie's hand a small pet before returning to playing with the silver cross at the base of her neck.

"Look, Evie, trust me, you could do everything right and still get it wrong in the end. We can't control other people—sometimes we can't even control ourselves."

The idea of losing control terrified Evie. This was one reason why she was having trouble reconciling her growing feelings for Ash with whatever Vivien and Alec were doing. It was even harder for Evie to accept that there are some things we can't control at all. She had always moved through life with one worn boot stubbornly placed in front of the other, meeting disappointment head-on. She had either set goals that she could achieve all on her own, such as cataloguing the Chawton Great House library, or coolly redirected her ambition whenever an obstacle was placed in her way. But as she got older, these new goals and directions seemed to be merging into an endless circle of frustration. Evie was beginning to fear that at the end of every new road would always be another Stuart Wesley, another Christenson, even another well-intentioned but restrictive Mr. Dutton.

Mimi topped up their tea again.

"You know, Evie, even as a movie star, I was no match for the studio bosses—the Jack Leonards and Monte Cartwrights of the world. My power, such as it was, was based on my looks."

"You always said looks fade."

"Indeed they do, and the men in charge count on that first grey hair showing up. Basing my fame on my looks—and, honey, there are a *lot* of talented gals out there—kept me in my place. I mean, think of it: the most power you'll ever enjoy, as an attractive young woman, is when you are least able to exercise it. It only declines with age." Mimi gave an unusually bitter laugh.

"If I could only get that book . . ." Evie muttered.

Mimi smiled patiently. "The book is only part of the solution. You're an academic. You say you want to confer value on the book, by restoring it to its rightful place in history. But then what? A name in a footnote, a new research position at another institution, only for this to happen to you all over again?"

"So you're saying, why bother?"

"No, I'm saying the opposite." Mimi paused again. "I'm saying, ask for *more*."

Mimi's ace delivery had always had a unique way of reaching Evie, whether on the screen or in person. She now told Mimi about her dream of reprinting the lost or neglected works of women authors from the past.

"Oh, Evie, I love that idea. I'd love to be a part of it someday."

"But I don't even know how to start."

"There is always someone who can help. Try and *find* them. Stuart Wesley is a toady from what I hear, but he's got that part right, at least."

As they finished their tea, Mimi brought Evie up to date on all the goings-on in Chawton. Evie let her thoughts wander to the founding of the original Jane Austen Society: four men, four women. Each of them so different from the other, but with one shared goal. *It takes all kinds,* Mimi had just said.

Evie had convinced herself that her way was always best because she had so often been forced to pursue things completely on her own. If she hadn't believed in herself, none of her successes would have happened. Now she needed to believe in something even bigger than that: that the rules themselves, as they applied both to and beyond her, might deserve to be broken.

CHAPTER TWENTY-SIX

RULE NO. 25

Staff shall not engage in activities that compete
with the business of the shop.

That same Sunday afternoon, two other employees of Bloomsbury Books were already breaking one of these rules. Like
many bookshop employees of their generation, both Alec and
Vivien used their one day off from work to try to create the very
thing they sold to others.

Alec's chosen domain was a cafeteria on Bayswater Road, with
a large street-front window through which London society could
be seen strolling in leafy Kensington Gardens across the way.
Alec felt more accountable in this environment—in his nearby
apartment, he was easily distracted. He also felt closer here to
the authors he most admired, such as Hemingway, Beckett, and
Joyce, who were infamous for spending hours in Parisian cafés,
getting stimulation from *cafés crèmes* and inspiration from the
real-life activity about them.

Of course, there was no real espresso to be found in London
for a *café crème*. England was still making its own brew from a
dismal blend of chicory and coffee essence, brought over in the
ration packs of US troops. Alec was fortunate enough to have enjoyed the real thing in Italy during his year abroad before uni-

versity and knew what the rest of England was missing out on. The depressed, war-weary nation, however, remained in love with instant coffee by virtue of its being new and American, and therefore fast and cheap.

As for inspiration from the world about him, Alec continued to search for that. Still unpublished as a novelist, he believed that only a great novel could give him the life that he sought. He aspired to be Hemingway in Key West or James Joyce in Paris; just like that line from Stephen Spender, Alec "thought continually of those who were truly great." As a result, he had set himself the goal of having at least one completed novel under his belt by age thirty. It pained him to admit that he had already missed this self-imposed deadline. Recent goings-on at the shop were only further slowing him down.

During his one month as acting general manager, Alec had not written a single creative word, finding himself too bogged down by ledgers, purchasing orders, and employee discontent to let his mind wander as it had done when he was safely perched on a ladder, looking down at the customers in the shop or absentmindedly watching Vivien. In fact, Alec almost always wrote about Vivien or women with her inimitable qualities. The literary result was a series of heroines quite similar in their petulance and daring, who would have been at home in a novel by Thomas Hardy or Henry James. Being away from Vivien when they had once shared such close quarters had done nothing to foster his imagination.

Alec already had enough concerns about the strength of his mind in that regard. Everything he wrote about, every character, seemed to end up a version of what had come before. His greatest compulsion to write remained rooted in the possibility of publication itself. As buyer for the Fiction Department, he was acutely aware of which concepts most attracted the discerning editor or casual customer. As a writer who feared the limits of his own imagination, he tended to build upon these existing ideas instead.

The outside world might stimulate such comparison and ambition in his brain, but access to its hidden compartments—its repressed other worlds—escaped him. During the recent literary luncheon, the prolific Daphne du Maurier had shared how her many ideas came to her, and Alec had grown only more disheartened. He had a facility with language and often found himself reworking other authors' phrases as he read. He also had no trouble being critical, as Vivien herself liked to point out. But ideas never woke him or came to him in the bath or needed to be jotted down on little scraps of cigarette or toffee wrapper, fished from a briefcase or front jacket pocket.

As a result, three unfinished manuscripts were now sitting in a drawer in his apartment, in addition to the current half-finished novel on the flecked Formica table before him. Alec carried the one hundred pages weight-like about him, stashed inside his monogrammed leather briefcase. He had been relying heavily on an outline from the start, only to discover that in execution the actual story fell apart. He found himself rigorously reworking phrases, changing points of view, moving scenes around, and trying all manner of techniques to make the writing reflect the high literary standard he had set for himself. Early feedback from an editor friend of his father's at Secker & Warburg had not been promising: "The prose has been edited down to the point of being bloodless; the three female love interests for our hero are in particular need of greater delineation from each other."

Alec stared out the cafeteria window at the sea of grey wool and muddy-brown tweed passing by. Except for the rich winter tones of the wealthier ladies' swing coats, most people were dressed in drab colours that merged seamlessly with the overcast sky. Alec recalled Vivien's penchant for wearing black instead of brighter, more feminine colours, and how striking and glamorous this looked on her. He thought back even further, to the little pots of rouge and eyeliner pencils scattered across the top of her bedroom dresser. Although rationing was finally coming to an end and makeup was more readily available, most women still kept to the simple regimen of mascara and Victory Red lipstick that had carried them through the war. Not so with Vivien. She had an almost preternatural intuition for staying one step ahead of current fashion. With her winged eyeliner, dramatic brows, and black formfitting sweaters, she stood out in every way.

The sheer force of her personality dominated Alec's thoughts and, consequently, his writing. He was not finished with her, for all she was seemingly finished with him. He wrote to understand her, and in so doing to better justify himself. He was just confident and privileged enough to not understand that he was the only reader in the world who would care about any of that. Unable to step out of his way when he wrote and wedded to his own notion of importance, Alec continued to produce a product of interest to an audience of no more than one.

Vivien wrote for no one—not even, strictly speaking, herself. That Sunday afternoon found her in her cold-water Hackney flat, curled up on the shabby antique French sofa with mahogany turned legs that she had bought from the Broadway Market up the road. Not long enough for a lie-down, the sofa rested under a window through which she faced the redbrick wall of the neighbouring building.

Vivien didn't mind the lack of view. When she wrote, she entered a world either so separate from her own mind, or so deeply buried, that everything she encountered was infinitely new and fascinating and surprising to her. Even her strong sense of self was no match for the wondrous feeling that her writing hand operated of someone else's accord. It wasn't quite the *automatic writing* that Gertrude Stein had so famously explored at Harvard under the tutelage of Henry James's psychologist brother, but it felt awfully close.

Unlike Alec, Vivien had no outline for what she wrote. She just sat down and did it because she couldn't help herself: it was the greatest happiness she knew. She was as guilty as Alec of neglecting to please an audience, but for a very different reason. She didn't need to write to understand herself—her infamous intuition came from an awareness of her emotions hampered only by an inability to hide them. Living so close to her feelings—and needing as a child to navigate her mother's—enabled Vivien to quickly pinpoint the emotional source of most of her behaviour.

Instead, Vivien wrote to keep pace with a talent that had been fostered in private and unsupported by the external world. She had lost the man she loved and been treated poorly by the only other one who had come close, and her years as a shopgirl had sapped much of her spirit; but the talent was something no one could take away.

What Vivien's own ego stopped her from seeing was the need for structure in her writing. She wrote without a destination in sight, and it showed. As Vivien sat in her apartment late that Sunday afternoon, letting the thoughts come to her unbidden, characters and events sprang to life before her eyes as if on a stage or through a movie camera. She could hardly write fast enough to keep up. She also wrote hurriedly from fear that the gift itself might dry up, although it never did. Instead, it met her on the page every time, as fearless and vital as she was. In that way, the gift was also her enemy. Its ease of appearance masked the diligence and self-control required to master it. More than anything else, Vivien needed a mentor—someone who recognised the talent but was unafraid to tame it.

This was why meeting Daphne du Maurier had been such a stroke of luck for Vivien. Ever since the disclosure of Lady Browning's other identity, she had inexplicably taken it upon herself to advise Vivien on her writing. It had all started during the cab ride home from Ellen Doubleday's Dorchester party, when the famous author had asked the now-starstruck shopgirl for a sample of her work.

"I actually have some on me."

As Vivien had started to retrieve her latest green coil-bound notebook from her handbag, Lady Browning had smiled knowingly. "Of course you do."

Vivien had then watched as the famous author read incredibly quickly, her fingers travelling over the handwritten lines, her lips mouthing the occasional sentence of dialogue half out loud. When she was done, she closed the notebook but kept it on her lap, resting her hands on it while staying deep in thought. When she finally spoke, it was not at all what Vivien had anticipated.

"But, my dear, you've got it all wrong. These little stories, this is not what you do. Your gift—and you most certainly have one—is dialogue. My dear, you are a *playwright*."

Vivien laughed at Lady Browning's solemn tone.

"I am most serious."

"Lady Browning, with all due respect, I can't even get the lowest of literary magazines to look at my work. I can't just wake up one morning and announce to the world that I'm a playwright. I assure you, the world will never care."

"But I care." Lady Browning smiled most enigmatically. "And that is sometimes enough."

"Why do you care? For that matter, Mrs. Doubleday, too—you are both being far too kind."

"Ellie told me about the St. Vincents and their shabby treatment of you. I've loathed Angelica St. Vincent for decades. Imagine having a future daughter-in-law like you—I'd show you off to the world." Lady Browning patted the notebook still resting on her lap. "This, too."

"Still, I wouldn't know the first thing about writing for the stage."

"I can help you. I once wrote an entire play based on Ellen. What if Ellen was English—what would happen to her then? It ran at the Aldwych for nearly a year. Let me put in some calls."

"I can't ask that of you."

"Why ever not? Vivien, dear, I am not without connections. People ask it of me all the time, although I hardly ever say yes. Even more rarely do I *offer* it."

Lady Browning explained how, as a young writer, she, too, had received help from an unexpected quarter: the legendary Cornish writer Sir Arthur Quiller-Couch, who wrote under the pseudonym Q. To this day, she had no idea why he had taken her under his wing and encouraged her writing.

"I suppose we first bonded over our love of the Brontës. He fiercely defended Emily—included her in his *Oxford Book of Verse*. 'Remembrance.'"

Vivien loved that poem. It was where she put so much of her grief over David, buried in the painful longing of the verse. She suddenly quoted out loud:

"'No later light has lighten'd up my heaven / No second morn has ever shone for me. . . .'"

Lady Browning patted Vivien's hand with affection and something akin to longing, before completing the quote herself:

"'Then did I learn how existence could be cherish'd / Strengthen'd and fed without the aid of joy.'"

"She's so brilliant." Vivien sighed.

"They all three were. They wrote for the reader, but an *ideal* reader, one they birthed into existence themselves. They gave us what we didn't even know we craved. How brave to have done that then. Or, really, even now."

Lady Browning fell unusually silent for several seconds before patting the green notebook on her lap again. "I like the spiral coil."

"My colleague Grace orders them in from New Jersey. She's keen on expanding our stock beyond books. These do quite well with the tourists and students who venture in."

"I need to visit this little shop of yours, this Bloomsbury Books." Vivien sighed. "It's a cesspool."

Lady Browning gave such an unexpectedly loud laugh that the taxi driver glanced at the rearview mirror in surprise. "Is the situation fixable?"

"Not on seven quid a week. I'm afraid there's only so much we women employees can do to improve our lot."

"Well, when you do think of it, you must ask Ellen or myself for help. For now, may I hold on to this notebook of yours?"

O f the many wonderful things that she and Lady Browning had talked about in the cab that night, this was the moment that had stayed uppermost in Vivien's mind. The very next day she had headed in to work and conceived with Grace the idea of a literary luncheon with Daphne du Maurier as their first featured guest. Since that event, several handwritten notes had occasionally arrived at the shop from Lady Browning, commenting on various extracts from Vivien's work.

In her most recent note, Lady Browning had repeated something that Q had taught her: "All great writing comes from a desire to escape, but you have to know what you are escaping to. The audience will follow anything you do if they are confident you know where you are going."

Vivien now sat alone in her flat, on the one full day that she could dedicate to her greatest passion in life. She chewed thoughtfully on the end of her pencil, her favourite tool for writing from her time behind the shop counter. She started to scribble down the words pouring out of her, then slowed down her hand and thought about her own audience of one, Daphne du Maurier, and what she would want her to say.

CHAPTER TWENTY-SEVEN

RULE No. 36

Staff shall recommend books to suit the interests of the customer.

The following morning, Vivien was standing bored behind the cash counter when an older man in his fifties approached, a rolled-up newspaper under one arm.

"I'm looking for a book."

Vivien put down her pencil and gave her practiced smile of forbearance in the face of the man's obvious remark. "Of course, sir. Any book in particular?"

"Nothing too fussy."

"Fussy?"

"You know." He made a face. "Old-fashioned."

"I see. Can you tell me a book you recently enjoyed?"

"I like that C. S. Forester."

"Ah, naval adventure then?"

"Not necessarily."

These conversations were, for Vivien, one of the most frustrating aspects of working in a bookshop. The customers who had no idea what they wanted out of the thousands of books in the world but presumed, for some reason, that the shop assistant did.

"Anything else?" she persisted.

"Noël Coward."

"Ah, drawing room comedy then? I have just the thing." Vivien emerged from behind the counter and led the man to the nearest new-fiction table.

"This is very popular." She held out a slender hardcover book.

"Love in a Cold Climate," he read aloud slowly. "By Nancy Mitford."

"Yes. One of our top sellers." Mitford's latest novel was Vivien's default recommendation with customers who had no idea what they wanted. Something about the infamous Mitford name, at least, tended to resonate with them.

"I don't read books by women."

"Come again?"

"Lady writers." He made another face.

"I see." Vivien bit the inside of her lip. "This then? Nevil Shute?"

This was her form of retail subterfuge. *A Town Like Alice* was one of the most heartily romantic tales Vivien had ever read, written by a former aeronautical engineer and pilot.

"Malaya in the war. Japanese POWs." She lowered her voice. "Torture."

Despite this deceptive plot summary, Vivien had never had a male customer return the book. The men must have ended up enjoying the story, which amused her greatly. The book would surely have been labelled a mere romance if authored by Daphne du Maurier or any other woman.

The man's eyes brightened at the idea of Australian soldiers escaping execution, and the sale was concluded. Vivien wrapped up the book in plain brown craft paper, around which she tied a length of ribbon in dark blue to match the exterior of Bloomsbury Books. Grace had recently ordered several spools from the haberdasher a few blocks north, then had the local engraver decorate each foot of ribbon with the name of the shop, its year of establishment, and the phrase *One Hundred Years of Fine Books*. This had all been hastily arranged in advance of Mr. Dutton's return, with enough ribbon ordered to last the shop through Easter.

The shop bell hit its casing, and Vivien glanced at the doorway at the exact moment that Alec peered down from his ladder. They both watched with interest as George Orwell's widow approached the cash counter just as the previous customer was walking away. Sonia Blair had returned to Bloomsbury Books to accept in person her invitation to the Beckett lecture.

"Yes," she announced in that soft, serious way of hers, which Vivien now recognised as grief, it still being only a few weeks since the death of Mrs. Blair's world-famous husband.

Vivien quickly understood what the other woman meant. "Oh, that's lovely. We are so pleased you can attend."

Just then Alec inched along the nearest wall on his ladder.

"Is there somewhere we could speak in private?" Sonia asked as Alec's lanky figure wheeled by, his enviable flop of hair shining in the morning sun.

Vivien looked at her in surprise and lowered her voice. "Shall I take my break a few minutes early?"

Sonia nodded while Vivien motioned upwards to Alec and artificially raised her voice. "I'm sure you heard all that. I'll be back by eleven."

The two women walked out together into the late-morning bustle of Lamb's Conduit. They grabbed tea in disposable cups from the coffee cart, each of them adding heavy doses of milk and sugar, then headed north towards Great Ormond Street and the quaint and relatively private Queen Square.

"I've always loved this street," Sonia was musing aloud, looking about at all the different trades and their window displays. "Perfect for a bookshop and quite literary in its own right. Eric— George—told me once that Yeats used to attend séances at number sixty-one. He called him an 'occult fascist.'"

Vivien laughed. "We have a few of those at work."

"So I've heard." Sonia hesitated. "You are aware of *Horizon*, the literary journal where I worked?"

"Yes, why?"

"It's why I came. To the literary luncheon."

The two women turned left onto Great Ormond Street and passed the famous children's hospital on their way to the entrance to Queen Square.

"I assumed it was to ask Lady Browning about 'The Doll.'"

Now Sonia Blair had to laugh. "Oh, how Eric would have loved seeing all that. A veritable storm in a Limoges teacup."

"The head of my department is still mortified."

"You seem to enjoy egging him on," observed Sonia.

"You don't miss a thing." This made Vivien wonder what it was that Sonia really wanted to discuss.

"No, I'm afraid I don't. I came to the shop, you see, to also meet you."

"Why on earth me?"

"Did you submit any writing yourself last autumn, to *Horizon*?"

Vivien nodded. "I received a lovely letter of rejection for one of my short stories."

"Yes, I know. I wrote it. On Mr. Connolly's behalf, of course. You see, Vivien—may I call you that?—we never do quite leave the secretarial work behind. Cyril was wonderful to his *ladies,* as we editorial assistants were called—better than most. But he was still, first and foremost, a man."

"You must have a prodigious memory, to recall any rejected submission of mine."

They were now passing through the stately gates of Queen Square, a long rectangular oasis in the heart of Bloomsbury, with its perfectly hedged garden beds and black wrought-iron benches and rails.

"I held on to all the female-authored submissions we rejected." Sonia motioned towards a bench up ahead. "With Cyril's permission, of course. Fortunately, he couldn't fathom why I cared."

They sat down next to each other on a bench that bordered the perimeter of the square. Before them clusters of snowdrops were beginning to emerge from the frozen ground, always the first sign of spring in London.

"Why *did* you care?" Vivien asked her bluntly.

"I often think of running my own press one day, an all-women one, perhaps in conjunction with a bookshop. With Eric gone and *Horizon* officially shut down, I feel at such a loose end. Everyone says I married him for his money; I might as well do something useful with it."

"But your readership would automatically be cut in half. And women don't buy the right books, or enough of them, I'm always being told."

"That's rubbish. I saw the subscription logs at work. Yet it's the same excuse the editors gave, time after time, in our meetings—how stories about women's concerns are of no interest to men, while male-authored stories appeal to all. Clarissa Spencer-Churchill and I both fought for your story, albeit unsuccessfully. Your imagination is quite wild, you know, and your dialogue razor-sharp in its bite. In many ways it reminded us of Anna Kavan."

Vivien was silently gratified by the comparison to one of her favourite authors and the praise for her own writing, which, aside from her many fruitless submissions over the years, she had shown only to Lady Browning.

"But the editors found the actual story too absurd and unbelievable. And, on this one point I might agree with them, too hurried."

"I admire how direct you are."

"I am sure you can handle it."

"It's odd, but I can." Vivien shrugged. "Writing is the one thing I never take personally. It doesn't even feel like it comes from inside me."

"As an editor of sorts, I've always been so fascinated by that."

"At least, it doesn't feel like it does." Vivien laughed. "I'm sure I'm wrong—after all, it has to come from somewhere."

Now it was Sonia's turn to shrug. "Not necessarily—I doubt great art can be so personal and contained. It has to strike a much more universal chord. We may none of us ever experience living at Manderley—not that that's Lady Browning's intention at all. Far from it, I suspect. But in a way we all dream of it. When it comes to women writers, however, men need to believe that the experiences come from somewhere real. How emasculating otherwise, if you think about it—that lack of access and control over our innermost thoughts and worlds."

Vivien stared at Sonia, her mind racing. "Do you really think that's what's behind it all?"

"I think everything begins and ends with feeling free, or at least in control—and threatened by the loss of it to the gain of others. The antithesis of cooperation. I am, after all, a committed socialist."

"Should you really be telling me any of this?"

"Only now that the magazine has folded. I had to wait until then. I would never approach you otherwise with any of the editorial decisions."

"So you came to the luncheon to meet du Maurier and me because you read our stories?"

"No, not entirely. I also read Mr. McDonough's. I wanted to meet 'the girl in the shop.'"

Vivien turned to face her in shock. Immediately her chest tightened with rage over her greatest fear being realised. She remembered stomping the journal under her bare right foot, pitching the brass nameplate into the wastepaper basket, and then throwing Alec's trench coat at his face immediately after. She had been determined that his last-ever view of her naked body would be as she marched away from him to retrieve her clothes from the back office.

"The story was clearly about you." Sonia seemed to hesitate in view of how furious her words were making Vivien. "You knew it got published, of course?"

"No, not until very recently."

"You had no idea of it?"

Vivien shook her head. "Alec doesn't let anyone in on the inner workings, such as they are, of his mind. I knew he was trying for years for publication. I didn't know he was trying to do it on the back of *me*."

"Does he know that you write, too?"

"God, I hope not."

"I thought Cyril should have chosen your story over Alec's. But the editorial team loved the character of the girl. More than the actual story, I'm afraid."

Vivien's head throbbed over the irony that she had come that close to publication only to lose out to Alec, of all people, and only because he had written about *her*. Was not even the story of her own life within her control?

"They all claimed the girl in the story reminded them of so many unmarried women who felt cheated by the war. It was obvious to me, however, that this was no composite. I don't think Mr. McDonough has enough imagination for that. Look," Sonia said more gently, "none of this is that unusual. For all their moaning about 'women's writing,' male authors are at least as guilty of using what they experience and know. After all, I am the girl in the Fiction Department, as Eric called me in *Nineteen Eighty-Four*."

"That doesn't bother you?" Vivien asked in disbelief.

Sonia shrugged again. "Most writers use real people for inspiration. The truly imaginative . . . well, take Lady Browning. One would be hard-pressed to find a scintilla of her life in those books."

"But Alec had to know that people would figure it out."

"Not necessarily. Clarissa Spencer-Churchill and I only figured it out accidentally. You were at a gathering at Ellen Doubleday's last month and met Clarissa, yes? Ellen told Clarissa—and Clarissa later told me—that you worked in a bookshop and had once been engaged to the future Earl St. Vincent. And there was something about a recent incident in your shop with a Cartier watch—the exact same model referred to in Mr. McDonough's story, which caused the two characters to bust up. That's what tipped us off and led me to your event."

"It's so frustrating," Vivien said bitterly. "I write about what I don't know, and everyone says it's not *believable* enough. Lady Browning gets criticized for making up the wildest, most nightmarish thoughts. Meanwhile, Alec gets published by telling my own story, no invention at all, no permission. The ego—the intrusion—of it all."

"Vivien, listen to me. Your writing is as strange, as beautiful, as any I've read. It's just not your time. I know no one wants to hear that. You'd probably rather be told you don't have talent if there's only to be effort with no reward. But sweet are the uses of adversity, as Shakespeare once wrote."

At these last words, Vivien looked over at Sonia curiously. "Mrs. Blair, I know a little of losing a husband. Why pay mind to any of this?"

"I suppose this is me using adversity." Sonia gave a sad smile. "I work best by losing myself in others. Eric always said that was part of the attraction to a larger cause—if one can't write." She took Vivien's gloved hands in both of hers. "I have no doubt that one day you will be a great success. But promise me to keep that temper of yours in check. And keep on writing. Just"—Sonia gave a rueful smile—"just not about Alec. I suspect he's nowhere near as fascinating as you."

The two women separated at the eastern entrance to the garden square. As Vivien headed back to the shop, she knew she was angrily stomping the very ground where T. S. Eliot had worked as an editor, Virginia Woolf had drawn inspiration for her novel *Night and Day,* and Thackeray had set his earliest chapters in *Vanity Fair.* Vivien could sell books by these and other authors, but that would probably be all. Even with the interest of Lady Browning or Sonia Orwell, her chances for a career in writing remained extremely poor. Besides, Vivien wanted something else even more now, and it wasn't to have her own version of her life published.

It was finally to feel in control of it.

A few hours later, Evie tentatively approached the kitchenette where Vivien was on tea-making duty.

"Hello, stranger," Vivien greeted her coolly.

Evie hung back in the doorway. She had studiously been avoiding Vivien ever since the du Maurier event, but her talk with Mimi the day before had had its intended effect.

"May I help?"

Vivien nodded as she filled up the kettle with water. "You know the drill."

Evie stood on her tiptoes to reach for the canister of black tea leaves in the open shelves above their heads.

"Everything all right?" Vivien asked brusquely as she plugged in the kettle.

Evie just stood there, not knowing what to say. She kept picturing Vivien and Alec tearing each other apart in Mr. Dutton's office, so angrily and almost violently—a memory that weeks later still left the young woman feeling shamefaced and confused.

"I know you've been looking through the books, Evie."

Vivien's knowing voice startled her. It wasn't what Evie had most feared being accused of, but it was close enough, and she could only wonder at what else Vivien might know. She was by far the most observant employee at Bloomsbury Books. Evie inwardly berated herself for not being more circumspect around her.

"You told me that first day," Vivien continued, "that you and Yardley were both part of the group that saved Austen's cottage. And that you'd first met Mr. Allen at an auction, at Sotheby's, isn't that correct?"

There was Vivien's razor-sharp memory to complete the artillery that the men in the shop always found themselves up against, just as Evie did now.

"Your showing up here wasn't a coincidence, was it, Evie?"

Vivien's voice had a slight edge now, an aggressiveness that Evie had only ever heard her use with men such as Alec and Master Mariner Scott.

"Evie . . . what are you up to?"

"If I find a book on another floor," Evie answered her instead, still not quite ready to tell Vivien everything, "'n' it's priced less than its true value, must I say so?"

Vivien was watching her curiously. "Well, we certainly know what Dutton and Allen would say about that. Sailor Scott would demand it merely on the grounds of trespassing. But it *is* knowledge gained in the course of employment, and I believe rule twenty-four is quite fulsome on the subject of *that*."

"But what do *you* think?"

Vivien unplugged the kettle and poured the now-boiling water into the teapot. "I think I'm totally fine with you ripping the rug out from under the lot of them."

She turned to Evie and gave her a smile so warm and understanding that Evie saw in it the forgiveness she hadn't known she needed.

"I want us to be friends, Evie. I don't think either of us will get very far on our own. At least, it hasn't worked for me yet." Vivien nodded in the direction of the back office. "And abusing friendship has worked out only too well for the Tyrant."

Leaving the kitchen, Evie realised that Vivien was being foiled by her own contingent at work, just as Evie had been at Cambridge. She had rarely seen anyone work as hard as Vivien, yet her ambitions remained thwarted. This made Evie question her own ability to improve her situation, whether at Bloomsbury Books or elsewhere. Finding and somehow acquiring *The Mummy!* might give her momentary acclaim and notice, much like the success of her catalogue behind the Chawton Great House dispersal. But without an accomplice of some kind, a new type of society, she was no match for the power structures in place.

As Evie returned to the third floor and her solitary duties, she recalled Mimi's recent advice over afternoon tea: to connect more—to *ask* for more. That had not been easy in the relatively small confines of Cambridge, where those in charge were few in number and held immeasurable sway. London was surely different. There was a lot up for grabs, and a lot of people reaching for it, in a city of over eight million. Evie wanted to do more than just grab, however—she wanted to build something new and lasting of her own. Something that no one could ever take away.

Cataloguing or selling books on behalf of men was simply not going to do it.

CHAPTER TWENTY-EIGHT

RULE No. 11

Staff shall take every opportunity to publicise
the work of Bloomsbury Books.

On Wednesday mornings, Evie and Ash had begun meeting for breakfast near King's Cross station on their way to work. Evie knew the area well—she had arrived often enough from Cambridge over the years to conduct research at the British Museum. She had recently introduced Ash to her favourite cafeteria in the area, where the waitresses were kept too busy by the morning commuter crowd to pay much attention to who was dining with whom. Ash always ordered the type of hearty English breakfast that tourists came in search of; Evie stuck to her usual porridge with a heap of brown sugar and creamy milk on top.

Facing a brisk fifteen-minute walk down to the shop, they left the café at 8:30 a.m. All about them, the winter sun cast the black suits and bowler hats of the businessmen into stark relief against the light overnight snow. After a few surprisingly mild weeks, winter had returned to London yet again. Evie regretted not wearing her trusty blue cardigan or navy knit dress under her wool coat. Instead, she wore one of her flatmate's dresses, cinched at the waist and in a deep emerald shade that made Evie feel conspicuous but that Charlotte had urged on her.

Crossing the street, Evie spotted a group of late-night revellers up ahead who were even more conspicuous than her, donned in a mystifying array of light, flowing Indian garments that left them exposed to the cold.

"How familiar," Ash observed dryly, and Evie found herself feeling awkwardly jealous at the sight of the three young women adorned in colourful saris with matching scarves about their heads. Their two male companions each wore a version of a Jodhpuri suit, complete with incongruous wool waistcoats and men's pleated flannel trousers underneath, and topped with turbans made from white bedding sheets.

At the street corner, Ash lingered behind Evie to grab a copy of *The Hindu* from the newsagent. As the revellers ahead started to pass, Evie glanced down at her feet, only to look back up in shock as a familiar voice jovially called out.

"Miss Evie Stone!"

Evie froze.

It was Stuart Wesley.

"Why, fancy seeing you here! You remember Caldwell. And this is my new fiancée, Sonia Christenson, and her friends from St Mary's." He waved grandly towards the young women at his side. "Ellen Cleaves and Claudia Davis-Jones."

Evie stared at the group.

"Speechless as ever, I see," Stuart continued. "All alone?"

Evie hesitated to make introductions as Ash now caught up to the group.

"And who's this?" Stuart grinned slyly.

Ash appeared inwardly amused at the various outfits the group were wearing, while Evie felt something else entirely: a deep sense of shame for the way so many people in England treated him.

"Ashwin Ramaswamy." He extended his hand towards Stuart, who shook it overly enthusiastically.

"Stuart Wesley. Evie may have mentioned me. You two missed quite the party at Albert Hall last night—the Chelsea Arts Mardi Gras Ball, you know?"

Of course, Evie thought. Of course Stuart and his friends would come down from Cambridge to attend London's most scandalous annual event. At that moment Evie realised, crestfallen, that Stuart Wesley did not need to follow the carnival in life: it would always follow *him*.

"The theme this year was 'Life in the Raj.'" Stuart smiled before nodding at Ash. "You'd have fit right in."

Evie watched as Vice-Master Christenson's daughter gave Stuart a not-so-friendly smack on his side with the back of her right hand.

"He's a good sport, I'm sure—right, Ramaswamy?" Stuart didn't wait for an answer as he now turned his attention back to Evie, who had still not said a word.

She saw it again, the constant avarice in his eyes. His ambition was the fulcrum at the centre of all his social extensions: the after-hours office calls, the balls, the champagne and confetti. Stuart made it so pleasant for others to stand in the shade of his practiced nicety, while the cold, hard ambition remained even further back than that. But Evie saw it because the shade of his nicety never extended quite as far as her. Worse, Stuart didn't care that she saw it because he knew for a fact—having recently stolen a job out from under her—that she was powerless to affect him. He just had to keep being nice to the people above him in order to continue being mean to someone as far beneath his concern as her. Having so often missed dangerous behaviour in others, Evie realised that her ability to perceive it now in Stuart did not make him less of a threat to her, but rather more so. He clearly felt able to do much more overt harm to her because she was beneath the concern of so many others as well.

"Well, we best be getting off to work." Evie tried to sound nonchalant and determined at the same time.

"Off to work?" Stuart repeated after her, looking widely about. "And where's that?"

"Just a shop," Evie answered as blandly as possible.

She was surprised to feel Ash by her side take her arm in his, as the glint in Stuart Wesley's eye sharpened.

"A shopgirl, heh? Hereabouts?"

She felt Ash's gentle grasp about her arm tighten so nicely at Stuart's invasive words, causing her pounding heart to quicken even more.

"In Bloomsbury," answered Ash instead. "And where are you running off to—the circus?"

Stuart narrowed his eyes at Ash so slightly that Evie could not wait to be rid of him.

"Not quite—although Cambridge does have its share of freaks, huh, Evie? Actually, we're heading back there now." Stuart turned to directly face Evie one last time. "I'll be sure to tell Kinross we bumped into you. He'll be most interested to know where you've ended up, and with whom. I guess London really is the centre of the world after all."

The merry group continued on its way, leaving Evie feeling both winded and nauseated at their retreat.

"Charming," Ash said under his breath.

"No, he's not."

Ash was still holding on to her arm, and now it felt less like support, and more warm and pleasant, and Evie let out her breath as he stepped back and pulled his arm away.

"Sorry about that. I just didn't like the way he was treating you. Thought it might distract him from asking too much about the shop."

It appeared to have done exactly that, and Evie was glad of

it—glad that Wesley had been left with such a flat, dismal impression of her life in London that he hadn't bothered to learn more. It boded well for his never thinking of her again, leading Evie to hope that this was the last time she would ever have to think of him as well. And she had so enjoyed the feel of Ash close to her. . . .

At that very moment, just as their arms were dropping back to their sides, a man bumped into them both so hard that Evie stumbled forward against Ash. As he caught her, Evie instinctively looked back in the direction of the shove, expecting a very quick "Terribly sorry" and the tipping of a hat. But the words the stranger hissed as he passed by were instead so vicious that Evie couldn't believe what she was hearing. It was as if the vile words hadn't really happened—as if they had come from another world altogether.

Protectively pulling Evie even closer to him, Ash flinched his face away from the other man as if he had been struck, but said nothing in return. Evie couldn't believe it. That wasn't like Ash. Ash wasn't intimidated by anyone.

"Did you hear what—" Evie stopped herself. She felt as if she was getting everything wrong: the seemingly innocuous presence of Stuart Wesley, the press of the crowd about them and the cost to Ash of having to ignore it all, the feel of his arm on hers—even her own feelings for him.

They resumed their walk to the shop in a silence that was anything but comfortable. Ash seemed frustrated by everything about him, even by her. Evie remembered something the village doctor in Chawton had once said: everything in life is either a warning or a cause. She had evaded Stuart Wesley again, that awful man on the street had long since passed, and Ash was walking beside her as he so often did. Yet this restoration of the usual—the status quo—felt deceptive to her in its ease. Something had shifted—something in her understanding of what she and Ash were up against and, she feared, something deep inside Ash himself.

A warning or a cause. The past, present, and future were all connected, even if she was not able to discern how. Evie knew that her strengths did not lie there. She was not a creator, and certainly not philosophically inclined. Instead, she hoped to share the words and ideas of women long gone from this earth, women who could no longer speak but, in their determination to not stay silent, could still have an effect, even now. Evie believed that her study of the past was worthwhile, but wanted what she discovered there to echo forward as well. It was 1950 and the world was once again being given a second chance, after another all-consuming war. People had only the past to learn from, yet already they seemed to want to forget and move on to the future. But there were no lessons to be found there, only promises instead. Evie had to wonder how empty such promises would turn out to be; not just for her, with her hands almost on Jane Webb's lost book, but for the women freed by war, the men moving to new lives in new countries, and all the harmed and hurt survivors left behind.

CHAPTER TWENTY-NINE

The General Manager shall have exclusive access
to the minute books of the shop.

It was two hours before the start of the Beckett lecture, and
Grace waited alone in the lavish restaurant on the eastern side
of Russell Square. Lord Baskin had asked her and Vivien to
meet for cocktails and a light supper at the Hotel Russell in advance of the evening's big event. This was so unusual that even
Vivien had been a little thrown off when the invitation had arrived by messenger at the shop.

"Are we being fired?" Grace had asked as they examined the
earl's engraved letterhead together.

Vivien shook her head. "That's not his style. And the man does
have style, I'll give him that. Besides, remember all that company information he shared with me after the du Maurier event?
That's nothing you'd share with staff you're about to boot out."
She paused. "What time did he say?"

"Sixish."

"Okay, I can just make it. I need to do one errand first and
then I'll meet you both there."

It was now well after six and Vivien had still not shown up.
Only Lord Baskin could be seen strolling through the adjoining
bar area towards Grace, easily navigating the many sofas and arm-

chairs in his way. The Hotel Russell had been the Baskin family hotel of choice for three generations, and the present earl clearly knew its maze of public rooms intimately.

"I'm so sorry, please forgive me," he said with a disarming smile, sliding into the other end of the curved corner booth so that he and Grace were facing each other. Glad of the distance he had put between them, she shifted uncomfortably under his gaze.

"We can put Vivien in the middle when she arrives," she said offhandedly. "Like a pettish child."

"Oh, I'm sorry again—did you not know?"

He was looking at her so earnestly that at first she didn't suspect a thing.

"Know what?"

"Miss Lowry can't make it. There was a note waiting for me at the front desk. Too late to reschedule at that point." He hesitated. "I hope that's all right."

It wasn't all right. She was a married woman after all, only out at night because of a whole other deception of her own.

Relations with her husband had reached their lowest point following his behaviour at the shop. Grace knew that someone as self-involved as Gordon would never understand how that moment in front of her co-workers had steeled her. For all that she had sacrificed for her husband in recent years, the bookshop remained her one bulwark against him—and the one thing she didn't want him coming near. This must be why she had turned back that morning in Lamb's Conduit, the hot, bitter taste of coffee still on her lips, and applied to the advertisement that in its elegant wording had masked Mr. Dutton's many quirks.

Relations with Gordon had reached such a low point that today Grace had told the first lie of her marriage. She had informed Gordon that she would be staying overnight at her mother's to help her with some medical appointments the next day. Grace knew she could trust her mother to cover for her should Gordon call. Privy over the years to more than a few instances of her son-in-law's moods, the older woman appeared to comprehend the situation only too well. Grace had always relied heavily on her mother's discretion in light of Grace's own unwillingness to discuss it.

Now the one thing that Grace had never intended—the main reason why married couples do so often lie to each other—had materialized before her against her will, facilitated by either Vivien or Lord Baskin, or both.

"You didn't know before?" she asked him, one eyebrow raised suspiciously. "About Vivien?"

"About . . . ?"

Grace watched as it now dawned on him, too.

"Oh, my goodness, how right you are." He stood up as if to go. "I'm so sorry for putting you in this position. I'd never do anything to suggest—to, ah, compromise—"

She motioned for him to sit down. Obviously upset, his willingness to leave so quickly appeared to prove his ignorance of any plotting by their co-worker.

"It's fine. We're here now as it is. I suppose one drink can't hurt."

He immediately motioned for the waiter and asked for her order.

"Dubonnet on ice," she said, catching the tight primness in her voice.

"Dry martini, my usual." Lord Baskin turned to Grace. "Mr. Westcott here has assisted my family for many generations, haven't you?"

Not served, Grace noticed. *Not worked for.* But *assisted*. Grace could tell that this choice of address meant a lot to its recipient, who accepted it with a polite yet gracious smile.

"Most certainly, Lord Baskin. Since his lordship was in his Little Lord Fauntleroy suit and curls."

Lord Baskin laughed heartily, and the waiter gave them both a slight bow before leaving.

"That was lovely," she commented.

"What was?"

"How you referred to him."

"How else should I?"

She smiled. Lord Baskin seemed unaware of how different he was from other men of his station, or from the ones that visited the shop. Or from Gordon. At this last thought, she stopped smiling and sat up straighter.

He was looking about the ornately decorated room. "Apparently Fitzroy Doll designed the restaurant on the RMS *Titanic* to be an exact replica of this one."

"That seems fitting."

"I'm so sorry—are you sure you're all right?"

His constant solicitousness towards her and others reminded Grace of something Ellen Doubleday had shared with them after the du Maurier event: that a good guest always acts like a host. Lord Baskin struck Grace as someone so grateful for his good fortune in life that he took none of it for granted, knowing he enjoyed it only on the backs of others. This was not her notion of the British aristocracy; certainly, it was not how any of their wealthier shop clientele behaved. Lord Baskin made her feel appreciated as his equal and encouraged to speak as one. Looking back, she would later recognise this as the moment when she had first begun to let down her guard.

"What was it you wanted to speak to Vivien and me about?" she asked, deciding it best to keep to business about the shop.

"Mr. McDonough."

It was not at all what she had been expecting him to say. "Alec? How so?"

Now it was Lord Baskin's turn to shift uncomfortably in his

seat. "He approached me . . . and, in good faith, I really should not be speaking a word." Lord Baskin looked about the room quickly before lowering his voice slightly. "But it's my understanding that he wants to buy the shop."

Grace stared at Lord Baskin. She knew Alec had money. The apartment in Knightsbridge, the apparel from Savile Row, the Patek watch: none of these things came easily, or at all, on a shopworker's income. His wealth also showed in the way that he hid his ambition with a deceptive air of unconcern—of having nothing to lose. This was Alec's envied energy about the shop. It enabled him to boldly pursue social connections in a manner that she and Vivien would never even dare to contemplate. That was one reason why the collective interest of Ellen Doubleday, Lady Browning, and Sonia Blair in Vivien was such a godsend to her. There would otherwise be no access to a better life for an unmarried woman lacking in family support, unless through the goodwill—and expectations—of a man.

"But he can't just do that. I mean, you'd have to agree, for one thing."

Lord Baskin nodded vigorously. "You're right, of course. It's just that the shop . . . well, the shop has become, not a burden exactly, just . . . well, firstly, the family property keeps increasing in value, but the books and other assets are worth only a fraction of their cost. Minus the outstanding debts, it would take only a few thousand pounds to buy out my half—five thousand at most." He hesitated. "And I'm not sure how much longer I can be involved."

"I don't understand."

"I'm finding it difficult, you see, to be at the shop."

He wouldn't look at Grace, not directly, which was how she finally knew that he was talking about her. It was the absolute most he could ever say to her as a married woman and remain the gentleman she knew him to be.

"Oh, I see."

He took a breath. "Working there was such a help, when Anna first left me, and during those final, endless, years of the war."

Grace was quiet as she let his words sink in. She thought about what that meant, to be left. She only ever thought about doing the leaving herself, lately more than ever as Gordon became increasingly irrational.

"You're always doing what you want now . . ." he would often complain, complaints that were beginning to spill over into his treatment of their two growing sons.

"What on earth does that mean?" she would be forced to ask, genuinely confused by what she might have done wrong.

". . . staying late at work, drinking and making a spectacle of yourself. . ."

"That was one night in—what, almost five years? Five years and the only time I've said yes to my co-workers and stayed—"

The argument would go round and round, always circling back to the after-party at the shop. For years Gordon had demanded to know exactly what she was doing at all times. Fortunately for their marriage, working as a beleaguered secretary to a man such as Mr. Dutton had left little to the imagination until now. Grace finally understood just how small her world was being kept by her husband—just how much he could completely enfold and contain it within his own. That was the bargain she had somehow silently, submissively made with him, and of which she despaired of ever seeing her end.

But to be left as Lord Baskin had been, by a beautiful woman whom he had obviously and passionately loved, so suddenly and without warning—what must such a betrayal do, especially to someone as generous, considerate, and proud as Jeremy Baskin?

"Do you ever feel," he now asked softly, watching her face carefully the entire time he spoke, "like we're still stuck back in the war? A war that's been over for nearly five years? It's as if we can't move forward. Why is that?"

"Guilt." Grace was startled by the declarative sound of her own voice. "It must be. Guilt for not doing more back then, even if we did do our best, because to what avail? All those lives lost and ruined all the same. And then more guilt, I suppose, for surviving, only to do what with it? Just the same old routine, same as before. Sorry, I shouldn't rattle on like that to you, of all people."

He looked surprised at the unusual note of pessimism in her voice.

"Perhaps that's what survivors have to do—hold on to what was."

She shook her head. "No, that shouldn't be. Look at Ash, coming here after the war, trying to build something new. Or even Evie Stone, for that matter. They haven't settled for their lot in life."

"What would you do differently, if you could?" Lord Baskin waited intently for her response. He always listened so patiently and expectantly to her, and it made Grace feel appreciated in a way that she rarely felt at work, and even less often at home.

"I wish I knew." She sighed. "I don't feel like I can do anything. Can't afford to. Not like Alec. He can play around at work and elsewhere: take over from his boss, make offers to the owner."

"I worry you may be right."

"Even if I'm not, it feels like I am."

"But what would you do if you could?" He must have caught the look of subtle warning in her eye, because he then said instead, "You are so excellent with the books, for one—always catching many a missing decimal or figure."

"Proper bookkeeping would require training, though. I can't spare time for that, not with a family at home." She shrugged. "I live in a much smaller world than you and Alec. There's nowhere to go. Nowhere to escape to, if things go wrong."

He smiled sadly at her. "No bookshop to hide out in."

She had to smile at his reference to himself during the war. "Owner's prerogative. But, if I'm being honest"—and it was the most that she, as a married woman, could say to him—"I took this job for similar reasons. And I'm glad I have it. For now."

"Right," Lord Baskin suddenly remembered, "we were talking about Alec."

"Is his offer serious, do you think?"

"I think so. But I should mention that Mr. Dutton and Mr. Allen also have a keen interest."

"I know."

He smiled. "Ah, yes, Vivien. You tell each other everything on those long bus rides home."

Tell each other everything. She remembered him saying those exact same words the last time they had sat together, a few hours before the du Maurier event. Then, as now, Grace could intuit the longing behind it and felt herself become flustered again under his gaze. "Not everything. But when it comes to the goings-on at the shop, we certainly do. You called Vivien here tonight as well as me, so I'll ask for us both—is Alec in a hurry? Could he beat Mr. Dutton and Mr. Allen to it?"

"I would always give them a chance to make an offer. I just want the shop to go to the best person possible, although I do worry about Herbert continuing to work given his health, and Frank so rarely here. For his part, Alec does seem to be in quite the hurry—I'm not sure why. Has anything happened lately to set him off?"

Grace shook her head discreetly. "Nothing more than usual."

They looked at each other in silent understanding.

"I thought things were improving there."

Grace said nothing. She still didn't know exactly what had happened between Alec and Vivien, just as she had not told Vivien everything about her marriage. For all that she and Vivien shared, some things were simply too painful to admit.

"I'm not sure he deserves her, for that matter," Lord Baskin added.

"Possibly. Although I'm not sure we should be talking about this."

"My ex-wife, Anna, and I had a similar dynamic. Very dramatic, it all was."

"Again, I really don't think we should be talking about any of this, do you?" It was her final attempt to keep them on course, and as Lord Baskin motioned to Westcott for the bill, she saw that it had worked. But she was also surprised to find that part of her didn't want it to. That afternoon at Hamleys together, she remembered wishing she could take her boys and run from her life—this time, she wished she could stay right here.

"Of course, you're right. You always are." He took a final sip of his martini and checked his watch. "It's getting close to seven and the shop must need readying for Mr. Beckett's arrival."

"Oh, I'm sure Vivien has started without me." Grace gave a tight but earnest smile.

He grinned back, looking visibly relieved at still being on a good footing with her. "I'm sure she has."

He escorted her to the front lobby and watched as she left. She wanted to say so many things to him but couldn't. She wanted to thank him, for being a friend. For always looking out for Vivien and her at the shop, despite their vast difference in station. And for seeing her as a person of substance, despite the small life she lived, bordered at both ends by a bus stop. But she couldn't say any of that—couldn't even tread near it. All Grace could do, instead, as the doorman held open the front door, was feel Lord Baskin's gaze follow her out onto the street, her head held high, her world so small and getting smaller still, for all the things she must not want.

CHAPTER THIRTY

RULE NO. 42

All shop events shall commence at precisely eight o'clock.

Samuel Beckett and Peggy Guggenheim surprised everyone by arriving at Bloomsbury Books together, high in spirits, and ten minutes late. They were without Suzanne Déchevaux-Dumesnil, Beckett's longtime companion and agent, who had had to return to Paris on business. The two former lovers had come straight from cocktails at the American Bar at the Savoy with Lady Browning and her own literary agent, Spencer Curtis Brown, who had set his sights on signing Beckett for the UK market.

Upon arriving, Beckett immediately raced his long, lean form up the stairs, murmuring the most gracious apologies to Alec, who led the way. The rest of the Bloomsbury Books staff were all standing at attention on the second floor, except for Mr. Dutton, who had left for home at precisely 5:30 p.m. on doctor's orders. He was now following the rules about his health as diligently as he had always run the shop. The staff were greatly relieved, none of them being eager to bear witness to a repeat of his horrific attack.

The History Department had once again been cleared for the

audience patiently waiting. Beckett approached the podium as Alec made his rather florid introduction, and everyone grew silent at the striking figure before them.

Alec stood behind and to Beckett's right, and Vivien stood to his left. Unlike Grace in her conservative red suit, Vivien was dressed all in black as befitted her mood, her tight-fitting wool polo-neck-and-pencil-skirt combination immediately catching Beckett's eye.

The rest of the audience sat rapt and expectant, many of the female guests still donned their furs and hats. Lady Browning was in the front row as one of Vivien's VIP guests, along with Ellen Doubleday and Sonia Blair. Peggy Guggenheim, her short, dark hair a frenzied mass of curls, was sitting casually across the aisle from them, playfully twisting her pearls in her right hand as if waiting for a show to begin.

Cradling a tumbler of Scotch in his left hand, Beckett announced that he would be reading from the first paragraph of *Molloy,* a book soon to be published in France. As he read, he spontaneously translated his writing into English, which gave halting pauses to what was already becoming a long reading. Alec grew restless, especially when Curtis Brown whispered behind him that the second paragraph of the book was rumoured to be eighty pages long.

Eventually, Peggy Guggenheim let out an audible, exaggerated yawn. Beckett gave her a playful glare, then let the pages of the bound manuscript fall to a close and invited questions from the crowded room before him.

Several gloved female hands started to flutter above heads, and Vivien had to suppress a smile. With or without a podium, Beckett was the most charismatic man in the room.

Things were proceeding smoothly until a male reporter from *The Times,* standing to the side of the audience, called out, "But don't you feel that the writing has to at least transport the reader somewhere comprehensible, if not recognisable?"

Beckett shrugged, his steel-blue eyes and close-cropped silver hair in attractive contrast to the dark knit polo neck and jacket he was wearing. "What is comprehensible?" he replied bluntly. "I mean, do any of you really understand what is going on here? We must experience first, in order to understand. I write to experience and then better understand myself: that is my only concern."

"*Your* only concern while you write, perhaps. But without basic narrative devices such as a *plot,* you are asking for a level of trust from the reader that the work itself has yet to earn. Surely the reader deserves to recognise something of the world as he knows it."

Beckett shook his head dismissively. "Recognition is ineffectual. What is the point of showing what we already know? I can assure you, the things that I recognise here tonight have no effect."

Vivien caught a teasing glance pass from Beckett to Peggy Guggenheim, his former paramour, in the front row.

"What we are responding to"—he now gave a small wave of his hand to the left—"when we do decide to act is the unseen. The completely new—the provocative."

Beckett looked over at Vivien in an unmistakable way. She let herself make the briefest of eye contact with him before turning back to the audience to see Peggy Guggenheim rolling her eyes at Beckett in a most familiar way.

"I'm trying to get at the essence of being." Turning back from Vivien, Beckett appeared to be finally starting to enjoy himself. "The one thing that drives us."

"You believe, then, in only one?" the newspaperman asked.

Beckett laughed. "In the case of men, yes."

At this the other men in the audience laughed, too, as well as several captivated women. Gazing across the makeshift stage, Vivien saw Alec looking a little less enthralled with the Irish poet and playwright than he had been at the start of the evening.

"But one could argue that, in a search for such *essence,* as you call it, the art becomes meaningless," the reporter gamely persisted. "Too minimal—too stripped of anything—and you risk leaving the audience out in the cold. After all, you need them as much as they need you."

Vivien had been watching Beckett carefully all night. He had a wonderfully satirical and mischievous eye, which was also part of his attraction, in addition to the daunting looks and boundless talent.

"I don't need the audience."

A murmur ran through the men in the crowd, that hushed noise of recognition that something was about to escalate.

"That's patently untrue." Sweat was breaking out on the reporter's brow. "If anything, you need us more than we need you."

Vivien looked over and watched in amusement as Alec's jaw markedly clenched.

"To do what? To write? I can write anywhere. Publish me or not."

"Why on earth are we here tonight, then?"

"You tell me."

The reporter snapped his small notebook shut. "Mr. Beckett, perhaps your refusal to acknowledge the needs of your audience explains why so much of your writing remains unpublished." This was a verbal windup, something the men in the room also recognised the sound of. Vivien recognised it, too—she had tried it often enough with Alec over the years. "Perhaps if you attended to its needs, rather than just your own, you would reach more people. And sell more books. After all, you can't have one without the other."

Beckett had had enough. He downed the rest of the whisky in the glass that he was balancing precariously on the lectern and simply stopped talking. Vivien watched him curiously, her spirits rising at his complete disinterest in pleasing. She wondered if she wrote so that she, too, could detach and disengage in this way—a way that men, or at least men like Beckett, got away with in real life.

Writing had always been the one safe place where Vivien could think and say whatever she wanted. She recalled another piece of advice from one of Lady Browning's handwritten notes: how writing for an audience required not only forgetting oneself, but getting out of one's way, so that there was both entertainment and emotional resonance for others. Lady Browning must know what she was talking about—her recent book, *The King's General,* had reportedly sold over one million copies in just three weeks, and in America her newest release, *The Parasites,* had just topped the *New York Times* Best Sellers fiction list.

Standing there watching Beckett shut his own event down, Vivien had to admit that she found him and his confidence intensely appealing, and not just because it was the confidence of genius. As the one positioned nearest to him on the left side of the lectern, Vivien could also feel the nice buzz of attraction between his body and hers. Everything was combining to raise her spirits much higher than they had been of late.

Alec's spirits, on the other hand, were visibly dampened by dismay. The guest author was, for all intents and purposes, gone. The only energy emanating from him seemed directed solely at Alec's former lover. Three people would later ask for their 10p admission fee back. There would be no group photo in any of the London papers, although there would be a tantalizing gossip item.

Sales, the next day, would be slightly down.

Throughout the lecture, Evie Stone had stood solitarily against the bookcase lining the north wall. From this vantage point, she could watch Beckett and the staff standing about the podium, as well as each of the women sitting in the first row. Evie immediately recognised both Daphne du Maurier and Mrs. George Orwell from the infamous literary luncheon. By now Evie also knew about Vivien's acquaintance with Ellen Doubleday, the recent widow of a famous American publishing magnate, following the incident at the shop involving two sister tourists and Vivien's Cartier watch.

The member of the audience who most fascinated Evie, however, was Peggy Guggenheim, an American heiress and gallery owner who currently resided in Venice. Evie understood from Vivien that Guggenheim had inherited a fortune after her father died on the *Titanic* in the arms of his mistress. In the years since, Guggenheim had amassed one of the world's most impressive art collections. Evie was intrigued by the idea of a woman spending huge sums of money on artwork before its proper valuation or appreciation over time. Evie's own experiences so far in both academia and commerce had left her constantly outbid by men.

To Evie, what all the female VIP guests tonight had most in common was money. She had learned from the salvation of the Jane Austen cottage just how critical financial security could be to accessing opportunity. Without a significant loan by actress Mimi Harrison, the society would never have been able to purchase the Knight family library, which had turned out to be so valuable in the end. Mimi had acquired that money from the many movies she had made, one of the few lucrative endeavours for a woman lucky to be born with film-star looks. Guggenheim had inherited the money that enabled her to compete in a world of men, Ellen Doubleday had married into it, and du Maurier had built one of the most profitable writing careers in the world—another rare profession for those women fortunate enough to have a room of their own.

Evie knew that Vivien and Grace were miserable in their jobs, but questioned how they could improve their situation without financial help. It was what Evie herself had first started to fear, sitting crestfallen in Christenson's hallowed office, and what Mimi had over tea recently counseled her about: hard work and diligence were not always enough. The girls of Bloomsbury Books made sufficient wages to survive and nothing more. There was not a spare shilling left to acquire an object that might increase in value over time or provide them with savings for future difficulties. As a result, Grace could not leave her husband and Vivien could only complain bitterly to no end. Evie worried that she, too, would end up similarly trapped, with fewer and fewer options.

As she let her eyes travel over all these women in the audience, she noticed that Grace seemed unusually tense tonight. Evie wondered if she feared a return of Mr. Perkins. Evie had never seen a married couple act like that. Her closest examples were her own parents and the married society members, all of whom had found love again relatively late in life and were well aware of their good fortune. Out of everyone at the shop, Evie admired Grace the most, with her intrepid mind and an inner stoicism that reminded Evie of her former employer, Frances Knight.

It was clear to Evie that the 11th Earl Baskin also admired Grace. On more than one occasion, Evie had looked down from the third-floor window and caught sight of Lord Baskin and Grace sitting together on a bench in front of the shop, sipping coffee and laughing easily together. Like Evie and Ash, Grace and Lord Baskin also came from very different backgrounds, even though they had both been born and reared on British soil. But they struck Evie as temperamentally similar in their solicitude for others and matching reserve about themselves.

These qualities were not remotely shared by Alec or Vivien, whom Evie had also been watching. Grace often referred to the feuding colleagues as unfortunate twins, and tonight the tension between them was at a fever pitch as they openly received the attentions of Guggenheim and Beckett, respectively. Ironically, Guggenheim's palpable attraction to Alec was helping Evie stay calm about the unmistakable interest Guggenheim was also showing in Ash. Openly flirting with one man in front of others was foreign enough to Evie that she couldn't begin to imagine showing such overt and simultaneous attention to *two*.

And then there was Ash himself. He often made a point of mentioning to Evie how different the two of them were. Yet it was obvious to Evie that they, too, were similar—at least in the ways that she believed mattered most. Evie especially related to Ash's career disappointments after seeing her own years of hard, solitary work lose out to Stuart Wesley's one-upmanship and Christenson's disinterest in someone as plain and uninteresting as her.

Next to Mimi, Ash was the only other person in whom Evie had confided her recent academic betrayals, but she wanted to share more than that with him. Being with Ash made her feel both content and strangely stirred up. In this curious emotional state, she was discovering new things about herself: in particular, how nice it was to not always do everything on her own. When she walked about London or dined without Ash, she missed the interesting observations he made by her side. Most of all, she loved hearing about India—about his love for a country that she had never seen, and that he had paradoxically come to believe he must leave.

Evie couldn't picture India at all—everything was a jumble of cinema newsreels during the war and the old maps and atlases she had discovered in the shop. She realised that in being so preoccupied with objects right in front of her, she had missed out on some of the romance and beauty of the world. Until now, she had had no yearning to travel. England had plenty enough books to keep her busy for a lifetime. But Ash had his own film reel in his head of a whole other set of images, a sensory collection that was unique to him. For the first time in her life, Evie wanted to understand, as much as her own mind, the inner workings of someone else's as well.

She loved the way Ash's mind worked, so precise and yet so wide. He knew every flower and tree that they passed. He could give everything a name, and not in the pejorative way that Vivien did. Ash made the world feel so expansive to Evie, for all that London's cramped streets and towering buildings often obscured the sky. There were over a million known species of insects in the world, and Ash wanted to learn each and every one of them. In this singular focus, he and Evie were perhaps most similar of all.

Evie wondered about India and what life there must be like. Perhaps one day she would even get to visit there herself. The thought would never have occurred to her before now, but she wouldn't be the first person to want to see a new corner of the world because of someone they had met. Evie thought of Jane Wells Webb and her forgotten novels, the marriage to the much older and crippled botanist John Loudon, and her subsequent career as a gardening writer partly to complement his interests. Marriage back then could not make space for two entirely separate existences of endeavour, but surely times had changed. Surely there was a way to combine career and marriage, if two people loved and respected each other enough.

Evie surprised herself at this sudden wish on her part and glanced about the room in embarrassment. Feeling the heat coming back to her cheeks, she recalled the first time she had met Ash, in the doorway to Mr. Dutton's office as he lay flat and immobile on the floor. Her cheeks had reddened then, too. Initially she had assumed that everything was of a piece with the confusion of the moment. But subsequent meetings with Ash had only increased the strange ache she experienced whenever she was around him.

Evie wondered if anyone else could tell how she felt about Ash. She was not used to having strong emotions that she couldn't hide.

Her fervid resentment towards the Cambridge contingent that had ruined her career was the closest she had come to that. Until now, Evie had been internally driven by self-appointed tasks, deadlines, and goals. Here was something provoking her emotions from the outside, beyond her control, and causing a reaction that she had never experienced before.

As she observed the pairs of mismatched adults before her, Evie wondered at everyone's willingness to telegraph their desires through silent signalling. Evie couldn't even articulate to herself what she wanted, let alone pull off such subtle—and unsubtle— flirting as that. London society life took the quiet cloistered existence of Cambridge academia and spun it on its head in such dizzying fashion. People in the city were much more transparent about what they wanted. Ambition was not frowned upon—work in and of itself did not need to be the sole reward, and money and fame were allowed to be. Samuel Beckett did not bow humbly before his audience; neither, for that matter, did Lady Browning.

Isn't that why we come? To find things we can't find anywhere else?

Ash had asked Evie this, the first time they had talked. Surely, there was no shame in wanting more, for all the men of Cambridge and Bloomsbury Books had tried to teach her otherwise. They promised vague rewards if she just stayed in her place and did what was expected, until they failed to deliver, at which point it was too late. Evie could see now that London would always reward the risk-takers and rule-breakers instead. This gave moments such as tonight a full-throttle energy: the feeling that anything could happen between any two people, with just the slightest inclination.

CHAPTER THIRTY-ONE

RULE No. 4

Staff fealty to the shop and its management must
be total and unwavering.

The audience was gone.

No one had approached the guest of honour at the end of the evening for a private word or two—everyone in the room had been far too intimidated by him. Beckett now leaned casually against the lectern while Guggenheim regaled the staff of Bloomsbury Books and her earlier drinking companions with tales from her own bookshop days. Vivien was fascinated by the dynamic of the two former lovers—when one withdrew, the other became more dominant. Du Maurier had earlier confided in Vivien what she knew of Beckett and Guggenheim's long-ago affair in Paris: "Four days they stayed in that room at the Ritz and only opened the door once—for a tray of sandwiches!"

From the moment Beckett and Guggenheim had entered Bloomsbury Books, the air of dust and stale books had transformed into something warm and invasive. Whereas the former lovers displayed towards each other an almost taunting, sibling-like energy, their attention to others was anything but. Vivien could tell Peggy Guggenheim was captivated by Alec's blond choirboy looks and solicitous manner as he worked hard to charm the night's special guests. Vivien wondered at Guggenheim's total freedom, which exceeded even that of Lady Browning, who was, after all, a married woman. Guggenheim had been divorced twice already and was rumoured to have had dozens, even hundreds, of lovers over the years. Vivien found herself unusually in awe. She had never met a woman who appeared to care less about what other people thought.

Guggenheim was telling them all about her unpaid internship thirty years ago at a Manhattan bookshop called the Sunwise Turn. "Which dear Nelson bought, of course, once it turned insolvent."

Guggenheim looked over at Ellen Doubleday upon mentioning her late husband. Vivien was starting to get the feeling that everyone in Manhattan—or at least everyone rich—somehow knew each other.

"It was a shop quite like this," continued Guggenheim, "but fully owned and operated by women."

Vivien looked quickly at Grace and then back at Peggy. "Really?"

"Oh, yes. And we published, too."

Evie's eyes widened perceptibly, and she took a small step forward in her eagerness. "Did you own your own press?"

"Absolutely!" Peggy turned to the room to laughingly add, "We had *many* machines to replace men."

Several of the women laughed back in recollection of the recent furor in this very same room over "The Doll."

"We printed poetry, essays, from anywhere in the world—a lovely Indian gentleman called Coomaraswamy"—Peggy Guggenheim turned to look suggestively at Ash—"even a gallery and performance space. This is where my fascination with modern art really took off, as these things don't just grow on trees." She gave a delightfully wicked laugh. "The women at Sunwise, like myself, always took on too much."

"Dr. Ananda Coomaraswamy," Ash spoke up. "He was actually from Ceylon originally. His father was a Tamil Brahmin, as was mine."

"And his mother was white, from Kent, as I seem to recall." Guggenheim now gave Ash a look of unabashed interest while the rest of the staff turned to him in astonishment at his choosing such a public moment to start sharing anything of his life.

"He graduated from University College with degrees in geology and botany," Ash continued, again to the other staff members' surprise. "Founded the Geological Survey of Ceylon. I have some of his earlier papers in the basement."

"How fascinating," Guggenheim said.

Beckett shook his head behind her, finally looking amused. "Marguerite, you could not be less fascinated by plants and rocks."

Guggenheim looked about the room. "He is the only one I let call me by my birth name. But it comes at a price, doesn't it, Sam?"

Beckett shook his head again and motioned to Alec to refill his whisky. Vivien was enjoying the spectacle of the recently reinstated head of fiction doing everything he could to salvage the evening, while Beckett remained singularly uninterested in him. Vivien did not think Alec would be invited to head out afterwards with Beckett for a nightcap, as Alec had done with so many other male authors in years past.

She wondered if an invitation might be forthcoming to *her*, however, in his stead.

From the second-floor window, Alec watched Vivien and Beckett on the pavement below, their heads bent together in intimate conversation. The gathering of widows and social rivals to whom Alec had looked forward for amusement was still milling about on the second floor, drinking merrily, but mostly amused by him.

"I suspect you've made a muck-up there," a woman's voice said from behind.

Alec turned around to see Peggy Guggenheim standing there, twisting the double strand of pearls about her neck in a taunting manner. "Miss Lowry has a mind of her own."

"I doubt *that* was the problem."

"We're just very competitive with each other at work."

"Are you sure that's what you're competing over?"

He started at her words, then looked back down at the street below. "What are you implying?"

Guggenheim stopped twirling her pearls long enough to take a sip of her champagne. "I hear she has many talents."

"I'll say."

"And you—do you have many?"

Alec's head started to pain him. He was not interested in bedding Peggy Guggenheim. Once again, he had been using the attentions of a wealthy shop visitor to make Vivien Lowry jealous. Instead, all it had done was drive her into the arms of one of the world's most enigmatic Irish storytellers and Resistance heroes: a double-barrelled threat to Alec's masculinity if ever there was one.

"What's a man like you really doing working in a shop? Surely you have writerly ambitions of your own?"

Alec turned back from the window to stare at Guggenheim, worried she could read his mind.

"That *is* usually the case, isn't it?" Guggenheim said pointedly. "Unless one is old and decrepit, and life has somehow passed you by. And that's certainly not you."

She put her hand out to rest it just slightly on Alec's arm. He responded by subtly leaning away to place his empty champagne glass on the ledge of the window frame.

Peggy must have picked up on his lack of interest, because immediately her entire demeanour changed. "Well, I guess we could call tonight a qualified success, on all fronts."

"Beckett certainly left them guessing."

She leaned forward to join Alec in looking down at the pavement below, where Vivien and the playwright stood closely together in animated conversation.

"He still is." Winking at Alec, Guggenheim returned to the roomful of women who had been amusedly watching the two of them.

Alec was now left in peace to observe the goings-on below: how Vivien leaned back against the old gas lamppost while Beckett had his left, writing arm stretched out and resting just above her head. Beckett was taller than Vivien by a good couple of inches, putting him nearer to Alec's height, and enabling him to look down at his potential conquest in a most intimate way.

Alec's jealousy was increasing by the minute. His feelings for Vivien had been all over the place of late. The incident with the watch and Vivien's one month as manager had strangely equalized things between them, enough so that they had succumbed yet again to the intense physical attraction that they hid behind their simmering insolence towards each other. After the du Maurier event, they had heard the footsteps running away as they made love in the back office, and they knew that someone on staff also knew about their temporary giving in. Alec had yet to determine who it was, although he had his suspicions. Then, due to his own childish game-playing, Vivien had inadvertently discovered how he had gained publication at her expense. She had immediately gone back to treating him like the enemy, and his heart had been broken all over again.

"Why don't you go down and talk to her?" a different female voice now asked.

Alec sighed at the prospect of having his love life analyzed by another meddling widow or divorcée, but when he turned around, he was startled to see that it was only Evie Stone.

Only Evie Stone was how the men at the shop often referred to its newest employee, who arrived promptly at work each morning and headed straight for the third-floor Rare Books Department. After that, she would be spotted only occasionally during the day, usually when making tea with Vivien or Grace.

"I'm sorry?" Alec asked, surprised by Evie's trying to initiate conversation with him, something she hadn't done before. He always got the feeling that she didn't quite trust him.

"You keep watching through the window."

"I just want to make sure that she gets home safely—that Mr. Beckett stays the gentleman."

Evie's eyes narrowed at him, and he saw that he didn't fool her one bit.

"Do you like her?" she asked instead.

So she had been the one to see them in the office that night. "Look, Miss Stone, it's not like in your books, all those women authors and romances and the like. Sometimes people simply don't care for each other. It doesn't have to mean anything more than that."

"What don't you like about Vivien?"

"I think it's more a question of her not liking *me*."

"Why?"

Alec stared down at Evie, at the penetrating coal-black eyes and innocent expression on the very young face. She looked nowhere near her stated age of twenty, with those pinkish cheeks of girlhood, bitten fingernails, and scuffed toes to the schoolgirl boots.

"Because I've messed up sometimes, like everyone. And I've apologized repeatedly, too. But nothing will ever be enough for Miss Lowry. And *that* is what I don't like about *her*."

"That sounds like pride, as my mother would say."

"How so?"

"You think your apology—your word—is enough. Not your actions. That's pride."

"Well, I'm certainly not going to beg her."

Evie shook her head. "I doubt that's what Vivien wants."

"That's the problem." Alec sighed again, starting to relax from the champagne and despite Evie's inquisitive gaze. "I have no idea what she really wants. I don't know what to do with her."

Evie shrugged, as if to say that it wasn't up to him. "She's a person, Mr. McDonough, no better and certainly no worse. Like you said yourself, she's not a character in a book."

He could only stare at Evie now, letting her abrupt, unfiltered words sink in as she wandered away. The last person from whom he would ever have expected advice on love would be Evie Stone. At that very notion, he grabbed his coat from the stand and left the party before there could be any further meddling from the women in the room.

L ady Browning, Ellen Doubleday, Peggy Guggenheim, Sonia Blair, Grace, and Evie were now the only people left on the second floor of Bloomsbury Books.

"All that nonsense up there—that not caring about the audience and such," Lady Browning was saying to the group, nodding at the empty lectern behind them.

"My old boss Cyril Connolly would agree," replied Sonia. "He once famously said, 'Better to write for yourself and have no public, than to write for the public and have no self.'"

"Surely there's a middle way?" a new voice called out. All of the women turned in unison to see Vivien standing in the doorway, smiling. "Ladies only?"

Peggy Guggenheim clapped her hands together. "Oh, I'd love to have seen his face when you declined," she said mirthfully. "He's so rarely turned down. The perks of fame."

Here Lady Browning nodded quite vigorously on her own behalf. "No argument there."

"Although male writers are a breed apart," added Ellen Doubleday.

"Writers in general, I should think," observed Guggenheim. "A piffling, insecure lot."

"Absolutely," agreed Ellen. "The number of disastrous dinner parties Nelson put me through. Excepting your presence, Daphne, of course."

"Now artists," Guggenheim continued, "they're the opposite of insecure. Far too Übermensch instead. But undeniably powerful in bed."

Grace and Vivien both turned to look at Evie, knowing she would be blushing at the reference, but the young girl appeared too stunned and captivated by Guggenheim to react.

"If you're all finished . . ." Vivien said with a laugh, then waited as the other ladies quieted down. "He didn't want to bed me—I'm sorry, Evie, *seduce me*—although I suppose that's always in the cards with someone like him."

"What on earth could he have wanted, then?" Peggy Guggenheim wondered aloud before more politely adding, "*If* you'll forgive my asking."

"He wanted to . . . *mentor* me. Oh, I see the looks on your faces. But apparently Lady Browning showed him my writing over drinks earlier tonight. I knew I should have asked for that notebook back."

Lady Browning made a gesture of blamelessness while she refilled her champagne glass from the silver tray on the desk. "I'm not sure I'd have ever been published without Sir Arthur Quiller-

Couch and his own advice. Don't look a gift horse in the mouth, as they say. Or, frankly, anywhere else."

"Well, that's not what young Mr. McDonough thinks was going on. Or"—here Peggy Guggenheim's dark eyes lit up in mischief—"was that part of the point?"

"Well, anyway," Vivien said in a more serious tone, "that's not actually why I came back up. The Sunwise Turn," she stated simply, turning to Guggenheim. "Tell us more."

"What would you like to know? We were all unpaid, swept floors, and sold thousands of books. And made a lot of tea. Not, I suspect, much different from any of you. Although they only allowed me and my lousy math near the till at noon, when it was quiet." Guggenheim grinned at the memory. "But we learned a lot, at a young age, when one has the time to. I wouldn't have had my own gallery on Cork Street without that experience."

As Guggenheim spoke, Grace felt her age. "I've been doing the exact same thing over and over for years."

"Which is . . . ?" asked Guggenheim.

"Essentially typing up the general manager's words."

"How scintillating," Lady Browning piped up.

"I started that way at *Horizon,*" Sonia Blair offered. "But I was lucky—Cyril Connolly loved women in the best of ways. Both Clarissa Spencer-Churchill and myself nearly had the run of the place by the end. Of course"—George Orwell's widow gave a self-deprecating, almost melancholy laugh—"it did just bust up, for what it's worth."

The women all laughed back.

"How much, though, would it take, I mean really? To run one's own shop?" Vivien looked at Guggenheim intently.

"What you want to do is build on something existing. It's the initial layout that's the greatest expense. The space, the shelving, the building up of inventory. You'll take a loss for a good year or two after all that." Guggenheim gave Vivien a sympathetic look before checking her watch. "I am afraid I do need to get going. Early train back to Venice tomorrow."

"May I have your card?" Evie asked Guggenheim, and Vivien and Grace both looked over at her in surprise.

"Why of course. You must look me up, if you ever get to Venice. You can come see my collection on the Grand Canal."

"Oh, I think she'll get to India first," Vivien said with a wink at Evie, who stared back as if the thought had never occurred to her.

Peggy Guggenheim pulled her gloves on slowly while watching Evie's face redden, then smiled suggestively. "Ah, now I see."

"I was born in India. In Calcutta," Sonia announced as she went to retrieve her coat from the nearby stand. "Eric, too, in what was then called Bengal. We both moved to England very young. It feels like a thousand years ago and a million miles away from this. It must be very hard for Mr. Ramaswamy to be so far from his family."

"What's it like?" Evie asked, while Vivien and Grace silently smiled at each other over her head.

"To my child's mind, it was so big and open, and as busy as a kaleidoscope. Yet everything felt shrouded in the absence of colour, in faded, empty white. Eric would have called it the air of oppression. He returned years later to work in Burma and came to despise the colonial order and how it controls people. I can see what he was talking about, although I would never presume to understand it like he or, more importantly, they did. Well, I must be off, too, I'm afraid."

The four female guests of Bloomsbury Books headed downstairs, hailed three cabs together to go off in only two different directions, then rearranged themselves laughingly as they realised their mistake. After waving from inside the shop as the cabs sped off, Vivien locked the vestibule doors before heading back upstairs with Grace and Evie to clean up.

"Those questions, about that Sunwise shop," Grace asked Vivien as they brought two trays of champagne saucers down to the kitchen to wash and put away, leaving Evie to stay behind to tidy up the second floor. "What was that about?"

"I've just had it up to here, haven't you? Nothing is ever going to change. There'll always be Mr. Allen missing in action, Master Mariner Scott biting off our heads, and Ash alone with his little microscope slides and bugs, not that anyone can blame *him*. And Mr. Dutton—the sweetest man, but not one to ever change even the few hairs on his head. Besides, he clearly shouldn't be back at work. The man looks positively yellow."

Vivien turned off the hot-water tap and banged the spout with the heel of her hand. "And here we are, washing up after the lot, making their tea just the way they like it, and selling out from under them every single time. Alec doesn't even have the decency to help out after his own failed event."

"We can always leave."

"Can we? Can you?"

Grace chose to ignore the pointed meaning of Vivien's words. "What do you propose, then? Starting a shop of our own? You heard Miss Guggenheim. I can't afford to live without income for even a few months, let alone take a loss."

"That night when Gordon came here, and Lord Baskin and I had that talk I later told you about . . ."

"Yes . . ." Grace replied absentmindedly as she finished drying off the last saucer.

"I felt like . . . I don't know . . . I felt like he was challenging me—challenging us—in a way."

They each took a tray of cleaned glasses and headed for the sparsely stocked liquor cabinet in Mr. Dutton's office.

"Challenging us to do what? To leave?" Grace knelt in front of the cabinet to put the glasses back in their place.

Vivien shook her head. "No, it was more subtle than that. You know all that talk about Mr. Allen and Mr. Dutton getting close to owning a majority of the shares together? A little over fifty, at fifty quid each?"

Closing the cabinet doors, Grace stood up and wearily leaned against Mr. Dutton's desk. Its entire surface was covered in neatly arranged piles of correspondence still awaiting his response in the wake of Alec's chaotic tenure.

"Baskin said they could buy him out for less than three thousand pounds." Vivien raised her right eyebrow at Grace suggestively.

Looking down at her hands folded in her lap, Grace started twisting about the simple plain wedding band on her left ring finger.

"What is it?" Vivien asked.

"I really shouldn't be saying anything, but Lord Baskin told me something tonight at the Russell. The real reason he called the *two* of us there for cocktails. Nothing to do with your meddling." Grace hesitated. "Now don't blow a gasket, but apparently Alec has already approached Lord Baskin about buying the shop himself."

"How? I mean, why? Why on earth would he want to be tied down like that?"

Grace raised an eyebrow back at Vivien. "It couldn't have something to do with you, could it?"

"With me?"

"Things between the two of you do seem awfully tense of late."

"But they've been awful for years . . . and besides, what about Mr. Dutton? And Frank? Why would Alec want to ruin their plans like this, when they've been like fathers to him?" Vivien stopped herself as if in recollection. "Oh, for goodness sake, that prig."

Grace exhaled deeply. "What a mess."

"Well, he can't buy it if we get to it first."

"Vivien, dear, wherever would we get that kind of money? And why would Lord Baskin sell to *us,* even if we did?"

Vivien shrugged. "Baskin doesn't seem too attached to any of this. At best he's popping by out of some misplaced sense of noblesse oblige. I doubt that's even the half of it."

Ignoring the intimation in Vivien's voice, Grace fiddled with the cuffs of her long blouse, which she had rolled up while doing the dishwashing.

"Are we going to talk about it?" Vivien asked gently, nodding at Grace's left forearm.

"Talk about what?"

"I saw, Grace. Your wrist. When we were washing up."

Grace shook her head dismissively. "It's fine."

"Has he struck you before?"

Grace looked at her in disbelief. "He didn't strike me."

Vivien stood there, waiting.

"He just grabbed me a little too hard, and it left a bruise. Don't look at me like that."

"Has he grabbed you before, then?"

Grace hesitated. "I can manage it. He's having a hard time."

"He's always having a hard time, Grace."

Grace turned away to sigh at the sight of all the papers on Mr. Dutton's desk. "There's so much work to do."

"Yes. We can blow it up, or we can start chipping away at it. But we need to start doing *something.*"

Grace gave a rueful smile. "I know what you want to do, Viv. About the shop. And about Gordon, too. Or even Alec, for that matter. I know you'd be more than happy to blow it all up. It's just not my way."

Vivien came forward and placed her hand gently on Grace's other arm. "Then start chipping away at it. Get everything in order.

Get a plan. He has a mother still, and somewhere to go. For that matter, so do you. It'll only get worse, trust me."

"And then what? I can't raise the boys alone on my salary here or anywhere else, not the way we women get paid. Gordon's stipend barely helps as it is."

"If we have our own shop, then we get to make the rules. *And* the salaries."

"Viv, I can live with the status quo. What I can't afford to do is end things only to make them worse."

"Desperate people—and Gordon looks that—will always force an ending on you, just never the one you're hoping for. With our own business, we'd at least have a chance for *that*. Grace"—Vivien squeezed her arm affectionately—"you know what you need to do."

"I liked it better when we were planning a takeover." Grace sighed.

There was the sound of a slight cough. Both women turned to see Evie standing in the office doorway, with the strangest look on her face.

"I think I can help" was all she said.

CHAPTER THIRTY-TWO

RULE NO. 37

Any error in stock or pricing shall be promptly reported.

Vivien and Grace followed Evie back up to the second floor. Vivien took a seat in Master Mariner Scott's well-worn armchair, shaking her head in amusement at Evie's grave demeanour. The young girl walked the length of the room towards the front street windows, removed a single, slender leather volume from a high set of shelves, and then just as solemnly returned. Without a word, she carefully held the book open to both Vivien and Grace to display the title page:

THE MUMMY!

A TALE
OF THE TWENTY-SECOND CENTURY.

"Why hast thou disquieted me, to bring me up?"
1 SAM., xxviii. 15.

IN THREE VOLUMES.
VOL. I.

LONDON:
HENRY COLBURN, NEW BURLINGTON STREET.
1827.

Taking a hesitant step forward, Evie handed the volume to Vivien, while Grace leaned over the back of Scott's chair in her eagerness to see. Vivien gently turned several of the pages before looking up at Evie, who was almost bursting with satisfaction as she stood there before them.

"So it's fiction then, and not history? Typical Allen. No wonder you had trouble finding it." Vivien continued to flip through the pages. "It looks like an imitation of *Frankenstein*. Is it any good?"

"They think it might be one of the very first science fiction novels ever written. It was completely forgotten about and only reprinted once, cheaply, in 1872. Until a few years ago, all the catalogues missed it." Here Evie turned slightly less satisfied with herself. "Well, all the catalogues except one. The book's apparently quite prescient about the future, with talk of railways, telegrams, electricity—even a form of television! *And* a female dynastic reign."

Vivien's face lit up.

"There's no name on it, though," Grace noticed. "Do they have any idea who wrote it?"

"A seventeen-year-old girl."

"You're joking!" cried Vivien.

Evie shook her head happily. She lived for moments like this. "Her name was Jane Webb. She became Jane Loudon, the—"

"—the gardening expert! Yes, how fantastic!" exclaimed Vivien.

"You knew about this?" Grace said in astonishment, leaning down over Vivien's shoulder to get a closer look.

Vivien closed the book in her hands and held it back out to Evie, who went to return it to its exact place on the shelves.

"Not really, just that Evie was up to something, snooping around the other departments . . ."

"How did you even know it was here?" Grace called out to Evie. "From your research at Cambridge?"

"Before that," Evie replied as she came back from the other

end of the room. "While I was cataloguing the library in Chawton, at the Great House there. This book was in the collection, but it looked like all the other second-rate Gothic tales on the shelves, and we valued it accordingly. When the contents of the library came up for auction at Sotheby's, Mr. Allen bought this and four other nineteenth-century texts for just a few dozen pounds. I kept a record of the sales."

"I bet you did," replied Vivien.

"Wait, so is that why you showed up here in the first place? You were looking for it all along?" Grace asked.

Evie nodded, again well pleased with herself.

Vivien laughed. "What did Allen bid for it in the end?"

"Twenty pounds. The reserve value. No one else bid."

"Any idea of the real value?" asked Grace.

"Right now, based on similar sales, I'd say a few hundred pounds at least, maybe five hundred." Evie watched as both Vivien's and Grace's expressions fell a bit. "Given its singular place in literary history, that amount should be much higher, but renewed appreciation has only just begun, primarily in the States."

"And one mustn't forget the sex of the author in these things." Vivien sighed. "Well, Evie, it's not life-changing money by any means. And Mr. Allen's pencilled-in price here, of thirty pounds— that's weeks of wages for you. I guess you could always nick it."

"Oh, no, miss. I hope you'd never suspect me of something like *that*." Evie looked stricken.

"No, of course not"—Vivien laughed disarmingly—"although you are certainly full of surprises."

"The key is to have the market properly recognise it," Grace interjected thoughtfully.

"Without being blinded by the sex of the author," added Vivien.

"Yes!" said Evie excitedly. "Remember what Miss Guggenheim told us tonight, about Berthe Morisot? How back in the 1800s her paintings were valued even higher than Monet's or Pissarro's?"

"Men." Vivien sighed again.

"This book should be worth at least a thousand pounds. The first American literary review of the one abridged edition was just last spring—I think it's only a matter of time before someone over here catches on. It was written a full century before we even had a word for science fiction, *that's* how far ahead of its time it was."

"Evie, I am most impressed," Grace said admiringly. "But whatever got into your head to go searching for it in the first place?"

"My research work at Cambridge. There was a reference to it in a letter by Thackeray that I came across at Trinity College."

"And you say an American journal has reviewed an abridged copy of the book?"

Evie nodded. "Just this past year."

Grace turned to Vivien. "How much did Lord Baskin say it'd take, to buy him out? Three thousand pounds?"

"Twenty-five hundred plus a few quid would get us majority control." Vivien quickly explained to Evie her recent talk with the earl and the current majority shareholder structure that could soon topple in favour of Dutton and Allen. "Evie, if we pool our money, do you think Mr. Allen would sell the book at cost?"

"You said twenty pounds was the reserve price at the auction, right?" asked Grace.

Looking back and forth between the two women, Evie nodded wordlessly, still trying to digest all the new information she was learning about the finances of the shop.

"Okay," Vivien said thoughtfully. "Let's try to raise the twenty quid together, and then Evie can buy the book on our behalf. They'll never suspect *her*."

"Mr. Dutton will never allow it." Grace sighed. "Rule twenty-five implicitly prohibits employee purchases."

Vivien bit her lip in concentration. "Damn those rules. Okay. Give me time to think. With the book misfiled here under Scott's one good eye, nothing will happen in the meantime. Then, once we own it, Evie can safekeep it for us until we figure out next steps. Deal?"

Evie looked at the two women, their faces full of excitement at the idea of taking over the shop. Although Vivien in particular might have no qualms about buying the book out from under their employer, Evie was discomfited by the notion. Mr. Dutton had hired her based in part on this very knowledge of rare books that she was being paid to exercise, and she remained mindful of rule twenty-four: *not using knowledge acquired in the course of employment for personal gain or benefit.* Evie understood Vivien's and Grace's frustrations at work and commiserated with their feelings of being undervalued and overlooked. But Evie was still not sure that the male management deserved to lose their shop out of it, despite her having experienced much the same frustrations at Cambridge and elsewhere in life.

For now, Evie kept this silent, nagging worry to herself. When she had first set out to find *The Mummy!,* she could not have foreseen Mr. Dutton and his ironclad rules. Her compulsive and literal nature tended naturally towards obedience—people like Stuart Wesley had taken advantage of that often enough. Evie felt loyalty to the man who had hired her, and whose obvious poor health had weighed on her ever since. The question now was how she could heed her employer and still help Vivien and Grace get what they most wanted: his overthrow.

CHAPTER THIRTY-THREE

RULE No. 26

No personal visits shall take place on the premises of the shop.

"W hy, hello."

Vivien looked up from behind the cash counter where she stood slouching, leaning on her elbows for support. She now rarely left the square confines of her station. This was in open defiance of Alec, who wanted her to continue to walk the floor as she had so successfully done during his brief tenure as acting general manager, driving up sales as a result.

"Good day, sir. How may I be of help?" Vivien asked in a rehearsed and muted tone.

The gentleman looked to be about forty, with a playful smile and keenly intelligent eyes. He was extremely well-dressed and somewhat short, so that Vivien—who in heels fell just a few inches shy of six feet—had to look down at him.

"I am looking for a Miss Evelyn Stone." He smiled winningly.

Vivien looked at him in surprise. "Rare Books. Via Dolorosa. Right this way."

He gave a sharp, confident laugh as they headed towards the front staircase. "You nicknamed the stairs—how delightful."

Reaching the open landing to the third-floor Rare Books Department, Vivien spotted Evie sitting as usual on her little stool near Mr. Allen's desk, a thick catalogue in her lap.

"This gentleman is here to see you, Miss Stone," Vivien announced formally, giving a respectful nod at the stranger standing behind her.

"Yardley!" Evie exclaimed with uncharacteristic excitement. She rushed over to shake the man's hand just as he bent to kiss her right cheek, causing them to knock their heads together and then laugh comfortably in unison. The man made a contrite face before finally pulling her in for a hug.

"You must forgive the informality. It's been far too long," he said in apology as he stepped back.

"Vivien, this is Mr. Yardley Sinclair, of Sotheby's."

A look of recognition passed across Vivien's face. "From the Jane Austen Society? That saved the house?"

The gentleman laughed. "Of sorts. Have you been taking good care of Evie here? You'll not find a harder worker."

"She is indeed that." Vivien winked knowingly at Evie. "Shall I make you both a spot of tea? All the better for catching up."

Yardley watched Vivien disappear down the stairs. "Via Dolorosa."

Evie laughed. "Vivien despises it here. She has a name for everything."

"The path to sadness . . ." he muttered as he looked about the floor. "My goodness, what a state this place is in. I knew Frank had been . . . preoccupied of late."

"It's fine. I like being alone up here all day."

"I am sure you do." Yardley ran his long, delicate fingers along the spines of a nearby set of books in a familiar manner. "Your mother's been wanting you home for a visit."

"I just, um, needed to get my bearings first, in the city."

He turned to survey her face carefully. "Evie, are you wearing lipstick? Mimi would be so proud!"

"Only a little. Yardley, why ever are you here?"

He walked over to Mr. Allen's desk and flipped through one of the many warehouse catalogues before looking back at her.

"I thought it was high time one of us paid you a visit. We were all surprised to learn from Adeline that you'd left Cambridge. Everything all right there?"

Evie nodded but she didn't hide her dismay from him. She never could.

"Ah, I wondered as much. Tell your old friend, hmm?" He motioned for Evie to sit down, and she obligingly returned to her little stool before answering him.

"I lost out on a research position to another student."

"A Stuart Wesley, by any chance?"

Evie's mouth fell open in astonishment. "How on earth do you know that?"

Yardley walked behind Mr. Allen's desk and pulled out his chair. "Hopefully Frank won't mind. May I?" He sat down and she noticed his always-inquisitive eyes travel over the many papers scattered about the desk. "It seems a Mr. Wesley, of Jesus College, Cambridge, has been looking into the Chawton Great House auction records of late."

"I'm sorry—what?"

Yardley nodded. "I caught wind of it from one of my assistants, who requested my permission to share information on a particular sale with this Mr. Wesley. A single book, in three volumes. With the strangest subtitle."

Evie's heart sank. She knew it before he even said it.

The Mummy!" she replied with a sigh.

She had always hoped her research process would somehow stay safe from Stuart Wesley's prying eyes, given how fundamentally lazy he was. She had obviously missed something with him yet again: the degree to which his ambition superseded his notable shortcomings. He must have found the letter from Thackeray that was referenced in her early research for Professor Kinross and then noticed a pattern with her other findings. Anyone motivated enough to examine her withdrawal history from the British Museum, as well as various Cambridge institutions, could have deduced her inordinate interest in *The Mummy!* and started retracing her steps from there. Evie recalled with new relief how Stuart, safe in the flush of his social success at the Chelsea Arts Mardi Gras Ball, had not pushed her for more detail on her lowly life as a girl in a shop.

"My goodness, yes!" exclaimed Yardley. "Now how on earth did *you* know *that*? Has he been here?"

"No, not yet. But knowing Wesley, it's only a matter of time. Will you be telling him who bought the book?"

Yardley spoke carefully in the face of her obvious distress. "Our auctions are an open event, but with highly valued retailers such as Mr. Allen, we have a gentleman's agreement to never disclose a buyer's identity without their permission first."

It was all becoming clear to Evie now. "Which is why you are here."

"In a way. I could always simply write or telephone Frank. But I really did want to see you, Evie. To make sure you were okay."

Evie thought of Yardley and Adam Berwick, with their little joint tenancy on the outskirts of Chawton, and all the other people she had left behind in the small village where she had grown up. Just seeing Yardley was making her miss home. No one there, at least, was trying to ruin her life.

"So, you will be asking Mr. Allen regardless?"

"I'm afraid I have to. Company policy."

"What if he says yes?"

Yardley stood without answering her as Vivien appeared in the doorway with the tray set for tea in her hands. She watched in surprise as Yardley came over to take it from her.

"Miss Stone and I don't stand on ceremony, not even here." Smiling graciously, he went and placed the tray down on the one clear space left on Mr. Allen's desk.

Vivien gave Evie an approving glance from behind Yardley, then headed back downstairs as the odd-looking couple sat down together on either side of the desk.

"I'll of course do my best to manage the situation with Mr. Wesley." Yardley poured the tea thoughtfully. "Although I have to wonder, what could be his pressing interest in such an obscure book?"

Evie knew that it was time to tell Yardley everything, despite his professional obligations to Sotheby's. It was her only chance to enlist his help in throwing Stuart Wesley off her trail. She told Yardley all about *The Mummy!,* stumbling across the reference in the letter by Thackeray, the missed entry in Block's *The English Novel, 1740–1850* and the recent American review, and the potential significance of a seventeen-year-old orphaned girl writing one of the first science fiction novels in the history of the world.

At first, Yardley covered his face in his hands and moaned rather dramatically at having missed all this himself. He then looked up and shook his head at the young woman in his usual impish way.

"My goodness, Evie, you've done it again. The Great House library and now *this.* Two such exemplary discoveries on the margins of academia. No one can ever overlook your abilities again— I'll see to that." His face turned serious, almost stern. "But the next time anyone tries to interfere with your promotion, you must let me know."

Evie nodded gravely. "I think I've learned my lesson when it comes to that."

"To that end, my dear, is there anything else you'd like to tell me, while I am here?"

She hesitated before quietly replying, "I think I met someone."

Yardley put the creamer jug down to stare at her. "Oh, Evie, how wonderful. Is he nice?"

She nodded. "He's the nicest man I've ever met. Besides Mr. Berwick, of course." She missed the look of pride on Yardley's face at Adam's name. "Smart. A little reserved."

Yardley laughed so uproariously that Evie had to join in with a smile.

"I shouldn't think it otherwise. You two must make quite the pair."

Evie took a sip of her tea in silence, then held the warm cup and saucer in both hands as she debated what else to tell him.

"How did you meet?"

"He works here, actually, in the shop. He's the head of the Science and Naturalism Department."

"Mr. Ramaswamy? Mr. Ramaswamy from downstairs?" An unrecognizable look now passed across Yardley's face.

"You don't approve?"

"Oh, my dear, no, not at all. I am very happy for you. It's just that I . . . I know what it is like."

"You do?"

He was watching her carefully and choosing his words equally so. "In a way. People don't like it when we do what's not expected, what's not usual. The *unknown*. It scares them, I think, that latitude and freedom so often missing from their own lives. Do the others here know?"

"I think so. I think they might have even known before me."

"Now why does *that* not surprise me!" Yardley grinned. "And Mr. Ramaswamy—does he like you?"

Yardley was looking at Evie so affectionately that she felt

herself soften inside. It made her realise how tightly wound she usually was—so tightly wound that she rarely let her guard down around anyone. Yardley, with his quickness to delight and utter disinterest in harming others, was one of the few people in the world with whom she ever truly relaxed.

"I'm not sure—how does one know?"

Yardley took a sip of his tea, then placed the cup and saucer gently down before him. "Sometimes, Evie, as hard as it is, you have to be the one to speak first. Even with—especially with—no promise of return." He reached out and patted her hand. "Now I know how bold that must sound to you."

"But what if he just likes me as a friend?"

"That's the best part, my dear—if you feel it, they almost always feel it, too." He leaned forward to teasingly add, "Although don't take my word for it. My job as an auctioneer *is,* after all, to raise expectations."

Despite the troubling news about Stuart Wesley, Evie was so happy to be visiting with Yardley again, surrounded by books. It reminded her of their times spent cataloguing the Chawton Great House library together, and the ecstatic joy they would forever share over its eventual record-breaking dispersal by Sotheby's.

Three years later, Evie had stood alone in her small flat on Castle Street, feeling the sting of Christenson's rejection, leaving the letter from her mother unopened by the threshold to the door. She had vowed at the time that she would not go back; she had done an excellent job of that so far. But this moment with Yardley was a reminder to not leave *everything* behind—to not become so focused on the future that what made you special in the first place had to be forged all over again.

Yardley had come back into her life for another reason as well. She would need to quickly warn Vivien and Grace about the other potential buyer circling out there. The three women would have to hasten their attempts to raise the purchase price in time to stop Stuart Wesley and any of his cohorts.

Evie wished she could share the women's secret plans with Ash but refused to burden him with information that could jeopardize his own job in any way. She decided to only tell him that Wesley was continuing to capitalize on research she had done while at Cambridge. As for her increasingly romantic feelings towards Ash, Evie could never be the one to speak first, despite Yardley's encouragement. She would be mortified to make her new friend uncomfortable around her in any way. She could only hope that, with time, Ash's own feelings towards her would become clear.

She could have no idea that, on both of these points, time was about to run out.

CHAPTER THIRTY-FOUR

RULE No. 31

Staff shall treat each other with pleasantness at all times.

A sh had taken to worrying about Stuart Wesley on Evie's behalf.

He had not been surprised to learn from Evie that Wesley was out in the world, secretly following her research work like a trail of breadcrumbs. During their encounter on the morning after the Chelsea Arts Ball, the young man's jocular demeanour towards Evie had struck Ash as not entirely genuine even then. Ash still wasn't sure what Evie was up to on the third floor of Bloomsbury Books—and he was keeping something from her in turn. This was complicating the protective and affectionate emotions he was increasingly feeling when it came to Evie Stone.

In addition to breakfasting together on Wednesday mornings, Ash and Evie now spent most Sundays strolling side by side along the Thames. This was their version of the very river walk that he had told her about over that first shared meal near the Natural History Museum. Ash would spend the workweek mapping out a particular section of the river for the two of them to explore, from the last nontidal stretch at Shepperton in the west all the way to just a few miles in from the sea. Knowing that Evie liked to have every step mapped out in advance, he would find the most efficient local transportation, be it bus, tube, or rail, to start and end their journey. Ash had found it best to avoid any areas of rising tidal waters that could leave a traveller stranded at certain times of the day, a risk that appeared to be of particular concern to Evie. On one of their daily chai breaks, he would then show her the map of where they were heading next. By now they had covered various stretches of the river together.

On the last Sunday in February, their plan was to meet on the south bank of Teddington and walk east towards Kew Gardens. By 2:00 p.m. they were standing by the Thames at low tide a mile down from Kew Bridge, watching as the river that drained the whole of the city left its catch of forgotten relics behind. The millennia of London life washed up on these pebbly shores: broken pieces of pottery that had belonged to the Romans, small clay pipes from Shakespeare's time, diamond-shaped shards of porcelain from the century just past.

Ash had recently introduced Evie to searching for buried treasure among the stones and mud. Expert at finding the most exquisite remnants, he now bent down to pick up a blue-and-white-painted piece of china before passing it to her.

"The survivors," Evie said with a smile. She turned the small piece about in the palm of her hand, then gently wrapped it in a handkerchief to store in her coat pocket. She had started a collection back in Charlotte's flat, keeping each and every fragment that Ash gave her in a large shortbread tin.

"More the remains," he answered her. "The parts that broke off."

Evie looked up at the note of resignation in his voice. "Is something wrong?"

He still didn't have the heart to tell her. Instead, he took her gently by the elbow and they ascended the embankment together.

At the riverside gate to Kew Gardens, Ash and Evie each put a pence in the turnstile to pass through to the park. Spring always came early to the south of England, and nowhere in London more vibrantly than here. This was the time of year when the air sweetened. Meadows of daffodils, hellebores, and snowdrops cascaded right up to the oak and birch trees that lined the young couple's way. Emerging from the canopy of the woodlands, they headed next to the Kew herbarium, with its view of the river and millions of plant specimens inside.

Ash wanted to examine the Petiver collection, which had been taken from India in the late seventeenth century, while Evie wanted to visit the library and archives also housed inside the Victorian building. She was in search of botanical drawings by a woman horticulturist named Jane Loudon, whose surname rang a bell with Ash. He remembered the first Sunday he had discovered Evie at the Natural History Museum, poring over the archives of John Loudon instead. Ash didn't press Evie further on this, however. He had learned not to press her too hard on anything, as it often made her turn silent and withdraw altogether.

Upon entering the herbarium, the two of them went their separate ways, agreeing to meet up one hour later for tea. At precisely four o'clock, Ash returned to the front entrance hall of the herbarium to find Evie deep in conversation with a much older woman. Her snow-white hair matched the laboratory coat she was wearing. Ash recalled having seen this woman before on past solo trips to Kew, although he had never tried speaking with her.

Elsie Maud Wakefield was the deputy keeper of the herbarium. She had graduated from Oxford in 1908 and been employed at Kew on and off since then, always overworked and understaffed. She had enjoyed several deserved promotions due to the absence of men at war, including becoming the head of Kew mycology in 1915. Wakefield's expertise in fungi had protected her from the fate of the women gardeners. *Their* employment by Kew Gardens during the First World War had ceased completely by 1922, until they were needed again with the outbreak of the Second.

Elsie's dark eyes, unsoftened by hesitation or too much external consideration, reminded Ash very much of Evie's own as he stood there watching the two women talking animatedly. He could picture Evie just like this one day, alone on a Sunday in a rarefied institution while families and lovers strolled the grounds outside. He didn't necessarily want such an insular life for Evie—with her tremendous capacity for loyalty and enthusiasm, Ash thought she would make an excellent helpmate to someone one day. What he didn't want to do was ruin any of that for her, or make things even one jot harder than they had to be.

"Ash, here, come."

Evie waved him over as Miss Wakefield turned to him with a boldly assessing gaze.

"Miss Wakefield has been here for *forty* years," Evie explained. "We've been discussing Blackwell's *A Curious Herbal*—we had a first edition back at the Great House library in Chawton. It sold to the British Museum."

Elsie Wakefield gave a sudden and loud snort of derision at the other institution's name.

"Miss Wakefield tells me Elizabeth Blackwell was the first woman to use your Linnaean system of organisation! Wrote her book to get her husband out of debtors' prison, no less."

Ash was surprised by Evie's sudden effusiveness, so different from how she had been those first few weeks at the shop. London must be having a real effect on her; she seemed to have taken to heart how the randomness of urban life forced people to create connections in a way that naturally existed in village life. Having to exert oneself to make such connections made them even more valuable and paradoxically less common in large academic and other structured institutions. From his own days at the University of Madras, Ash knew how easy it was to be socially lazy in such places. He wondered if he, too, could have been better at connecting while in London, despite the obvious obstacles in his way.

"Miss Stone here has been telling me all about you," Miss Wakefield stated in a loud and authoritative voice that rang through the empty central hall. "An entomologist." Everything Elsie Wakefield said was a declaration, as if she labelled the world of people along the same Linnaean lines as her specimens. "Did you find the Petiver collection?"

Ash only nodded, surprised by how intimidating he found her. He rarely felt intimidated by anyone—this was one reason why his new life in England had been so difficult to endure. He had always been the best at whatever he took on, yet desirable opportunities here remained entirely cut off from him. He felt constantly reduced in the eyes of almost everyone around him to the colour of his skin. Few seemed able to see past that, and he couldn't conceive of this ever changing. He was a pragmatist to Evie's optimist and envied her ability to overlook the reality right in front of her. She had confided in him some of what had happened to her at Cambridge, and he marvelled at how quickly she had changed tack and thrown herself into the shopgirl position at Bloomsbury Books.

"Good," Miss Wakefield was saying. "The Petiver is our oldest collection. Almost as old as me."

Evie laughed merrily, and Miss Wakefield took a second to smile at her before turning back to Ash.

"Now, young man, take Miss Stone to that tea you promised her."

Ash nodded again, this time cracking a smile himself.

"Of course, it's not the original tea pavilion," Miss Wakefield explained. "Suffragettes set the whole thing on fire back in 1913. Burned it to the ground. The men hereabouts called it a queer way to get the vote. But for all that, they do still talk about it!"

As the three of them said their goodbyes, Evie asked for Miss Wakefield's card, which the older woman looked only too pleased to provide. Ash watched as Evie ran her little ink-stained fingers across the embossed lettering that set out Elsie Wakefield's impressive title at Kew. They left her standing alone in the doorway to the herbarium, surrounded by the white-painted columns and portico, waving vigorously as they exited the front wrought-iron gates.

It was just a five-minute walk to the refreshment pavilion, but Ash knew Evie well enough by now to know that her appetite could not be ignored much longer. They sat down on folding French bistro chairs at the end of a long farm table placed directly under the bare branches of a towering oak tree.

At their arrival, Ash noticed the party next to them shift their chairs slightly farther away. He was both relieved and a little irritated that Evie did not seem to notice, so preoccupied was she with the choices on the menu. Ash motioned to the server for a pot of tea, while continuing to watch Evie out of the corner of his eye.

She looked so young, sitting there in her little woollen coat and matching beret, trying not to think about how hungry she was. She had so much ahead of her, and so many dreams. He thought about her idea for the printing press, the mysterious Loudon research, the passion for neglected women writers. His feelings for her—her possible feelings for *him*—could ruin all that. Ash thought again of Miss Wakefield and the herbarium over which she so happily ruled. Recalling the many other women who had recently come into the bookshop and their lives—the married, the widowed, the divorced, all of them of independent means—Ash realised that Elsie Wakefield might be the closest specimen to a grown-up Evie Stone that he would ever find. He knew now was the time to speak.

"Evie."

"Mm-hmm . . ." She continued to examine the long list of cakes on the menu.

"Miss Wakefield . . ."

"Wasn't she wonderful? Never even takes a Sunday off."

"Such dedication."

Evie laughed. "I don't think that's it. I think she knows she has to. Outwork the men, I mean."

"But you love working all the time." He raised a knowing eyebrow at her. "The first time we met, you were doing research on a Sunday, after all."

"As were you."

He had to smile. "I guess that's true. But I'm quite alone here, in England. You could go home to Chawton on your days off."

"I will. In time."

"So, you'll not be returning home anytime soon?"

Evie shook her head. "I love London. It's like a hundred villages rolled into one. You could live here forever and never get to the bottom of it."

"I've decided . . ." Ash stopped to clear his throat as the waitress placed the teapot down between them. "Evie?"

"Hmm? Oh, yes. Lemon drizzle, please."

"A rather considerable slice, if you can," Ash added to the waitress, who surprised him with an understanding smile. "As I was saying, I've decided to return home."

"Oh . . . yes, of course, right after tea . . ."

"I mean return home to India."

Evie looked up from the menu in confusion. "I don't understand. On a trip?"

"No, for good."

"But you just got here."

"A year ago."

"That's not so long."

"It feels long to me. I came here to be a scientist. Not to sell books."

"I didn't go to Cambridge to sell books." Evie closed the menu hard between them.

"It's not the same thing."

Evie stared at him wordlessly, visibly hurt.

"Look." He sighed in frustration, convinced that he could never make her understand. "I have no regrets. But it's obvious I'm not wanted here. It gets more obvious all the time, and I'm still just a novelty. What will happen if I ever become more than that?"

She was shaking her head at him in confusion. "A novelty . . ."

"I just meant that right now I'm not a threat to anyone. I'm invisible. That's still not enough. It won't ever be enough. Better to just go than be someone I'm not and still be a threat for all that."

He sighed again, feeling helpless in the face of her silence and resentment.

"I'm sorry if you can't see things the way that I do. But my going really is for the best—for both of us."

With the mystery and finality of his words hanging in the air between them, Ash reached for the teapot and poured out Evie's tea. She refused to drink it or to look at him at all. He hadn't pressed her on anything, yet she had withdrawn all the same. He was trying to make the best decision for them both before things got out of hand. As they each sat there sullenly, no longer enjoying what would turn out to be their last Sunday together as employees of Bloomsbury Books, Ash had a horrible feeling inside that he was already too late to stop that.

CHAPTER THIRTY-FIVE

Staff must remain at their stations at all times,
except as herein permitted.

Septimus Feasby, principal keeper of printed books at the British Museum, paid four quarterly visits to Bloomsbury Books each year from his nearby offices. Full of eagle-eyed intent, he would spend the morning going through Frank Allen's latest estate acquisitions, all of which were invariably still in their shipping crates or in disturbingly high piles on the floor. Dr. Feasby was infamous in his profession for never having missed out on a key acquisition either at auction or under advisement.

Septimus Reginald Feasby had been christened by parents who, in this choice of names, clearly intended their child for a career connected to the past. To that end, he had graduated with a First in English from Jesus College, Cambridge, alongside the future Vice-Master Christenson, whose overlooking of Evie Stone's academic achievements had led to her current role as shopgirl at Bloomsbury Books.

Like Christenson, Dr. Feasby had evaded service in the Great War by the mere good fortune of being six months too young to serve by its very end. The two men had, however, graduated in time to pursue Cambridge's new degree of Doctor of Philosophy.

Feasby's doctoral thesis on the entirety of English drama had been supervised by Sir Arthur Quiller-Couch, King Edward VII Professor of English Literature, a fellow of Jesus College, and du Maurier's esteemed mentor, who had fretted over his charge's "relentless" consumption of books. Ambitious to a fault, Dr. Feasby had built his career at the British Museum as a keeper and curator in its Department of Printed Books, his connection to Cambridge continuing through external membership on various councils including that of the Senate. It was to both his and Christenson's disappointment when the latter council voted to allow women full graduation from Cambridge, precipitating the arrival shortly thereafter of young Evelyn Stone, full of her own ambition and eagle-eyed intent.

The curator timed his visits to Bloomsbury Books for precisely 9:30 a.m., arriving at the store the minute it was due to open. Standing there, tapping impatiently on his wristwatch, he often surprised Vivien with his intense hawkish face in the window as she approached to unlock the door to the street. On one memorable occasion, Dr. Feasby had ended up locked between both vestibule doors in a bizarre chain of circumstances that had led to the upbraiding of various staff and a lasting obsequiousness on their part towards Dr. Feasby that was neither genuine nor earned.

It was somewhat surprising, therefore, when he showed up at noon on the last day of February, fully one month ahead of his next quarterly visit.

"Dr. Feasby," Vivien greeted him. "How have we been?"

Giving his usual curt nod, Feasby brushed right past her on his way to the staircase.

"Shall you see yourself up?" Vivien called after him, knowing there would be no response. She had always despised Dr. Feasby but almost wished she had an excuse to accompany him, if only to watch how he would react upon encountering the newest employee of the shop.

E vie was sitting on her little stool in front of the cabinet that contained Bloomsbury Books' most valuable antiquarian selection. She remained in low spirits from last Sunday's visit to Kew Gardens with Ash, who the next morning had given notice to Mr. Dutton of his intention to resign. In an unusually brief staff meeting, Mr. Dutton had announced that Ash would be leaving his position by the fourteenth of April, the start of the New Year in his home state of Madras. Evie had not spoken more than a few words to Ash since learning of his decision. She was far too new to being in love to manage bewildering heartbreak as well. Keeping to herself was her only way of coping, especially when her pride was involved.

Evie was also still upset by what Yardley Sinclair had recently come to the shop to warn her about. She kept looking up at the doorway at the slightest noise, half expecting to see Stuart Wesley himself standing there, an inescapable part of the world from which she had effectively been banished. Evie had tried to leave that world behind and never look back; how disheartening to realise that not even looking back was remotely within her control.

Hearing footsteps first approach, then halt suddenly behind her, Evie peered over her shoulder to see a familiar-looking man standing on the upper landing. He was leaning forward into the open space, looking exactly like the twisted centuries-old mulberry tree that Ash had once shown her. Evie felt another pang inside at the memory.

"Where's Mr. Allen?" the man asked loudly.

"At an estate sale in Wales," Evie replied calmly. He did not intimidate her—he struck her as almost too cartoonish to be worrying.

"Hmmph." He looked about the room, then back down at her. "And you are . . . ?"

"Evelyn Stone."

"I mean, what do you *do*?"

"Mr. Dutton took me on in the New Year, to help catalogue the rare books."

"Took you on? From where?"

"From Girton College. At Cambridge."

He made a type of grunting sound that she had never heard before. "I *know* where that is. I'm from Jesus. Septimus Feasby, doctor of philosophy."

Evie knew who he was, too. She had heard Professor Kinross boast often enough about his friendship with the famous curator. She had also seen his name on the letter from the British Museum that had permitted Kinross to examine certain archival materials in such a state of decay that access was severely limited except in matters of grave national importance. Fortunately for Kinross and his team, Dr. Septimus Feasby had decided that a years-long endeavour to annotate *Vanity Fair* fell within that category.

"Dr. Feasby. Of course." Evie stood up. "What brings you here today?"

He ignored her and looked around. "Allen's lost complete control of this place. How the deuce am I expected to find anything in a mess like this?"

"Perhaps I can be of assistance."

Dr. Feasby went over to the desk and started to flip through one of the large Sotheby's catalogues left out from Mr. Allen's last time in the office.

"I highly doubt that," Dr. Feasby finally answered her, almost as an afterthought.

Evie remained standing by her stool, watching his snooping with an increasingly suspicious eye. He was now carefully examining the current ledger of annual sales.

"I really think—"

He turned back to her and made a shushing sound. "Just get back to whatever it is you were doing."

She watched as he made his way over to the section of shelves dedicated to the later Georgian period and started poking around.

"Is this everything from the late 1820s?" he called back to her over his stooped shoulder.

"I'm afraid I'm not sure. Things are quite scattered 'round."

"How well do you know these books?"

"Fairly well, I'd say."

"And are things often 'scattered 'round,' as you say?"

She nodded.

"When is Allen back again?"

"Monday."

He finally turned to face her, almost grudgingly, as if she were otherwise too unimportant to be directly addressed. "Then *you'll* help me. I am trying to locate a copy of a book from 1827 called *The Mummy!*"

Evie started to think quickly. She was surprised he was tipping his hand like this, but he clearly did not think her a threat in any way. Evie wondered what Wesley or Kinross might have said to Dr. Feasby, both about the potential value of the book and her own knowledge of it. Cambridge and the British Museum often competed to acquire important literary artifacts for their collections. The Cambridge academics must not have been too forthcoming, given how little Feasby was trying to hide his search from her until the book was in his grasping, withered hands. Unless she was simply too far beneath his concern to even matter. It was all becoming quite a muddle. Somehow, she had to turn his obvious disinterest in her to her own advantage.

"I'm afraid I don't recall seeing that book up here," she replied slowly, knowing that this was more of an omission than an outright lie.

"You are aware of it?" he asked her pointedly.

She nodded casually, trying to appear as disinterested as possible. "If you are interested in early science fiction—"

He put his hand up for her to stop talking. "I am interested in what I am interested in. It is not for you to guess at. You're only to help me *find* it."

Evie was now in a state of full inward panic.

"I know for a fact that Mr. Allen acquired the book at auction. It was confirmed to an, um, associate of mine. By Sotheby's itself. The book is here, and you are to locate it for me."

Evie swallowed. "I'm afraid I can't. I know of no such book on this floor."

"Check those sales ledgers on the desk then. Back to September 1946. By the looks of things, you sell only a handful of old books a week, if that, so it shouldn't take long."

Heading dutifully over to the desk, Evie opened each of the annual ledgers that had tracked the department's weekly sales for the past four years while Dr. Feasby continued rummaging through the shelves. She ran her shaking finger down every page but did the task quickly, given her years of research work at Cambridge, her recent examination of the ledgers, and her knowledge that what she was searching for was not there. After twenty minutes, she looked up and shook her head as he now stood before her, a fixed expression of impatience tightening his features like a screw.

"Then take me to the other floors. Judging from the chaos of this department, a book could be anywhere in the shop."

"I can't. I can't leave my station."

"You most certainly can."

"Actually, no, it's shop policy. Rule number twenty-two."

He stared in shock at her refusal. "You will take me to the other floors, and you will help me find what I am looking for."

Evie shook her head. "I really cannot leave this floor except on my allotted breaks. But if you want to ask the other department heads for help—"

He was eyeing her now extremely carefully. She could not read him at all. She wished she could size up exactly how dangerous he might be to her. She thought back on Wesley, Kinross, and Christenson, and all the signs she had missed there, too, as she had slaved away unheeded and unremarked in Cambridge's many libraries. Evie knew she should pay more attention to how others actually felt about her, but she just couldn't see it. It was a world of unwritten rules, and unlike Grace and Vivien, Evie had never minded how Mr. Dutton spelled everything out.

So she refused Dr. Feasby one more time, hoping that somehow he would give up and try to find what he wanted another way. Hoping that things weren't as momentous and dire as they were starting to appear. Hoping that by adhering to the rules and not explicitly lying to him—in his zeal, he had failed to more precisely ask her, a total nobody in his eyes, for the truth—she could somehow escape his venom.

Not for the first time, Evelyn Stone had severely underestimated the situation.

CHAPTER THIRTY-SIX

RULE No. 3

Any conduct unbecoming of staff towards a customer
or in general, shall result in immediate termination.

Septimus Feasby marched straight down to the back office, where Herbert Dutton sat quietly, sipping a cup of turmeric tea on the suggestion of Ash Ramaswamy. Despite being back at work nearly a month, Mr. Dutton still suffered from a range of troubling symptoms including constant stomach upset, occasional headaches, and a fluttering heart, and he had been only too happy to take Mr. Ramaswamy up on his medicinal knowledge of herbs reputed to heal such ills.

Dr. Feasby stood coldly before Mr. Dutton and demanded that the girl on the third floor immediately be fired for insolence or he would take his business elsewhere. He gave no further details than that, believing that this one statement alone was enough— a belief that he would one day infinitely regret. He had then marched out of the shop self-satisfied, muttering that he would return after his lunch and expected the girl to be gone by the time he got back.

In his thirty-two years at Bloomsbury Books, Herbert Dutton had never seen anyone be fired. Under his own rules for the shop, he alone had that authority. For the first time in his role as general manager, Mr. Dutton regretted this power but feared his only choice at present was to exercise it. The Department of Printed Books at the British Museum was by far the largest institutional buyer from Bloomsbury Books.

Mr. Dutton reluctantly called Evie in. First, he asked for her side of the story out of respect for her as one of his staff. Next, he reiterated that, pursuant to shop rules two and six, she was required to always prioritize the needs of the customers and to uphold the store's reputation as a purveyor of fine books at the highest level. Finally, he informed her that her employment at Bloomsbury Books must, as of that moment, come to an end.

Evie stood there in shock as Grace came rushing in, followed shortly by Vivien, who had also caught wind of the situation. Alec was due to leave soon for early drinks with Norman Mailer, whom he was hoping to secure for a future evening lecture. Allan Wingate had recently published the UK edition of Mailer's wartime novel, *The Naked and the Dead,* to great acclaim, and in light of the Beckett debacle, Alec was now eager to promote a young up-and-coming author without any attendant controversy. Master Mariner Scott was already lunching at the pub the Lamb at the very top of the street. Ashwin Ramaswamy was, as usual, eating at his desk in the basement, unaware of all the commotion taking place on the main floor.

Mr. Dutton sat there alone, meekly, staring at the three women before him. He forced himself to take the deep, meditative breaths that his GP had recommended, all the while wishing he could flee.

"This is unbelievable!" Vivien was exclaiming.

"Miss Lowry, please," Mr. Dutton pleaded, desperate to maintain order. "I know we are all upset, but it behoves you, as a fellow staff member, not to interfere with the treatment of your colleague. Without managerial or supervisory capacity of your own—"

"Oh, please," Vivien said forcefully, banging her hand on the edge of his desk while Grace shot her a subtle glance of warning. "Everyone knows Septimus Feasby is an old fusspot without an ounce of patience *or* humanity. It's high time someone refused one of his ludicrous demands."

"Miss Lowry, I'm begging you, if you continue in this insolent manner, I will have no choice but to terminate you, too."

At these words, Alec appeared in the doorway to the office. "What on earth's going on?"

Herbert Dutton put both his hands up in the air as if in helpless surrender. Vivien explained the situation to Alec while keeping her furious face trained on Mr. Dutton the entire time.

"Herbert, the girl's been here only a few weeks," Alec said in an almost pleading tone as he took a step into the room. "Surely we should give her another chance?"

Vivien and Grace both turned back to stare at Alec in open confusion.

Mr. Dutton shook his head. "I'm sorry, my decision is final."

"But she clearly isn't a—"

"I said *final*."

It was by far the most censorial that any of Mr. Dutton's staff had ever seen him, causing Alec to storm out of Dutton's office for the first time as well. In that moment Grace, who was always so attuned to shifts in atmosphere—having honed this skill so thoroughly at home—realised the full magnitude of what the three women were up against. She started to think quickly about all the recent takeover talk while Mr. Dutton sat there, roundly settled back in his chair, immovable for once by anyone's pleas and totally unaware of what was really at stake.

Grace gave Evie one last, motherly look before deciding that the best course of action would be to get the one thing that could stop anything like this from ever happening again.

"Mr. Dutton, I think you would agree that Evie has been an

otherwise exemplary employee these past seven weeks." Grace
kept the tone of her voice as measured as possible. "And she is still
on probation, falling short of the three months of service required
for severance pursuant to rule forty-nine, correct?"

Mr. Dutton nodded, relieved to have someone else quote the
shop rules in full for once.

"So, you will not be giving her any missed wages?" Grace
asked.

Mr. Dutton nodded his head again in response. Grace noticed
that Evie was watching her with an evolving mixture of panic,
dread, and awe on her face.

"Then we, in our capacity as staff, would like to make a gentle
suggestion. To present Evie with a gift, just a small one. A me-
mento, if you like, of her time here in the shop."

Mr. Dutton gave an audible sigh of relief that did not escape
any of them.

"Of course, we are well aware of the rules prohibiting employee
purchases of any kind," Grace calmly continued.

Mr. Dutton now nodded gamely, clearly relieved to no longer be
fighting them on the issue of termination itself.

"And we all know how difficult that must be, for someone as
passionate about books as Miss Stone here herself."

He continued to nod, all the while breathing deeply.

"Might we suggest, then, that Evie be allowed to take one book
from the shop, not from the Rare Books Department, of course,
given their value . . . just one book of her choice, as a small token
in remembrance of her time here, as well as in gratitude from us
all?"

Evie stared openly at Grace in amazement, while Vivien began to quietly move back from the desk in appeasement.

"All right," Mr. Dutton finally muttered. "Take anything you
want, Evie, from one of the other departments. I know you to have

been a most diligent and hard worker. Mr. Allen in particular is most grateful for all you have done, in light of his own lengthy absences of late. I only ask that you then collect your things quickly and be gone before Dr. Feasby gets back. It would be such a help in this rather charged situation. You do understand?"

Evie bit her bottom lip and looked down at her feet, overcome by both the intense emotion of the moment and the words about to escape her.

"Now there, child," Mr. Dutton couldn't help saying in the face of her distress. "It will all be fine. I shall be happy to provide a letter of reference to assist you in securing new employment. Dr. Feasby can, admittedly, be quite difficult and ornery. I am sure that, with time, you will bring your own obvious talents and perseverance to a brand-new endeavour."

Evie tried to give him the forgiving smile he was so clearly hoping for, and as she turned her brightening face back up towards his, his heart softened yet again.

"Tell me, my dear, do you know which book you would like to take with you, as our parting gift?"

Evie took one look at Grace and Vivien, thought of Stuart Wesley strolling Cambridge lanes full of discarded champagne corks and confetti, and then said, very simply and declaratively:

"*The Mummy!*"

When Dr. Feasby returned after lunch, he marched straight back into Mr. Dutton's office and demanded to know that the girl was gone and to receive the assistance that was his due.

Mr. Dutton felt bad for Evie, but the shop needed Dr. Feasby and his curatorial business more. The British Museum had been acquiring from Bloomsbury Books for nearly one hundred years.

So it was with some measure of relief that Mr. Dutton now sat at his desk, still not feeling physically quite right, but at least confident that this latest little fire had been thoroughly tamped down.

"Of course, Dr. Feasby. A rare book of some kind?"

Septimus Feasby's crooked features began to slowly realign, as he felt the restoration of the respect and order that he demanded from those that served him.

"Yes. Frank's lost complete control of his department and that snit of a girl outright refused to help me."

"I am so sorry for all your trouble," Mr. Dutton replied placatingly. "How exactly may we assist you?"

"I know for a fact that Frank acquired a certain book at auction a few years past, but it's nowhere upstairs."

"Perhaps it sold?" Mr. Dutton gently suggested.

"Don't be a ninny. I already checked on that. It has to be on another floor."

Mr. Dutton stood up, not wanting to aggravate the curator any further. "Of course. I will take you to the History Department myself and we will get started there. We will turn this place upside down if we have to. But I can assure you, we will find you your book."

Mr. Dutton left his office ahead of Dr. Feasby to escort him to the second floor. Whenever Mr. Dutton strolled through the shop, he always felt most keenly the import of his position as general manager. His problematic heart swelled with pride at everything operating smoothly about him like the finely tuned Cartier on Miss Lowry's slender wrist. All fifty-one rules being firmly adhered to and everything in its place.

They had not lost a book yet, for all of Frank's carelessness. With supreme confidence Herbert Dutton ascended towards the landing of the second floor, looking down from the stairs to see Alec's angelic blond head watching from the top of a ladder and

Vivien's scowling face and lithesome figure behind the front cash counter. Somewhere outside, little Evie Stone roamed the streets of London, surely disconsolate right now, their small parting gift of a book inside the battered leather bag she always carried about. Mr. Dutton had recognised her special qualities right from the start, the minute he came to consciousness, saved by those same qualities of quick thinking, diligence, and perseverance. He felt a nagging sense of guilt at the memory of how she had saved his life. This was how he must repay her in order for Bloomsbury Books to survive. It was simply business, he told himself, as he surveyed his kingdom below. Everything in business must be forgiven and forgotten because it all shared the same desired end. For businesses to survive, individuals had to make room for them and not the other way around. Nothing personal, he reminded himself.

Dr. Feasby was waiting impatiently on the first step below the second-floor landing where Mr. Dutton now stood, surveying his small but unshakeable world. Truth be told, he had never cared for Septimus Feasby. But pleasing the customer always came first, Dutton reminded himself, just as he had minutes ago reminded Evie.

Giving a most gracious and practiced smile, he turned back to the curator to ask, "And what is the name of this book you are looking for?"

A s quickly as she had first appeared, Evie Stone was gone.
     She left no parting address, given that she was not due any further wages. Mr. Dutton had neglected to capture her particulars for the shop's files upon her hire. This unusual mistake on his part reflected his physical turmoil at the time, which was now being rapidly revived by stress.

Dr. Feasby held firm to his earlier threat of taking his business elsewhere.

Frank returned from Wales to learn that a rare and invaluable volume under his care had been lost within the shop.

And Master Mariner Scott returned from the pub to discover that his department had housed a groundbreaking and historic work of fiction.

Little could any of them guess that this very same book, written by a seventeen-year-old girl, would soon turn the worlds of Gothic literature and science fiction on their heads.

CHAPTER THIRTY-SEVEN

RULE No. 8

Staff must demonstrate courtesy, readiness, and zeal at all times.

Friday afternoon was usually the most relaxed time of the week at Bloomsbury Books, reflecting the mood of the customers who wandered in. These were mostly small clusters of students now free from lectures, businessmen taking their time getting home, and society ladies who had just had their hair and nails done in anticipation of evening events still many hours away.

But this Friday at the shop was a dismal affair, given Evie's involuntary departure earlier in the week. Grace and Vivien left together at precisely 5:30 p.m. as usual, but without a word to any of the men. They held their black handbags out in front of them, stiff and armour-like, as if to intimate that they were not to be similarly messed with. For the first time in recent memory, Grace had not approached Mr. Dutton's office doorway to call out cheerfully, "Do you need anything else before I go, sir?" Ever respectful of his staff's start and end times, Mr. Dutton would always just shake his head with a tightly polite smile, aware of the looming hours of work he still often faced. Grace's refusal to inquire of him tonight was a gauntlet being thrown down, if only he could see it.

Ash left quietly for home soon after the two women, followed

by Master Mariner Scott, who headed straight to the pub for dinner. Alec was alone behind the cash counter when Lord Baskin
appeared in the front vestibule, having just exited a cab from the
street.

"You missed all the excitement," Alec greeted him wryly.

"So I heard." Lord Baskin nodded in the direction of the back
offices, where Mr. Dutton and Mr. Allen could be seen through the
windows in deep conversation.

Alec closed the purchase order book that Vivien had taken to
neglecting in her dangerous new mood. "I was just finishing up."

"Big plans for tonight?"

"Not very. You?"

"On my way to Syon House for the weekend. Care for a pint at
the Lamb before you head home?"

Alec hesitated. He was still upset with Mr. Dutton and not
eager to discover in Lord Baskin any shared support for Evie
Stone being sacked. But despite his anger, Alec reminded himself that the earl had always proven to be a most gracious and
eminently reasonable owner. Alec shoved the order book back under the counter and walked through the rear swinging door to
join him.

The Lamb public house was at the very north end of Lamb's
Conduit Street. Built in 1729, the pub's current façade was a mix
of austere Georgian structure, elaborate Victorian style, and an
Edwardian return to the cleaner lines of its eighteenth-century
origins. Inside, the central bar still retained nineteenth-century
snob screens with movable glass panels, originally intended to
hide the customer from the publican while ordering, as well as
to obscure the different classes of patrons from each other. Alec
was inwardly amused at the notion that one hundred years ago a
doctor's son such as himself would rarely have been seen grabbing
a pint with an earl.

The current proprietor was the recently widowed Mrs. Bessie Rosenberg. She had taken over the pub following the death of her husband, Arthur, in 1944, but was sadly rumoured to be in declining health now herself. Entering through the street door, both men caught sight of Master Mariner Scott already seated inside and having a word with Mrs. Rosenberg. Baskin gently put his hand on Alec's back and steered him towards a small round table in the opposite corner of the room.

"I suspect we'll be needing our privacy." Lord Baskin motioned to Alec to take the more comfortable booth seat before them.

"You'll be hard-pressed to find privacy at the Lamb—Scott practically lives here." Alec looked about the rest of the room. "You mentioned Syon House, earlier."

Lord Baskin nodded. "The duke is contemplating opening the house to the public—something I've been discussing with Mother for years. Changes all afoot. Now, what can I get you?"

Alec was surprised by the offer. Over the years, he and Lord Baskin had always socialised while being elegantly served in different hotel restaurants and cocktail lounges. Yet the earl did not look out of place at the Lamb as he sauntered over to the bar to give their order. In fact, Alec observed, Lord Baskin never looked out of place anywhere. Alec envied this about him.

Lord Baskin returned to the table with two lagers and placed one down across from Alec. "I suspect you must be needing this, too."

"Will you be speaking with Herbert and Frank later?"

Lord Baskin nodded. "But I wanted to hear from you first."

Alec sighed in frustration. "It's just that Dutton himself devised those rules. Evie'd only been two months on the job—not even—and was simply following it all to the letter. There has to be some acknowledgement of *that*. If nothing else, at *least* missed wages."

"She got a book out of it, I understand." Lord Baskin raised his eyebrows at Alec in amusement.

"I've never seen anyone as angry as Feasby in that moment. Dutton still hasn't recovered from the set-down he got."

Baskin nodded again thoughtfully. "I don't think Herbert's recovered at all."

"You mean his health."

"Not necessarily. I understand his health is improving, although certainly not by leaps and bounds. No, I meant the humiliation, for a man like Herbert, of losing all physical control in the workplace. In front of his entire staff, no less." Baskin paused until he caught Alec's eye. "In front of . . . the *women*."

Lord Baskin's emphasis of his last word now caught Alec's ear as well. "What are you implying?"

"He came back in advance of doctor's orders, after all. Perhaps he's feeling vulnerable from many directions." Lord Baskin paused again. "Tell me, how are *you* feeling about possibly taking on the shop?"

Alec knew this was coming. And his own answer—for once spontaneous, and truly genuine—surprised him. "Less certain, given recent events. Staff morale is exceedingly low."

"You can always make adjustments."

"Like Mr. Dutton just did?"

"Not quite. But staffing at the shop could arguably use some redress. We men are all very alike, very much stuck in the past. The women are a much more interesting mix. Tell me"—Baskin leaned forward keenly—"what are you hoping to achieve with ownership?"

Alec shrugged. "I suppose I feel it's time for a change."

"For the shop, or for you?"

This was the question Alec had been wrestling with for several weeks now.

While he pondered it, Lord Baskin sat back in his chair, look-ing surprisingly calm and pensive despite the spiralling situation at the shop. "I try to think about my job as bringing out the best in others. I fear most owners tend to think in terms of control. But it's not about directives, for all Mr. Dutton's efforts. We're selling books, after all, *not* plutonium."

"I just feel stuck. The war's been over for years now. I should get a move on."

"And owning the shop is the solution?"

"Well, it's the only logical next step given where I am. And I have the financial means, as I understand them from you."

"Certainly."

The two men looked over at the sound of Mrs. Rosenberg laugh-ing boisterously at something Master Mariner Scott had just said. A waitress approaching their table gave a knowing wink at Alec. "He's quite the charmer, that one. Coming in 'ere year after year."

Alec and Lord Baskin looked at each other and then back at the waitress in surprise.

"And now the two o' them finally making merry, just when the missus is takin' a turn for the worse, lord bless 'er. You two gen-tlemen all right?"

Alec was so astonished, he barely recalled what he said next in response to her forthrightness.

"Well, now we finally know what Scott's been up to all these years." Lord Baskin laughed as the waitress went on her way. "That sly dog."

"Not to sound like a snob, but Mrs. Rosenberg is so . . ."

"Different? Perhaps. Perhaps that's why it works. You never want to be too alike."

Alec caught the note of insinuation in Lord Baskin's voice and wondered to whom he might be referring. In his month as acting general manager, Alec had picked up on Lord Baskin's subtle but unmistakable interest in Grace Perkins whenever he stopped by, which he had been doing much more often of late.

"A good marriage is like a good team. One should complement the other, if possible." The earl took a sip of his lager. "There can be such a thing as too much competition."

"You're talking now about Vivien."

"I'm talking now about Vivien."

Alec was unsure of how much Lord Baskin might have guessed over the years. "I've thought about elevating her entirely to head of fiction should I take control."

"How generous of you."

"You don't think it will work?"

"On the contrary. But I don't think it will fix what ails the two of you."

Alec sighed. So Lord Baskin had guessed correctly, after all. "Probably not. Probably nothing will."

"You'll never be able to contain her. I know something about that."

Alec was surprised by Lord Baskin's hinting reference to his ex-wife, Anna, who had long ago decamped to the States with her American second husband. Baskin rarely discussed his love life with the men at work; for the first time, Alec wondered if Grace might be the reason why.

"I suspect many have tried to contain Miss Lowry her entire life," mused Lord Baskin. "She won't abide it."

"Contain how?"

"You can go far with looks like hers, but only in one direction, and with only one discernible end. I see it every season. But then the Lord St. Vincent was taken in battle, along with an entire generation of eligible men, and suddenly it's the 1950s. Vivien might even be used to it by now, the being on her own."

"It's hard to feel sorry for her. She's always so angry."

"Palpably so, yes. But aren't you, too? Aren't we all, in a way?" Lord Baskin sighed. "Herbert's decision about Evie came from somewhere. Maybe anger. Maybe fear. It was clearly the wrong decision, whatever it was. And now I have to somehow fix all that."

"Poor Evie Stone," Alec muttered aloud with unusual feeling. Both the lager and the commiseration of the earl were making Alec relax. He suddenly didn't feel so committed to, or trapped by, the path ahead. He felt, strangely enough, as if Lord Baskin was giving him a way out. "I feel sorry for *her* at least, if no one else."

"We certainly have failed her. But Dr. Feasby's reaction also makes me wonder."

"About what?"

Baskin took a final sip of his lager, then gave a mischievous grin. "About how sorry for Miss Stone we might actually end up feeling in the end."

CHAPTER THIRTY-EIGHT

RULE No. 5

Rebellious or mutinous behaviour by staff, in congregate
or alone, shall not be tolerated.

Late on Sunday afternoon, Lord Baskin made a small detour
before heading home to Yorkshire from Syon House. He agreed
to meet with all three of his female staff in the American Bar
of the Savoy Hotel.

"We want to buy the shop," Vivien announced as he took a seat
across from them and ordered a whisky neat.

Lord Baskin's eyes immediately went first to Grace before
turning back to Vivien.

"We?" he asked, notably confused. "You mean, your . . . husband?
Families?"

Vivien shook her head. "No, us three."

"I don't understand."

Vivien laughed. "Grace, why don't you explain? I think he'll
understand it better coming from you."

Seated between Evie and Vivien, Grace was exhausted from
all the recent upheaval at work and at home. She had moved in
with her mother the previous weekend, taking both boys with
her, all under protest from Gordon. He had telephoned every hour
on the hour, until her mother—now fully cognizant of what her

daughter had been up against all these years—disconnected the line. The boys had been upset at the hasty and horrible removal from home and kept threatening to run away. All Grace could do was hope that she had fostered and built something, all those years, to attach them to her. She couldn't have done any more than that. So much of it was out of her hands.

The threat of solicitor bills also weighed heavily on her. Gordon claimed to be determined to gain custody of their rambunctious sons. Again, Grace could only hope that, with time, the quiet around the house would calm her husband's inner turmoil and give him a small measure of the peace and compliance that he tried so constantly to extract from those around him. An extraction that had led to the painful chipping away of Grace's soul until she would be left with nothing in the end but her own inner turmoil.

Grace turned to address Lord Baskin, who was patiently waiting for her with his elegant yet slightly ruffled manner and warm, hazel eyes. Whenever she was with him, Grace felt such a strange, wonderful feeling of being silently appreciated and understood, with absolutely nothing demanded in return. She recalled the bus ride, the dropped keys under the bench, and the spilling of her coffee, all the little moments that had marked their first meeting. Moments that had served—in conjunction with Alec's calling out from the doorway, the advert in the window, and the achievable typing speed—to mask what had really happened that day: the day she had fallen in love.

It had taken over four long, hardworking years to get to this point, and there was more work ahead. But as her eyes met his, Grace took strength in that feeling of understanding, which she now knew to be another form of love. Being understood, appreciated, and not judged: these, surely, were the cornerstones of real love. The love that helps us move forth in life, no matter what it throws at us, no matter what we lose. That love, at least, is always there, even if we can't do anything about it.

Lord Baskin smiled encouragingly at Grace, as if he knew all this, too, as well as what she was about to say.

"We want to buy your half of the shop—your fifty-one per cent—and run it ourselves. Fully owned and operated by women."

"And you have the money?" he asked in surprise.

Grace nodded, while Vivien now spoke up. "There'll be an announcement soon. Then you'll know exactly how we're planning to pull it off."

He stared curiously at the three women before him, each of them sitting so seriously and upright in the American Bar of the Savoy. Although a surprising choice, the hotel on the Thames Embankment was distant enough from both Bloomsbury and the bookshop to provide some degree of anonymity for an ambitious takeover such as this.

"Choosing this location now seems very apt, given its history," he observed with a smile. "All those war leaders meeting Churchill here, or dining at the Grill Room . . . de Gaulle and Masaryk scheming . . ."

"I can assure you," Evie finally piped up, "it's not improper in any way."

"No, no, my dear, of course not. I have no worries in that regard. I'm just . . . surprised . . . given the sum of money involved." He looked back at Grace. "I should confess something to you. Alec's pulling back. I think he's none too pleased with Mr. Dutton's decision to let Evie here go."

"Then we've only Mr. Dutton and Mr. Allen to worry about?" Grace asked.

Lord Baskin nodded. "Do they suspect anything at all?"

"No. We don't think so. Not yet. They may figure it out soon enough though."

"Then again they might not," Vivien added dismissively.

"But you'll still have to buy out their half, you know," Lord Baskin continued. "They won't just walk away."

"We're hoping to increase profits enough to eventually do exactly that," replied Grace. "Or secure extra financing if need be—perhaps from a few new partners along the way."

"We're also vastly underpaid in comparison to the male employees and used to it," Vivien added. "If the men all go, that should ease up enough cash to start buying up the rest of the shares within the year, as well as start paying ourselves more fairly."

"All the men? Gone?" he asked with surprise.

The three women nodded in unison.

"Mr. Ramaswamy is heading back to India next month anyway." Grace gave Evie a quick look. "Master Mariner Scott is well past his prime and should have retired years ago on his naval pension."

"Mr. Dutton's obviously still recovering and with his weakened heart probably shouldn't even be at work," Vivien pointed out with rare sympathy. "And Mr. Allen would clearly rather be somewhere—anywhere—else."

"And Mr. McDonough?"

"Alec, too, for that matter," Vivien replied. "I'm sure all he really wants to do in life is boss others around. Look, if they want to stay, we're very open to it. Of course, a lot will be changing in the shop that they might not care for. New rules and guidelines and all that."

"And a new name!" exclaimed Evie. "The Sunwise Turn."

"From east to west," Lord Baskin answered her. "Scottish, isn't it, for the 'prosperous path'?"

"Exactly," replied Evie, finally warming up to his presence in the conversation.

Lord Baskin had to laugh. "When I first told Vivien about the shop's share structure, I thought I might be stirring up some kind of a hornet's nest. But nothing nearly as stinging as this. I have to say, I am impressed. But is it a done deal?"

All three women nodded together again.

"I'm still your landlord, though. You won't be getting rid of me so fast." He gave Grace another look at these words, and this look even young Evie caught.

"All we need is twenty-five hundred pounds, correct? Plus another fifty?" asked Evie, and Lord Baskin nodded. "Then we should know by the fifteenth of March. The Ides of March."

"The settling of all Roman debts," Vivien declared triumphantly.

He laughed again.

The three women now sat alone in the curved booth of the American Bar. Surrounded by notepads, envelopes, and loose sheets of paper, they were each scribbling furiously.

"How's yours coming along?" Grace asked Vivien next to her.

As they laid out the letters that they had been working on side by side to compare, Grace caught sight of Evie rubbing her eyes from fatigue.

"How are you faring, Evie?" Grace asked with motherly concern. Evie usually had those rosy cheeks of youth that Grace loved in her two boys, but today the young woman looked quite drawn and pale.

Evie shook her head. "I have to keep going. There's barely enough time till the fifteenth. I've calculated everything down to the minute."

"Of course you have." Grace sighed. "Well, at least Lord Baskin is on our side."

"Of *course* he is," repeated Vivien. "You didn't tell him, though. You should have."

"Tell him what?" Evie asked in alarm.

Grace shook her head at Vivien in reproach. "I didn't want to burden you with this, Evie, but I've left my husband. Taken my boys and moved in with my mother for now. But please don't worry—it has nothing to do with the shop."

Evie looked confused. "Then why would you tell Lord Baskin? Even if he does admire you."

Grace stared at Evie in surprise. "What makes you say that?"

Vivien scoffed. "Grace, please, if even Evie could spot it . . ."

"Especially from the third-floor windows," Evie added, and the two older women burst out laughing. "Does this mean you like Lord Baskin back?"

"Ladies, please, just let me do everything on my own time. Just like Evie here." Again Grace sighed. "There's so much at stake— and so many people to keep quiet. What if it all blows up in our faces?"

Evie looked at both women in eagerness and asked with all the optimism of youth, "But what if it all goes *right*?"

CHAPTER THIRTY-NINE

RULE No. 51

Staff must provide two weeks' notice of their intention to resign.

O n Monday, March 6, Herbert Dutton arrived at Bloomsbury Books at exactly 9:00 a.m. to start his day. After opening the front street door, he extended a gloved hand to find the inner vestibule door still locked. This surprised him, as one of the staff would usually have arrived by now to ready things for the coming day.

He peered inside at the empty shop. The low morning sun was streaming in from the windows at the back, and in the orange and yellow rays Mr. Dutton could see the dust he had always tried so hard to manage through a rotating cleaning schedule with the girls in the shop. Just one more sign that his protracted absence had led to a slipping of the usually high standards at Bloomsbury Books.

Mr. Dutton let himself in and walked through the empty fiction floor. Vivien was not yet standing inside the cash counter as if visibly trapped, and Alec was not high up on his ladder perch nearby. Reaching the back offices, Dutton noticed that Grace's desk, too, sat empty. There was not a sheet of paper on its polished wood surface, which gleamed in the early-spring sunshine.

This was unusual as well, for as proficient a worker as Grace was, she rarely caught up to Mr. Dutton in his outstanding correspondence.

Entering his own office, Mr. Dutton stopped short at the frayed edge of the carpet where he had collapsed two months earlier. Yet again he pictured himself lying there, poor Evie Stone ministering to him at his side. He wished he could stop thinking about his attack and its lingering impact on his health, but the aggressive medicating of his heart made that difficult. And now Evie was gone, and Dr. Feasby and the museum's patronage had quickly followed in her wake. Herbert Dutton had miscalculated badly on all fronts, and his lack of support for his newest and most vulnerable staff member had left him with lingering doubts over his leadership and judgment. After all, he was the one who had set all fifty-one rules of the shop that Evie Stone had simply refused to disobey.

Dutton hung up his bowler hat and wool-lined trench to sit down at his overflowing desk. He saw no sign of catching up anytime soon on the mounds of *couches* and correspondence that Mr. McDonough had let accumulate during Dutton's recent medical leave. He could not bring himself, however, to take Alec to task for his negligence. For one thing, Herbert remained mortified by how Alec had learned his and Frank's secret. They may not have owed anyone the truth, but their silence on the subject with Alec surely undercut the strength of their friendship and the young man's regard. Herbert and Frank had not trusted Alec, and that must have stung, for all that the two men had turned out right in worrying that their relationship would upset him. Since Alec's surprise visit to their home, he had become increasingly remote and distracted at work. Mr. Dutton found himself studiously avoiding Alec in turn, Mr. Allen had resumed his lengthy estate travels, and the group friendship was, for all intents and purposes, seemingly gone.

Hearing the shop bell ring, Mr. Dutton was grateful for the commencement of a normal day at the shop. He relied heavily on a clockwork routine to calm his fragile nerves. The fifty-one rules had been enacted not only as guidance for his staff, but as the one thing Herbert Dutton could rely on in a life and world where the typical rewards were beyond his reach. Not for him and Frank would be the pleasures of a shared life outside the secrets of their home. But at the shop and on paper, Mr. Dutton was in charge and in command of whatever catastrophes arose.

At the sound of high heels clicking across the old oak floors, Dutton looked up to see both Grace and Vivien standing in the doorway, still wearing their hats and coats, each with a black handbag hanging in the crook of her left arm.

"Why, hello—did you come in together, then?"

He peered more closely to discover that they each also held an envelope in their hands. "What's this?"

They came forward to place the letters down on the desk before him.

"We're resigning," Grace stated simply, with just the slightest catch in her voice.

"In protest of the wrongful firing of Evie Stone," added Vivien with nothing but cold, implacable resentment in hers.

Mr. Dutton opened each envelope methodically and laid the two short letters on the blotter before him, side by side. As he read, he could feel small beads of sweat returning to his brow.

"I don't understand. What will you do? Where will you go?"

"Those questions are nothing to keep us here," Vivien replied sharply. "It's a matter of principle. Something management would also do well to remember."

"We are both very grateful for the opportunity to have been a part of the shop," Grace added. "But this is not how we treat staff here. Or should do."

"And without notice? You plan to leave right now, today, in violation of rule fifty-one and that clear requirement?"

"The rules apply to all or they don't apply to anyone," Vivien answered him in a bitter voice.

"That's not how it works," he countered, uncomprehending anger starting to rise in his.

"Then fire us, too," Vivien answered, and the two women turned on their heels and marched down the book-lined corridor and out the front door together, just as they had done every workday since the end of the war.

With the women all gone from the shop for good, the men were left scrambling. Alec McDonough would be manning the main floor all on his own, and Mr. Dutton now had sense enough of Alec's work habits to inwardly panic over the supply-and-order chaos that would surely result. Frank grudgingly agreed to stay in the shop as much as possible, which would cause him to miss several spring estate sales coming up. With Mr. Ramaswamy soon departing Bloomsbury Books as well, Herbert Dutton felt as if his well-oiled bookselling machine of the past thirty years was grinding to some mysterious and irreversible halt. Worse still, he no longer felt as if the gears were even in his own hands.

Herbert and Frank were sitting together at dinner, complaining about several disasters that had followed the women's departures that morning and were sure to only increase in their wake. The two men then retired to the front parlour after their pudding, just as they did every evening when Frank was at home. Herbert started to methodically read his two separate editions of the evening paper, while Frank cursorily flipped through travel brochures and the *National Geographic*.

As Herbert turned the pages of *The Times* one by one, Frank resumed his complaints about how removed and absentminded Alec McDonough had been throughout the day.

"Perhaps he relied on Miss Lowry even more than we suspect," Herbert replied.

"I *told* you that you should have made her assistant manager upon your return."

Herbert shook his head as he turned the pages of his newspaper. "The power would most certainly have gone to her head. It would have thrown off the male customers, as well as made things difficult for Alec."

"The golden boy," Frank muttered with a rueful grin. "Although perhaps not so golden anymore, hmm?"

"He should never have been subject to our private business. That was *our* fault."

Frank put down his copy of the *National Geographic* to sigh at his partner of nearly twenty years. "No, none of this is our fault. We've all been put in a most untenable position. Hiding as if our lives—this life—depended on it."

"Well, it does." Herbert was always the calmer voice at home.

"Just think what it would be like, though, if it didn't. And then Alec would have to deal with it, *really* deal with it. And learn, hopefully, and not just about *this*"—Frank waved his long elegant arm about the room—"but about himself, too. He's clearly in love with Vivien and has absolutely no clue what to do about it."

"Would you?"

The two men looked at each other and laughed at both the irony and the absurdity, their first genuine moment of levity together in days.

"I miss travelling." Frank picked the *National Geographic* back up. "I was glad Miss Perkins suggested that we bring in this magazine. I will certainly miss her. And now Mr. Ramaswamy is going, too. We could have done more there."

Herbert looked at the man he loved. The smooth, confident—

but easily distracted—man, so different from himself. They had been friends, lovers, and housemates for many years, and for all those years Herbert had told himself it was enough. As he had lain in bed for weeks, worried sick about the increasing frailty of his heart, he had been both surprised—and profoundly moved—by Frank's degree of devotion. To be so cared for and needed by someone else was, Herbert now understood, the greatest privilege of being loved. Yet they had been encumbered as a couple from fully experiencing that love, in a way that Herbert had convinced himself was bearable. Necessary. Understandable.

He had convinced himself of all that in order to survive, and he had fired Miss Stone for the same reason. He had put safety and comfort ahead of everything else, and in that unbalanced approach to life, he had created an isolated perch for himself that could only topple in the end.

Surely that was what the universe—in the now-departed form of Vivien and Grace—was telling him, as the men panicked over how to keep the shop seamlessly going. Despite Herbert's muddled efforts, Dr. Feasby had still taken his business elsewhere, furious at the loss of the book he had been so determined to acquire. Herbert's desperation in firing Evie, merely to hold on to a most difficult but long-standing customer, was reflective of how badly the shop needed every penny it could get. Bloomsbury Books' annual profits were reliably thin. He and Frank could continue to accept shares from Lord Baskin in lieu of a few weeks' wages until next year, when they would own the shop—that's how tight things were.

Herbert was no longer even sure that he wanted to keep his financial interest in the shop, let alone increase it. After this latest struggle with his health and Frank's unwavering attendance at his side, Herbert was beginning to wonder if it made more sense to plan for his retirement and let Frank pursue interests of his own. He had always seemed to enjoy the travel more than the books, never needing to be in the shop all day in the way that Herbert happily was. Owning the shop together would only contain Frank even more.

Perhaps the dream of ownership had been something else all along. Perhaps it had really been—like the fifty-one rules—the dream of control, of a true partnership, when as two homosexual men they had felt like anything but masters of their fate and life together.

Herbert Dutton turned to the final pages at the back of *The Times* where announcements were posted daily for various upcoming auctions, sales, and other events. He almost missed the notice from Sotheby's, but then his eye caught the name of Yardley Sinclair, their longtime contact, who had always been such a support to the shop.

The newspaper dropped to the floor.

"What? Herbert, my dear, what is it?" Frank asked in consternation at the paleness in Herbert's face. "Is it another attack?"

Herbert Dutton shook his head, then gave the strangest sound as the colour quickly returned to his complexion, turning it red with all kinds of emotion.

"No." He gave a groan that bordered on a laugh.

"It's Evie Stone."

The large notice in *The Times* stated that a previously lost first edition of *The Mummy! A Tale of the Twenty-Second Century* had recently been discovered in a London bookshop. The new private owner had retained Sotheby's to auction off the historically significant find on the fifteenth of March at its offices at 34–35 New Bond Street. The auction was to be presided over by Yardley Sinclair, the director of museum services, in a rare nod to the importance of the proceedings.

With an impressive reserve price of five hundred pounds, the London and global acquisitions markets quickly took note, and reporters from both *The Times* and the *Daily Mail* were dispatched to cover the newsworthy event.

The day before the notice of auction appeared, Yardley had been surprised to receive Evie Stone's note, asking him to meet her for tea in the Thames Foyer of the Savoy, where she was secretly staying as a guest of Mimi Harrison.

As surprised as he was by the location for their meeting, Yardley was even more astonished when Evie carefully extracted the delicate first edition of *The Mummy!* from her leather bag. She calmly but forcefully explained that the extremely rare book had been a publicly bestowed gift from her employer upon her involuntary and unjustified departure the previous week, that she had indisputable rights of ownership as a result, and that she wanted to arrange an auction for its sale as quickly as possible.

Yardley wanted more time, both to conduct a proper assessment and to build anticipation. As invaluable and noteworthy a find as the book surely was, it was still part of a burgeoning canon in science fiction. The three volumes also suffered from the relatively mild interest in their creator, a woman heretofore only known for gardening manuals directed at housewives. Yardley was concerned that male academics and curators in particular would continue to overlook the book's true value, leaving the unemployed Evie with only a few hundred pounds for her efforts.

But Evie was adamant that the auction be held as quickly as possible, at a reserve price of five hundred pounds. Yardley countered with a suggested minimum reserve of two hundred pounds instead. Aware that Evie had lost out on yet another job and was all alone in London, Yardley wanted to ensure that the book did indeed meet the minimum amount required for sale. In his expert opinion, two hundred pounds was reasonable, achievable, and represented almost half a year's wages for the young woman. Evie, however, held firm and won out.

A few days after the announcement in *The Times,* Yardley was surprised to learn from an irate Frank Allen of the sudden and joint resignation by the remaining female staff of Bloomsbury Books on the same day as the notice of auction. Yardley would always wonder which ignominious event had come first. Either way, he suspected that the public posting of the sale had led to such chaos and fury on behalf of the bookstore's management that the women had selected their time to leave most wisely.

Having already conceded to Evie on several substantive points, Yardley had more happily obliged in one more: the selection of the fifteenth of March for the auction of the book. This date had been communicated to him by Evie on behalf of Vivien Lowry, Evie's former colleague at Bloomsbury Books. Yardley was fully aware of the date's historical significance as the Ides of March.

The deadline for Romans to settle all debts, and the day on which the reign of the *dictator perpetuo* Julius Caesar had come to its infamous end.

CHAPTER FORTY

RULE No. 34

Staff shall not confuse work with pleasure.

Alec McDonough was working late at night alone in the shop. His heart was no longer in the job in more ways than one. Recently he had grabbed a quick pint at the Lamb with Samuel Beckett. Alec had invited the playwright out for drinks in the hope of getting advice on his own writing, just as he had done with many prominent guests of the shop over the years.

Beckett had closed the pages of Alec's latest short story and laughed. "Why don't you just bed her, man, and get it over with."

Alec was mortified to feel his cheeks redden like a schoolboy's.

"Look"—Beckett shifted in his seat and put both hands on the small oak table before him—"writing's a blood sport. You have to want it more than anything. Do you?"

Alec didn't want to come across as a dithering amateur, but in the face of Beckett's piercing gaze and deeply lined brow, the younger man suddenly felt like one. He knew that someone as famously no-nonsense as Beckett would not give much time or thought to anything but the cold, hard truth.

"I love everything about writing *but* the writing."

"Well, that's honest, at least. I respect that." Beckett sighed and pushed his small round spectacles up onto his brow.

"What do I do, then? Besides work in a shop shelving books."

"I fear there's only one thing left." Beckett's blue eyes crinkled with good humour. "Become an editor."

A week later, Alec sat sullenly at Mr. Dutton's desk, trying to catch up on all the stock purchase orders he was quickly becoming delinquent on. The shelves in the main-floor fiction section were already beginning to look noticeably bare, which was never an attractive sign for customers strolling in. Vivien must have been even more efficient than he'd feared, Alec sighed to himself as he worked hard to catch up to her.

He had been trying to catch up to her for a long time now, and not just at work. Still, he could not pin her down. She refused to conform to anyone's notions of how a woman should act, least of all his. As a highly eligible bachelor, Alec had always found it hard to believe that Vivien would rather forego romance with him altogether than forgive any past callous words of his. In a strange way, she behaved as much the widow as Ellen Doubleday or Sonia Blair. How little did future paramours seem able to measure up to the man who had been lost—symbolized by the date on the back of the watch, the one sentimental attachment Vivien had ever displayed about anything. The inscription continued to bother Alec greatly, as much as it had that first morning in bed: how the mere memory of another man might be more than enough for Vivien, or at least matter more than *him*.

Evie Stone had been completely right in chalking up his behaviour to male pride. No wonder he had taken such satisfaction from conquering the workplace that he and Vivien had shared together, while finding her own ambition rather unseemly—another irony that until now had escaped him. Fueled by his ego, he had worked hard—and unknowingly sacrificed much—to make everything look the way that he thought it should.

It had all led to an empty, Pyrrhic victory in the end. Because he was doing all the wrong things to win—and because Vivien was as competitive as him—he had set himself up to fail in a most spectacular fashion. The one thing he deep down wanted to win—Vivien herself—had been lost forever.

Ironically, the other men in the shop had turned out to be just as unsuccessful at separating love from work. Alec now knew all their business dealings to have been a façade for more emotional yearnings, while the women appeared to have kept their eyes mostly on business all along. For Herbert and Frank, the shop was only one aspect of their partnership; Master Mariner Scott had been pitching woo at the pub proprietress up the street; even Lord Baskin appeared to have an ulterior motive in his continued visits to the shop.

Furthermore, the shop had proved invulnerable to change, providing the type of stifling routine that Alec had originally been so eager to escape in choosing Bloomsbury Books over an office job. Certainly, the shop benefitted aesthetically from looking exactly as it had one hundred years ago, when the 9th Earl Baskin had won it gambling. There was comfort in the well-trod wooden floors with the Georgian cut nails and the old oak shelving with the handcrafted joints. The customers were also wonderfully loyal, although many a morning Alec opened the front door to a line of aging men, umbrellas and newspapers tucked under their arms, creatures of the past themselves. They struck Alec as a dying breed, taking him along with them, with his failed attempts as a writer, lover, and friend. For on that last point, he had failed Mr. Dutton and Mr. Allen as well.

When Alec had joined the shop on the heels of the Second World War, he had been in need of a new start. The men at work had quickly become like brothers to him—Herbert almost like a father. He had mentored and challenged Alec to his full potential in a way that had been completely generous and gracious. Alec had known he was the golden boy long before Frank had nicknamed him that—long before Vivien had declared him the Tyrant.

What was he still begrudging Herbert and Frank? By now he

should be over their having kept such a secret from him. If it was their homosexuality itself, why couldn't he just separate the person from the act? He recalled the disastrous Beckett lecture where Daphne du Maurier had openly flirted with both him *and* Vivien, and how uncomfortable that had made him feel. Vivien, on the other hand, had taken it all in stride as just one more compliment. Certainly—and here Alec felt the sickening pulse of jealousy—she had been only too pleased to receive Beckett's appreciative looks all night.

Alec had to face the fact that he was a prude. He had no idea why. He couldn't attach it to anything specific in his life. He had felt this way for as long as he could remember. Something about the transgressive nature of sex and attraction was off-putting to him, a revulsion that was only liberated for him by the act of sex itself. It was what he had felt in common with Vivien from the beginning, from the night of their first mistake—the shared, silent understanding that a whole other world was out there for the taking, a world that most people would never dare to explore.

After the beginning, they had made the same mistake again, following Vivien's success with the literary luncheon. But this time the mistake had also undoubtedly become the end.

In a way it had been the last dying gasp of his stifled imagination. Sex with Vivien was where he had set it free. And it would now stay there, trapped, in bed with her, and in the back office in the moonlight, a moment both transgressive and completely, beautifully real. Trapped, he now feared, with the memory of Vivien herself, of her once-long chestnut-brown hair and un-made-up face lying next to him. Years ago, following a much more successful evening lecture, a famous author, famously drunk, had confided in Alec that he remained celibate for the entire time that he wrote a book. There was a connection, the author had felt certain, between the storing up of his sexual energy and the release of his imagination onto the page.

Alec slammed the order book shut and went to return it to the cash counter. He was tired—tired of thinking about all of this, around and around, to no avail. Tired of not being able to leave that bed with Vivien, despite her slamming of doors soon after, until she had fully receded from his view. And now she was gone. He wouldn't get to argue or spar with her anymore. He wouldn't get to compete with her over the business of the shop.

Are you sure that's what you're competing over? Peggy Guggenheim had asked, as he stared out the second-floor window and watched Samuel Beckett try to whisk Vivien away into the night.

Maybe he and Vivien had been rivals over something else altogether. His bruised ego wanted it to be about love. He was hurt that Vivien had so willingly moved on from him. He stayed up on that ladder, perched on a tower of pride, and she stayed behind the cash counter, trapped like him, but not at all willingly.

Alec put the purchase order book away in its place under the counter. A few other books and catalogues were stashed under there, and as Alec shoved them about with his hand, he felt the cool metal edge of a coil. Reaching in deeper, Alec pulled out the notebook that Vivien had most recently been scribbling in throughout the day, until walking out in protest with Grace.

In the moonlight, the green shade of the cover almost glowed. Everything else in the shop was so often a varying shade of dull suitcase brown. Trust Vivien to pick out the brightest, most vibrant notebooks from the stationery-and-gifts section for which Grace had had to repeatedly petition Mr. Dutton over the years. Alec couldn't blame either woman for being fed up with all the fighting and walking away. Things would not be easy for them outside the safe confines of the shop. The economy was still struggling. The average weekly income was under ten pounds. What would either woman find for employment without the kind of referral that one could usually rely upon from such an upstanding man as Herbert Dutton?

Alec opened the green notebook and started to read. None of it was familiar. None of it made sense to his linear, unimaginative mind. The thoughts were disjointed in places, large sections were asynchronous, and there was an overreliance on active verbs and metaphor. But there was poetry in there, too, in the seams and in the spaces between the perfectly selected words. Most of all there were pages and pages of dialogue, so rich and real, despite being nothing like how people actually speak. Yet it captured so powerfully how they *are*.

Alec was both shocked and impressed at how little any of it connected to the world he knew to be Vivien Lowry's. Her secret writing was coming from somewhere else, a creative subterranean universe that she did not balk from, ignore, or judge. She remained the freest person he had ever known, in two different worlds, when he had barely explored the one.

He had once written an entire short story about his unresolved feelings for Vivien. Reading through the notebook, he realised that he had been doomed to lose her all along, but not for the reasons he had thought. It wasn't a question of ill-fitting temperaments or grudges to bear. He simply didn't deserve a woman like her. That, he now saw, was what his pride had really feared—and fought against—all along.

There was nothing more to be done. The moonlight cascaded across the old oak counter full of markings from so many different quill, fountain, and Biro pens over the past one hundred years. Alec fished about in the old empty tin that they used at the cash counter for storing pens and pencils and took out an erasable red one. Then he did the one thing Vivien had left him, the only thing left to do.

He began to edit.

CHAPTER FORTY-ONE

RULE No. 33

Staff shall not interfere with the personal possessions
of their colleagues.

Vivien turned her key in the door to Bloomsbury Books one
last time.

She had neglected to hand it in before walking out with
Grace earlier in the week. She had also forgotten to retrieve her
current writing notebook from under the front cash counter. She
was now returning late at night to do both those things under the
cover of darkness, in no mood to deal with management any longer.

But first she had met up with Samuel Beckett at the Dorchester Bar. In arranging the meeting, Ellen Doubleday had called
the location a "demarcation line," reminding Vivien of their joint
penchant for nicknaming things.

Over cocktails, Beckett had returned to Vivien the older coil-
bound notebook that Daphne du Maurier had given him, now
marked up with red-ink swirls, doodles, and scribbles in his barely
legible hand. Vivien wondered if one day that notebook would end
up the most valuable object in her possession, especially if her
own writing inside remained unvalued and ignored.

As Beckett had sat at the bar next to her, the notebook taking
up space between them, he had expounded on all the challenges

a young playwright faced. Vivien had listened respectfully, astonished to have the time of such a reputable artist. But Samuel Beckett had once slept with Peggy Guggenheim, who knew Ellen Doubleday, who was loved by Lady Browning, whose literary agent was Spencer Curtis Brown, who had known George Orwell, who had married Sonia Brownell, who now knew Vivien. It was this type of connective tissue that had led to the first—and presumably the last—literary luncheon at Bloomsbury Books. The success of Vivien's event had led to the friendship with Sonia Blair and to Alec's rebuttal with the Beckett lecture, the failure of which had led to tonight.

Rejected by the 7th Earl and Countess St. Vincent for her staunchly middle-class upbringing and lack of social connection, Vivien wondered what her late fiancé's family would make of her now. The best part of these new connections was that she had not strategically sought them out—they had found her instead. A Cartier Tank watch, a hotel hallway encounter, a misbegotten short story inspired by that same middle-class life: these disparate elements had reeled in a coterie of wealthy women who were reeling from marital loss or disappointment themselves. In coping with pain, however, they all harboured the one hope that privilege can bestow: the ability to anticipate, and seek, a new horizon. If the money trapped them in some ways, it also provided an escape that Vivien, Grace, and—so far as yet—young Evie Stone could not foresee in their own lives.

Vivien stepped over the wire across the vestibule threshold, preventing the clapper of the shop bell from hitting its metal casing as it did throughout the day. Latching the door behind her, she moved slowly past the tables of books, letting the moonlight lead her way. She looked about the rows of shelves and felt surprisingly wistful. Whatever happened next, the days of Bloomsbury Books were gone.

A small light had been left on in Grace's office. Vivien headed down the corridor to turn it off, in a rare and final act of obedience.

"Oh." She stopped short at the sight of Alec sitting at the small, cleared desk, looking like a schoolboy with his sleeves rolled up, waistcoat undone, and blond hair in his eyes.

"You're back." He instinctively put his hands over his work.

"Only to return my key." She peered through the darkness at the familiar glint of metal coiled about the edges of the paper before him. "And to get my notebook . . . Alec . . ."

He pushed back from the desk sheepishly. "Vivien, I had no idea."

She rushed forward angrily to grab the notebook from him, but he put his own hand out gently over hers.

"Vivien, can we talk? For once?" He gave a sad smile. "Your temper."

Vivien pulled back. She was indeed always angry. Daphne du Maurier shared Vivien's anger with the world, but Ellen Doubleday refused to give in to it, and Sonia Blair had advised against it that day in Queen Square. Vivien wondered if she and du Maurier both used the anger as fuel for their writing, and at what cost to themselves.

"Fine. Talk. Heaven forbid I stop you."

"I had no idea that you were writing, not like this. Why didn't you tell me?"

"I didn't think we were close enough."

He shook his head at her in obvious frustration. "I do know people. I could have helped you."

"Or used it in your next story."

"Vivien, you know that it wasn't really about you."

"I'm the last person you need to convince of that. And the only person who will ever believe you." She bit her lip to keep from raising her voice. "You should have warned me and you know it."

"I should have done a lot of things differently. I let my pride get in the way. In my writing, and here, in the shop. And with you." He held the notepad out to her. "It's very good. I'm quite envious."

She wasn't past taking pleasure in that. Alec's taste in books was arguably narrow but impeccable.

"And I'm sorry I looked at it without your permission. I couldn't help myself. I guess I never could." He hesitated. "I didn't think you'd ever be back."

She heard the new note of pain and regret in his voice and felt the cage coiled about her heart start to unclasp itself. She quickly steeled herself against it; this was no time to start getting soft. But she did need to start taming her anger, given the challenges of the days ahead. Vivien wondered just how civil she could become with Alec. He'd always represented the recklessness and ease of wealth to her: the snobbery rampant in England, from the derision over an accent to the subtle standing of a wristwatch. She had her looks on her side, but looks could only get you so far. No wonder someone like Ash, so self-possessed and direct, had decided to leave it all behind.

"Where will you be going, you and Grace?"

She shrugged.

"Well, I should tell you that I'm going, too."

Vivien raised one eyebrow at Alec in genuine surprise.

"I should tell you something else." He motioned for her to sit down across from him. "I actually considered trying to buy out Lord Baskin's interest in the shop with some of my inheritance. Dutton firing Evie certainly didn't help matters." Alec hesitated. "You don't look surprised."

"I'd put nothing past you." She reluctantly sat down across from him.

"Still, it was a pretty fleeting decision in the end."

"What changed your mind?"

Alec sighed. "I only ever wanted to be a writer, but it's hard for me, in a way that few things are. It's not just a skill you can train yourself into. There has to be some imaginative spark, some awareness of feeling. There's nothing going on up here." He smiled self-deprecatingly and pointed at his head.

"I could have told you that." Her old teasing manner was starting to replace some of the perpetual resentment she felt towards him.

"It's not hard for you, though, is it? Flows right out of you."

"Just a pretty vessel."

"No, not at all. Just . . . very real."

She looked at him curiously.

"I always thought your anger was a wall against feeling anything. But that's not it, is it? It's *because* you feel." He nodded at the notebook in her hands. "I guess it has to go somewhere."

"If that's true, it's nothing I'm conscious of."

"That doesn't make you any less talented."

"I didn't say it did," she retorted gamely.

They both stared at each other, then laughed.

"So, I've made a decision." Alec put up both his hands to bring their fingertips gently together. "I'm starting in two weeks at Faber, over in Russell Square. As an editorial assistant."

He was watching her eagerly, and she saw how much her opinion, her approval, meant to him. How they had each tangled up that need for approval with resentment over needing it at all. Was that what the war had done to them all in the end—made needing anything or anyone so risky that it was better to harden and deaden oneself inside instead?

Again, Vivien felt herself start to soften. It was most troubling, how this moment did not feel like goodbye after all. Even the past felt like something else. No longer a mistake or a beginning, but maybe a prelude instead, to something much more unexpected.

"An editor?" She was surprisingly pleased by the news. "But, Alec, that's so perfect—of course."

"You think? I'm glad. Beckett seemed to think so, too."

"Beckett?"

"Yes. He told me I couldn't write for toffee."

Vivien had to bite her lip now to keep from laughing.

"It's all right." Alec's own laugh escaped him. "Turned out he knew one of the directors at Faber and made an introduction. Or maybe he was just trying to eliminate me as competition when it came to *you*."

Vivien made a face. "No worries there, Alec. I reject you solely on the basis of your personality."

They laughed together again, sitting there so comfortably, finally the colleagues they had never been. For the first time in years, Vivien felt as if she could trust him and found herself wanting to confide in him about Evie and the book. But it wasn't just her secret to tell.

"Well, Alec, I have to say, I'm proud of you. You didn't buy your way into something for once."

"Thanks, Viv."

"No, I mean it. It takes a lot to completely pull up sticks like that and try something new."

He shook his head. "I'll be fine. But I worry about you, and Grace. And poor Evie."

"Oh, I'll find something. Don't you worry about me."

"I do, though. I always will."

There was nothing left to say, for now. Bloomsbury Books might soon be gone, but there was always the promise of something new arising in its place. Whatever it was, it would only come about by completely breaking with the past. Vivien wondered if the same could be said for her and Alec, with enough time and distance between them.

"What will you do next?" he asked.

She stood up, her green coil-bound notebook in one hand.

"Take over the world," she said brightly, dropping her key on the desk with the other hand, before leaving Bloomsbury Books for good.

Ashwin Ramaswamy agreed to meet Evie Stone one last time. Upon her termination, she had completely disappeared from Bloomsbury Books and his life. The following Monday, Vivien and Grace had also marched out of the shop, in a manner that seemed entirely too coincidental. This was when Ash first suspected that something was up. His suspicions only increased when he opened that evening's *Times* to discover Sotheby's announcement of the upcoming auction of *The Mummy!* The very book that Evie had asked for, and received, and slipped into her little leather bag; the very book that Dr. Septimus Feasby had railed about less than an hour later, so loudly that several customers had immediately fled the store, along with all future business from the British Museum.

Ash hated how things had been left between Evie and him, so he had been greatly relieved—and a little nervous—when her note appeared at his hostel a few days before the auction. In her usual direct but polite manner, Evie had written to ask that he meet her near the Natural History Museum, at the same tearoom where they had taken their first meal together. There had been many shared meals and walks since then, mostly under the intrusive and hostile stares of people trying to make sense of something that they refused to understand. Just like the Scottish waitress who now stood by their table, waiting impatiently and dismissively all over again. Ash wanted to say something to her, but he knew it was useless. Besides, he was going away soon, too, and he didn't want her rudeness to be any part of his and Evie's last time together.

"I won't miss the looks," he said to Evie instead, after the waitress had left them with a loud smack of the notepad against her hand.

Evie sat there quietly across the table from him, still visibly upset with his decision to return home. "People look oddly at me, too, sometimes. Although I know it's not the same."

"It's not. You're right. And the difference is everything. They still think they know you. They don't know me—why I came here, what I want from them, because I *must* want something—and that makes them hate me, the not knowing. I'm just tired of it."

"So that's why you're going?"

"No. It just makes it easier."

Evie shifted uncomfortably in her seat as if she wanted to say something else.

"What is it?" he asked softly.

"It's just . . . you don't seem like someone who wants things easy."

"I want them fair." He cleared his voice. "Just like you."

She nodded quickly. "What if you had a crystal ball?"

"Come again?"

"A crystal ball. A friend back home, Frances—my former employer actually, she's quite a bit older than me—she used to say it's best in life to pretend to have a crystal ball 'n' try to picture 'n it how everything ahead of you that could go well has done so. And how the bad stuff you kept worrying 'bout happening never did. Right now, you don't know for sure that things won't get better."

"You mean hope."

"More, takin' it day by day, inch by inch. Till you know for sure what you're up against. Ash . . ."

"Yes, Evie?"

"I don't want you to go." She looked down. She wouldn't look at him. "I love you."

He hadn't expected this—couldn't conceive of these words coming first from her, so young and resolute and proud. Of course, he didn't want to leave her, either. But just like Lord Baskin, he would never put the woman he loved in a position of having to speak of something she couldn't. His needs could never extend as far as his innate gallantry towards hers.

Most of all, he could never ask the woman he loved to give up so much for him. His plans to leave were due in large part to that. The difficult decision would eventually make life easier for them both. It would cut off contact and force them to move on to what was "proper," as the British liked to say. It was easy to love Evie, the purest, most direct, and bravest person he had ever met. But a life with him would be so unnecessarily hard. He had not forgotten the shoving and slurring by the stranger on the street after Stuart Wesley had ambled off and Ash had released Evie's arm, the only time they had ever really touched. How could he subject her to such constant abuse when her life was hard enough already, and especially so now?

"Evie . . ."

She shook her head. "Don't. Please."

"Evie, I can't ask this of you. You must know that. You deserve the world." Here his voice caught in his throat. "I can't give that to you."

"Some of it I can get myself."

She finally looked back up at him, and he saw a new glint of determination in her eyes.

"You don't know how hard it will be," he persisted. "No one can prepare you. I can't—no matter how I feel—I just . . . can't."

"You don't love me."

"It's not a question of that. Even love is no match for how awful it will be—for how people will act towards you, towards . . . us."

"I've never cared about other people. If anything, I should care more."

"It's not just about you, or me." He hesitated. "It would also be about any children."

His even mentioning the idea of this brought tears to her eyes. Ash started to fumble for his handkerchief to lend her, the display of such sudden emotion from her so rending to his own heart.

"You're being just like Mr. Dutton."

"Excuse me?" he asked, startled.

She nodded as the tears started to fall. "You have your own rules, 'n' everyone must abide 'em." She wiped her eyes with the handkerchief he now held out to her. "But what about what I want? What I'm willing to fight for?"

It was only starting to dawn on Ash that in making this decision for them both, he was nonetheless depriving her of some say in the matter. He thought of Grace and Vivien, whom he had always quietly admired, and how they, too, seemed kept by men from the kind of love and happiness that they deserved. So often something happened to women—really, to many people—along the way, that kept them on a path not wholly of their own making, and never the path to true prosperity as a result.

As Evie stood up and hurriedly left the table, still crying, Ash realised that he, too, was keeping her on a path not wholly hers. The very thing he so deplored in his own life. It was a form of practical servitude, in a way, this not being able to live the way you wanted to. To keep things as they were, the people in power needed people like him, Evie, Grace, and Vivien to also stay in their allotted station. By returning to India, Ash knew that he looked as if he were giving up. But *that,* at least, felt like a choice. Not these ugly stares of the waitress or the whispered slurs of others, both of which constantly put him in his place. It was no place he wanted to be. But, most of all, it was not a place to which he would ever want to subject Evie.

He had been worried about her, from that horrible moment in the shop when he had raced upstairs from the basement just in time to see her leave Mr. Dutton's office, her face tearstained and red, and head straight for the second floor. No one had followed her—he wondered if that had also been intentional on the other women's part—and she had soon after descended Vivien's Via Dolorosa all over again, clasping the battered leather bag against her side, holding tightly on to the one precious treasure that she alone in the world had found.

He would always remember that moment, the victory snatched from defeat, by a unique and determined girl.

Whatever might happen next, he would carry the memory with him always, far more precious than any book.

CHAPTER FORTY-TWO

RULE No. 7

The reputation of the shop must never be called into question
in any forum, public or otherwise.

T he auction was about to begin.

Yardley Sinclair surveyed the main room on the lower level of Sotheby's, filled to capacity with potential buyers, intrigued onlookers, and various members of the press. The room was so packed that extra chairs had been brought in from some of the other rooms downstairs. Yardley was unusually nervous on both Evie Stone's and his own behalf, and he looked about for faces he might know. For a second, he thought he recognised a familiar-looking heart-shaped face in the back row, but the hair was an unfamiliar peroxide blonde, and the row of heads in front obscured the other features.

The rest of the crowd was mostly made up of male representatives from museums, libraries, and other prestigious institutions. Yardley noticed a few more women in the room than usual, all of them of a "certain age," as he liked to say. Probably wealthy Americans on the London leg of their winter Continental tours.

Ascending the podium to open bidding as the director of museum services, Yardley surveyed the sizable crowd one last time. Out of the corner of his eye, he caught sight of Evie Stone staring hard across the room. Following the direction of her penetrating gaze, Yardley spotted the young man named Stuart Wesley, who had come to call at Sotheby's a few weeks ago regarding *The Mummy!* He was sitting at the end of the first row, three seats down from Dr. Septimus Feasby of the British Museum. Yardley hoped the young man knew what he was doing here. Yardley himself would never want to be on the receiving end of one of Evie Stone's determined glares.

Professor Fredrik Christenson, the new vice-master of Jesus College, Cambridge, and his colleague, the now–Senior Fellow Robert Kinross, sat sandwiched between Feasby and Wesley on the bamboo chairs with intricate needlepoint seat cushions. The four men took up one full row to the far left of the podium, on the side of the room opposite the mirrored wall with its double entrance doors. Christenson was checking the new Rolex Tudor Oyster watch that he had gifted himself following his recent assumption to the vice-master role. He looked up in visible irritation when the doors opened one last time, mere seconds before the exact hour and start of the auction. A slender woman dressed all in black quickly sneaked in and proceeded straight to the rear of the room, seating herself in the farthest available corner, followed by a wealthy-looking middle-aged woman who remained standing by the doors in her fur coat, and the flustered *Daily Mail* newspaperman who had so recently challenged Daphne du Maurier on a much less glamorous stage.

"We have before us today," Yardley announced in his typically ominous tone, "a most spectacular and rare find: *The Mummy! A Tale of the Twenty-Second Century*. A first edition from the London publishing house of Henry Colburn, anonymously published in 1827 by a young woman who would later become Jane Loudon, the much-heralded gardening expert. Three volumes, bound in leather with marbled boards and lettering embossed in gold, and

in uncommonly pristine condition. One of only two editions released by Colburn, one of only three printings ever made, and
at present the only known copy of the first edition in existence.
Recently and most enthusiastically, preeminent critics and cat-
aloguers of the novel as a form have embraced this book as one
of the earliest examples of science fiction, one of literature's most
fascinating and emerging genres. *The Mummy!* is prescient in
both theme and content, and Sotheby's is most honoured to bring
this historic find to you today. Bidding now opens at two hundred
pounds."

Dr. Feasby raised his hand. He had full authority to bid within
his discretion on behalf of the British Museum as its principal
keeper of longest standing and the highest repute.

"Two hundred pounds from the gentleman in the first row. Do
I hear two hundred and fifty? Two hundred and fifty pounds."

Vice-Master Fredrik Christenson bid next. Along with the
prestige of his new role, Professor Christenson remained the preeminent expert in nineteenth-century English literature at the
University of Cambridge. He had full discretion to bid upwards
of the reserve price to one thousand pounds, an amount both unlikely and not overly worrying. Although Christenson was in competition with Dr. Feasby and the British Museum, the closeness of
their relations would always allow for the loaning of academically
significant material between the two institutions.

"Do I hear three hundred, then? Three hundred pounds?"
Yardley tried to keep any note of premature excitement from his
voice, but he was quietly thrilled that Evie Stone might indeed
get her reserve price in the end.

"Four hundred."

All heads turned in the direction of the female voice coming
from their midst. Her face was obscured by a large, brimmed hat,
from under which peeked a pair of heavy black eyeglass frames.

Dr. Feasby started to twitch in his chair.

"Four hundred and fifty," he declared without waiting for Yardley's prompt, clearly eager to meet the reserve price and finish with the proceedings.

"Four hundred and fifty!" Yardley intoned. "Do I hear five hundred, the reserve price? At this point any winning bid will be fully binding on the seller."

"One thousand pounds," announced a new female voice with a strong mid-Atlantic accent. Immediately all heads swivelled in excitement to see the woman sitting in the very centre of the room. This woman looked vaguely familiar to Yardley, with short, curly hair and a long string of pearls that she twisted about in her hands. She did not appear to do so from nerves, however, as she looked merrily about at the astonished onlookers.

Yardley swallowed nervously in excitement. "One thousand pounds. Do I hear one thousand one hundred?"

Dr. Feasby refused to look about the room at his competitors. Instead, he gravely and confidently lifted his right index finger towards Yardley.

The parameters to Vice-Master Christenson's discretion had now been exceeded. He leaned forward to confer with Kinross and Wesley on his right, then tapped Dr. Feasby on his left with a gentlemanly muttering of good luck. None of the men in the front left row displayed any concern over the proceedings. In his decades as the principal keeper of printed books at the British Museum, Septimus Reginald Feasby had never lost out on anything.

"Fifteen hundred."

The room gasped at the sudden American female voice ringing out from near the entrance.

Yardley looked over at Evie, whose earlier glaring face was now lit up in a way that he remembered only too well. He was thrilled for her good fortune, but professionally stupefied as to what was going on. First edition works of literature rarely captured more than a few hundred pounds unless they were from the canon: the Shakespeare folios, a hand-illustrated original William Blake, early formative works such as *Don Quixote*. Aside from Jane Austen, Yardley could not recall the work of any female author ever approaching more than one thousand pounds in the history of Sotheby's.

Bidding now furiously proceeded between Dr. Septimus Feasby and an assortment of women scattered throughout the room, until two thousand pounds was reached.

"Twenty-five hundred," exclaimed another American female voice, this one from the woman with blonde hair in the back row. Yardley tried to make her out again—her voice sounded hauntingly familiar.

"Twenty-five *hundred* pounds!" he announced with delight, then waited impatiently to see what would happen next. Yardley had estimated the value of the book to be one thousand pounds at the absolute most, based on past sales of works of literature by women. *The Mummy!* might be valuable as a forerunner of modern science fiction, but where did it leave the few recognised classics by women—*Middlemarch, Pride and Prejudice, Jane Eyre,* even *Frankenstein*—if bidding on an until-now-obscure Gothic novel were to reach several thousand pounds?

Dr. Feasby sat in the front row as implacable and unreadable as stone. Yardley watched the older gentleman's hawkish, deep-set features dim as he tilted his face downwards in both contempt for his competitors and concentration.

"Three thousand," he calmly called out.

Cheering broke out at the eminent curator's declaration.

Yardley used his gavel to silence the room. "Three thousand pounds!" he exclaimed with unrestrained jubilation. "Going once, going twice . . . sold, for three thousand pounds to the British Museum!"

The gentlemen in the front left row were in deep conference now, heads bent together. As usual, they were not paying attention to what was going on behind them. They did not see four women and young Evelyn Stone rise in unison from their chairs to join the American woman by the doors before departing the room together, or hear the sounds of the many press cameras clicking in their direction.

E vie stood alone on the pavement outside Sotheby's, the disperser of great treasures past and present, as the women now passed her by.

The woman with the dyed-blonde hair. The woman in the large hat and glasses. The one with the pearls. The one in fur. The one in black.

Evie waved happily as each clambered quickly into a waiting taxi to head off in four very different directions: Cornwall, Boston, Venice, New York. Evie had held many secret meetings the past two weeks in the Thames Foyer of the Savoy, and Lord Baskin had been eerily on point when he had referenced Churchill, de Gaulle, and Masaryk all meeting there during the war in similar scheming fashion. Evie had indeed felt like the leader of a strategic campaign as she had sat there over tea with each woman, obscured by tiered silver trays and potted palms, and discovered a brand-new skill in herself: inspired coordination.

The taxis sped off ahead of a surge of cameramen and newspaper reporters, everyone crowded together on the pavement outside the stately entrance to the world's leading auction house. There was much jostling, shouting, and craning of heads as the male bidders for the lost book *The Mummy!* now also quickly emerged from its doors and made their own, ignominious retreat. As the cameras flashed furiously after them and the sea of black bowler hats began to part and recede, Evie looked through the crush of men and saw standing there before her, as if he had been waiting all along, the one man today whom she had dared not hope to see, his hand outstretched towards hers.

"You're not going?" she asked, astonished.

"No." Ash took her hand in his before bowing to kiss it in full view of the dispersing crowd. "Not when I've finally found something I can't find anywhere else."

And in that moment, Evie knew she had won the world for herself after all.

As for those who had just lost, and the reason behind their defeat, there would later be names to caption the photographs hurriedly captured as Yardley's gavel had given its final, resounding thud.

Mrs. Ellen Doubleday, recent widow of Nelson Doubleday, Sr.

Miss Mary Ann "Mimi" Harrison, actress.

Lady Browning; Daphne du Maurier, author.

Miss Marguerite "Peggy" Guggenheim, heiress and collector.

Mrs. Sonia Brownell Blair, recent widow of the author George Orwell (born Eric Blair).

CHAPTER FORTY-THREE

RULE No. 1

The shop at 40 Lamb's Conduit Street, Bloomsbury, shall be known, in perpetuity, as Bloomsbury Books & Maps.

The clearance sale of much of the stock of Bloomsbury Books took place two weeks later.

The thirty thousand volumes were whittled down in half, book by book, over a period of many days. During this time, Evie stood guard over the rare books floor to ensure that only those items that had been properly assessed by her and Yardley left the premises in customers' eager hands. In this way the rare books collection remained relatively intact, having the most value of all the departments in the shop.

The History Department ended up the most heavily liquidated, Master Mariner Scott not having kept his stock in pace with any kind of readership. The Science and Naturalism department became the second-most depleted, following a visit from Miss Elsie Wakefield, deputy keeper of the herbarium at the Royal Botanic Gardens in Kew. Having over the years endured many a dustup with the keeper of printed books at the British Museum, Miss Wakefield had enjoyed learning of Dr. Feasby's commercial comeuppance over the lost book *The Mummy!* Through her gleeful correspondence afterwards with Evelyn Stone, Miss Wakefield had been offered the opportunity to peruse the shop's botany and other scientific books ahead of their sale to the public. Greatly impressed by the knowledge and currency of the collection, Miss Wakefield acquired a huge lot before offering the unemployed Ashwin Ramaswamy a position as the new head librarian at Kew.

With the profits from the clearance sale rolled back into the liquid assets of the shop, Evie, Vivien, and Grace now owned shares in Bloomsbury Books valued at approximately seven thousand pounds, a significant increase from the three thousand pounds they had recently paid Lord Baskin with their profits from the sale of *The Mummy!* Lord Baskin remained the owner of both the real property at No. 40 Lamb's Conduit and its fixed assets (including furniture, shelving, and kitchen and other equipment). This limited the three women's investment in the shop to the value of its stock, which greatly mitigated their financial exposure and risk, as well as enabling Lord Baskin to retain a personal and financial stake in the business being conducted on his land.

Mr. Dutton and Mr. Allen also now owned shares worth significantly more than when they had first considered early retirement from the book trade. Both men agreed to redeem their partial ownership interest in Bloomsbury Books after a visit to their home by Lord Baskin. The earl had explained the recent sale of all of his shares to the three former female employees of the shop, giving the women majority control as a voting block. With their own sudden influx of cash, Herbert and Frank planned to incorporate a travel agency in Dulwich now that the British were vacationing abroad in much greater droves as the economy continued to strengthen. Herbert would focus on the logistics of flight, ocean voyage, and other arrangements, while Frank would lead charter tours and set up working relationships with various hotels and other providers, in an effort to offer their clientele competitive pricing and unique travel experiences.

Master Mariner Scott promptly retired at the news that the

future bookshop at No. 40 Lamb's Conduit was to be fully owned and operated by women. He and Bessie Rosenberg, the owner of the Lamb, were married in early April, following which Scott took up station in a corner booth of the historical public house and regaled anyone who would listen with his tales at sea. To the surprise of all of the local shopkeepers, Scott also became a devoted caretaker to his wife, nursing her through a prolonged decline and helping with the business of the pub.

The annotation of *Vanity Fair* by Senior Fellow Kinross of Jesus College was discovered by Cambridge University Press to contain several egregious errors and incidents of plagiarism, all attributable to Stuart Wesley, a former research assistant on the project. Sonia Christenson called off her engagement to Wesley following the ensuing scandal, which also led to his immediate departure from the research team of Vice-Master Christenson of Jesus College. Dr. Septimus Feasby continued in his curatorial role with the British Museum, albeit in an even worse mood than before.

Finally, to fulfill the redemption of all of Dutton's and Allen's shares, the three newest shareholders of Bloomsbury Books— Evelyn Stone, Vivien Lowry, and Grace Perkins—had been required to buy out the two men. This purchase was enabled by a series of loans from the five women who had so ably assisted in the historic sale of *The Mummy!*—loans that were then promptly repaid with a 45 per cent interest in the company divided equally among the five female lenders. With so much investor cash, the shop's new female management planned to replenish stock, as well as carry out several other initiatives in line with their vision for the shop.

These initiatives included filing on April 14, 1950, a change-of-name registration for Bloomsbury Books with Companies House, the United Kingdom's registrar of companies. The long-standing bookshop at No. 40 Lamb's Conduit Street would now be called

Sunwise Turn, in honour of one of the first bookshops in America to be fully owned and operated by women. New signage, stationery, labels, and packing slips were being designed in a vibrant hue of orange, a most effective "selling" colour according to Grace, to reflect the new name.

Opening day was planned for that same day in mid-April.

Grace and Lord Baskin sat on the bench in front of Sunwise Turn, each of them holding a cream-coloured mug of coffee from Jonny's cart with one hand, their other hand discreetly clasped in the other's. They were looking up together at the third floor of the shop, where Evie was happily waving at them while eagerly peering up and down the street. She was watching out for the arrival of a large handpress printing machine that had been manufactured at the turn of the century and recently acquired at an appropriately discounted price. With the Science Department having been both purged by Elsie Wakefield and relocated to the rare books floor, the handpress was to be installed in the basement in its place. Here Evie planned to employ a young female trade unionist to typeset and print the neglected works of women writers from the past.

When the lorry finally pulled up, Evie's pixie face disappeared from view as she raced down Via Dolorosa to supervise the delivery.

"Tell me again," said Lord Baskin, laughing, as Evie's tiny feet could be heard rushing down the staircase and out the front doors being propped open by crates of books for the much-anticipated arrival. The deliverymen emerged from the rear of the lorry, struggling under the weight of the cast-iron machine. Evie directed them towards the basement stairs next to the kitchen doorway, where Vivien stood watching in amusement as the large hulking contraption passed by.

"Evie knew she needed a good two weeks to transcribe, by

hand, all six hundred and some pages of *The Mummy!* before releasing it to Sotheby's for the auction," Grace explained to Lord Baskin.

"So, the Ides of March wasn't just a symbolic date."

Grace shook her head.

"And you didn't think you could trust me with any of this?"

She gave his hand an affectionate squeeze. "I had two other business partners to oblige. You of all people know what *that* is like."

"Fair enough. But still, the amount of work that would take . . ."

"About thirty to forty pages, ten hours a day. Holed up in the Savoy she was, merry as a cricket. I trained her in some of the basics of Pitman shorthand, and she took to it like the brilliant scholar she is."

"So, her complete handwritten copy makes Septimus Feasby's latest acquisition less exclusive in the end. How perfect. And she has other titles ready to reprint?"

"Yes, a lengthy list compiled from years of cataloguing the Great House library in Chawton and her research work whilst at Cambridge. And, if she ever gets her nerve, Daphne's 'The Doll.' But right now, of course, the greatest interest is in *The Mummy!*, following the success of the auction. The initial reprint order already stands at one thousand subscriptions. That should help pay the landlord, who, as I in my new bookkeeper role understand it, always comes to collect."

Lord Baskin took this as his cue, and rightly so, to sneak in a quick kiss while the other shop managers were preoccupied with the arrival of the press.

Back inside the kitchen, Vivien made two large pots of tea. Like Evie, she had her own lists of books from which to continue the work she had started during her brief but memorable reign as the acting head of fiction. The clearance sale had left Vivien with quite a wide berth for incoming new stock, and her days were filled with purchase orders, invoices, sales visits with representatives from England's publishing houses, and transatlantic phone calls to many other ones abroad. She did not have much time for writing, but with a piece currently on submission at Faber and Faber through the assistance of its newest junior editor, Alec McDonough, Vivien was grateful to be kept busy and distracted.

Vivien loaded up a tray with one pot of black tea and one of steeping chai, along with a pitcher of steamed milk and a bowl of sugar. She made her way carefully towards the front staircase and ascended the steps leading to the second-floor gallery space. As she approached the landing, she could hear the laughter of the several women already gathered inside. Peggy Guggenheim was in the centre of it all, hanging up the different paintings she had brought over by cab in two bulging Louis Vuitton suitcases.

"I miss my London gallery days," Guggenheim was musing out loud as Vivien placed the tray on the pedestal table in the east end of the room, where Master Mariner Scott's old beaten desk had once dominated the space. Other recent additions to the second floor included two comfortable wingback chairs on either side of the round table, a newly restored fireplace to foster a cozy, library-like atmosphere, and a permanent sideboard amply stocked with cups, saucers, and glasses for shop events both formal and spontaneous such as this one. Vivien retrieved enough dishware from the sideboard for everyone gathered, and the ladies all stopped what they were doing to help themselves.

"The tea—and the printing press—have arrived," Vivien announced.

Sonia Brownell Blair jumped up from her seat on a pile of cushions in the middle of the empty floor. Most of the shelving in Scott's former department had been relocated to the third floor, where the remaining history and science volumes were now being housed along with the still-substantial collection of rare books, all under the managerial eye of Evelyn Stone.

"I must see this," Sonia Blair said, grabbing a cup of chai on her way to the stairs. She had recently arranged for the sale to Sunwise Turn of several of the rejected female-penned stories that she had collected over the years from the now-defunct literary journals *The Criterion* and *Horizon*.

Vivien smiled in satisfaction at Sonia's excited departure, while Peggy Guggenheim and Lady Browning returned to readying the second floor for future events. Peggy was enjoying reliving her time as an unpaid intern at the original Manhattan bookshop in honour of which Bloomsbury Books had been rechristened. Shortly after the auction, Ellen Doubleday had returned to America on the first spring-season voyage of the RMS *Queen Mary*. In her absence, Lady Browning and Peggy Guggenheim had become fast friends, discovering in each other a matching sense of mischief and low tolerance for fools. They both planned to visit Ellen on Long Island in the summer season along with Mimi Harrison, who had also returned to the States following a week of standing in for Vivien Leigh at the Aldwych.

As the two women resumed hanging up the various paintings on loan from Guggenheim's massive personal collection, Vivien headed towards the front windows to gaze down at all the street activity below. She could see Grace and Lord Baskin sitting on the bench, amiably chatting together, and Evie saying goodbye to the movers as Ash approached from farther up the road with a small bouquet of flowers from Kew Gardens in his hands.

It was all so very different from that second day in January, when Mr. Dutton had collapsed and the shop had been full of ambulance attendants and frantic employees. All three women managers of Sunwise Turn had been relieved and gratified when both

Mr. Dutton and Mr. Allen had politely accepted the handwritten invitations on new store stationery to attend opening day—and Vivien had found herself secretly pleased by Alec McDonough's acceptance of the same. Their work together as writer and editor was advancing surprisingly well over at Faber and Faber.

As Vivien stood at the open window, the breeze carried up to her the mixed scent of tobacco, coffee, and cherry blossom that distinguished this small corner of Bloomsbury. The shops on the street below were leaving out more and more wares in the warmth of the sun, and the pavement was full of passersby who couldn't help but peek inside the front window of the bookshop that was soon to reopen.

Mid-April was a time of year so full of the promise of spring that even Vivien could not fail to appreciate it.

EPILOGUE

THE RULES OF SUNWISE TURN, LTD

est. April 14, 1950

PROPRIETORS:
GRACE PERKINS
VIVIEN LOWRY
EVELYN STONE

Everyone, employee and customer alike, shall be treated at all times with the utmost dignity and respect. No exceptions.

Each department head shall develop, in conjunction with each employee, a career plan allowing for the taking on of increased responsibility and challenge commensurate with their desires and talents.

All staff are welcome and encouraged to make suggestions of new titles for stock, regardless of their area of expertise.

Employees shall receive a discount of 15 per cent on all in-store purchases.

In the conception and execution of events, attention shall
be paid to the greater community at large, so that the selection of
authors and other speakers reflects its needs and interests.

Every member of Sunwise Turn is responsible for making her,
or his, own tea.

ACKNOWLEDGMENTS

This book was written while I was housebound during a global pandemic. I could not have done so without the help and support provided to my family by the following dear friends: Tim Liznick, Sarah Eves, Andrea Nairn, Vicky DeVries, Chris Stoate, Patti Harbman, Jordan Morelli, and Candice Scholaert. We are also indebted to the superior and compassionate medical assistance provided to us during this difficult time by Dr. Nathan Hambly, Dr. John Yates, Dr. Ayesha Chaudhry, Dr. Eugene Downar, Dr. Marissa Joseph, Maysa Deif and Cherry Jin of Rexall Pharmacy, and Michel Rizkallah and Mina Fanous of Morelli's Pharmacy.

Neither this book nor my debut novel, *The Jane Austen Society,* would exist without the wise, sensitive, and unflagging counsel of my agent, Mitchell Waters. He has changed—and saved—my life more than he can ever know.

I am so grateful to everyone at St. Martin's Press for their infectious enthusiasm for both of my books, and for their tireless, creative, and thoughtful promotion during a time of unprecedented difficulty for the publishing industry. I am particularly indebted to my editors, Keith Kahla and Alice Pfeifer, who know exactly what is right for a story and exactly how to extract it from me; publicist Dori Weintraub, who knows exactly how to share it; and Marissa Sangiacomo, who markets it all so expertly.

Thank you to my team at Brandt & Hochman, especially Marianne Merola, who has dealt with a disrupted global translations market with tremendous responsiveness and calm.

If you are lucky enough to have a book of interest to film and TV, you are especially lucky to have Lucy Stille of Lucy Stille Literary on your side.

As a former lawyer, I know my good fortune in having Ian Cooper of Cooper Media Law and Ronald Davidzon of Davidzon Law each share their time and legal acumen so generously with me.

The following wonderful authors were kind enough to read drafts of this novel at various early stages, and I am extremely thankful for their support, wisdom, and encouragement: Laurel Ann Nattress, Molly Greeley, Rose Servitova, Barbara Heller, Martha Waters, Dr. Nguyễn Phan Quế Mai, Elle Croft, and Brooke Lea Foster. One of the best parts of writing historical fiction is the excuse it gave me to reach out to authors, curators, archivists, and historians around the world for the benefit of their expertise, which was so graciously bestowed by Dr. Paula Byrne, Jane Healey, Nick Holland, Katie Childs, Dr. Gillian Dow, Kathryn Rooke, Dr. Seb Falk, Victoria Ogunsanya, Louise Ansdell, and Anita Felicelli. On a personal note, my road to publication has immeasurably been eased by three amazing Canadian writers who also happen to live within biking distance of me: Samantha Bailey, Jennifer Hillier, and Hannah Mary McKinnon.

Inspiration in writing comes from surprising sources. It was a rewatch of the wonderful movie *84 Charing Cross Road* (based on the equally wonderful book of the same title by Helene Hanff) that led me to the beginning of my story. A fascinating post by Emily Midorikawa on the blog *Something Rhymed,* which celebrates female literary friendship, lit the spark of my story's middle. Tripping across a fantastic article by Ted Bishop on the real-life Sunwise Turn, and a recent new edition of the 1923 memoir by co-founder Madge Jenison, most serendipitously led me to its end.

My book also owes tremendous creative and imaginative debt to two women-run shops in London: The Second Shelf in Soho, which specializes in rare and rediscovered books by women, and Persephone Books (formerly of Lamb's Conduit Street in Bloomsbury and now based in Bath), an independent publisher of neglected works by mid-twentieth-century women writers. I was also inspired by the Heywood Hill bookshop in Mayfair and *The Bookshop at 10 Curzon Street: Letters between Nancy Mitford and Heywood Hill, 1952–73*, edited by John Saumarez Smith. In this epistolary account, I loved how Heywood Hill referred to the shop's steep staircase as *via dolorosa* and have fictionally—and brazenly—adopted that concept here as well. As a former independent-bookshop owner, I urge you to learn more about all three of these wonderful establishments.

In all the ways that really matter, I write every word for an audience of two: my husband, Robert, and our daughter, Phoebe. If the words resonate more broadly than that, it is icing on the cake. They have the entirety of my heart.

Finally, I am so grateful to my mother and father, Pat and Roger Jenner, for making me a writer. No one has ever had more supportive parents at any stage of life, and to this current one I can now add my father's superlative copyediting skills. Their enthusiasm for both my books has been the greatest part of getting published, and I am extremely lucky to be able to share this journey with them both.